Praise for *New York Times* bestselling author
Joseph Finder and his novels

VANISHED

"Financial thriller wiz Joe Finder has fully and seamlessly entered the world of Lee Child and James Rollins. A rousing, lightning-paced thriller from the first page to the last. "   —*Providence Journal*

"If Jack Reacher met Nick Heller in a dark alley, my money's on Reacher. But it would be ugly. Or would it? Actually, I think they'd go for a beer together and set the world to rights—because Joseph Finder has given me a terrific new hero to root for. This is an action-packed, full-throttle, buy-it-today-read-it-tonight series that you definitely shouldn't miss."

—Lee Child

"Cliffhangers galore, the fascinating tradecraft of corporate espionage, and an engrossing story will propel readers through this outstanding thriller. Highly recommended as a great summer read."

—*Library Journal* (starred review)

"Written in staccato chapters that are emotionally supercharged and action-packed, this thriller will more than satisfy adrenaline junkies and have them guessing until the very end."   —*Publishers Weekly*

"Breakneck pace and labyrinthine schemes . . . ingenious."   —*Booklist*

MORE...

"A bloody, rollicking thrill ride...the plot moves at light speed."   —*Richmond Times-Dispatch*

"The action is swift...keeps the plot bubbling and the pages turning."   —*Wall Street Journal*

"Thrilling. . . Start *Power Play* this afternoon and you'll have the nightstand lamp burning at bedtime."
     —*Pittsburgh Post-Gazette*

"A finely crafted excursion into the dark heart of executive-suite skullduggery...plenty of action and suspense."   —*Forbes*

"[A] masterpiece...strong plotting, memorable characterization...a readability quotient to the degree that it almost seems as if putting the book down at any point before finishing it is akin to a criminal act...A fabulous offering."   —Bookreporter.com

KILLER INSTINCT

"Unstoppable."   —*USA Today*

"Masterful."   —*Houston Chronicle*

"Explosive...wickedly fun."   —*Entertainment Weekly*

"Master of a complex suspense formula...flawlessly executed violence, crisp dialogue, and taut pacing."
     —*The New York Times Book Review*

"A first-rate thrill ride."   —*Pittsburgh Post-Gazette*

"A roller coaster of a read."   —*Cosmopolitan*

"It starts off with a bang and doesn't slow down until the last page."   —*Ottawa Sun*

COMPANY MAN

"Finder skillfully places his story of corporate intrigue (who is trying to sell the company, and why?) in counterpoint to the unraveling of a family's secrets (why is Nick's son Lucas so disturbed?), and the plot, which also features rogue cops and at least one homicide, accelerates to a headlong finish."   —*New Yorker*

"It's everything a thriller should be: suspenseful, entertaining—and, above all, thrilling."   —*Chicago Sun-Times*

"Once again, Finder has produced a page-turning corporate thriller with enough twists and turns for any reader."   —*Denver Post*

"The thriller is rejuvenated by Joseph Finder with *Company Man*. That's because Finder puts the emphasis on sharply created characters instead of potentially eye-glazing business minutiae."   —*Chicago Tribune*

PARANOIA

"A high-octane thrill ride."   *—San Francisco Chronicle*

"The most entertaining thriller of the year."
—Publishers Weekly

"Jet-propelled…this twisting, stealthily plotted story…
weaves a tangled and ingeniously enveloping web…
[with a] killer twist for the end."
—The New York Times

"Riveting…perhaps the finest of the contemporary
thriller novelists. . . You may think you've read one
mystery too many. Find Finder and you'll think
again."   *—Pittsburgh Post-Gazette*

"Page-turning perfection…Finder has that rare knack
for instantly pulling the reader into the story and then
tops that with surprises within surprises."
—Cleveland Plain Dealer

"Fast, funny, and very, very topical."
—Toronto Globe and Mail

"Imaginative and original, this is a gripping thriller
with three characteristics too rare in the genre: humor,
heart, and good writing."   *—Detroit Free Press*

Also by
JOSEPH FINDER

FICTION

The Moscow Club

Extraordinary Powers

The Zero Hour

High Crimes

Paranoia

Company Man

Killer Instinct

Power Play

NONFICTION

Red Carpet: The Connection Between the Kremlin and America's Most Powerful Businessmen

VANISHED

Joseph Finder

St. Martin's Paperbacks

For Molly Friedrich
Agent, adviser, friend

VANISHED

Copyright © 2009 by Joseph Finder.

Cover photograph © Michal Besser / Alamy

For information address St. Martin's Press, 175 Fifth Avenue, New York, NY 10010.

Library of Congress Catalog Card Number: 2009013029

ISBN: 978-0-312-94651-7

Printed in the United States of America

St. Martin's Press hardcover edition / August 2009
St. Martin's Paperbacks edition / August 2010

St. Martin's Paperbacks are published by St. Martin's Press, 175 Fifth Avenue, New York, NY 10010.

10 9 8 7 6 5 4 3 2 1

PART ONE

Behind every great fortune lies a great crime.
—Honoré de Balzac

PROLOGUE

Lauren Heller's husband disappeared at a few minutes after ten thirty on a rainy evening.

They were walking to their car after dinner at his favorite Japanese restaurant, on Thirty-third Street in Georgetown. Roger, a serious sushi connoisseur, considered Oji-San the best, most authentic place in all of D.C. Lauren didn't care one way or another. Raw fish was raw fish, she thought: pretty, but inedible. But Roger—the Mussolini of maki, the Stalin of sashimi—never settled for less than the best. "Hey, I married you, right?" he pointed out on the way over, and how was she supposed to argue with that?

She was just grateful they were finally having a date night. They hadn't had one in almost three months.

Not that it had been much of a date, actually. He'd seemed awfully preoccupied. Worried about something. Then again, he got that way sometimes, for days at a time. That was just the way he dealt with stress at the office. A very male thing, she'd always thought. Men tended to internalize their problems. Women usually let it out, got emotional, screamed or cried or just got mad, and ended up coping a lot better in the long run. If that wasn't emotional intelligence, then what was?

But Roger, whom she loved and admired and who was probably the smartest guy she'd ever met, handled stress like a typical man. Plus, he didn't like to talk about things. That was just his way. That was how he'd been brought up. She remembered once saying to him, "We need to talk," and he replied, "Those are the scariest four words in the English language."

Anyway, they had a firm rule: no shop talk. Since they both worked at Gifford Industries—he as a senior finance guy, she as admin to the CEO—that was the only way to keep work from invading their home life.

So at dinner, Roger barely said a word, checked his BlackBerry every few minutes, and scarfed down his nigiri. She'd ordered something recommended by their waiter, which sounded good but turned out to be layers of miso-soaked black cod. The house specialty. Yuck. She left it untouched, picked at her seaweed salad, drank too much sake, got a little tipsy.

They'd cut through Cady's Alley, a narrow cobblestone walkway lined with old red-brick warehouses converted to high-end German kitchen stores and Italian lighting boutiques. Their footsteps echoed hollowly.

She stopped at the top of the concrete steps that led down to Water Street and said, "Feel like getting some ice cream? Thomas Sweet, maybe?"

The oblique beam of a streetlight caught his white teeth, his strong nose, the pouches that had recently appeared under his eyes. "I thought you're on South Beach."

"They have some sugar-free stuff that's not bad."

"It's all the way over on P, isn't it?"

"There's a Ben & Jerry's on M."

"We probably shouldn't press our luck with Gabe."

"He'll be fine," she said. Their son was fourteen: old enough to stay home by himself. In truth, staying home alone made him a little nervous though he'd never admit it. The kid was as stubborn as his parents.

Water Street was dark, deserted, kind of creepy at that time of night. A row of cars were parked along a chain-link fence, the scrubby banks of the Potomac just beyond. Roger's black S-Class Mercedes was wedged between a white panel van and a battered Toyota.

He stood for a moment, rummaged through his pockets, then turned abruptly. "Damn. Left the keys back in the restaurant."

She grunted, annoyed but not wanting to make a big deal out of it.

"You didn't bring yours, did you?"

Lauren shook her head. She rarely drove his Mercedes anyway. He was too fussy about his car. "Check your pockets?"

He patted the pockets of his trench coat and his pants and suit jacket as if to prove it. "Yeah. Must've left them on the table in the restaurant when I took out my Black-Berry. Sorry about that. Come on."

"We don't both have to go back. I'll wait here."

A motorcycle blatted by from somewhere below. The white-noise roar of trucks on the Whitehurst Freeway overhead.

"I don't want you standing out here alone."

"I'll be fine. Just hurry, okay?"

He hesitated, took a step toward her, then suddenly kissed her on the lips. "I love you," he said.

She stared at his back as he hustled across the street. It pleased her to hear that *I love you,* but she wasn't used to it, really. Roger Heller was a good husband and father, but not the most demonstrative of men.

A distant shout, then raucous laughter: frat kids, probably Georgetown or GW.

A scuffling sound from the pavement behind her.

She turned to look, felt a sudden gust of air, and a hand was clamped over her mouth.

She tried to scream, but it was stifled beneath the

large hand, and she struggled frantically. Roger so close. Maybe a few hundred feet away by then. Close enough to see what was happening to her, if only he'd turn around.

Powerful arms had grabbed her from behind.

She needed to get Roger's attention, but he obviously couldn't hear anything at that distance, the scuffling masked by the traffic sounds.

Turn around, damn it! she thought. *Good God, please turn around!*

"*Roger!*" she screamed, but it came out a pathetic mewl. She smelled some kind of cheap cologne, mixed with stale cigarette smoke.

She tried to twist her body around, to wrench free, but her arms were trapped, pinioned against the sides of her body, and she felt something cold and hard at her temple, and she heard a click, and then something struck the side of her head, a jagged lightning bolt of pain piercing her eyes.

The foot. Stomp on his foot—some half-remembered martial-arts self-defense class from long ago.

Stomp his instep.

She jammed her left foot down hard, striking nothing, then kicked backwards, hit the Mercedes with a hollow metallic crunch. She tried to pivot, and—

Roger swiveled suddenly, alerted by the sound. He shouted, "Lauren!"

Raced back across the street.

"What the hell are you doing to her?" he screamed. "Why *her*?"

Something slammed against the back of her head. She tasted blood.

She tried to make sense of what was going on, but she was falling backwards, hurtling through space, and that was the last thing she remembered.

1

It was a dark and stormy night.

Actually, it wasn't stormy. But it was dark and rainy and miserable and, for L.A., pretty damned cold. I stood in the drizzle at eleven o'clock at night, under the sickly yellow light from the high-pressure sodium lamps, wearing a fleece and jeans that were soaking wet and good leather shoes that were in the process of getting destroyed.

I'd had the shoes handmade in London for some ridiculous amount of money, and I made a mental note to bill my employer, Stoddard Associates, for the damage, just on general principle.

I hadn't expected rain. Though, as a putatively high-powered international investigator with a reputation for being able to see around corners, I supposed I could have checked Weather.com.

"That's the one," the man standing next to me grunted, pointing at a jet parked a few hundred feet away. He was wearing a long yellow rain slicker with a hood—he hadn't offered me one back in the office—and his face was concealed by shadows. All I could see was his bristly white mustache.

Elwood Sawyer was the corporate security director

of Argon Express Cargo, a competitor of DHL and FedEx, though a lot smaller. He wasn't happy to see me, but I couldn't blame him. I didn't want to be here myself. My boss, Jay Stoddard, had sent me here at the last minute to handle an emergency for a new client I'd never heard of.

An entire planeload of cargo had vanished sometime in the last twenty-four hours. Someone had cleaned out one of their planes at this small regional airport south of L.A. Twenty thousand pounds of boxes and envelopes and packages that had arrived the previous day from Brussels. Gone.

You couldn't even begin to calculate the loss. Thousands of missing packages meant thousands of enraged customers and lawsuits up the wazoo. A part of the shipment belonged to one customer, Traverse Development Group, which had hired my firm to locate their cargo. They were urgent about it, and they weren't going to rely on some second-string cargo company to find it for them.

But the last thing Elwood Sawyer wanted was some high-priced corporate investigator from Washington, D.C., standing there in a pair of fancy shoes telling him how he'd screwed up.

The cargo jet he was pointing at stood solitary and dark and rain-slicked, gleaming in the airfield lights. It was glossy white, like all Argon cargo jets, with the company's name painted across the fuselage in bold orange Helvetica. It was a Boeing 727, immense and magnificent.

An airplane up close is a thing of beauty. Much more awe-inspiring than the view from inside when you're trapped with the seat of the guy in front of you tilted all the way back, crushing your knees. The jet was one of maybe twenty planes parked in a row on the apron nearby. Some of them, I guessed, were there for the weekend, some for the night, since the control tower closed at ten o'clock. There were chocks under their wheels and traffic cones around each one denoting the circle of safety.

"Let's take a look inside, Elwood," I said.

Sawyer turned to look at me. He had bloodshot basset-hound eyes with big saggy pouches beneath them.

"Woody," he said. He was correcting me, not trying to be friends.

"Okay. Woody."

"There's nothing to see. They cleaned it out." In his right hand he clutched one of those aluminum clip-boards in a hinged box, the kind that truck drivers and cops always carry around.

"Mind if I take a look anyway? I've never seen the inside of a cargo plane."

"Mr. Keller—"

"Heller."

"Mr. Keller, we didn't hire you, and I don't have time to play tour guide, so why don't you go back to interviewing the ground crew while I try to figure out how someone managed to smuggle three truckloads of freight out of this airport without anyone noticing?"

He turned to walk back to the terminal, and I said, "Woody, look. I'm not here to make you look bad. We both want the same thing—to find the missing cargo. I might be able to help. Two heads are better than one, and all that."

He kept walking. "Uh-huh. Well, that's real thought-ful, but I'm kinda busy right now."

"Okay. So . . . Mind if I use your name?" I said.

He stopped, didn't turn around. "For what?"

"My client's going to ask for a name. The guy at Tra-verse Development can be a vindictive son of a bitch." Actually, I didn't even know who at Traverse had hired my firm.

Woody didn't move.

"You know how these guys work," I said. "When I tell my client how Argon Express wasn't interested in any outside assistance, he's going to ask me for a name. Maybe he'll admire your independent spirit—that go-it-alone thing. Then again, maybe he'll just get pissed off so bad that they'll just stop doing business with you guys. No big deal to them. Then word gets around. Like maybe you guys were covering something up, right? Maybe there's the threat of a huge lawsuit. Pretty soon, Argon Express goes belly-up. And all because of you."

Woody still wasn't moving, but I could see his shoulders start to slump. The back of his yellow slicker was streaked with oil and grime.

"But between you and me, Woody, I gotta admire you for having the guts to tell Traverse Development where to get off. Not too many people have the balls to do that."

Woody turned around slowly. I don't think I'd ever seen anyone blink so slowly and with such obvious hostility. He headed toward the plane, and I followed close behind.

There was a hydraulic hum, and the big cargo door came open like the lift gate on a suburban minivan. Woody was standing in the belly of the plane. He gestured me inside with a weary flip of his hand.

He must have switched on an auxiliary power unit because the lights inside the plane were on, a series of naked bulbs in wire cages mounted on the ceiling. The interior was cavernous. You could see the rails where the rows of seats used to be. Just a black floor marked with red lines where the huge cargo containers were supposed to go, only there were no containers here. White windowless walls lined with some kind of papery white material.

I whistled. Totally bare. "The plane was full when it flew in?"

"Mmm-hmm. Twelve igloos."

" 'Igloos' are the containers, right?"

He walked over to the open cargo door. The rain was thrumming against the plane's aluminum skin. "Look for yourself."

A crew was loading another Argon cargo jet right next to us. They worked in that unhurried, efficient manner of a team that had done this a thousand times before. A couple of guys were pushing an immense container, eight or ten feet high and shaped like a child's drawing of a house, from the back of a truck onto the steel elevator platform of a K-loader. I counted seven guys. Two to push the igloo off the truck, two more to roll it onto the plane, another one to operate the K-loader. Two more guys whose main job seemed to be holding aluminum clipboards and shouting orders. The next jet down, another white Boeing but not one of theirs, was being refueled.

"No way you could get twelve containers off this plane without a crew of at least five," I said. "Tell me something. This plane got in yesterday, right? What took you so long to unload it?"

He sighed exasperatedly. "International cargo has to be inspected by U.S. Customs before we do anything. It's the law."

"That takes an hour or two at most."

"Yeah, normally. Weekends, Customs doesn't have the manpower. So they just cleared the crew to get off and go home. Sealed it up. Let it sit there until they had time to do an inspection."

"So while the plane was sitting here, anyone could have gotten inside. Looks like all the planes just sit here unattended all night. Anyone could climb into one."

"That's the way it works in airports around the

world, buddy. If you're cleared to get onto the airfield, they figure you're supposed to be here. It's called the 'honest-man' system of security."

I chuckled. "That's a good one. I gotta use it sometime."

Woody gave me a look.

I paced along the plane's interior. There was a surprising amount of rust in the places where there was no liner or white paint. "How old is this thing?" I called out. My voice echoed. It seemed even colder in here than it was outside. The rain was pattering hypnotically on the plane's exterior.

"Thirty years easy. They stopped making the Boeing seven-twos in 1984, but most of them were made in the sixties and seventies. They're workhorses, I'm telling you. Long as you do the upkeep, they last forever."

"You guys buy 'em used or new?"

"Used. Everyone does. FedEx, DHL, UPS—we all buy used planes. It's a lot cheaper to buy an old passenger plane and have it converted into a cargo freighter."

"What does one of these cost?"

"Why? You thinking of going into the business?"

"Everyone has a dream."

He looked at me. It took him a few seconds to get that I was being sarcastic. "You can get one of these babies for three hundred thousand bucks. There's hundreds of them sitting in airplane boneyards in the desert. Like used-car lots."

I walked to the front of the plane. Mounted to the doorframe was the data plate, a small stainless-steel square the size of a cigarette pack. Every plane has one. They're riveted on by the manufacturer, and they're sort of like birth certificates. This one said THE BOEING COMPANY—COMMERCIAL AIRPLANE DIVISION—RENTON, WASHINGTON, and it listed the year of manufacture

(1974) and a bunch of other numbers: the model and the serial number and so on.

I pulled out a little Maglite and looked closer and saw just what I expected to see.

I stepped back out onto the air stairs, the cold rain spritzing my face, and I reached out and felt the slick painted fuselage. I ran my hand over the Argon Express logo, felt something. A ridge. The paint seemed unusually thick.

Woody was watching me from a few feet away. My fingers located the lower left corner of the two-foot-tall letter A.

"You don't paint your logo on?" I asked.

"Of course it's painted on. What the hell—?"

It peeled right up. I tugged some more, and the entire logo—some kind of adhesive vinyl sticker—began to lift off.

"Check out the data plate," I said. "It doesn't match the tail number."

"That's—that's *impossible*!"

"They didn't just steal the cargo, Woody. They stole the whole plane."

2

WASHINGTON

"I think I saw her eyelids move."

A woman's voice, distant and echoing, which worked itself into the fevered illogic of a dream.

Everything deep orange, the color of sunset. Murmured voices; a steady high-pitched beep.

Her eyelids wouldn't open. It felt as if her eyelashes had been glued together.

Against the blood orange sky, stars rushed at her. She was falling headlong through a sky crowded with stars. They dazzled and clotted into odd-shaped white clouds, and then the light became harsh and far too strong and needles of pain jabbed the backs of her eyeballs.

Her eyelashes came unstuck and fluttered like a bird's wings.

More high-pitched electronic beeps. Not regular anymore, but jumbled, a cacophony.

A man's voice: "Let's check an ionized calcium."

A clattering of something—dishes? Footsteps receding.

The man again: "Nurse, did that gas come back?"

The husky voice of another woman: "Janet, can you page Yurovsky now, please?"

Lauren said, "You don't have to shout."

"She made a sound. Janet, would you please page Yurovsky *now*?"

She tried again to speak, but then gave up the effort, let her eyelids close, the lashes gumming back together. The needles receded. She became aware of another kind of pain, deep and throbbing, at the back of her head. It pulsed in time to her heartbeat, rhythmically sending jagged waves of pain to a little spot just behind her forehead and above her eyes.

"Ms. Heller," said the man, "if you can hear me, say something, will you?"

"What do you want, I'm shouting!" Lauren said at the top of her voice.

"Now I see it," one of the female voices said. "Like she's trying to talk. I don't know what she said."

"I think she said 'Ow.' "

"The doctor's on rounds right now," one of the women said.

"I don't care *what* he's doing." The husky-voiced woman. "I don't care if he's in the medical supply closet screwing a nurse. If you don't page him right this second, I will."

Lauren smiled, or at least she thought she did.

She felt a hard pinch on her neck.

"Hey!" she protested.

Her eyelids flew open. The light was unbearably bright, just as painful, but everything was gauzy and indistinct, like there was a white scrim over everything. She wondered whether she'd fallen back asleep for several hours.

A hulking silhouette loomed, came close, then pulled back.

A male voice: "Well, she's responding to painful stimuli."

Yeah, I'll show you a painful stimulus, Lauren thought but couldn't say.

Actually, two silhouettes, she realized. She couldn't focus, though. Everything was strangely hazy, like every time you saw Lucille Ball in that dreadful movie version of *Mame.* Lauren had played the snooty Gloria Upson in the Charlottesville High School production of *Auntie Mame,* and she'd seen the Rosalind Russell movie countless times, but couldn't stand the Lucy one.

"Mrs. Heller, I'm Dr. Yurovsky. Can you hear me?"

Lauren considered replying, then decided not to bother. Too much effort. The words weren't coming out the way she wanted.

"Mrs. Heller, if you can hear me, I'd like you to wiggle your right thumb."

That she definitely didn't feel like doing. She blinked a few times, which cleared her vision a little.

Finally, she was able to see a man with a tall forehead and long chin, elongated like the man in the moon. Or like a horse. The face came slowly into focus, as if someone were turning a knob. A hooked nose, receding hair. His face was tipped in toward hers. He wore a look of intent concern.

She wiggled her right thumb.

"Mrs. Heller, do you know where you are?"

She tried to swallow, but her tongue was a big woolen sock. No saliva. *My breath must reek,* she thought.

"I'm guessing it's a hospital." Her voice was croaky.

She looked up. A white dropped ceiling with a rust stain on one of the panels, which didn't inspire confidence. Blue privacy curtains hung from a U-shaped rail. She wasn't in a private room. Some kind of larger unit, with a lot of beds: an ICU, maybe. A bag of clear liquid sagged on a metal stand, connected by a tube to her arm.

An immense bouquet of white lilies in a glass florist's vase on the narrow table next to her bed. She craned her neck just enough to see that they were calla lilies, her favorites. A lightning bolt of pain shot through her eyes. She groaned as she smiled.

"From Roger?"

A long pause. Someone whispered something. "From your boss."

Leland, she thought, smiling inwardly. *That's just like him.* She wondered who had ordered the flowers for him.

And how he knew what had happened to her.

She adjusted the thin blanket. "My head hurts," she said. She felt something lumpy under the blanket, on top of her belly. Pulled it out. A child's Beanie Baby: a yellow giraffe with orange spots and ugly Day-Glo green feet. It was tattered and soiled. Tears welled in her eyes.

"Your son dropped that off this morning," a woman said in a soft, sweet voice.

She turned. A nurse. She thought: *This morning?* That meant it wasn't morning anymore. She was confused; she'd lost all track of time.

Gabe's beloved Jaffee—as a toddler, he couldn't say "Giraffiti," the name printed on the label. Actually, neither could she. Too cute by half.

"Where is he?"

"Your son is fine, Mrs. Heller."

"Where is he?"

"I'm sure he's at home in bed. It's late."

"What—time is it?"

"It's two in the morning."

She tried to look at the nurse, but turning her head escalated the pain to a level nearly unendurable. How long had she been out? She remembered glancing at her watch just before they got back to the car, seeing 10:28. Almost ten thirty at night on Friday. The attack came not long after that. She tried to do the math. Four hours? Less: three and a half?

Lauren drew breath. "Wait—when did Gabe come

by? You said—you said, 'this morning'—but what time
is it—?"

"As I said, just after two in the morning."

"On Saturday?"

"Sunday. Sunday *morning*, actually. Or Saturday
night, depending on how you look at it."

Her brain felt like sludge, but she knew the nurse
had to be wrong. "*Saturday* morning, you mean."

The nurse shook her head, then looked at the
horse-faced doctor, who said, "You've been unconscious
for more than twenty-four hours. Maybe longer. It would
help us if you knew approximately what time the attack
took place."

"Twenty-four . . . hours? Where's—where's Roger?"

"Looks like you got a nasty blow to the back of the
head," the doctor said. "From everything we've seen,
you haven't sustained any injuries beyond a small spiral
fracture at the base of the skull. The CT scan doesn't
show any hematomas or blood clots. You were extremely
lucky."

I guess it depends on your definition of luck. She
recalled Roger's panicked face. The arms grabbing her
from behind. His scream: "Why *her*?"

"Is Roger okay?"

Silence.

"Where's Roger?"

No reply.

She felt the cold tendrils of fear in her stomach.

"Where *is* he? Is Roger okay or not?"

"A couple of policemen came by to talk to you," he
said. "But you don't have to talk to anyone until you feel
up to it."

"The police?" Tears welled in her eyes. "Oh, dear
God, what happened to him?"

A long pause.

"Oh, God, no," Lauren said. "Tell me he's okay."

"I'm sorry, Ms. Heller," the doctor said.

"What? Please, God, tell me he's alive!"

"I wish I could, Ms. Heller. But we don't know where your husband is."

3

Woody Sawyer ran after me, his boots clanging on the steel air stairs. "What are you saying?" he yelled over the clamor of the K-loader and the roar of a jet engine starting up nearby. "This isn't our plane?"

I didn't answer him. I was too busy looking around. A minute or so later I found what I was looking for.

It was the plane I'd seen being refueled earlier. A white Boeing 727 parked on the far side of the Argon jet that was being loaded. It looked identical to the two Argon jets—they could have been triplets—only it had the name VALU CHARTERS on its fuselage.

"Let's take a look inside," I said.

"That's not our plane!"

"Can you get a couple of your guys to roll one of those air stairs over here?"

"You out of your mind? That's not our plane!"

"Have you ever seen a Valu Charters jet around here before?"

"The hell do I know? These dinky little companies come and go, and they lease space from other companies—"

"I didn't see any Valu Charters listed on the airport directory, did you?"

Woody shrugged.

"Let's take a look," I said.

"Look, I could get in some serious deep trouble for boarding someone else's plane. That's illegal, man."

"Don't worry about it," I said. "I'll take the fall."

He hesitated a long time, shrugged again, then walked back to where the crew was loading. A minute or so later he came back, rolling a set of air stairs up to the Valu Charters plane. He climbed up to the cockpit door with visible reluctance.

Just as I suspected, underneath the Valu Charters logo—which also peeled right off—was the orange Argon Express Cargo logo. Painted on. Remnants of tamper-resistant tape adhered like old confetti to the doorframe of the cargo hatch.

When the door came open, I could see that it was fully loaded with row after row of cargo containers. Each one had a different set of numbers affixed to its sides—really, stick-on letters and numbers of random sizes, sort of like the cutout newsprint letters in a ransom note.

"Do the numbers match your manifest?" I said. I knew they would.

There was a long silence.

"I don't get it," Woody finally said. "How'd they switch planes?"

"Easy," I said. "It was a whole lot easier than off-loading and driving it out of the airport, and it only takes two guys—a pilot and a copilot."

"I don't follow."

"Didn't you just say you can buy one of these old junkers cheap? All they had to do was paint it white and fly it in here in the middle of the night after the control tower's closed. Park it nearby and slap on a couple of vinyl decals. Probably took two guys ten minutes, and no one was around to see them because everyone had gone home. But then, they were already on the airfield, so they were *supposed* to be here. No one probably gave them a second look. Honest-man security, right?"

"My God. Jesus. That's . . . *brilliant*."

"Well, almost. By the time they flew in last night, the fuel-service guys had gone home, too, I bet."

"So?"

"So that's why the plane's still here. They couldn't fly it out without filling the tank. Which they just finished doing. I'm guessing they were going to wait to take off until everyone went home."

"But . . . who could have done it?"

"I really don't care who. I wasn't hired to find out who."

"But—whoever did it—they must be around here somewhere."

"No doubt."

"Look, Mr.—can I call you Nick?"

"Sure."

"Nick, we both want the same thing. We agree on that."

"Okay."

"We're basically playing on the same team."

"Right."

"See, I really don't think Traverse Development needs to hear the little details, you get me? Just tell them we found the missing cargo. Or you did—I don't care. No harm, no foul. Some kind of mix-up at the airport. Happens from time to time. They're going to be mighty relieved, and they're not going to ask a lot of questions."

"Works for me."

"Great. Thanks."

"But first, would you mind opening this can right

here?" I approached one of the big containers. Most of the igloos were stuffed with hundreds of packages for a lot of different customers, but the routing label on this one indicated that it had originated in Bahrain. All of its contents were destined for the Arlington, Virginia, office of Traverse Development. Through a Plexiglas window, I could see tightly packed rows of cardboard boxes, all the same size and shape, all with Traverse Development's logo printed on them.

"I'm sorry, I can't do that," he said.

"You have the keys, Woody."

"Customs hasn't even inspected it yet. I could get in some deep kimchi."

"You could get in some even deeper kimchi if you don't."

"That supposed to be a threat?"

"Yeah, basically," I said. "See, my mind keeps going back to the parking-space thing."

"Parking space? What about it?"

"Well, so, whenever one of your planes lands and parks for the night or whatever, your crew has to record the number of the space it's parked in. Standard operating procedure, right?"

He shrugged. "What's this about?"

"Your Argon jet flies in from Brussels yesterday and parks in space 36, right? That's in your computer records. Then our bad guys do this big switcheroo with the decals, so what *looks* like your plane ends up in the wrong space. Number 34, right? Only the problem is, someone already entered 36 in the computer log, couple minutes after it landed. Which isn't so easy to backdate. And which could be a problem when the guy from Customs comes to check things out, and he's going to go, 'Huh, how'd that plane get moved overnight, like by magic?' So someone wrote the *new* space, number 34, on the whiteboard in your office. That would be . . . you. Woody."

Woody began to sputter, indignant. "You don't know the first thing about how our operations work."

I tapped on the Plexiglas window of the cargo container. "Why don't you pop this open, then we'll talk. I'm really curious what's in here that would make you and two of your employees risk such a long stretch in prison. Gotta be something totally worth it."

He stared at me for a few seconds, then whined, "Come on, man, I open this, I could get in trouble."

"Kind of a little late for that," I said.

"I can't open this," he said, almost pleading. "I really can't."

"Okay," I said, shrugging. "But you got a phone book I could borrow first? See, I want to call around to some of the aircraft boneyards. There aren't that many of them—what, six or seven airparks in California and Arizona and Nevada? And I'm going to read off the serial number of that old junker over there and find out who sold it. And who they sold it to. Oh, sure, it'll probably be some dummy company, but that'll be easy to trace."

"I thought you don't care who did it," Woody said. His sallow face had turned deep red.

"See, that's my problem. Kind of a personal failing. I get my hooks into something, I can't stop. Sort of an obsessive-compulsive thing."

He cleared his throat. "Come on, man."

I tapped the Plexiglas window of the igloo. "Let's pop the hood here so I can take a quick look, then you can get back to your Sudoku." I tried to peer through the window, but the Plexiglas was scratched and fogged, and all I could see were the boxes. I turned around and gave Woody a smile and found myself looking into the

barrel of a SIG-Sauer P229, a nine-millimeter semiautomatic.

"Woody," I said, disappointed, "I thought we were
playing on the same team."

4

"Hands up, Heller," Woody said, "and turn around."

I didn't put my hands up. Or turn around. I waited.

"Let's go," he said. "Move it." There was a tic in his right eye.

"Woody, you're making things worse."

"You're on private property here, and I asked you nicely to leave, okay? So move it. Hands up."

I brought my hands up slowly, then thrust my left hand up quickly and suddenly and grabbed the barrel of the SIG and torqued it downward while I smashed my right fist into his mouth. He yelped. Like most guys who brandish weapons, he wasn't prepared to defend himself without one. He tried to wrest his gun from my grip, and at the same time he turned his head away, thereby offering up his ear, which my right fist connected with, and he yelped again. Then I levered the pistol's barrel upward until his index finger, trapped in the trigger guard, snapped like a dry twig.

Woody screamed and sank to his knees. I pointed his SIG-Sauer at him and said, "Now would you mind unlocking this container, please?"

He struggled to his feet, and I didn't help him up.

"There's a seal on it," he said. "They're going to know I opened it."

"I'll take care of Customs."

"I'm not talking about Customs."

"Who are you worried about?"

He shook his head, then shook his right hand, moaned. "You broke my finger."

"Awful sorry," I said, not sounding very sorry.

Groaning the whole time, he walked around to the back of the igloo and inserted one of his keys in a padlock, then rolled up a panel.

"You got a box cutter?" I said.

He pulled one out of a holster on his belt and handed it to me. I tucked his gun into the waistband of my pants, sliced open one of the cardboard cartons, and pried the flaps apart.

When I realized what was inside, I smiled. "No wonder my client was a little antsy about it."

"Good God Almighty," Woody said.

The box was tightly packed with shrink-wrapped packages of brand-new United States currency.

Hundred-dollar bills: the new ones, of course, with the off-center engraving of Ben Franklin looking constipated. Each oblong bundle—"bricks," they're officially called—was stamped in black letters REPORT ANY DISCREPANCIES TO YOUR LOCAL FEDERAL RESERVE OFFICE and had a bar code printed at one end.

These were fresh, unopened packs of money from the U.S. Bureau of Engraving that somehow had ended up in Bahrain, in the hands of some company in Arlington, Virginia, I'd never heard of before that morning.

"I had no idea," Woody said. "I swear."

"What's the volume of this thing?" I thumped the side of the igloo.

"I don't know, like around five hundred cubic feet, maybe? Just shy of that."

I thought for a moment. I'm pretty good at math—one of the few remaining legacies of my father, who was not only a math whiz but an immensely rich man before he went to prison.

I unwrapped one brick and counted forty packets of bills. Each packet contained a hundred bills; they always do. That meant that each brick was worth four hundred thousand dollars. One cubic foot, I figured, was a bit less than three million dollars.

Assuming that each box was packed with bricks of hundred-dollar bills, just like this one, the container held almost a billion dollars. Maybe more.

A billion dollars.

I'd never seen a billion dollars up close and personal. I was impressed by how much space it took up, even in hundred-dollar bills.

"A little spending money, Woody?"

He'd stopped nursing his broken index finger. He was gaping. "My God . . . My God . . . I had no idea."

"What did you think was in here?"

"I . . . I had no idea. Honestly, I didn't! I'm telling you, I had no idea—they didn't . . ."

"No idea at all, Woody?"

He didn't look up. "They didn't give me details."

"But someone knew. A lot of time and money and thought went into this. And the risk of hiring you and a couple other guys in your company."

"I just did my part."

"Which was to make sure the switch went through no problem."

He nodded.

"I'll bet they gave you an emergency contact number. In case something got screwed up."

He nodded.

"I want that number, Woody."

He glanced up at me, then down.

"See, Woody," I said, "this is where the road forks. You can either cooperate with me and make things better. Or not, and make things even worse. A whole lot worse."

He said nothing.

My cell phone started ringing. There was no one I needed to talk to. I let it go to voice mail.

"Woody, you sure as hell didn't pull this off by yourself. No offense. So why don't you give me a phone number?"

"I thought you didn't care who did it," Woody said once again.

"I do now," I said.

Everyone who served in the Iraq war knew the stories about the missing American cash. Not long after the U.S. invaded Iraq, the U.S. government secretly flew twelve billion dollars in cash to Baghdad. I know it's hard to believe, and it sounds like it was made up by one of those wacko left-wing conspiracy-obsessed blogs on the Internet. But it's a matter of documented fact. Twelve billion dollars in U.S. banknotes was trucked from the Federal Reserve Bank in East Rutherford, New Jersey, to Andrews Air Force Base outside Washington, where it was put on pallets and loaded on C-130 military transport planes and flown to Baghdad.

The idea, I guess, was that this was the only way to pay our contractors working in Iraq and run the puppet government: in stacks of Benjamins. Baghdad was awash in crisp new American banknotes. Gunnysacks full of cash sat around, unguarded, in Iraqi ministry offices. Bureaucrats and soldiers played football with bricks of hundred-dollar bills.

And here's the best part: Somehow, nine billion dollars just disappeared. Vanished. Without a trace.

I had an idea where some of it might have gone.

My cell phone started ringing again. Annoyed, I fished it out of my pocket, glanced at the caller ID. It said Lauren Heller—my brother's wife. In Washington, D.C., it was around one in the morning. She wasn't calling to chat.

I answered, "Lauren, what's up?"

"It's me."

Not Lauren. The voice of an adolescent boy. Lauren's fourteen-year-old son, Gabe.

I hadn't spoken to my obnoxious brother in months, but I liked his wife a lot, and her son—Roger's stepson—was a great kid. Gabe and I talked on the phone at least once a week, and I did stuff with him as often as I could. He was the son I didn't have, might not ever have; and I was, I guess, the father he lacked. Having ended up with Roger as his stepfather instead.

"Hey, bud, I'm sorry. I can't really talk now. I'm with a client." I glanced at Woody, pulled his SIG-Sauer from my waistband, and wagged it at the guy. Like some overworked customer-service representative, I said apologetically: "I'll be right with you."

"Uncle Nick," Gabe said. "You need to get over here."

"I'm not in D.C., Gabe. What's wrong?"

"It's Mom. She's in the hospital."

"What happened? Is she okay?"

"I think she's in a coma."

"A *coma*? How—"

"No one's telling me anything. She got mugged or something, but—"

"Where's your dad? Is he out of town on business?"

"I don't know where he is. *No* one does. *Please*, Uncle Nick. Can you get back here now?"

"Gabe," I said, "I'm in the middle of something, but as soon as I can—"

"Uncle Nick," he said, "I need you."

5

WASHINGTON

She must have fallen asleep again—a fitful, distressed sleep, troubled by dreams that were far too real. Gabe visiting her in the hospital, his curly hair a mess, crying when he saw her. A doctor with a long chin and a high-domed forehead peering into her eyes with a bright light. She awoke, slowly this time, unsure which if any of these things had actually happened.

When she opened her eyes again, she could tell right away she'd been moved. None of that frantic intensive-care cacophony, the jumbled voices and quick footsteps or the dissonant symphony of electronic beeping. One machine beeping quietly, but not much else. Quiet whispers.

The quality of light was different somehow. Daylight, maybe. There had to be a window somewhere nearby. She'd slept through the night. Another night, come to think of it.

Two men in jackets and ties stood at the foot of her bed. One a lot older than the other. *Cops,* she thought.

For a moment she thought she might still be dreaming. She closed her eyes and went away for a while, but when she opened them again, they were still there, talking quietly to each other. One of them glanced at her, approached.

He was around sixty, with thinning white hair and a scraggly white beard that she guessed had been grown to conceal a weak chin. "Mrs. Heller, I'm Detective Garvin from the D.C. police department." He was holding a giant Dunkin' Donuts cup. "And this is Detective Scarpino."

The guy standing behind him—cute, dark-haired, the innocent face of a boy and the body of a linebacker—looked barely thirty. "How's it going?" he said, smiling, and she couldn't help smiling back.

They each took out leather badge holders and flipped them open. She saw only a flash of gold, a glint of silver.

The older one sat slowly, gingerly, on the only chair, as if he had a bad back. "How are you feeling, Mrs. Heller?" His partner went scrounging for another chair from somewhere beyond the blue curtains, the boundaries of her world.

"Where's my husband?" she said.

Garvin went on as if he hadn't heard her. "One of the nurses gave us the heads-up that you were okay to talk, but if you don't feel up to it, we can come back."

"What time is it?"

"Around nine. In the morning."

"Are you here about my husband?"

Garvin wore steel aviator rim glasses with thick lenses that grotesquely magnified his bleary pale eyes—gray? blue? Hard to say. "Mrs. Heller, we'd like to ask you some questions about what happened."

The throbbing behind her eyes was back with a vengeance. "Are you . . . homicide detectives?" she asked in a choked voice.

He shook his head, gave a prim smile. "We're from the Violent Crime Branch."

The words made her stomach flip over. "Detective, where's my husband?" she said, heart thudding. "Have you found him or not?"

"No, ma'am. Nothing."

"What do you mean, 'nothing'?"

"Every hospital in the city and the surrounding area has been called. Medical examiners' offices, even the central cellblock."

"Cellblock?"

"We don't want to rule anything out. A notice went out on WALES—the Washington area law-enforcement network."

"And . . . ?"

"Nothing, ma'am. I'm sorry. At this point, we're treating this as a missing-persons case."

"How do you know he wasn't—harmed? Or worse?"

"Our crime scene squad didn't find any cartridge casings or bloodstains or anything else that would indicate bodily harm."

" 'Missing persons' . . . ?"

He hesitated. "Missing Person Critical, actually."

Scarpino returned with a molded plastic chair and scraped it into place behind his partner's.

"Why 'critical'?"

"Suspicion of foul play."

"But you just said you didn't find anything."

"Because of what happened to you."

"How do you know I wasn't just mugged or something?"

"Because, ma'am, you were identified by the contents of your purse. Someone saw you lying in the street and called nine-one-one, and because you still had your wallet, we knew who you were and who to call."

His stare was penetrating, downright unnerving.

"So?"

"Tells us you probably weren't mugged, right? So

maybe you could tell us as much about the incident as you remember."

She told them everything she could. Garvin asked all the questions; Scarpino, clearly the recessive gene, said nothing, took notes.

"The attacker—was there only one of them?" Garvin asked.

"As far as I know. I mean, some guy grabbed me from behind, and I guess he hit me on the head with something, though I don't remember that part. And . . . yes, I think he put a gun to my head."

"Where?"

"Right here." She pointed to her temple.

"Before or after you were hit in the head?"

"Before."

"What makes you so sure it was a gun?"

"I—I don't know, it was hard and round and it felt like metal and—I mean, I suppose it could have been anything, but—"

"You didn't see it, though."

"No, but—actually, come to think of it, I remember hearing a click. Like a revolver being cocked."

"You know what that sounds like?"

"My dad kept one in the house. I don't think he ever fired it, but he showed me and my sister how to use it."

"Did the attacker try to get your clothes off?"

"No. But he might have been scared off when Roger showed up."

"Let's back up a little. You and your husband went out to dinner, just the two of you, right?"

"Right."

"A special occasion?"

Date night, she wanted to say, but instead she replied, "Just dinner."

"Whose idea was it to go out to dinner?"

"What difference does it make?"

"We're just trying to get the big picture here."

"It was Roger's."

"Did you go out for dinner often, just the two of you?"

"Not often enough. We used to go out every week, but recently that's sort of . . . Well, it's been months, probably."

"Did your husband have any enemies that you know of?"

"Enemies? He's a businessman."

"Mrs. Heller, are you and your husband wealthy?"

Lauren hesitated. What a question. She didn't know how to begin to answer that. Wealthy compared to whom? To a police detective? She made a good salary, but it was still a secretary's salary. Roger made a lot more than she, as a senior vice president, but in the six figures. Not the million-plus that the top corporate officers earned. They lived in a nice house in Chevy Chase. Compared to the house where she and Maura had grown up in Charlottesville—a tiny split-level ranch—it was Versailles.

On the other hand, compared to the kind of money Roger's family once had, they were paupers.

"We're well-off," she finally said. She hesitated. "My husband's family used to be quite rich, but not anymore."

Garvin blinked. "Oh?"

"You might have heard of his father, Victor Heller."

A pause. "Sure." A blank look clouded his eyes. Not an uncommon reaction, she'd found. Victor Heller was famous, and not in a good way. "You think people might assume the family still has money?"

"How would I know? Anyway, if someone thought he was rich, wouldn't there be a ransom demand? Wouldn't they kidnap me instead of him? Or my son?"

"Just exploring every possibility, that's all. Did you

notice any change in your husband's behavior recently? Did he start to act differently toward you?"

"I'm not sure I understand what you're getting at."

"Let me ask you something, and please don't take this the wrong way: You and your husband—how was your relationship?"

"What's that supposed to mean?"

"Was there any talk of divorce? Do you think he might have been having an affair?"

"You're really clutching at straws, Detective."

"Not at all. It's standard procedure—we never want to leave any stone unturned."

"Our relationship was—fine."

"Not great? Just fine?"

"We had our ups and down like any married couple. But no, he wasn't cheating on me. And we never talked about divorce."

"Did he ever threaten you, Mrs. Heller?"

"Oh, this is ridiculous."

"Look, Mrs. Heller, we all want to find out what happened to him, too, but we can't do that without your help. We really can't. I know this is a stressful time for you, and I know you're in a lot of pain, but time is really crucial here. The faster we move, the more likely we are to solve this thing."

"Isn't it possible that my husband was attacked, too, and he's wandering around in a state of amnesia or something? Or maybe he's been badly hurt. Or . . . or worse. And meanwhile you two are sitting here spinning out all sorts of wacky scenarios. You're guessing, that's all. *Guessing.*"

"Yeah, well, guessing is a lot of what we do. I get good at guessing. And yeah, maybe we're clutching at straws. But that's all we got at this point, Mrs. Heller. All we know is that you were the victim of a random-seeming attack in a part of the city where that doesn't happen very often. You weren't mugged, and apparently they didn't try to rape you. We have no reason to believe your husband was killed. He's gone, and we don't know more than that. Without evidence, without a motive, we're not going to get anywhere, do you understand?"

"You don't sound very optimistic."

"I don't want to give you false hope, is all."

Someone made a throat-clearing sound, and they all turned around.

Gabe was standing there. His dark ringlets wild and scraggly. He was staring at her, an expression of grave concern in his liquid brown eyes. Black jeans and a black hoodie sweatshirt with a weird cartoon character on the front: Invader Zim, she remembered. He looked even scrawnier than usual.

"Gabe," she called out.

"Excuse me, Officers," he said sternly. "My mother needs to rest. You need to leave now."

The younger cop grinned until he caught the sharp edge of Gabe's adolescent glower, then the two detectives began to gather their things.

6

"Hey," she said hoarsely, when the cops had left.

"Hey."

Tears in his eyes, she saw. In the last year her sweet boy had become a remote and often surly teenager. But once in a while there were flashes of the adoring son he'd once been and would, she hoped, be again. Her love for him swelled in her chest, like a physical object, expanding her ribs, her collarbones.

"Thanks."

"I'm serious. They shouldn't be here."

She noticed the dark circles under his eyes. They appeared whenever he was sick or overtired or just worried. Which was often. More than a few pimples on his cheeks, which hadn't been there two months ago.

In his right hand he was clutching his beat-up school notebook, spiral-bound, ST. GREGORY'S on the cover. The notebook had nothing to do with school, though. She wasn't allowed to look at it, which made it all the more tempting, though she never had. All she knew was that it contained some epic-length comic book he'd been working on for a year or more. She'd caught a glimpse once before he snatched it away and was astonished at the quality of the drawings.

"Thanks for lending me Jaffee," she said. She reached out a hand, held his. He squeezed her hand back. That was about as much affection as he ever showed her anymore. He hated being kissed or hugged, tended to shrink from her caresses as if she had some grotesque infectious disease.

"Your blood pressure is really bad," he said.

"Why do you say that?"

"That machine keeps beeping."

"It's supposed to do that. Don't worry about it. I'm fine."

"You don't look fine."

"I look worse than I feel."

"Lot of flowers," Gabe said.

"From Lee."

She meant Leland Gifford, the CEO and son of the founder of Gifford Industries. He'd find someone to cover for her, of course—likely Noreen, who worked in the same executive suite as Lauren but was underemployed as the admin to the CFO and lusted after Lauren's job. She was a disaster, though: not too bright, not very detail-oriented, not half as competent as she thought she was. Now Lauren had something else to worry about. Leland ran a multibillion-dollar corporation, but he barely knew how to send e-mail.

Half to herself, she added, "Somebody must have told him what happened."

Gabe shrugged. "I e-mailed him from your computer at home."

"You e-mailed him?"

"What, I'm not supposed to e-mail your boss?"

"No, it's—I'm impressed, that's all. Thank you." She fumbled with the bed's controls, raised the head of the bed so she was finally upright. She murmured, mostly to herself, "I've got to get myself released from this place. I've got to get back there."

"Mom, you have a serious concussion, and you just woke up from being unconscious for twenty-four hours. Leland Gifford will be fine for a while without you." Abruptly, he added: "Okay, Mom. Where is he?"

"Who?"

"You know who I mean. Where's Dad?"

She hesitated for a few seconds while she tried to think. Her brain was operating at half speed. She blinked, silent for a beat too long. What had they told him? She tried never to lie to him. Even if she wanted to, he was too smart to lie to.

The kid scared her sometimes, he was so smart. She wondered where he inherited it. Not from her gene pool, that was for sure. Richard, her first husband and Gabe's father, was smart enough but no genius. She also wondered from time to time whether being so precocious made him an outcast at his private boys' school. It couldn't be easy.

"He went on a business trip," she finally said. "Sort of an emergency. A last-minute thing."

Now Gabe's eyes went flat. "Don't, Mom. The cops came to the house yesterday looking for him."

"You—you were alone, Gabe?"

"Of course I was alone. I'm fine. I'm fourteen."

"Oh, God, Gabe."

"Chillax, Mom, okay? It's all good."

" 'Chillax'?"

"I'm just freaked out about Dad, that's all. They wouldn't tell me anything, but . . ."

"But you overheard what they were saying to me."

He nodded.

She bit her lower lip, shook her head, and after a few seconds, she said, "Look, I don't know where he is."

"Did he—did he, like, go somewhere?"

She finally returned his gaze with a look that was equally fierce, yet also sorrowful and compassionate at the same time. "It's possible he got hurt in the attack—"

"Like he's lying somewhere bleeding to death?"

She shook her head. "The police assured me that he's not in any hospitals or . . ."

"Or morgues," he added.

"Which is a huge relief, Gabe. That means that he's—he's probably fine, just—"

"He's dead. You know he is." He swallowed, blinked rapidly, tears flooding his eyes.

"No, Gabe. No, he's not. Don't think that way."

"How do you *know* he's not?"

"Gabe, there'd—there'd be . . ." She couldn't continue.

"Do you think it's possible these guys who hurt you grabbed Dad or something? Like, kidnapped him?"

Finally, she replied, defeated, "I don't know what to think."

"Maybe Uncle Nick can find him."

"I know you love Uncle Nick. Me, too. I just don't think he can find anything the police can't. He does corporate work, mostly."

"Well, we'll see," Gabe said. "I called him and he told me he's on his way home now. He promised me he'd find Dad."

7

I'm not married, even though I've come dangerously close a few times, and I don't have a family of my own. My "family of origin," as the shrinks say, had been pretty well shattered by my father's very public arrest and the squalid events that followed. So my nephew, Gabe, means a lot to me. I'm extremely protective of him.

Strictly speaking, I'd finished my work in L.A. anyway. I'd done the job I'd been sent there to do: I'd located the missing shipment. As I waited at L.A.X. for the first flight to D.C. that had an available seat, I got on my BlackBerry and fired off an e-mail to Jay Stoddard with the details. As much as I wanted to stay on and indulge my own curiosity and dig into what had really happened there, that was a luxury I no longer had. I had no intention of dropping it, of course. I never drop anything. But I had to get back to D.C. and make sure that Gabe and his mother were okay.

Because whatever had happened to his father—my brother—didn't sound good at all. He'd been missing for two days.

The truth was, Roger and I hadn't been close since Dad's trial. Maybe that was a euphemistic way of putting it. I didn't like the guy, and he didn't like me either. We barely tolerated each other.

But damn it, he was my brother. And maybe more important, Gabe's stepfather.

And I couldn't suppress a feeling of gnawing anxiety, of growing disquiet.

The earliest flights were sold out, so I didn't get to Washington until the late afternoon. In the cab, I called Lauren's cell, expecting Gabe, and was surprised when Lauren picked up. The doctors were letting her go home. She told me what had happened, in broad outline, anyway. She sounded a little groggy but otherwise fine.

Which was a huge relief. Some of the tension I'd been feeling over the last several hours, like a low-level nagging headache, began to ebb away.

I stopped by my apartment, a loft in a converted warehouse in the Adams Morgan section of Washington. I'd bought it because there was parking in the building, and it came furnished. The agent talked about "hip modern urban living" and its "industrial aesthetic." A sign out front said, obnoxiously, "You. Are. Here." To me it looked like what it was, an old warehouse with raw concrete ceilings and a lot of painted ductwork. It had all the charm of an airplane hangar. Gabe thought it was cool, of course. He referred to it as my Fortress of Solitude.

A few hours later I pulled into the driveway of my brother's house on Virgilia Road in Chevy Chase, a big old Georgian Revival on a leafy street surrounded by other big old houses. It was made of red brick with black shutters and white trim. It was imposing from the front, and even more imposing inside: six bedrooms and seven and a half baths, five fireplaces, a big pool in the backyard that they never used.

Roger once cracked to me that my entire apartment could probably fit in his media room. I replied that his entire house could probably fit in the conservatory of our childhood home in Bedford. That shut him up. We both knew what it was like to have a lot of money. We never thought about it. But after we lost it, I actually felt relieved, like I was taking off tight shoes.

Whereas Roger became obsessed, like Ahab and his damned white whale, with what we'd lost.

I found Gabe sitting on the front steps. He was wearing a black hoodie sweatshirt and frayed black sneakers and had iPod earbuds in his ears. He was drawing in his mysterious notebook, the one he never let anyone look at. He closed it quickly as I approached.

"Hey," he said, pausing the music on his iPod, yanking the earbuds out. "Thanks for coming."

"Hey." I leaned over to give the kid a hug, and he got up only partway, and we embraced awkwardly. Gabe was small for his age. I could feel his bony shoulders and rib cage. "How's Mom?"

"I don't know why they let her out of the hospital so soon. She was in a coma for twenty-four hours."

I shrugged, turned my palms upward. "Was she badly hurt?"

"Enough to give her a concussion."

"You think she shouldn't be home?"

He shrugged, palms up, an unconscious imitation. "I'm not a doctor."

"Ah. No word from your dad?"

"The police were asking Mom if they had relationship problems. They think maybe Dad ran off."

"That doesn't sound like your dad."

He was watching my face closely. "Or maybe he was kidnapped. Isn't that possible?"

"Kidnapped? I doubt it. Look, we'll figure this out. I don't want you to worry, Gabe."

"Yeah," he said dubiously. "Sure."

I turned toward the door, and he said, "Uncle Nick, will you teach me how to use a gun?"

"It's late. We'd piss off the neighbors."

"I mean, like, at the range or the gun club or whatever."

"I don't belong to a gun club, and I don't shoot at a range. In fact, I rarely use a gun. I always prefer to use my hands."

His eyes widened. "To kill people?"

"For database searches, mostly," I said.

"I'm serious, Uncle Nick. I want to learn how to use a gun."

"I don't think teenagers who wear all black should use guns," I said. "Bad stuff tends to happen. Don't you watch the news?"

"I'm talking about protecting Mom. And self-defense and like that."

"Sorry," I said.

I opened the front door, and he said, "Uncle Nick?"

I turned.

"Thanks, man," he said. "For being here, I mean."

8

I'd always thought that the only smart decision Roger ever made was to marry Lauren. She was strikingly attractive—glossy black hair and milky white skin and caramel brown eyes; lips that pulled down at the sides when she smiled. Lauren was a beautiful and elegant woman.

But most of all, I thought, she was a really good human being. Totally unself-centered. She'd devoted her life to three difficult men: her husband, her son, and her boss, Leland Gifford. That couldn't have been easy. Just being the administrative assistant to the CEO of a major company was more than a full-time job; it was more like a marriage. No doubt Roger was jealous of her devotion to her boss. And maybe her boss was jealous of her devotion to her husband.

She gave me a big hug as I entered, and I stared in shock for a few seconds. Even though I knew she'd been hurt, seeing the evidence of that attack was unnerving. She had a bandage on her head, and the left side of her face was scraped up, with yellowish bruising around her eyes.

She thanked me for coming, and I asked how she was doing and told her she looked good.

"I just lost respect for you," she said with a disappointed shake of her head. "I always thought you were a real straight shooter."

"You're right. I lied. You look pretty rough. I'm worried about you."

She laughed. "Thanks for your honesty. But I do feel better than I look."

She led me through the marble-tiled foyer and into their huge kitchen, which smelled like gingerbread or maybe pumpkin pie. She handed me a mug of coffee: black, the way I like it. The mug had a shield on it and said ST. GREGORY'S, Gabe's private boys' school. She sat on a stool at one corner of the big black granite island, and I sat facing her.

"The hospital let you go home already?"

"The doctor thinks I'm okay as long as I take it easy. And I can't leave Gabe alone in the house."

"No word about Roger?"

She shook her head slowly.

"Listen," I said. "The first thing is, I don't want you to assume the worst." She needed me to be calm and unworried, and I did a fairly good job of faking it.

Tears came to her eyes. "I don't even know what the worst *is*."

"Tell me what happened," I said.

9

I listened, asked a lot of questions, and mostly tried not to feed her worst fears. But the more I listened, the stranger it seemed.

A sudden, unexplained attack as they were walking to their car. No blood on the ground, no signs of struggle: nothing to indicate that my brother had been killed or even wounded. The hospitals and morgues had been checked for bodies, and no one matching his description had turned up.

There had been no word from him in the two days since the attack.

It didn't look good. In the pit of my stomach, I knew that he wasn't likely to turn up alive. I didn't want to tell her that. Yet I also didn't want to mislead her.

"How many of them were there?" I asked.

"I don't know," she said. "Probably just one. But he had a gun."

"How do you know?"

"I felt it."

"How?"

"He held something against my temple that felt like the barrel of a gun. And I heard that little click a revolver makes when you cock the hammer."

"So it was a revolver, not a semiautomatic."

"You don't cock a semiautomatic, Nick."

I just smiled. I didn't want to get all firearms-geeky on her. Actually, you do cock a semiautomatic when you rack the slide. But the point she was trying to make was basically right: nothing else sounds quite like the hammer on a revolver being pulled. "Male or female?"

"Male, for sure."

"Why?"

"I don't know, I—well, I guess, the strength—"

"There are some awfully strong women around."

"Maybe I felt arm hair or something."

"His arms were bare, then."

"No . . . I . . . it *smelled* like a guy, if you know what I mean. Cologne. Cheap cologne, mixed with cigarette smoke."

"Did you get the sense that Roger knew the attacker?"

Her eyes roamed the room. "No, I don't think . . ."

"Gabe said the cops were wondering if you and Roger were having marital difficulties."

She winced. "He said that?"

I nodded. "Basically."

"What does that mean? Like he tried to have me bumped off?"

"I guess."

"That's just stupid. If Roger wanted to leave me, he'd just leave."

"Did he ever talk about that?"

"Not you, too."

"Nah. Roger's not the divorce type, I'd say. He'd rather just grind you down."

She frowned, but not with her eyes. "I know you two have . . . issues. I realize he can be annoying some-times, but—"

"Annoying? White guys who call each other 'dude' are annoying. Hot-air hand dryers in public restrooms are annoying. I wouldn't call Roger annoying." *He's a jerk,* I didn't say. *An asshole.* In other circumstances I might have said this aloud. But not that day. And the fact was, she loved the guy, and so did Gabe, so who was I to impose my opinion on them? It was irrelevant.

She looked up suddenly, sniffed the air. "Oh, God, the sweet potato." She ran over to the toaster oven on the counter near the refrigerator (a Sub-Zero, of course, roughly the size of a Humvee) and came back shortly with her foil-wrapped baked sweet potato and a fork.

"Want some?"

"I'm good."

"You have any supper?"

"You know me. I eat when I'm hungry."

In their house, the kitchen was normally Roger's domain. I have a great respect for male friends of mine who can cook. Just not for kitchen fascists like my brother. He always had to have the right high-end appliance or expensive pan, the right cold-pressed extra virgin olive oil, the right thirty-year-old balsamic vinegar. Once food becomes that important, you've got a problem that Umbrian white truffle oil can't solve.

"In the hospital, they kept feeding me Jell-O and ginger ale, and all I could think about was baked sweet potato for some reason."

"Is your boss going to survive without you?"

She smiled fondly. "He's been great. He told me to take as much time as I need. But I want to go back soon."

"You're well enough?"

"Like I said, I only look a train wreck. I'm feeling fine. Gabe has school, and I'll just go stir-crazy sitting around the house."

"I assume Leland Gifford knows about Roger's . . . disappearance."

"Of course."

"You've talked to him about it?"

"Just briefly. I called him this afternoon."

"And?"

"He's offered to do anything he can. The police interviewed him about Roger."

"Did he have any theories as to what might have happened?"

"Lee's as baffled as anyone."

I nodded. "Do you have any idea what Roger's been working on recently?"

She paused to chew a big mouthful, looking at me with narrowed eyes. "We rarely talked about work. Sort of house rules."

"So he didn't mention anything he was especially worried about."

She shook her head. "Nothing interesting, as far as I know."

Of course, that pretty much described all of Roger's work at Gifford Industries. He structured deals, arranged financing. It would take me pots of black coffee to get through a single one of his mornings without lapsing into a boredom-induced coma. I always had the feeling, though, that Roger regarded himself as overqualified—that he'd never been promoted to a level he considered commensurate with his talents. Not that such a level could ever possibly exist in corporate America.

"Hmm," I said.

"You're thinking this had something to do with his job?"

"Not necessarily. Just covering all the bases. It could be anything. But I doubt it was a random mugging. If he was attacked"—I deliberately avoided the word "killed"—"there'd probably be some evidence of that. Something would have turned up by now." A body, I didn't say.

"Then what are you suggesting?"

"We can't rule out some sort of abduction or kidnapping."

"A *kidnapping*? You're not serious." Her voice got high-pitched, scornful, as if to mask her fear. "The cops said the same thing. But who'd kidnap Roger? We're not rich. That's crazy."

My eyes slid toward the humongous hulking stainless-steel eight-burner Vulcan commercial range that threw off enough BTUs to serve a good-sized restaurant. I knew they'd dumped a quarter of a million bucks at least into redoing their kitchen to Roger's maniacal specifications. "No doubt," I said.

"I mean, sure, we're well-off, but Roger and I both work for a living."

"I know." Once Victor Heller's considerable assets were seized, Roger and my mother and I were left without any money. But Roger, at least, inherited Dad's genius for making it and investing it. Just one of many ways he and I were different.

Lauren had been Gifford's admin, a divorcée with a young child, when she met Roger, and she'd made it clear from the outset that she loved her job, loved working for Leland Gifford, and would never give it up. She continued working because she wanted to, not because she had to. Roger made enough to support them, and he invested well.

"Anyway, if he's been kidnapped, wouldn't I have gotten a ransom demand by now?"

"Not necessarily. Sometimes they wait, just to increase the desperation level. But I agree, that's not likely."

"Then what *is* likely?"

"Just a theory, here, but maybe he stuck his nose into something he shouldn't have. Got into trouble with the wrong sorts of people."

"Like who?"

"Your company's involved in gigantic, billion-dollar construction projects around the world. Maybe he ran up against some organized-crime syndicate that thought they had some project nailed but lost out to Gifford Industries. Maybe Roger helped elbow them out. Something like that."

"You make Gifford Industries sound like some sort of two-bit Mafia-owned New Jersey garbage-hauling company."

I thought of a few rejoinders—I'm just wired that way—but I held my tongue.

"Forget the Mafia," I said. "The criminal underworld's gone transnational. The Russians, the East Europeans, the Asians—they've all gotten sophisticated. Now they invest. They use legitimate businesses to launder their money. They trade commodities. They're into oil and precious metal and insurance companies and banks. All over the world. What if Roger came across something about one of these organizations while he was negotiating a deal, something they didn't want him to know . . ."

She looked at me for a few seconds, then her eyes shifted from side to side as if she were reading something off a TelePrompTer. I had a feeling she was thinking that possibility through to its logical conclusion, which wasn't a happy one.

"You don't really believe things like that happen, do you?" She sounded almost scornful.

"Not really," I admitted. "Rarely. But the world's a dirty place. Who knows."

"Then what? What do you think happened?"

"Wish I had something to tell you." I thought for a moment. "Listen, Lauren. When I asked you if Roger knew the guy, or the people, who grabbed you, you hesitated."

"I did?"

I'd noticed a flash of uncertainty appear in her face; maybe she wasn't consciously aware of it. "Was there anything in Roger's face, his expression or whatever, that might have indicated he wasn't totally surprised by what was going on?"

She was silent for a few seconds, pensive. "You know, I just remembered something."

"Okay."

"It's what he said when we were attacked. The last thing I heard him say."

"Okay."

"He said, 'Why her?' "

" 'Why her,' " I repeated. "Which implies, 'Why not me?' "

"Like he *knew* them. Like maybe he knew who they were."

I thought for a moment. "I think it tells us something more important."

She raised her eyebrows.

"That maybe he was expecting this to happen. And the question is why."

Quietly, a tremor in her voice, she said: "Expecting it? Expecting *what*?"

"Maybe he'd been warned. Maybe it was an attempt to scare him."

"For what? That's—that's too bizarre, Nick."

"You wouldn't believe some of the stuff that goes on."

"Try me."

"Someday I'll tell you the real reason I got booted out of the Pentagon. Things aren't always the way they appear from the outside. There's usually more to the story."

She shook her head, as if to dismiss the wild speculation. Then she fell silent for ten or fifteen seconds. "You don't think he's alive, do you?"

"I'm sure he's fine."

"I don't believe you."

I didn't believe it either. "Don't worry," I said.

"I'm losing respect for you again."

"Whatever happened to him, I'm sure he's okay. Keep the faith. I'm here for you guys, you know that."

"I know. That means a lot. But Nick, I didn't want to involve you in this. That was Gabe's idea, not mine."

"Involve me?"

"You know what I mean. Professionally, or whatever. I told Gabe I doubt you can find out anything the cops can't."

"Well," I said, "truth is, my firm has resources law enforcement doesn't."

"You're not suggesting I hire Stoddard Associates, are you?"

"Jay Stoddard wouldn't take the case. I'd have to do it on my own. Off the books."

"That wouldn't be—I don't know, complicated?"

I hesitated, but only for an instant. "No," I said. "I don't think it would be complicated."

"I mean, given, you know, the way you and Roger . . ."

"He's my brother. And your husband. And Gabe's dad. That's not complicated."

"So maybe it would be . . . you know, cleaner . . . if I hired you directly, paid you off the books. If you're willing to help out, I mean."

"I won't take money from you."

She hesitated. I could see she was struggling. "Roger's done really well," she said with a nervous smile. "You were in the army, and then you worked for the government . . ."

Yeah, yeah, I thought. *I served my country, while my brother served himself.* That was what she meant but would never say out loud. The fact was, I did what I did, chose what I did, in order to escape. In other words, for wholly selfish reasons.

But I'd never say that out loud either.

"Give me the names of the cops who interviewed you," I said. "I'll talk to them. Why don't we start there?"

"Are you sure?"

"Not a problem, Lauren. And maybe you could also give me the names of Roger's close friends. You know, anyone he might have confided in."

"Well . . ." She faltered. "You've known Roger a lot longer than me."

"He didn't really have any close friends, did he?"

"Not really."

I wasn't surprised. He'd always been sort of a loner. Going back to when we were kids, he tended to hang out with my friends. Even though he considered us uncool, since we were a few years younger. And even though he was never really the hanging-out type anyway.

"Nick, are you sure this is okay?"

"More than okay," I said.

She jumped up and threw her arms around me, and after a few seconds she began sobbing.

10

The offices of Stoddard Associates looked like the most posh, high-end law firm you'd ever seen: dark mahogany paneling everywhere, antique Persian rugs, burnished fruitwood conference tables. Hushed elegance. Old money. Even a prim middle-aged British receptionist.

The firm's founder and chairman, Abner J. Stoddard IV—Jay, as everyone called him—sometimes joked that the décor he'd selected, down to the last detail, was nothing more than what he and his CIA buddies used to call "window dressing." That's tradecraft jargon. *Every good front needs a plausible cover,* he'd say.

He was only partly joking. After all, Stoddard Associates was a high-powered private intelligence firm. A corporate espionage agency, though Jay Stoddard would never use those words. An august and influential, if shadowy, enterprise. Not some cheesy gumshoe operation with frosted-glass windows and the lingering stench of stale cigar smoke. We occupied twelve thousand square feet of the ninth floor of a sleek office tower at 1900 K Street in Washington, with a curved façade of glass and stainless steel and slate spandrels. K Street, as everyone knew, was the Champs Élysées of Washington lobbyists.

And Jay wasn't just some ex-spook who did investigations for big companies and the government and very rich people. He was the consummate Washington insider, a guy who knew where all the bodies were buried and was willing to exhume them for the right price. He was a fixer. He knew everyone who counted. He understood how things really worked in this town, as opposed to what they taught you in civics class or what you read in the papers, and he had a strong enough stomach to deal with all the creepy-crawlies you found when you turned over the rock.

Whenever he met with some politician who had qualms about hiring him to do oppo research—digging up dirt on a rival—Stoddard liked to quote Governor Willie Stark from *All the King's Men*: "Man is born in sin and conceived in corruption and passeth from the stench of the didie to the stink of the shroud. There is always something."

Jay Stoddard knew that everyone had dirt.

He was a tall, lanky guy in his early sixties, with a proud mane of silver hair he kept a bit too long. He wore handmade English suits and Brooks Brothers shirts with frayed collars, which was his way of announcing that he had taste and family money and appreciated the finer things in life but didn't really think about any of that stuff. More window dressing, I suspected.

We were wrapping up our Monday morning Risk Committee meeting, which was basically twelve of the firm's most senior staff members sitting around the big conference table and voting on which cases to take and which to turn down. It was your typical undercaffeinated Monday morning gathering: stifled yawns and low energy, throat-clearing and doodling, and furtive glances at BlackBerrys. Except for Jay, who paced around the room because he couldn't sit still for more than five minutes.

Most of the cases we'd voted on were pretty boring, standard fare. A big data-storage firm wanted us to find out whether their Indonesian manager was embezzling. The CEO of a huge investment bank wanted us to find out if two of his top executives, a man and a woman, were secretly having an affair. (I wondered why the CEO didn't want to use his own internal security guy. I also wondered why the CEO cared so much; I had no doubt he was looking for a pretext to fire the two executives for some other reason. The case smelled fishy to me. We voted yes, of course.)

Everyone perked up when Stoddard mentioned a request he'd gotten from the Metropolitan Museum of Art. One of their curators was about to go on trial in Ankara for trafficking in looted antiquities—ancient gold coins that the Turkish government said had been stolen from a state museum. I had visions of some Manhattan society dame, with her Burberry scarf and Louis Vuitton bag, huddled in a dank squalid Turkish prison out of *Midnight Express*. We voted to investigate further.

But the case that took up most of our time that morning was a request from one of the biggest oil companies in the world. They were trying to acquire a midsize but highly profitable oil field-service company—a hostile takeover bid. And they wanted us to compile some deep background research on the CEO of the target company.

As usual, the voice of sanity was our forensic data expert, a lovely African-American woman with mocha skin and extremely short hair and big eyes named Dorothy Duval. Dorothy had a smoky voice and a blunt, earthy manner. I'm sure they'd hated her at the National Security Agency, where she had worked for nine years before Stoddard hired her. Stoddard was shrewd enough to realize how smart she was. Or maybe he just found her amusing.

"Look, can we have some real talk here?" Dorothy said. "They want a full-out data haunt. Cell-phone tracking, electronic monitoring, the whole deal. They want the guy's phone tapped."

"You're totally making that up," said a senior investigator, Marty Masur. "They never said anything of the kind." Masur was small and bald, arrogant and abrasive. He'd been a Senate investigator until he pissed off one too many senators. Just then he was in the process of pissing off everyone at Stoddard Associates.

"That's because they're too smart to say it outright," Dorothy replied. "Nobody puts a request like that in writing. They don't have to."

"So you're just point-blank refusing?" Masur shot back. "You wanna keep your hands clean, is that it?"

"Weren't you the guy who wanted to take on that 'collection job' for Hewlett-Packard?" she said, pursing her lips. "Tap the phones of their board members? Wonder whatever happened to the firm they did hire."

"They were amateurs," Masur said. "They got caught."

"There was also that little detail about how it was against the law. Like this job would be. I won't do it."

Masur snorted, shook his head. His face flushed, and he looked like he was about to say something really nasty when Stoddard broke in: "Nick, your thoughts?"

I shrugged. "Dorothy's right. It's a huge risk. We might end up paying more in legal fees than we can bill on this."

Masur muttered something, and I turned to him. "Excuse me?"

He shook his head.

"No, I want to hear it, Marty," I said.

He gave me a wary look. I'd always thought he was intimidated by me. I'm six-foot-two, served in the Special Forces in Iraq, and I'm still in decent shape. Also, there were rumors about my dark skills, things I'd done in Iraq and Bosnia, that swirled around me. None of them were true, but I never bothered to set the record straight. I didn't really mind having a scary reputation. I think Masur was afraid that if he got on my bad side, I'd get him in an alley one night and slice off one of his ears or something. I liked letting him think that.

" 'Being cautious is the greatest risk of all,' " he finally said. "Nehru said that."

I nodded sagely. "If we don't succeed, we run the risk of failure."

Masur looked at me quizzically.

"Dan Quayle said that," I added. Whether he actually did or not, I liked the quote.

Dorothy gave me one of her dazzling smiles.

"All right, ladies and gentlemen," Stoddard said and cleared his throat. "I will never allow this firm to be put in jeopardy," he said. "As tempting as the money might be, there's just no question that we have to do the right thing here. We're going to pass."

As the meeting broke up, Stoddard grabbed my elbow. "Come into my office for a sec?"

"Sure."

We walked down the hall, past the black-framed photographs of Stoddard with politicos and world leaders and celebrities. My favorite was the photo of him and Richard Nixon. Nixon was wearing a light blue suit and was clasping Stoddard's hand awkwardly. Stoddard was even lankier then, black-haired and movie-star handsome. He had been working in the CIA's Operations Directorate until the Nixon reelection campaign had hired him to do oppo research. They needed someone to dig up dirt, discreetly. I'd heard that Nixon had hired Stoddard to compile dossiers on certain key Democratic senators in order to discourage them from demanding his resignation. But Stoddard was far too discreet ever to discuss it. Stoddard's work was legendary, and he cashed in by setting up his own shop right after the election.

Nixon had signed the photograph, in his knifelike script, "With deepest thanks for doing your part to keep the election honest."

I loved that.

"Great job on that Traverse Development thing," he said.

I nodded.

"You're good. Sometimes I forget how good."

"It was easy."

"You only make it look easy, Nick. You've got *sprezzatura*. You know what that means?"

"I'm on Zithromax," I said. "Supposed to get rid of it."

He glanced at me, then chuckled. "*Sprezzatura*'s an Italian word. Means the art of making something difficult look easy."

"Is that right," I said.

As we entered his office, I mentioned the name of the big oil company we'd all just been talking about, and I said, "That's an awful big contract to turn down, Jay. I'm impressed."

He looked at me. "Come on, man—you think I'm letting that one slip through my fingers? In this economy? The house on Nantucket needs a new roof." He winked. "Always cover your ass, Nicky. Sit down. We gotta talk."

11

Visitors to Jay Stoddard's office were always surprised. They expected the standard ego wall of framed photographs of Stoddard with the rich and famous and powerful. But those he'd banished to the hallway. Which was either modest or clever—or just his way of putting his fingerprints all over our offices.

Instead, the walls of his office were lined, floor to ceiling, with books. There were first editions—Victor Hugo and Trollope—but mostly there were big picture books on architecture. Strewn artfully across his glass coffee table were magazines like *Architectural Record* and *Metropolis* and a big orange book called *Richard Meier Architect*.

He was an architecture nut. Once, over his fourth glass of single malt at the Alvear Palace Hotel in Buenos Aires, he confessed to me that, as a young man, he'd desperately wanted to go to the Yale School of Architecture. But his father, who'd been in the OSS during World War II, forced him to join the CIA. Jay wasn't morose about it, though. "Dad was absolutely right," he said. "I'd have starved to death. I thought all architects were *rich*!"

He shrugged off his suit jacket and hung it on a mahogany valet in the corner. Over his threadbare blue button-down shirt were bright red suspenders—which he called "braces," because he was an Anglophile—with little pictures of golfers on them.

"You need a cup of coffee," he announced, pushing the intercom button on his desk phone. "Intravenous, looks like. Hungover, Nick?"

"I'm okay," I said. "I never drink on plane flights." It was true. One of the secrets of business travel, I'd learned. That and always fly first class. "No coffee, thanks."

His assistant's voice came on: "Yes?"

"Sorry, Heather, cancel that," he said to the speakerphone as he sat behind his desk. He never drank coffee, himself. He said he didn't need it, which made it hard to trust him. I don't need a lot of sleep, but this guy was almost an android. He was incredibly energetic. He played squash, I was told, like a Roman gladiator on speed.

Jay leaned forward and put his elbows on his desk, propping up his head, staring off somewhere behind me. This made him look bored and disengaged.

He often came off as casual and shambling and loose-jointed, but his desk told you everything you needed to know: It was always perfectly clean. Nothing marred the wide polished expanse of mahogany. He was a Type-A personality, an obsessive-compulsive, a clean freak. He was great at banter, never seemed to take anything seriously, sometimes even appeared to be muddleheaded. But he missed nothing. His mind was a steel-jaw trap: Once you got caught in its teeth, you'd have to chew off your own limb to escape.

"So you got in to the office early today?"

I shrugged.

"Looking into Traverse Development, huh?" he said. His blue eyes seemed to have gone gray.

"I like to know as much as possible about my clients," I said. I'd run Traverse Development through our standard corporate registration databases and found nothing. I'd also run a search on the cell-phone number that Woody gave me back in L.A., the emergency contact number for whoever had hired him. But no luck. It came back as "private."

Did someone tell Stoddard I'd been searching? Or did my computer search trigger some kind of notification?

"Maybe not the best use of your time."

"Don't worry, I did it on my own time."

He paused. "And?"

"It doesn't exist," I said.

"Strange," Stoddard said. He was toying with me. "The check cleared."

"No business registration in the city of Arlington. Or Arlington County. Nothing in SearchSystems. The address on that shipment turns out to be bogus—a rented mail drop. A place called EasyOffice, which is one of those business suites you can rent by the hour or by the week. The rent was paid in cash. So obviously it's a front."

"Oh, please. Don't be so suspicious. Companies use fronts for all kinds of legitimate reasons. Like avoiding taxes."

"You know what was in that container, don't you?" I said. "What was being shipped out of Bahrain?"

"I didn't ask." Jay was too skilled to look evasive.

"But you know anyway," I said.

He laughed. Sometimes talking with him was like fencing. "Don't ask, don't tell."

"I think you know damned well what was in those boxes." I said it in a good-humored way, not wanting to come off as confrontational. Confrontational rarely worked with him.

He chewed the inside of his cheek, which was always

the giveaway that he was trying to decide whether to tell a lie. The "tell," as they say in poker. Stoddard was practiced in the art of deception, but my skill at reading people is better. I give full credit for this to my father, who was a liar the way some people are alcoholics. He lived and breathed dishonesty. It was a useful education for a kid.

"If you opened a sealed shipment, Nick, you don't want to brag about it. You could get the whole firm in trouble. If you're going to break the law, you do it for the client. Not to work against the client."

"It was a messy recovery, Jay. A couple of boxes broke open."

"Why do I doubt that? Point is, whatever you found, that's outside of the scope of our work. They hired us to do a very specific job. Nothing beyond that. In addition to which, as you well know, anything we come across in the course of an investigation that might be detrimental to a client we always keep confidential. Otherwise, we'd go out of business in a week. I don't need to tell you this."

This was one of the things I didn't love about my job. Often, a client would hire us to investigate some alleged wrongdoing inside the company, and later, after we found it—embezzlement or fraud or bribery or whatever—we'd discover that what the client really wanted was to see if it could be found. Sort of like a game. A scavenger hunt. If we couldn't find it, neither would the Justice Department. And they always insisted that we bury our findings. Clean up the mess for them and keep our mouths shut. If you didn't go along with them, they might refuse to pay. And the word would get around that you were, well, maybe a little too fussy. A pain in the ass. Not the kind of firm you could really be comfortable with.

This sort of thing happened far more than we or

anyone else liked to admit. Which was why you had to be careful about who you signed up to work for. You didn't want to find yourself complicit in covering up someone else's crime.

"This has the potential to blow up in our faces," I said. I lowered my voice. "There was close to a billion dollars there in cash. Sealed in bricks by the U.S. Treasury."

"So?"

"So there's this annoying little law. The bulk-cash smuggling law of 2001. If you're shipping more than ten thousand bucks in cash, you've got to fill out paperwork."

"Oh, please. Not if the government does it."

"This wasn't a government flight. This was a private cargo shipment."

"The government uses private cargo firms all the time these days. You know that."

"For a billion dollars' worth of cash? I'm dubious."

"Bottom line, this isn't your problem, Nick. Grow up. Don't be naïve."

Now he was pulling out the heavy artillery. There was nothing worse, in Stoddard's mind, than being naïve about how the world really worked. He had no patience for it.

"I'm not taking a moral position, here, Jay. I'm just saying that this is the sort of thing that ends up splashed all over the front page of the *Washington Post,* and suddenly we're dragged into it. First as a sidebar. Then we become our own separate front-page story."

"Only if it's truly illegal, which we don't know, and only if someone talks. Barring that, we're on totally solid ground."

"You really do have faith in the ultimate goodness of mankind, don't you?" The only successful way to argue with Jay, I'd learned, was to outcynical him.

He laughed loud and long. Jay had a good smile but a lot of gold fillings at the back, and they caught the light. "Look, Nicky. The world's a dirty place. I'm sure your father could tell you a lot more about that than I could. Give him a call. Ask him."

He arched a single brow, which was something I'd always wished I could do. Stoddard wasn't trying to be snide, I didn't think. He probably just intended this as his coup de grâce, his knockout punch.

"I don't think they allow incoming phone calls at his prison," I said. "Though I admit I've never tried."

If you took a really close look at some of the biggest, most notorious scandals of the last thirty or so years, you'd find Jay Stoddard lurking somewhere in the shadows. As an investigator or a fixer or an adviser, I mean. Whether it was the Iran-Contra hearings in the Reagan days or a Canadian media mogul on trial for fraud. Or one of a dozen Congressional sex scandals. And a whole lot more situations that might have exploded into ugly public imbroglios if it hadn't been for Stoddard's work.

But you'd have to know where to look, because Jay didn't like to leave traces. And he always preferred to be on the winning side.

One of the very few times he picked the wrong side was when he agreed to work for my father. Victor Heller was arrested and charged with massive accounting and securities fraud and grand larceny, and being the smart and extremely well-connected guy that he was, he hired the finest investigative firm in the world to assist his legal defense. Unfortunately for both Jay and Dad, the facts got in the way. He was sent to prison for thirty years.

In fact, I'm convinced that it was because Jay Stoddard felt guilty about letting my father down that he hired me, the black sheep of the family who'd dropped out of college to enlist in the Special Forces. Who'd joined the army instead of Goldman Sachs. Later, though, Jay began bragging that I was his best hire. "Something in those Heller genes," he'd say.

"Larceny," I liked to reply.

He'd shake his head, a mournful look in his eyes. "Your dad's a brilliant man. It's just a damned shame . . ."

Now he said, "Anyway, odds are the whole thing's perfectly innocent. Let's just leave it there, okay?"

"If I ran a check on some of the serial numbers, I wonder if it would turn out to be part of the cash that went missing in Baghdad a few years ago."

"Maybe. But why would you?"

"Curiosity."

I was starting to piss him off. His tone got increasingly exasperated. "Nick, we've all got a lot of work to do around here. Let's just move on, okay?"

I shrugged. I wasn't interested in getting into a fight with him. Certainly not a fight I couldn't win. And maybe he was right. "Forget it, Jake," I said. " 'It's Chinatown.' "

Quoting one of the best lines from one of Jay's favorite movies seemed to mollify him. He laughed heartily. "All right," he said, "as far as I'm concerned, this never happened."

I was being forgiven. As if I'd accidentally insulted his wife. Very few people were as affable as Jay when he wanted to be.

"Don't worry about it," I said.

I wish I'd left it there.

12

When I got to my office, which was about a quarter the size of his, I saw that my voice-mail light was blinking. All calls came through our main switchboard and were answered by Elizabeth, the British receptionist. Most callers just left a name and number and she e-mailed me the message. Sometimes I missed those old pink "While You Were Out" message slips that used to stack up when I worked at McKinsey & Company. But once in a while, especially if the matter was confidential, or the caller didn't want to leave a name, she'd put them right into my voice mail.

I played the messages over the speakerphone while I sat in my desk chair and spun it halfway around to stare out the window at K Street. A pretty young girl in an orange shirt came out of the restaurant across the street and knelt in front of the menu easel on the sidewalk. She kept tossing back her long brown hair while writing the day's specials on the chalkboard in a neat cursive hand.

One of the messages was from an old army buddy about our weekly basketball game. Another was from a woman I'd been seeing on an extremely casual basis.

But nothing from Lieutenant Garvin of the Washington Metropolitan Police. I'd left him two messages. So I tried him again, got his voice mail, left him a third message.

In the meantime, I had a few other phone calls to make.

Jay Stoddard had explicitly told me to stop asking questions about Traverse Development, but that was like waving a red flag at a bull. I've never liked following orders, which was one of the reasons I was happy to leave the army, then the government. I'll admit, though, that this didn't make me an ideal employee.

In any case, I wasn't asking questions about Traverse Development, whatever that was. I was asking about the almost one billion dollars in cash that Traverse was shipping, and technically that was a different matter. Hairsplitting, maybe, but whatever works.

The plastic wrapping on the bricks of currency had identified it as being from the Federal Reserve Bank of New York in East Rutherford, New Jersey. That was the location of the largest cash vault in the country. They had people there whose entire job was to analyze the movement of cash around the world—which is probably one of those jobs that sounds more interesting than it actually is. I called the international cash operations unit of the East Rutherford Operations Center and identified myself by my real name and firm and told them that, in the course of an investigation, I'd found a small bundle of cash in a briefcase belonging to a suspected drug trafficker. I gave the woman one of the serial numbers.

It took her more than five minutes to return to the phone. She had all sorts of questions for me. Where exactly was this drug trafficker based? How much cash? What was the range of serial numbers, and were they sequential?

I told her the serial numbers on the hundred-dollar

bills all began with DB—at least, the ones I had looked at.

"Well, sir, the first letter, D, means that it's the 2003 series. And the second letter—B?—that means it was issued by the New York Fed."

"Well, that helps," I said. "But what I want to know is, was this part of any bulk shipment of cash?"

"I can't tell you that, sir." The woman's voice had gone from bored-but-friendly to officious-and-stern.

"That's too bad," I said. "Because when the Fed won't help law enforcement recover cash that's stolen from one of their shipments, that's serious indeed. Just the sort of thing that my buddy, the chairman of the Committee on Oversight and Government Reform, would love to sink his claws into. You know how they love scandals like this. How do you spell your last name, again?"

If there's one thing a bureaucrat fears more than having to work past five o'clock, it's having to testify before Congress.

By the time I hung up, I'd confirmed my suspicions. Sure enough, the cash on that plane was part of the famous nine billion dollars that had gone missing in Baghdad a few years back.

But I still hadn't cracked the mystery of who or what Traverse Development was, and that wasn't going to be easy to do out of this office. Not with Jay Stoddard looking over my shoulder. And not without asking questions about it, as I promised Jay I wouldn't do.

I had an old friend named Walter McGeorge, who was an expert in TSCM, which is the industry shorthand for Technical Surveillance Countermeasures. In simple terms, Walter was a bug-sweeper, the best I'd ever met.

Walter had been a communications sergeant on my Special Forces team. He'd been trained in all the usual stuff—radio equipment and wire communications, burst-code radio nets, and so on. Everything from encrypted satellite transmissions to old-fashioned Morse code. Somewhere along the line, "Walter" had become "Hognose," because of his passing resemblance to Porky Pig, and then "Merlin," as he earned the admiration of his teammates. He was recruited to the same Pentagon intel team as me but survived longer. When he finally decided he wanted out, I got him a job doing bug sweeps for a TSCM firm in Maryland. He'd done a number of projects for me since Stoddard Associates didn't have TSCM specialists on staff: That was a specialized skill these days. All the big investigative firms outsourced those jobs now.

I reached him on his cell. The connection was crackly, and I asked whether I'd disturbed him on a job.

"Yeah," he replied crankily. "A job involving bluefish."

Merlin was a serious sport fisherman and kept a small boat in the Harbour Cove Marina on Chesapeake Bay.

"I need to send someone a package," I said. Before he had the chance to make a crack about how he wasn't my secretary, I went on: "I have the address of a drop site, and I want to send them a GPS tracking device. You think you could send out a FedEx package with one of those letter loggers inside?"

"You looking for historical data?"

"Historical?"

"If you're talking about the GPS Letter Logger, the one that's like a quarter inch thick and fits in a number-ten business envelope, well, that just records where it's been after the fact. It's not real-time. You have to get it back to download the data. And I got a feeling you're not going to get it back."

"I need real-time. I'm figuring the FedEx package will get delivered to the drop site and probably transferred to some actual office, where it'll get opened."

"Maybe. Maybe not."

"Maybe not," I conceded. "Still, it's worth a try. Once they open it and see a tracker inside, they're going to destroy it. But at least I'll get the real location that way."

"You think so, huh?"

"I hope so. That's why I'm calling you."

"Well, here's the deal. If you want a GPS logger that can broadcast its location in real time, it's gonna be a little beefier than that Letter Logger device. It'll send out real-time position data as SMS text messages. Lithium-ion battery. Should stay powered for ten days."

"Think you can pop one in the mail later on today?"

"Soon as I get back to the office."

Another call was coming through. I recognized the number, told Merlin where to send the package, and said, "Thanks, man. Good fishing."

Then I picked up line 2. "Lieutenant Garvin," I said. "Thanks for getting back to me."

"Good to hear from you, Mr. Heller," the cop said. "Funny coincidence, actually. I've been wanting to talk to you about your brother."

13

The headquarters of the Violent Crime Branch of the Washington Metropolitan Police was hidden away in the back of some dismal shopping center in southeast D.C., off Pennsylvania Avenue. I headed over there right after work. I was buzzed in and entered a dimly lit corridor that smelled of vomit, the stench not quite masked with some deodorizing spray that was almost as bad. I passed an open conference room that had crime-scene tape stretched across the doorway, probably to keep people from accidentally stepping into the mess on the floor.

Detective-Lieutenant Arthur Garvin met me halfway down the hall. He wasn't quite what I expected. He had an almost professorial appearance: thick steel-rimmed glasses, scraggly white goatee, red-rimmed nostrils. On the way over, I'd called in to the office and asked Dorothy to do a quick backgrounder on the guy. He was sixty-four, with thirty-two years of service, and had gotten a retirement waiver. The police and the fire department had a mandatory retirement age of sixty, but they made exceptions in special cases. Most cops want to retire as soon as they can, I've found. The ones who get retirement waivers are the ones who love what they're doing.

He wore a light blue shirt with a button-down collar,

neatly creased; he had his shirts professionally laundered, and they came back in boxes. Not a polyester kind of guy. Neat and orderly, though a large dark grease stain in the middle of his shirt pocket marred the effect.

He shook my hand. His was damp. "Come on back to my office. Ordinarily, we'd talk in the conference room, but it's undergoing maintenance."

"Smells like someone couldn't hold their Jack Daniel's," I said.

He scowled. "Nah, something's going around the office. Some kinda stomach virus." He sounded congested, kept sniffling.

He didn't share an office since he was a lieutenant. His was cramped and windowless, with a bad rug and wood-veneer paneling and a lot of framed certificates and awards. It reminded me of a home office in someone's finished basement.

Garvin sat behind his desk and took a long swig of coffee from a giant mug. "Coffee?"

"No, thanks."

"So, snake-eater, huh?"

I shrugged. He'd checked me out, too.

"Isn't that what they call you Green Berets?"

No one I knew in the Special Forces ever used the term "snake-eaters." We all went through a pretty nasty training program called the Q Course, but you didn't actually have to cook and eat snake. Maybe in the old days you did. No one ever called us "Green Berets" anymore, either. Not since John Wayne.

"Guess so," I said.

"You've been with Stoddard Associates for about three years."

"That all? Seems a lot longer."

"Now, I assume you're here for personal reasons and not on business."

"Right," I said.

He sneezed, pulled out a crumpled handkerchief, blew his nose loudly. He sneaked a surreptitious glance at the contents of his handkerchief before crumpling it back up and stuffing it into his pants. "Sorry. I shouldn't have come in to work today, and now you're gonna catch this damned thing."

"I don't get sick," I said.

"Bad luck to say that. Now you're really gonna get hit bad."

"I'm not superstitious either," I said. "Where's your partner? Scorpino? Scardino?"

"Scarpino. Tony's on another case. He's been reassigned."

I knew what that meant. The case had been deemed low-priority. Only one cop on it now.

"Thanks for taking the time to see me," I said. Cops are overworked and underpaid, overstressed and undervalued, and I always try to let them know I appreciate them. They also tend to be resentful of people who do roughly the same work they do but get paid a lot more. I can't blame them.

He sneezed again. "Ah, Jeez," he said. He took out his handkerchief and went through his ritual all over again, right down to the furtive inspection.

"I'm grateful for everything you're doing to find my brother. I want to help any way I can."

"You and your brother are pretty close, huh?"

He peered at me for a few seconds over the rim of his coffee mug. The thick lenses of his eyeglasses magnified his eyes, made them look weird, like some space alien's. If I had been guilty of something, I would definitely have been intimidated. He was probably quite effective in interrogations.

I shook my head. "Not in years."

"Must be hard, living in the same town and all."

"We travel in different circles."

"Uh-huh." He put down his mug, turned his chair to face his computer monitor. "How about you and Mrs. Heller? Don't get along with her either?"

"We get along great. I like her kid."

"*Her* kid? You mean, *their* kid?"

"Well, Roger's stepson. But Roger's been his dad since Gabe was two or three."

"So you're in touch with her?"

"From time to time. Gabe and I talk about once a week."

The thought crossed my mind that he might consider me a suspect. Ex–Special Forces, which meant that I was capable of scary stuff. Unmarried and not currently in a relationship. So naturally I must have conspired with my brother's wife to kill her husband and set this whole elaborate thing up.

But fortunately he didn't seem to be going down that path. "She ever talk about their marriage?"

"No. She and I don't really have that kind of relationship."

"I assume your brother never talked about that sort of stuff with you either."

"Right."

"So there could be serious problems between the two of them that you might not know about."

"Theoretically, sure. But I'd probably have noticed."

"Any drug use?"

"Not that I know of."

He tapped at his keyboard. "Do you know if he was involved with bookies?"

"Bookies? Roger? I don't think he's ever seen a horse race. Lieutenant, I think you're barking up the wrong tree."

"What tree should I be barking up, Mr. Heller?"

"My brother was involved in some complicated financial arrangements at Gifford Industries. The stakes are pretty high—business partners, competitors, all that. Wouldn't surprise me if he made some enemies. Bad actors."

"He have any enemies that you know of?"

"I don't want to give you carpal tunnel syndrome."

"That many, huh?"

"Roger has an abrasive manner. I'm sure he pissed people off all the time."

"Maybe the wrong people."

"Could be."

"People he'd want to run away from."

"It's possible." I watched him tap at the keys for a few seconds, then said, "I assume you've flagged all his credit-card accounts."

He typed a while longer, sniffled, then turned to me. "Huh. Hadn't thought of that." His sarcasm was bone-dry. I liked that.

I let it pass. "Nothing popped up, I take it. You ran his name through all the standard databases—NCIC and so on?"

"Another excellent suggestion," he said. "So glad you stopped by. Wouldn't have thought of that either." He sneezed, and blew his nose, but this time he didn't bother with the examination. "Any other tips for me?"

"How about checking those closed-circuit crime cameras you guys have all over the place?"

"Actually, Mr. Heller, we don't have a single crime camera in Georgetown."

That was news to me. "No crime in Georgetown, huh?"

"No budget," Garvin said. "I think this is what they call backseat driving."

I ignored him. "Then what about traffic cameras? I've seen plenty of them around Georgetown."

"They don't record anything. They're monitored, but only for traffic-related incidents."

"Like running a red light."

"Like that."

"Still, there have to be dozens, maybe even hundreds, of private security cameras in that part of Georgetown. Businesses, embassies, probably some apartment buildings, too. Anyone canvass the area?"

He gave me one of his styptic, space-alien glares. "Maybe we can bring in the National Guard to assist us. I don't think we put in that kind of effort to look for Osama Bin Laden. What makes you think we've got that kind of manpower for a missing-persons case?"

"Of course you don't," I said in a matter-of-fact tone. "But let's speak frankly, Lieutenant. This is probably a homicide."

"Think so?"

"The odds of my brother being alive at this point are negligible. You know it as well as I do."

"Hmph. Interesting. Well, you're the expert." He sneezed twice, did his handkerchief thing. "Being a high-priced investigator with Stoddard and all."

"Lieutenant Garvin," I said, "this is your case, not mine. I get that. I just want to help."

"Yeah? Then maybe you could explain something to me."

"Okay."

"Since you're so sure your brother was abducted by unnamed 'enemies' and probably killed. How do you explain the fact that about half an hour *after* he and his wife were attacked, he went to a Wachovia Bank ATM and made a withdrawal?"

I stared at him.

"Kinda raises the odds of your brother's being alive, doesn't it?" he said, and he sneezed again.

14

"You don't seem surprised."

"Because it wasn't him," I said. In fact, I was pretty much blown away at first, but I've got a decent poker face. So Garvin had put a flag on Roger's bank accounts. "You might want to ask for the ATM videotape," I said, just to watch his reaction.

Garvin began to sputter with indignation, but then he grinned. "Got me," he said. "Wachovia's sending it over as soon as they pull it."

"Whoever abducted my brother grabbed his card and forced his PIN out of him. He didn't withdraw the money of his own volition."

"Yeah, right."

"Nothing else makes sense. I'm sure my brother has several bank accounts. Which one?"

"His personal checking account. The one he uses most often to get cash."

"What time was this?"

"Eleven oh-nine P.M. Sixteen minutes after we got the nine-one-one call from someone who saw his wife lying on the ground."

"Gotta be a holdup, then," I said. "If someone abducted him for some reason, they'd never jeopardize it for, what—a thousand bucks? The maximum Roger could withdraw at any time?"

"Probably."

"A holdup that went bad, then."

"If by 'went bad,' you mean they killed him, where's the body?"

"You tell me."

"Right," Garvin said with muted disgust.

"It's also possible they're still holding him."

"Your big kidnapping theory again, that it?"

"Look, Lieutenant, you guys are stretched way too thin. You don't have half the resources my firm has. It's not fair, but it's true." I ignored his cold stare. "We've got access to some very powerful, and very expensive, investigative databases. How about I put some of that firepower to work? Case like this, I figure you can use all the help you can get."

Garvin took off his glasses and set them down on top of a neatly stacked pile of folders. He closed his eyes and massaged his eyelids with his fingertips, pressing hard. "Believe it or not, Mr. Heller, this ain't my first rodeo."

It was never anyone's first rodeo, was it? "I'm only talking about the investigative tools we have at our disposal."

"Thanks, but no thanks."

"We've got asset locator services and corporate databases and law-enforcement databases that you probably think only the National Security Agency has. We've got access to international records that the CIA and the NSA *wish* they had. Don't tell me you'd turn away a lead if I handed you one."

"Actually, yes. I would turn it away. I can't use anything you find, Mr. Heller. It wouldn't be admissible in court. I can't establish the chain of custody."

"Forget about trial. If I can piece together what happened to Roger, you're not going to ignore what I come up with."

"I know you want to find your brother," Garvin said. "I get that. But if you start meddling in my case, you're going to screw it up. You start talking to a potential target before we have our ducks in a row, you'll tip our hand before we're ready. The target's going to start destroying evidence and building alibis in advance. I can't have that."

"It ain't my first rodeo either."

"Yeah, well."

"You're the pro here, not me," I said. "I'm not here to bust your butt, and I sure as hell don't want credit. If an envelope happens to turn up in your mailbox with some interesting information in it, don't throw it away. That's all I'm saying."

"I didn't ask you do to anything," Garvin said.

"Absolutely not."

"And certainly nothing illegal."

"Never," I said.

Garvin looked at me for a second or two, then nodded. "Good. Just so long as we're clear on this. I don't want you doing a damned thing."

"Hell no," I said, and smiled. I handed him a business card. "Here's my cell number. Let me know if you find anything interesting, okay?"

My car—or maybe I should say truck—was an old, rebuilt Land Rover Defender 90. It was rugged and utilitarian and indestructible and totally reliable. Not at all luxurious. Not a living room on wheels like the Range Rover. It was a tall steel box with hand-cranked windows and a Spartan interior, and it could tow cars and drive through rivers. A true off-road vehicle, even though my off-road driving, since I started working for Stoddard, was mostly limited to gravel driveways in Nantucket.

The Defender was a gift from a grateful Jordanian arms dealer after I made the mistake of admiring it while advising him on protection at his Belgravia estate. He had it reconditioned, repainted the same glossy Coniston green, and shipped over. It was a 1997, but it looked brand-new.

I climbed in just as my cell phone started ringing.

"Yeah?" I said.

"Nick." It was Lauren, and she was whispering. "Can you come over?"

"What is it?"

"I just got an e-mail," she said. "From Roger."

15

Lauren was sitting in front of a computer screen in the small nook off their living room that served as her home office. She was wearing a T-shirt and sweat-pants, and she was barefoot. She looked up as I entered. She'd been crying, I could see. Her eyes were bloodshot.

She tilted the screen so I could see it. I read a few lines, then stopped.

The e-mail was from Roger.Heller@InCaseOf Death.net.

"'In case of death'?" I said. "What the hell's that?"

She looked at me for a long time. "I just looked it up. It's an e-mail service that sends out e-mails to your loved ones," she said. "After you die."

We were both silent for a few seconds.

"I've never heard of such a thing," I said.

Lauren spoke haltingly. "It's sort of morbid, really. But I guess it's a useful service. You know, if there are things you want to tell your family after your death . . ." And she bit her lip.

"Okay," I said. I put a hand on her shoulder.

She swallowed, wiped away her tears with the backs

of her hands. "You sign up for these automatic e-mail notifications. For up to five people. The e-mails go out after you've died."

I said gently, "And how do they know you're dead?"

"I'm not sure, Nick. . . . It looks like they automatically e-mail you as often as you request—weekly, monthly, whatever—and you have up to a week to hit REPLY, and if you don't . . ."

But I'd stopped listening. I'd moved closer to the screen and started reading Roger's letter.

My sweet Lauren,
This has to be the strangest letter I've ever written. Because if you get it, that means I'm dead.

I looked up and saw that Lauren was standing.

"I need to make sure Gabe's doing his homework," she said.

I nodded, kept reading.

How it'll happen, I have no idea.
But first things first. I want you to know how deeply I love you. I'm not an easy man to be married to, so you might not always have realized it—and for that, all I can do is ask your forgiveness. I've never been good about expressing affection, but I hope at least you know I tried my best.
Who knows what they'll do? Will they try to make it look like I committed suicide? You've known me for 9 years—you know I enjoy my life far too much to be suicidal. Or maybe they'll set it up so it looks like I drove drunk—even though you know how rarely I drink, and that I never ever drink and drive.
Or maybe they won't even leave a body—no

evidence. I have no idea what they might try. But if you get this, that means they finally succeeded.

I can only hope that you actually receive this e-mail. I'm not sure you will. The people who are trying to stop me have the ability to intercept e-mail. Given what I know them to be capable of, that's the least of it. So one copy is going to your work e-mail address, and one copy to your personal one, and I hope you get at least one of them. I'm certain they can, and will, read this e-mail.

Whether or not I can save myself, I've taken precautions to protect you and Gabe—to give you the means to hold them off. You'll know what I mean.

But whatever you do, you must never trust anyone.

I thought long and hard about e-mailing Gabe separately, but in the end I decided to leave it to you. You'll know how to handle it. Tell him whatever you think best. Just make sure to tell him I love him immensely. That if there's an afterlife, I'll be cheering him on, and I know he'll grow up to be a terrific man.

And for all the ways I messed up your life—for all the wreckage I'm leaving behind—please forgive me.

I love you so much.

Roger.

P.S.: Please say good-bye to the librarian.

When I finished reading, I sat there for a minute and stared at the screen in a kind of fugue state.

Then I heard Lauren's voice, and I turned around. "He wants you," she said.

It took me a few seconds to realize she meant Gabe.

16

Gabe's room stank of sweat and old laundry. I'd been in monkey houses at zoos that smelled nicer. Dirty clothes were heaped everywhere: on the floor, on his desk, on top of the CD player with the big speakers. Lauren had long ago given up cleaning up after him, and their housekeeper, who came three times a week, refused to enter his room. I could barely make my way to his bed. The only clear spot seemed to be on his desk in front of his computer.

The walls were painted bright orange, his choice, and an odd assortment of posters hung on the wall. A poster for the movie *The Dark Knight* with Heath Ledger wearing creepy eyeliner and lipstick; the only word was "Ha," dripping blood. A movie poster for *Watchmen*: a guy getting thrown out of a tall building, shards of glass in his wake, a yellow smiley button floating in midair with a splotch of red blood on it. And the words JUSTICE IS COMING TO ALL OF US. NO MATTER WHAT WE DO. His desk was piled high with comic books and a big softcover of the comic-book artist Will Eisner.

Gabe lay in bed reading a paperback called *Joker* by Brian Azzarello. The front cover was a grotesque closeup of the Joker's feral grin, with jagged yellow teeth and smeared lipstick. Gabe was wearing headphones hooked up to an iPod Touch. Music blasted in his ears so loud that I could hear it, tinny and distorted and really awful.

My thoughts were still careening, still trying to make sense of Roger's strange and cryptic e-mail. *If you get this, that means they finally succeeded,* he'd written. So he was expecting to be killed. *I've taken precautions to protect you and Gabe,* he'd said. *The means to hold them off.* What could that be? Would Lauren know? And what was that bizarre postscript—*Please say good-bye to the librarian*—supposed to mean? A code, surely, but what?

I sat on the side of Gabe's bed, and he pulled the headphones off and hit the PAUSE button on his iPod.

"Whatcha listening to?" I asked.

"Slipknot."

"Well, *obviously*. Which cut?"

" 'Wait and Bleed,' " he said. "But you knew that."

He didn't smile, but there seemed to be a twinkle in his eye. He enjoyed the game. He knew I didn't get the emo-screamo stuff he'd started listening to recently, and never wanted to.

"You call that music?" I said. Just like old farts have been saying to teenage kids for generations. I imagine Mozart's dad said something like that, too.

"What do you listen to?" Gabe said. "No, wait, let me guess. Coldplay, right?"

Busted. But I just gave him a steely stare.

"And what else—Styx? ABBA?"

"All right, you win," I said. "How's the comic book?"

"It's a graphic novel," he bristled.

"Same thing, right?"

"Not even close."

"When do I get to see it?"

He blushed, shrugged.

"Not for public consumption, huh?"

He shrugged again.

"I'd love to read it sometime."

"Okay. Maybe. I'll see."

"Anyway. You wanted to talk to me?"

He wriggled himself around until he was sitting up. I noticed he was wearing a black T-shirt with Homer Simpson looking into the barrel of a nail gun. It said CAUTION: MAN AT WORK. He also had a stuffed animal in the bed with him, a ratty-looking giraffe Beanie Baby he'd named Jaffee.

Gabe was a strange kid, no doubt about it. He was fourteen, almost fifteen, and had only just entered adolescence. He was a remarkable artist, entirely self-taught, and he spent most of his time—when he wasn't reading comic books—doing panel drawings with an ultrafine black pen. He was scary-smart, brilliant at math and science, and he affected a world-weary cynicism. But every once in a while a crack would appear in his brittle shell, and you'd catch a fleeting glimpse of the little boy. He didn't seem to have any close friends. They called him a dork and a nerd at school, he told me once, and I felt bad about what he must be going through. Adolescence was hard enough for a normal kid.

He wasn't easy to spend time with, which was why I made a point of spending as much time with him as I could. I'd take him to the Air and Space Museum or the Museum of Natural History or the National Zoo, or just for a walk. When he was younger, I taught him how to throw a baseball, and for one disastrous season I coached his Little League team (at the end of which he decided he wasn't cut out to be an athlete). We tried fishing once, but we both found it boring. Recently, I'd been taking him to comic-book stores a lot, and once, a year or so ago, he made me take him to a comic-book convention at a Quality Inn somewhere in Virginia, for which I truly deserved a purple heart.

"That e-mail was about Dad, wasn't it?"

I looked at him for a few seconds while I decided how to reply.

"You don't have to tell me," he said. "I figured it out."

"Were you spying on your mom?"

"Of course not. I don't have to."

"You don't read her e-mail, do you?"

"No way."

"Okay. Good."

"Uncle Nick. He left us, didn't he? He ran off with someone."

"Why in the world would you say that?"

"I can tell. I know things. What did his e-mail say?"

"That's between you and your mom. But no, he didn't run off. Nothing like that."

"Don't lie to me, Uncle Nick."

"I won't. And I'm not."

"Are you going to take off, too?"

"What's that supposed to mean?"

"Like Dad." He said it with a kind of scalding hostility, but that was only to mask the fear, the vulnerability.

"You wish," I said. "But sorry. You can't get rid of me that easy."

He smiled despite himself.

From downstairs I heard Lauren calling, "Nick?"

"All right," I said, standing up. "Good night. Don't worry. We'll get to the bottom of this. We'll find your dad."

"Nick?" Lauren said again, her voice distant and muffled.

Gabe hit the PAUSE button on his iPod and put his headphones back on.

I closed his bedroom door behind me.

"Nick?" Lauren's voice echoed in the stairwell. Something in her tone made me quicken my pace. "Can you come here?"

17

Lauren was standing in front of her computer, hunched over.

"Take a look," she said, swiveling the screen toward me.

I looked, saw nothing unusual. "Yeah?"

"Look again."

"I don't see anything."

"Right." She began scrolling through her e-mail inbox. "It's gone."

I leaned over, watched her move her cursor up and down the list of messages she'd received that day. Roger's e-mail did seem to have disappeared.

"You think you might have accidentally deleted it?"

"No. I'm positive. His e-mail is gone. I don't understand this." Her voice rose, approaching hysterical. "It was right *here*."

"He sent a copy to your work address," I said. "Can you sign on to your work e-mail from here?"

"That's what I'm doing."

Her fingers flew over the keyboard. Then: "Jesus."

"It's not there either," I said.

She shook her head.

"Did you print out a copy?"

"Of course not."

"Or save it on your computer?"

"Why would I? Nick—" She turned around. "I'm not imagining this, right? You saw it."

"Maybe there's a way to get it back. We have someone at Stoddard Associates who's a whiz at data recovery."

"It's like someone reached into my e-mail and just deleted it." She opened a browser on her computer and went to InCaseOfDeath.Net. It was the cyberequivalent of a funeral home—floral bouquets in the borders. Photos of somber people coming up, then fading in flash animation—elderly folks, young parents, and kids—and quotes about death and grieving scrolling across the window. "Never leave anything unsaid!" a banner shouted. "The things you mean to say, the things you haven't said."

There was a MEMBER LOGIN box, and below that a line: "Forget password?"

We both saw it at the same time. "He must have had an account," I said. Even before he could finish, she was typing in Roger's work e-mail address, then she clicked SEND PASSWORD.

A line came up in red:

INCORRECT EMAIL ADDRESS WAS ENTERED.

"Try his home e-mail," I said. She typed it in.

INCORRECT EMAIL ADDRESS WAS ENTERED.

"He must have used some e-mail account I don't know about," Lauren said. "Damn. But what could we find out anyway, come to think of it?"

"Who knows," I said. "When he opened the account. What address he used. Maybe nothing. Maybe we're just grasping at straws."

She walked into the living room and sat on one of the

giant cushy black leather sofas. I followed her in and sat on another couch facing her. Some entertainment news show was on their huge flat-screen Sony. The sound was off. Paris Hilton or one of those interchangeable Hollywood celebrities dodging the paparazzi.

"So Roger was right," I said. "He said 'they' can intercept e-mail. Whoever 'they' are. He called them 'the people who are trying to stop me.' "

"But who's he talking about?"

"I was hoping you might have some idea."

She shook her head. "He never said anything about . . ."

"About people threatening to kill him?"

"It sounds paranoid. Crazy. But his e-mail sounded totally rational, don't you think?"

"You think he wrote it himself?"

She looked at me, furrowed her brow, gave a skeptical smile. "I hadn't thought about that. But it sure sounded like him. I'd say it was definitely Roger."

"I agree. Though it sounds more . . . emotional than I would have expected."

"Nick, you have no idea." She sounded annoyed. "I don't think you ever saw that side of him. The affectionate side."

"He kept it pretty well hidden."

"Maybe he was just different with me."

"No doubt."

She was quiet a moment. "That was the last thing he said to me, you know."

"What was?"

" 'I love you.' "

"Interesting."

"Why interesting?"

I shook my head, and we didn't say anything for a while, and then she asked, "But why didn't he come right out and say what he'd found or who he was afraid of?"

"To protect you, I'd guess. Maybe he figured you'd be safer if you didn't know anything. Since he thought his e-mails were going to be read."

"Then what was the point of his sending any e-mail at all?" she said. "I mean, to go to the trouble of signing up with this morbid 'in case of death' website so he could have an e-mail sent to me that told me almost nothing—why?"

"But I think it tells you a lot. In ways that other people won't understand. Like this line he added about a librarian. What do you think he's referring to?"

"I have no idea. I can't think of the last time he even went to a library."

"He didn't say 'library,' he said 'librarian,'" I pointed out.

"Right," she said. "Librarian."

"Is 'librarian' a code for something?"

"Not that I can think of."

"Or the word 'library'?"

"I really have no idea."

"Well, it's a signal of some sort," I said.

"What about the police? Did you talk to them?"

I nodded.

"Do they have any leads?"

I thought for a moment. "So far just one," I said, and I told her about the withdrawal from Roger's bank account *after* the attack.

"I don't get it," she said. "If they stole his ATM card, wouldn't they need his PIN code to withdraw money?"

I nodded again.

"So it's possible they forced it out of him? At gunpoint or something? Which means maybe they have him alive?" There was such hope in her face that I felt bad.

"Yes, it's possible," I said. The other obvious possibility, which I didn't want to suggest to Lauren, was that once they got the money from him, they no longer needed him alive. She was too fragile. She might have lost her husband, the stepfather to her child. I didn't want to make things even worse for her.

"Where does Roger keep his laptop?"

"His study." She glanced at her watch. "It's late. I've got to be at the office early tomorrow morning."

"You sure you're up to it?"

"Yeah, I think so. Leland needs me back there. No matter what he says."

"You know," I said, "you may be able to help out."

"How?"

"Find out what Roger was doing before—before this happened. What he was working on."

"Ask around, you mean."

"Be discreet about it. It may help explain things."

"Or it may not."

"Agreed. But at this point, we need to sweep up everything. Then we see what we have. Okay?"

"I have to be careful. Being the CEO's admin and all that."

"Of course."

"I'll do what I can, Nick."

"Good. You don't mind me poking around in Roger's study for a bit, do you?"

"Of course not. Actually . . . would you like to spend the night in one of the guest rooms?"

"No need. Thanks anyway."

"No, I mean . . . would you mind spending the night here? I'm just feeling really spooked. That terrifying e-mail from Roger, then the way it vanished? That just scared the hell out of me, Nick. I'm scared about whatever's going on with Roger, and I'm scared for Gabe, and . . . Jesus, Nick, I'm too scared to even think clearly about anything anymore. Would you, please?"

"Of course. Though I'll have to get out of here early so I can stop at my place and change."

"I'll probably be gone by the time you leave. I get to work early."

"What about Gabe?"

"He gets picked up by his car pool. Don't worry about him, he'll be fine. He's used to being alone here in the morning."

"Roger always left early, too?"

She nodded. "Sometimes we drive in together, unless he wants to get in to work before me."

I noticed that I'd referred to Roger in the past tense—as if he was dead—and she didn't catch it.

"Poor Gabe," I said. "Latch-key child."

"Yeah, right," she said, getting up and giving me a quick peck on the cheek. She picked up a couple of remote controls, and switched off the TV and the cable box.

On her way out of the living room, she stopped. "I'm sorry," she said. "I think you know me well enough to know that I'm not, you know, a scaredy-cat. I don't panic, you know that. But after the last couple of days, when I think of Gabe, and I think—"

"You don't have to explain."

"I'm scared out of my mind. Okay? I'm just flat-out terrified."

She turned around quickly, as if she was embarrassed she'd been so open, and she walked toward the door.

"Lauren," I called out.

She stopped, turned her head.

"I'm not going to let anything happen to you guys," I said.

Lauren whirled around, half walked, half ran toward me, and threw her arms around me. "Thank you," she whispered.

Then just as quickly she let go. "I'll get your room ready."

18

I never thought I'd see a home office more grandiose than my father's. Until I saw my brother's.

Dad's library made a certain pompous kind of sense, since it was located in a thirty-room mansion built in 1919 on a ninety-acre estate in Bedford, New York. That's horse country, of course, where women do their shopping in jodhpurs or jeans with holes at the knees and men walk around in flip-flops and everyone gets Lyme disease.

Roger, though, had carved his library out of a far more modest, suburban house. He'd knocked out a couple of rooms on the second floor to create a two-story stage set, complete with a catwalk, and lined with leather-bound books he'd never even opened, probably sold by the yard. Here, my brother got to feel as important, as baronial, as I was sure he didn't at work, where he no doubt just pissed people off.

I found his laptop right where it belonged, on his ornately carved mahogany desk. It was next to an open copy of a book called *Field Guide to Birds of Eastern and Central North America*. Roger was a "birder": a bird-watcher.

That was a hobby I didn't get, like most aspects of my older brother. I have no hobbies, but I basically understand why a guy might want to restore vintage muscle cars or brew his own beer or collect sports memorabilia. I know accountants who wield nothing more dangerous than a sharpened number two pencil at work but have workshops in their basements with table saws that could slice off your thumb in half a second. I know mild-mannered pediatric pulmonologists who race remote-control monster trucks or rock out on their Fender Stratocasters by themselves when they get home at night.

But getting up at three in the morning to get pooped on by a Black-capped Gnatcatcher? I wasn't sure I understood the excitement.

I powered up the laptop, and while I waited, I did a quick walk around his office. He had several framed pictures of Mom and Dad together, one at home and one in a banquette at a nightclub. A photo of Dad in his office on the top floor of the Graystone Building in New York, wearing a three-piece suit, the Manhattan skyline behind him.

Built-in cherrywood file cabinets were neatly labeled—bills, taxes, investments, and so on. I pulled open a couple of drawers and saw that he kept paper copies of his phone bills, which made things easier for me.

I checked out the French doors that opened to the backyard, tried them, and was satisfied that they were securely locked. I knelt, noticed the rudimentary security system in place—the magnetic contacts wired into an alarm system, so if someone tried to force the doors open, the alarm would sound.

Something about it looked wrong, though.

But before I could give it a second look, I heard a high-pitched tone coming from Roger's computer.

It didn't look good. The screen was deep blue and

covered with incomprehensible text—white letters and numbers, garbage that made no sense to me except for one line that I understood quite well:

> *A problem has been detected and Windows has been shut down to prevent damage to your computer*

It was what computer geeks called the Blue Screen of Death.

Roger's computer was dead. It had either crashed or—more likely—it had been wiped.

I had a theory how that might have happened—how someone might have gotten into his study to do it—and I went back to the French doors and knelt again.

Sure enough. One of the magnetic contacts on the doorframe looked like it had been hastily screwed into place. As if someone had unscrewed the contact switch, pulled out the connected wire, then jumpered the switch before screwing it back in—sloppily. In other words, someone had disabled the magnetic contact so the alarm wouldn't go off when the French doors were opened.

Meaning that someone had probably already done a covert entry.

Someone had slipped into Roger and Lauren's house. To search, perhaps. Or for some other reason.

And maybe was planning to do it again.

19

I spent the next forty-five minutes circling the perimeter of the house, looking for evidence of any other intrusions, using a little LED penlight I found in the kitchen that someone had gotten at a trade show. The usual stuff: disturbances in soil patterns, broken shrubbery, jimmied locks, wood shavings, and the like. But I didn't find anything else. No surprise there: Whoever had broken into the house through Roger's study didn't need any other way in. What did surprise me was how primitive the security system was. That would have to change.

I didn't see any point in telling Lauren about the break-in. Not yet, anyway. There was no need to frighten her more.

So I went upstairs to get some sleep.

The guest room was midway between the master bedroom and Gabe's room. It was furnished in classic WASP-grandmother style—oval braided rug, little bedside tables with tiny reading lamps. Hand-colored antique wood engravings of birds on the wall, in little gold frames. An old-fashioned white bedspread made out of that tufted, nubby fabric called chenille. I think.

On top of the toilet in the guest bathroom was a

wicker basket that held a little travel-size tube of Colgate toothpaste, a shrink-wrapped travel-size toothbrush, little bottles of shampoo and conditioner, small hand soaps from Crabtree & Evelyn. I brushed my teeth, undressed, and hung my clothes up on the mahogany valet.

I got into the bed, naked. Found myself staring at some of the weirder-looking birds on the wall—the Ruffed Bustard, the Sacred ibis, the Balearic crane—and wondering if they were extinct, or found only in Madagascar or some Amazonian jungle.

I couldn't sleep. Maybe it was the unaccustomed sounds of a strange house. Maybe it was the fifteen-hundred-thread-count Egyptian cotton sheets, or whatever they were, which I wasn't used to. Too slippery.

More likely, though, it was because I was on alert for any noises that might indicate someone was trying to break in.

I found myself thinking about my brother. About our childhood bedrooms, which we insisted on being right next to each other's. When, given the size of our house, we could easily have been separated by half a mile.

For most of our childhood, we were best friends. We shared almost everything. We were brought close by the weird isolation imposed upon us by my father's money. Or maybe it's more accurate to say, by the way my father chose to live, since I've known rich people who are vigilant about giving their kids a normal life. They send their kids to public schools, they conceal their wealth as best they can, they drive ordinary cars and live in ordinary houses.

But not Victor Heller. He was a brilliant wheeler-dealer who rose from a working-class background to rule Wall Street, and he wanted everyone to know it.

Hence the estate in Bedford, with the horses and stables and clay tennis courts and the collection of antique
roadsters. For years he commuted to and from work in
his own Sikorsky helicopter, which landed on a pad in
our backyard, until the town authorities took him to
court to make him stop.

Mom was the prettiest girl in his small-town high
school, with looks that rivaled Grace Kelly's, and her
early photos confirmed it. Victor Heller won her over
by the sheer brute force of his charisma, by his indom-
itable will, his outsize ambition.

To the world, she seemed to be the perfect society
wife, though she was anything but. She was too smart to
play the role he'd assigned her—arm candy and cheerful
volunteer for the charities he supported. Her chief pleasure in life was being a mother, yet Victor made sure she
wasn't around much to enjoy it. He insisted she go to all
the dinner parties and balls and weekends in Verbier or
Mallorca or Lake Como, though she never seemed to
take pleasure in any of it.

As a result, Roger and I spent more time with our nan-
nies and gardener and caretaker and household staff than
we did with our parents. This didn't make for a great
childhood, but it did at least bring us together. Roger and
I were born less than two years apart—eighteen months,
a closeness in age that could have made us intensely ri-
valrous. Instead, we were more like fraternal twins. We
did everything together.

Our personalities couldn't have been more different,
though. I was the rebel, the troublemaker, and the athlete. Roger was the intellectual, far more bookish, basically a solitary type. Yet he was also a troublemaker in
his own quiet way. One of our housekeepers called him
Eddie Haskell. We'd never seen that old TV show *Leave
It to Beaver,* but years later when I saw a couple of

reruns on late-night TV, I realized that our housekeeper really hadn't liked Roger. Eddie Haskell was an unctuous, conniving brown-noser. He was the two-faced character who'd politely compliment Mrs. Cleaver on her lovely dress while instigating some evil prank that would inevitably get her son, the Beaver, in trouble.

Roger wasn't as bad as Eddie Haskell, though, and I wasn't the Beaver.

Still, Roger did enjoy tormenting me with magic tricks. He spent a lot of time at a magicians' supply house in the city called Tannen's Magic, and he was as good at sleight of hand as I was at throwing a pass. There was one trick he liked to do that I never figured out. It involved sticking his thumb through a hole that he'd cut into two blue cards stuck together, then sliding a red card between the blue cards like a guillotine, apparently slicing through his thumb. I'd beg and plead, but he'd never tell me how he did it.

My brother was a skilled amateur magician, but his greatest talent was always keeping secrets.

20

I was lying in bed, staring at the cracks in the ceiling, when there came a soft knock at the door.

I said, "Yeah?"

"Nick?"

Lauren's voice, hushed and tentative.

"Come on in."

"You sure it's okay?"

"Sure." I sat up, pulled the covers up over my lap. The door opened slowly, squeaking on its hinges, and she looked in.

She noticed my bare chest, and said, "Oh, my God, I'm sorry."

"It's fine," I said. "Don't worry, I won't get out of bed."

She entered. Now she was wearing just the oversized T-shirt, but it was long and roomy enough that it wasn't immodest. Her hair was tousled. "I couldn't sleep."

"Me neither."

She sat in the reading chair next to the bed. "How's the bed?" she said, concerned.

"It's great. What happened to your head bandage?"

"I don't need it. The cut's not bad, and it's healing. It only looks bad."

Her eyes dropped to my chest, for just an instant,

then she quickly looked away. "I meant to leave you a set of Roger's pajamas."

"I usually don't sleep in pajamas. Anyway, they probably wouldn't fit."

"True." She was quiet for a few seconds. "You think Gabe's doing all right?"

"Hard to tell," I said. "He's a teenager."

"What'd he want to talk to you about?"

I shook my head. "I never rat out my nephew."

"Gabe scares me sometimes. He sees too much."

"You should hear what he listens to."

"He's always on the computer with his headphones on, listening to that horrible music."

"Too bad he's outgrown those video games he used to play all the time—Halo 3 and Call of Duty 4, those games where you just try to see how many people you can kill. Healthy stuff like that."

She shook her head, gave a pensive smile. "And then there's his notebook. That comic book he's always working on. Which I'm not allowed to look at."

"Graphic novel."

She nodded. "Did he show it to you?"

"No. Not yet."

"You know how much he admires you."

"I don't know why."

"He thinks you're cool."

"No. He knows I'm *not* cool."

"Well, he thinks you're terrific."

"Sure, why not? I drop by once a month or whatever, and I don't nag him to do his homework."

"No, it's—it's like you're the kind of dad he's always wanted to have. He once said . . ." She looked embarrassed, seemed to have changed her mind, decided not to say whatever she was about to say. "Don't get me wrong—Roger is as good a stepfather to Gabe as he can be. He always treated Gabe like his own. But it can't have been easy for him, marrying a divorced woman with a little kid. And he's not naturally the most—you know, the warmest . . ."

Her voice faded, and I said, "Well, our own father might not have been the best role model. My parents' marriage didn't exactly inspire imitation."

"Is that why you haven't gotten married?"

I shrugged.

She said, "Haven't found the right woman yet?"

"I've found plenty of the right women."

"So . . . ?"

"Marriage is great—for some people. I just don't think it's in my skill set."

She seemed to be thinking hard about something. She bit her lip. Stared at her hands for a while.

"Lauren," I said, "why does Gabe think Roger ran off with some woman?"

"What? He does? Oh God, is that what he told you?"

I nodded.

"That's heartbreaking."

"What makes him think so?"

"Because he has a rich fantasy life. The comic books are only the tip of the iceberg."

I smiled, but she wasn't joking. "I need to ask you something very personal."

"You mean, was Roger having an affair?"

"It's really none of my business," I said. "Unless it has some bearing on what happened to him."

"I understand, and no, he wasn't."

"You're sure."

"Am I a hundred percent sure he never cheated on me? Who can ever be a hundred percent sure of anything? But I sure don't think so, and I think I'd have found out."

"Not necessarily. He was always really good at keeping secrets."

"I think women always know. On some level, conscious or subconscious, they just know."

"And you've plumbed the depths of your subconscious."

"Look, Nick, I know."

I nodded. "Got it."

But I was convinced she wasn't telling me everything.

21

A car alarm woke me at around four thirty, and I decided to get up for the day and begin combing through my brother's files for any interesting leads. I padded downstairs to the kitchen, found the lights, then spent a few moments puzzling over the coffeemaker. I'm good at mechanical things, but since I didn't go to M.I.T. and wasn't trained as a nuclear physicist, that one was beyond me. Eventually, I found a switch that lit up a row of green LED lights. Coffee beans started grinding. A minute or so later, coffee started trickling out of a steel tube—espresso, by the look of it. I had no idea where they hid the coffee mugs, but I found a clean one in the dishwasher. Missed the first shot of espresso but figured out how to extract more.

Soon I was sitting in Roger's study with a large mug of espresso. Somewhere, water was running through a pipe: a toilet flushing. Lauren, I guessed. Probably a much lighter sleeper than Gabe. Particularly after her husband's disappearance.

I was half hoping that his laptop would have healed itself overnight, but no. It still had the Blue Screen of Death, covered with those hieroglyphics.

Unfortunately, the filing-cabinet drawers I was most

interested in—the ones that held Roger's bank statements and financial records, according to their labels—were locked. They were your standard Chicago pin tumbler locks, the spring-loaded kind that pop out when they're unlocked. Not all that complicated. A child could pick it—well, a child with unusual manual dexterity and a decent lock-pick set.

So I started with the unlocked drawers and found a long row of folders bulging with credit-card statements. All neatly placed in order by credit card (platinum American Express, various MasterCards and Visa cards) and, within each folder, by date.

I had nothing specific in mind. Mostly I was looking for patterns: recurring charges, unusual charges. Travel, restaurants, or whatever. Anything that might tell me something about my brother that I didn't know.

Pretty quickly I learned more about Roger than I wanted to know.

Such as the fact that he colored his hair—an itemized Rite-Aid bill that listed Just For Men hair dye along with various purchases like Preparation-H hemorrhoidal suppositories and other things I wish I hadn't seen. Nothing wrong with a man coloring his hair, of course. But Roger had always bragged that it was his regular cardiovascular activity that kept him looking so youthful.

Nope. Just For Men, Medium-Dark Brown.

And the occasional Botox treatment, I discovered. At Advanced Skin Specialists of Silver Spring. Fifteen hundred bucks a pop.

Apparently my brother was a bit more vain than he let on.

Then I found a couple of recurring charges to Verizon on one of his MasterCard statements. One was for residential landline telephone service, and it listed the phone numbers. Three other charges were to Verizon Wireless, for three different cell-phone accounts.

So I looked for his phone bills and found them pretty quickly in another drawer. Apparently he had two land-lines at home. One barely got any use. That was proba-bly the one they used to send faxes on, back in the day when people sent faxes. The other line, their primary home number, listed calls to a whole array of numbers I didn't recognize. Most frequent were calls to Virginia Beach, where Lauren's sister, Maura, lived. Second most frequent were calls to Charlottesville, Virginia, where Lauren's mother lived.

Then, the cell phones. Roger's main mobile phone ac-count was one of those primo, unlimited-minutes call-ing plans. He obviously used it for work—there were a lot of calls every day to Alexandria, probably to Gifford Industries corporate headquarters. The occasional call home, a few to Lauren's mobile number. A second cell-phone account was Lauren's, with Gabe added on to hers as part of a "family plan."

But I couldn't find the billing records for the third cell-phone account, no matter how much I searched. So I made a mental note to ask Lauren about it, then I looked around for the key to the locked drawers contain-ing Roger's financial statements. Nothing in all the usual places where people hide their keys. So I found a small screwdriver and a paper clip in one of Roger's desk drawers and set to work picking the lock.

I heard a throat being cleared, and I looked up.

Lauren was standing in the doorway, arms folded, watching me. She wore a beautifully tailored navy suit over a white silk blouse, and she looked amazing. Even with the fading scrapes and bruises.

"You're up early," I said.

"Leland's flying to Luxembourg."

"Okay."

"But he always starts early anyway. That car alarm wake you up?"

"Yep."

"Sorry about that."

She crossed the room to Roger's desk and opened the top drawer. "I don't mean to take the fun out of it," she said, pulling out a small manila envelope and handing it to me, "but it might be easier just to use the key."

"Hiding in plain sight," I said. "I think Edgar Allan Poe wrote something about that."

"Can I ask you what you're looking for?"

"Any large withdrawals. Checks. Transfers into or out of any of his accounts."

"What would that tell you?"

I shrugged. "If he got money from anyone unusual. Or paid any out. Particularly any large amounts. A money trail always helps."

She nodded. "Well, I don't know when you have to leave for work, but Gabe gets picked up for school around seven forty-five. Can you make sure he eats some breakfast? I don't think he eats breakfast. He really should."

"Sorry. That's above my pay grade."

"Well, whatever you can do."

"No promises. Lauren, did Roger use this computer often?"

"Every day. Why?"

"When was the last time you saw him use it?"

She squinted, tilted her head first to one side, then to the other. "The last morning he was here. Why do you ask?"

"It's fried. Totally gone."

"That's weird."

"If you don't mind, I'm going to take it to work with

me to see if any of the data can be recovered. And one more thing. Do you usually set the alarm during the day?"

"Sometimes. Why?"

"From now on, I want you to keep it on anytime you're not here. And when you and Gabe are asleep, I want you to use the night settings. In fact, I want to get someone in here to upgrade the system. Put in something a little more sophisticated."

"You really think that's necessary?"

"I just want you to take precautions."

"You really think a home-security system is going to keep anyone out who wants to get in here?"

"Of course not. But I want to make it as inconvenient for them as possible."

She smiled, but I could see the strain in her face, the tightening of the muscles in her jaw, the lines around her eyes. The yellowing bruises.

As she turned to leave, I said, "Oh, one more thing. I haven't been able to find all of Roger's cell-phone records."

"They should all be there. You mean, you're missing some of the statements or something?"

"I can't find any billing records for one of the numbers," I said, and I read it off to her.

"That's not Roger's cell phone."

"It's a Verizon Wireless account."

"That's not a number I've ever heard before," she said. "Are you sure that's his?"

"It's his."

"Sorry, Nick," she said. "I can't help you with that. That's a mystery to me. Roger always paid all the bills, not me."

"Interesting," I said.

"But he'd never keep something like that from me.

He'd never keep a secret cell-phone number. That's not Roger."

She shook her head emphatically and walked out of the room, and I thought: *Maybe you don't really know Roger.*

22

On the way in to work, Lauren listened to her office voice mail in the Lexus, hands-free.

Most of the messages were from Leland. Whenever he thought of something he wanted her to do, he'd leave her a voice mail.

It had taken him years to get the hang of e-mail—he used to dictate e-mails for her to type, but finally he'd evolved his own two-finger hunt-and-peck method and liked to do it himself. He'd taken to the BlackBerry right away, even though he complained that his fingers were too thick for the Lilliputian keys.

But when he was traveling or just on the road, it was a lot easier for him to leave her voice mail. The first couple of messages were apologetic: "I don't want to overwhelm you on your first day back," one of them began; and then, "Also—but if you're not feeling up to it, don't worry about it, I'll ask Noreen."

Noreen Purvis, the CFO's admin, worked in the executive suite, too, in the same open bullpen, within shouting distance. She was a disaster, even though Leland was too polite to say as much. She was older than Lauren and had worked at Gifford Industries far longer. She made no secret of the fact that she'd expected

Leland to pick her as his admin when Cynthia, Leland's longtime secretary, had retired more than ten years earlier.

Leland didn't like Noreen, though. He considered her disorganized and even slovenly, and he was annoyed by her smoking, even though Noreen never smoked indoors. Plus, he didn't want to grab someone else's admin. Instead, he hired Lauren.

Noreen, of course, had no idea how Leland really felt about her. She'd wanted the job that Lauren got and never failed to let Lauren know, in all sorts of passive-aggressive ways, that she was far more qualified to be the administrative assistant to the CEO.

The Parkway was choked with traffic, as it always was at this time of the morning, but she didn't mind.

She needed time to think.

She was determined to arrive at work ready to focus on Leland, not distracted by all the trauma in her personal life. She wanted to give Leland her all for the few hours he was in the office.

Long ago she'd realized that she was, in many ways, like a wife to him, but without the sex. (Then again, she thought ruefully, it wasn't as if she and Roger had had much of a sex life in the last couple of years either.) In certain respects she knew Leland better than his own wife. But unlike so many marriages where you grow to detest your partner (like her own starter marriage), her relationship with Leland Gifford kept getting better. Her affection and respect for the man had only deepened. She'd come to know all his flaws, and she loved the man despite them all. Maybe even because of them all.

She couldn't allow herself to think about Roger just then, about where he might be at that very second. Thinking about what might have become of him gave her a terrible, gnawing anxiety.

No. She had to put those thoughts out of her mind, at least for a few hours. She had to arrive at the office with a clear head.

She drove into the Gifford Industries office park and eased the Lexus into a space close to the building. She didn't have a reserved spot: Those were just for the executive team. But it was early enough that there were still plenty of spaces, and she didn't have to park half a mile away.

The soft morning light glinted off the gray-green glass skin of the Gifford building. It was a strange, futuristic-looking tower, a twenty-four-story parallelogram. She couldn't decide if it was ugly or beautiful. It was a "green" building—ecofriendly, energy-efficient. Built of concrete made from slag. Floor-to-ceiling insulating high-performance glass windows. On the roof, a rainwater harvesting system and a one-megawatt solar array.

As she walked toward the main entrance, someone called out to her. It was a senior vice president, Tom Shattuck: tall, broad-shouldered, blond.

"Lauren, I'm so sorry to hear about your husband," he said with the somber concern of an undertaker.

She wondered how the word had gotten around so fast and whether everyone assumed Roger was dead.

"Thanks," she said.

"If there's anything I can do, you know I'm here for you."

He was always extremely cordial to her, but she knew all about him from his admin. He was a tyrant to the woman who worked for him all day. The admins all talked, of course. Didn't their bosses realize that?

She smiled, nodded, and kept walking. She waved her badge at the proximity sensor, stepped into the revolving door, and entered the cavernous atrium. Right in the center, surrounded by tropical foliage, was a huge bronze globe, the continents sculpted in sharp relief. On the front of the globe, set at a jaunty angle, was the Gifford Industries logo, which couldn't have been more hokey: retro squared-off streamlined script that must have looked futuristic when it was designed in the 1930s.

A couple more people waved at her, flashed sympathetic looks, and she ducked into the express elevator to the twenty-fourth floor. She slid her security card into the slot, and the elevator rose.

The lights in the executive suite were already on, which surprised her. She was normally the first one in. She passed her prox badge against the sensor until it beeped, then pushed open the glass doors. When she rounded the corner, she saw someone sitting at her desk.

Noreen Purvis.

23

Gabe's room was as dark as a cave.

He was asleep under the covers, a barely discernible lump. His crappy music was semiblasting from the speakers on a big black clock/radio/CD player on his desk, his iPod docked into the top of it.

The music was the audio equivalent of needles being stuck in my eyeballs. I flipped on all the lights. He groaned.

"Let's go," I said. "You should have been up twenty minutes ago."

He pulled the blanket over his head, and I said, "You can run, but you can't hide."

He made a surly sound and burrowed in deeper.

"You can't get rid of me that easy. Move it, or you'll experience firsthand how I flushed those al-Qaeda terrorists out of their caves at Tora Bora."

His head slowly emerged from the covers like a turtle from its shell. "That's such crap," he said. "You guys never even found Osama bin Laden."

"Hey, don't blame me."

He mumbled something vaguely caustic, and I said, "Anyone ever tell you you're a smart-ass? Turn off the music."

He did. "What are you doing here?"

"Making sure you get to school. Move it."

"I'm staying home. I don't feel good." He pulled the covers back over his face.

"You sleep with that stuff on all night?"

"No, it's my . . . alarm." His voice was muffled.

"No wonder you overslept. The music's too lulling. Don't you have anything more strident? Celine Dion, maybe?"

He grunted, unamused. As much as I liked Gabe, he was a difficult kid. Fortunately, he was someone else's problem, not mine. The thought of having a kid, or kids, gave me the heebie-jeebies, but raising a teenager truly seemed like a horror show. I didn't understand how people did it, though evidently people did. My mother, for one. (Dear old Dad, smart guy that he was, took off when I was thirteen. He missed out on most of the fun.)

"Come on, kid," I said. "Get up."

"You can't make me."

"Oh yeah? You didn't know I have police auxiliary authority? I can have you arrested right now for truancy." It sounded almost plausible.

Gabe slowly pulled down the covers just enough to peek out at me. He uttered a pretty hard-core curse word.

"I can also have you arrested for obscenity."

"Is that what Grandpa's in prison for?" he said.

"You're quick."

"I'm staying home today."

"What's the problem, Gabe?"

He mumbled something I didn't understand, and I moved in closer, yanked the covers down. "I didn't hear you so good," I said.

He put a hand over his eyes to shield them from the light, and croaked, "It's like all over school anyway."

"What is?"

"About Dad."

"What's all over?"

He sat up, hung his legs over the side of the bed, and stood. Reaching over to his desk, he ran a finger across the touchpad of his MacBook, and the screen came to life.

It was his Facebook page. His picture in a box at the top and a bunch of other little boxes and things. I said, "What am I looking at?"

He tapped the screen. I looked at where he was pointing, an area of the page called "The Wall," which had a column of little pictures of what I assumed were junior-high-school kids, mostly face pictures but some weird posed shots. Some of the guys had baseball caps on backwards. Next to each picture was a name and some comment, like "What was English homework??" and "quiz on verbs 2morrow?!" Apparently this was how Gabe and his friends communicated.

On one line was a blue question mark instead of a picture. And the comment:

"hey Gay Gabe, you loser, your dad ditched you, can't blame him, why don't you just kill yourself?"

I looked at Gabe, saw the tears in his eyes. "Who wrote this?" I said.

"I don't know."

"There's a name here. Can't you just click on it?"

"It's fake. Someone made a fake Facebook page."

"You think it's someone from school?"

"Gotta be."

"Is this what they call cyberbullying?"

"I don't know."

"Back in the day, someone called you names, you'd wait for him after school and beat the crap out of him."

"Oh, please," he said. "You went to some fancy private day school in Westchester County. Like, in a limo with a chauffeur."

"Granted," I said. "But that doesn't mean we didn't have fistfights."

I came close to telling him how often I beat up kids who made fun of his father, after Victor's arrest. But I didn't think he'd want to hear that his uncle Nick had been his father's defender. Especially since Roger was my older brother.

"'Why don't you just kill yourself,'" he said, bitterly. "Maybe I will."

"That'll show them," I said, then realized that sarcasm was probably a bad idea at this point. "Come on, Gabe. You can't pay attention to jerks like this. You know what I always say—never let an asshole rent space in your head."

He sat back down on the side of the bed, resting his head in his hands.

"Move."

Gabe started getting dressed—jeans so tight he had to squeeze into them, his black hoodie, black Chuck Taylors. He grabbed an already open can of Red Bull and took a long swig.

I looked at my watch. "Ten minutes before your car pool gets here. Your mother wants you to have breakfast."

He toasted me with his Red Bull. "What do you think this is?"

I shrugged. The last thing I wanted to be was this kid's authority figure.

"Gabe, why do you think kids at school say that kind of stuff about your dad?"

"Because they're assholes?"

"No question. But what makes them say crazy stuff like that, do you think?"

A sullen look came over him. "How do I know?"

"No idea where the kids at school might get that idea?"

"Maybe it's true."

Softly, carefully, I said, "You said that before. What makes you think so?"

He looked supremely uncomfortable. "I told you, I just see stuff. I notice stuff."

"Did he tell you something?"

"No," he said scornfully. "Of course not."

"So what did you see? What did you notice?"

"Nothing. It's just . . . I don't know, like, a feeling."

"A fear, maybe?"

"Maybe."

"That's understandable."

"I have to go to school."

"Now look who's concerned with the time all of a sudden," I said.

While I waited with him for the car pool, I asked, "Gabe, do you use your dad's laptop?"

"Why would I? I have my own."

"Any idea why it might have crashed?"

"Crashed?"

"Blue Screen of Death."

"Oh. He asked me how to do a disk wipe. He said he was planning to get a new one. Maybe he screwed it up. Wouldn't surprise me."

"He was trying to wipe it clean? Delete its contents?" So much for my theory about someone breaking in to tamper with Roger's computer. Still, the alarm contacts on the French doors to Roger's study had been quickly and sloppily disabled; that much I knew. Meaning that someone had made a covert entry for some reason. To snoop around, maybe. Or maybe for another purpose I hadn't yet figured out.

"I guess."

"Why?"

"Who knows. Why were you looking at my dad's computer, anyway?"

"Because I thought there might be a clue there as to what happened to him."

"Why would he leave a clue on his laptop?"

"He wouldn't," I said, but before I could explain, a big blue Toyota Land Cruiser pulled into the driveway.

"See you," Gabe said.

"Remember what I told you about assholes."

"Yeah. Never let them rent space in your head. Wish it was that easy."

He slung his backpack over his shoulder and went out to the car.

And I couldn't shake the feeling that he, like his mom, was keeping something from me.

24

"Look at you!" Noreen Purvis scolded, getting right to her feet. "You should be home in bed!"

"I'm okay," Lauren said. "Really."

"Oh, honey, I mean it. I can take care of things here for as long as it takes you to recover properly."

"And I appreciate it. But I'm fine."

Noreen was a big, horsy woman with ash-blond hair that she wore in a short, no-nonsense style—sort of Princess Diana circa 1990. On Princess Di it had looked good.

She was wearing her fake Chanel scarf and a brown pantsuit and a pair of black Tory Burch pumps with the huge gold Tory Burch medallions on the toes. They were probably fakes, too. She reeked of tea rose perfume and cigarette smoke.

"Why is the door closed?" Lauren said, glancing at Leland's office, which was next to her desk.

Noreen shrugged. "He's been in there since I got here, maybe twenty minutes ago."

"Who's he talking to?"

She shrugged again, began clearing her things off Lauren's desk. "Well, I should fill you in on the arrangements for Leland's trip, I guess."

"I'll be right back," Lauren said. "Need to use the girls' room."

She locked herself in a stall, lowered the toilet seat, sat down, and began to cry.

It was as if a dam had burst. Damned Noreen sitting at her desk, talking about Leland in that proprietary way.

And Roger. She was frightened. She didn't know what to think. Not knowing about Roger.

My God. Not knowing: *That was the worst thing.*

She pulled out a length of toilet paper to blot the tears. After about five minutes, she was all cried out. She left the stall and went to the sink and reapplied her makeup. Then she washed her hands in cold water—the taps came on automatically for a few seconds when you waved your hands under them, but not long enough for the water to turn warm. The paper-towel dispenser shot out an annoying small rectangle of perforated brown paper.

Everything was irritating her now. Everything upset her.

She'd been back barely half an hour and already she needed a vacation.

25

As soon as Gabe got in the car, I called my old army buddy Merlin, the TSCM expert, and asked him for another favor.

I asked him to stop by Lauren's house later and help me put in a decent home-security system. Granted, asking Merlin to do a security system was a little like asking Bill Gates for tech support on Microsoft Word. Sort of overkill. But Merlin was gracious about it and said sure.

Just as I was backing out of Lauren's driveway, my cell phone rang. I glanced at the caller ID and said, "Lieutenant."

"You might want to stop by."

Arthur Garvin's voice was hoarse and adenoidal. He sounded even worse than the day before.

"You got the tape?"

"I did."

"And?"

"I'll be here until around eleven."

"I've got a meeting in the office," I said. "Do you think you could courier a copy over to me?"

He coughed noisily for a few seconds. "Yeah," he

said, "why don't I send my personal courier over. On his mounted steed."

"All right," I said. "I'll be right there."

Lieutenant Garvin turned his computer monitor, an ancient Dell, around so we could both watch. He offered me coffee, and this time I took it.

A fuzzy color image was frozen on the screen. I couldn't make out anything beyond a couple of indistinct silhouettes on a street. The ATM was, I assumed, located outside. Near a gas station. Cars zipped by in the background.

In the frame around the image were numbers—date code, time sequence, all that sort of thing.

Garvin futzed with the mouse, clicking and double-clicking first the left button, then the right one. Finally, he got it working, and I could see a couple of smeary blobs making funny abrupt movements toward the camera.

"I should warn you in advance," he said. "The resolution's lousy."

"Oh, yeah?"

"And that's not all. I thought it was video they were sending over. It's not."

"What is it?"

"A couple of still photos."

"What do you mean?"

"This ATM had a recording rate of one frame every ten seconds."

I groaned. "To save hard-disk space, I bet."

"Who the hell knows? I don't know why they even bother."

It's sort of ironic that so many banks invest so much money in their security systems, installing high-tech digital video recorders in their automatic teller machines that transmit compressed video signals to a central server. All very fancy and high-end—and then, to save space, they set their cameras to record at the slowest possible rate. Ten to fifteen frames per second is slow. But one frame every ten seconds was little more than a stop-action camera.

Garvin clicked something, and the frame advanced, and I could see a man in a suit leaning forward toward the cash machine's screen. The face was clear.

It was Roger.

There was no doubt about it at all.

His rimless glasses, his large forehead, the dark brown hair parted at the side. The hair was mussed, and his glasses were slightly crooked. He was wearing a dark suit and white shirt and tie, but one lapel of his suit was sticking up and his tie was askew. He looked like he'd been injured. It was hard to see much of his facial expression, but from what I could tell, he looked frightened.

Roger had survived the attack.

For the first time, I knew that for sure. But where he was right now, or even whether he was still alive, I had no idea. The mystery I'd stepped into—or been dragged into—had suddenly gotten a whole lot more baffling.

And probably a lot more dangerous.

26

"That him?" Garvin said.

"That's him."

"I owe you an apology," he said.

"I'll take it. But for what?"

"You were right about this being an abduction."

"Was I?"

"Your brother wasn't acting on his own volition. That's pretty clear."

"Based on what?"

"Watch. Check this out. I *think* I know how to do it." He double-clicked the mouse, shifting the frame to the left. Then he clicked some more, centering in on the figure next to my brother.

It was a guy in a hooded sweatshirt, back turned to the camera. Lieutenant Garvin touched the screen with his index finger, drawing my attention to what looked an awful lot like a gun.

"You get the guy's face?"

"Nope. The whole transaction lasted a minute ten seconds. Seven frames. And you don't see the guy's face on any of them. Not even a partial."

"I'd like to see all of them, if you don't mind."

Garvin nodded. I expected at least a sigh of frustration, but his attitude toward me seemed to have softened a bit. I was no longer the annoying brother of the victim, or the intrusive, competing investigator. Now I was almost a colleague helping him solve a problem.

He clicked the mouse and advanced frame by frame, from the beginning. This time we were viewing just the left half of the image, the part that had earlier been outside the frame. You could see the hooded figure very close to Roger, his back always to the camera. He never raised his weapon. He kept it at his side, pointed at Roger.

"Did Wachovia security say if there was another camera?" I asked.

"This is the only one."

"Where's the ATM?"

"Georgetown. M Street, near the Key Bridge."

I nodded. "Couple blocks from where they were attacked. So whoever grabbed him just wanted cash? Sorry—I still find that hard to believe."

He shrugged. "They got four thousand nine hundred bucks. His account allowed him to withdraw up to five thousand a day, turns out. That ain't chump change."

"Granted. But I doubt money was the primary motivation."

"Five thousand bucks is plenty of motivation."

"Sure. But that's not it."

"Got a theory you like better?"

"Well, it's not plain-vanilla kidnapping. Not without a ransom demand."

"Yet."

"It's been long enough. No. You just called it an abduction, and I think you're right. That I get."

"How come?"

"Because Roger was expecting an attack of some kind."

"You know this how?"

"What he said to his wife that night. He said, 'I love you.'"

"So?"

"That's not like him."

"Not like him to tell his wife he loves her? Real sweetheart, huh?"

"You don't want to go there. Point is, he knew he was going to be grabbed. He knew he might not ever see her again. He was saying good-bye."

"Maybe." He sounded dubious.

"And then, when he saw they'd grabbed Lauren, he said, 'Why her?'"

"Huh. Like, 'take me instead.'"

"Right."

"Doesn't mean he knew them, though."

"You're right. It doesn't."

"No blood, no trace evidence, no ransom demands. Your theory still doesn't get us any closer."

I paused for a moment. One of my abiding principles is never to tell anyone anything he doesn't need to know. Loose lips and all that. But Garvin and I were, in a sense, partners by then. The only thing that counted was finding my brother, and the more Garvin knew, the more helpful he could be.

So I told him about what looked like an attempted break-in at Roger's house. And about the InCaseOf Death.net e-mail.

"He was being threatened," I said. "Which is why he arranged that e-mail. Because he was afraid they'd try to make it look like he killed himself."

Garvin sneezed while I was talking, blew his nose loudly. I was beginning to wonder whether it wasn't just a cold but maybe Ebola virus.

"Can I see a copy of this e-mail?" he said.

"It's gone," I said, and I explained.

"Well, there's got to be a copy somewhere."

I shook my head.

"Gotta be some high-priced computer geeks in your high-priced firm who can bring it back."

"I can ask."

"You say he was 'threatened.' Over what?"

I shook my head. "Don't know. Maybe to force something out of him."

"Like what?"

"My guess? He had some information someone wanted. Or he wasn't supposed to have. Something business-related. Like a big project he was financing."

"That's pretty vague."

"Like I said, it's just a guess. I don't actually know. But he tried to delete everything on his laptop at home."

"To get rid of evidence?"

"Or to protect his family."

"How so?"

"Cover his trail. Let's say he'd been collecting information on his laptop, and he didn't want these guys to know he had it."

"You got the laptop?"

"Yeah," I said vaguely. I had other plans for it. "I think so. I'll look around."

"Okay. So now I think I get it."

"Get what?"

He began tidying things on his desk, moving folders into piles. "I asked our Homeland Security division to check on all flights out of the country. Told them to flag your brother's passport. That was when I was thinking fugitive, not abduction."

"And?"

"Turns out your brother's on the No Fly List."

"No Fly List?"

"Yep. You know, that new TSDB watch list."

"TSDB?" I said, but I remembered the new acronym just before he said it.

"Terrorist Screening Database."

"My brother wasn't a terrorist," I said.

"Neither are most of the people on the list," he said.

I grunted. Like most people who've come into contact with the sharp end of the U.S. government since September 11, 2001, I'd seen more than my share of abuses of law enforcement. Things like the USA PATRIOT Act were used to justify all kinds of invasions of privacy.

"You know what bycatch is?" Garvin said.

I shook my head.

"It's like when commercial fisheries go trawling for tuna, and they end up catching other stuff in their nets, like sea turtles and dolphins. The bycatch."

"Dirty fishing," I said. "Isn't that what it's called?"

"Right."

"But that implies catching something you don't intend to catch," I pointed out. "You don't put someone's name on the No Fly List by accident."

"Okay," Garvin conceded. "So maybe it's no accident. Maybe you're right. Maybe your brother made some enemies. Maybe whatever he was doing, he got into some kinda stuff he shouldn't have. National security stuff, maybe."

"He does finance at a construction company."

"Gifford Industries is a construction company? Like Home Depot is the corner hardware store. Maybe there's something about him you're not telling me."

"I've told you everything I know."

"Then maybe there's something about him you don't know," Garvin said.

27

Actually, there was plenty about my brother I didn't know.

Like how his mind worked.

Just because we were brothers didn't mean that we shared anything but a strange upbringing and fifty percent of our DNA. We couldn't have been more different.

Still, for a long stretch of our childhood—right up until the day Dad left—we were best friends.

Dad was a remote, unfathomable, larger-than-life character to both of us. He seemed to laugh louder than most people, got more angry, was smarter, more intense, more everything.

We loved going to his office in Manhattan. His firm occupied the entire top floor of the Graystone Building, an art deco ziggurat near Grand Central that had been built to resemble a Babylonian temple. In the lobby was a huge mural by some famous artist of Prometheus stealing fire. The elevator doors were ornate brass. His office always smelled like pipe smoke and old wood and leather and brass cleaner, and it was suffused with the ozone of power. It had a breathtaking view of the city. Silhouetted against the Manhattan skyline, Victor Heller stood mightier than any of the spindly skyscrapers in the distance, a colossus astride the globe.

We were terrified of him. When he got angry, you didn't want to be within a mile. One day he was looking for something in our bathroom, the one Roger and I shared—who knows what he was looking for, maybe a roll of toilet paper—when he found a half-used pouch of chewing tobacco. It said RED MAN on the label.

He stormed into the game room, where we were playing Risk, and he demanded to know which one of us was using chewing tobacco.

We both denied it. I didn't even know what chewing tobacco was.

Furious, Dad whipped us both with his crocodile-leather belt. I don't think he really cared about whether we were using tobacco. He just didn't like having his authority undermined.

Afterward, Roger and I consoled each other. We both knew we'd been unfairly punished, which hurt even more than our backsides. Roger slid down the waistband of his Jockey shorts a few inches and showed me the damage Dad had done. His buttocks were crimson. Mine were, too.

"Hey, Red Man," he said, and we both burst out laughing.

It turned out that the chewing tobacco had been left under the sink by Sal, one of the caretakers, who'd been fixing a leak. But the incident also left us with a nickname for each other, a secret code: "Red Man." Never in front of others. Only between us.

"Hey, Red Man," we'd say to each other on the phone, and it was like a nudge, a wink. It instantly evoked a whole world—of archeological digs on the far reaches of the property that enraged Yoshi, the elderly Japanese gardener; of pranks that made our favorite cook,

Mrs. Thomasson, giggle; of getting into trouble and covering for each other.

It made us feel like fellow conspirators. Which was nice. It brought us even closer.

Until we turned against each other.

28

By some strange spin of the genetic roulette wheel, I grew up big and broad-shouldered and muscular, while Roger became stringy and gawky. He needed glasses; I didn't. He became defiantly bookish while I was the athlete who pretended not to care about school. He was the smart one; I was the strong one. He was a bully magnet, and even though he was older, I became his defender. He didn't like that.

By the time we entered our teens, it became clear that Roger wanted to be just like Dad. He told everyone he was going to work "in finance."

One day, when I was thirteen and Roger was almost fifteen, we got home from school to find Mom waiting for us in the gloomy library, sitting in a big leather chair in the circle of light cast by a reading lamp. She said she wanted to talk to us.

She got up, gave us both hugs, and told us that Dad had been arrested at work that morning. Right in front of his employees. They'd handcuffed him and led him out through the trading floor.

"Why?" Roger said.

"The Justice Department wanted to embarrass him."

"No, I mean, why did they arrest him?"

She explained, but it didn't all sink in. Something about securities fraud and insider trading. Something about an SEC investigation that had been going on for months. Since I barely understood what Dad did for a living, I had no idea what he'd been arrested for.

We didn't see Dad until the next day. He was at home when we returned from school, which was strange. Normally, he didn't get home until after dinner.

He took us into his study and told us that he'd spent the night in jail, locked up at the Metropolitan Correctional Center with a bunch of drug dealers. That morning he'd been taken before a magistrate and arraigned and released on bail.

He told us not to worry. That the charges were trumped up. He'd made some powerful enemies, and they were trying to drag him through the mud. But he had great lawyers, and he'd fight this thing, and we'd all get through it, and we'd all be fine.

"But I want you boys to know one thing," he said fiercely. "I'm innocent. Never forget it."

"I don't understand," Roger said. "How could they arrest someone who's innocent?"

Dad leaned back in his chair and laughed raucously. "Oh, good Lord, kiddo, you've got a lot to learn about the world."

The next morning, when Roger and I were on our way to school, our car stopped at the end of the long driveway. The driver—yes, we had a driver—cursed aloud, and we looked out the front windshield.

There was a mob in front of the gates—cameras, reporters with bulbous microphones, people swarming the car, screaming at us.

The driver backed up and took us out the back way.

School wasn't much fun that day. Everyone had heard about the arrest of Victor Heller. A rich-kid school like that, you can believe everyone's parents were talking about it at the breakfast table, and with undisguised glee. There was a lot of pent-up resentment over our father. A lot of jealousy.

Our friends were sympathetic, but there were plenty of kids who hurled insults.

And that was when I learned to fight.

Anyone who dared say anything nasty about my father had to deal with me. Anyone who said anything to my brother had to face me, too.

We were a family under siege. Both parents were around far too much, except for the times when Dad's lawyers came to the house and met with him in his study for hours on end. The phone kept ringing, but my parents wouldn't answer it. They stopped going out.

Mom, who until that moment had always seemed a recessive gene, swung into action, helping the lawyers coordinate a legal defense. Suddenly, she felt useful. She knew nothing about Wall Street or white-collar crime, but she was smart and determined to stand by her husband.

She saw the cuts and scrapes on my face when I came home from school, and she said nothing. She knew. She just bandaged me up and told us we'd all get through it.

When Dad emerged from his strategy sessions with his lawyers, he'd rattle around the house or practice his serve with the tennis pro, and he talked to us a lot, assured us that he was innocent, that all the charges would be overturned, and this nightmare would be over. Soon.

About a week later I was awakened by a car starting up in the middle of the night. I sat up, went over to my window. Saw the distinctive beehive taillights of Dad's 1955 Porsche Speedster. Went back to sleep.

In the morning, Dad was gone. Never said good-bye. Mom's eyes were bloodshot, her face puffy, and we could tell she'd been crying. She said only that Dad had had to leave suddenly to take care of some business.

He wasn't back when we returned from school.

Nor the next day.

It took three days before Mom told us that Dad wasn't coming back anytime soon. He'd left the country. She didn't know where he'd gone.

All she knew, she said, was that he was innocent. He hadn't done anything wrong. But innocence didn't always mean you could get a fair trial.

The indictment was handed down four days after he fled. Victor Heller had been charged with wire fraud and income-tax evasion and securities fraud, even racketeering. The newspapers began referring to him as the "fugitive financier."

But I didn't have to defend my father's honor anymore at our fancy private school. The next day we stayed home from school and helped Mom pack up the house. A moving truck came the day after that.

The government had seized all of Dad's assets, which meant everything—the Bedford house, the duplex penthouse on Fifth Avenue at East Sixty-fourth Street, the house in Palm Beach that Roger and I hated, the chalet in Aspen, the ranch in Montana. All bank accounts. Every last cent.

We piled into the old Subaru station wagon that Mom liked to tool around Bedford Village in and headed for her mother's house, north of Boston. After we crossed the Massachusetts border, Mom stopped in Sturbridge to get some lunch, and she went to an ATM to get cash and began crying. Her personal bank account had been seized, too.

We had nothing.

Roger and I were starved, as only teenage boys can be, but we said nothing.

"You okay, Red Man?" Roger said to me.

"I'm okay," I said.

We didn't stop until we got to Malden and our grandmother's cramped, pink-painted suburban split-level ranch house. The house Mom grew up in. No tennis court. No stables.

No Dad, either.

We didn't see him again for more than ten years.

29

After five years of working the dark side of Washington, D.C., both in the government and out, I had a pretty good Rolodex. Not like Jay Stoddard's, but not too shabby. I knew someone in just about every three-letter government agency.

Granted, no one actually uses Rolodex card files anymore. In fact, as a figure of speech, I prefer the concept of the favor bank. You do a favor for someone, help someone out of trouble, put someone in touch with someone else, make a connection . . . the odds are the person you helped out will pay you back.

They don't always. Some people are jerks. Past performance is no guarantee of future returns and all that. Plus, deposits into the favor bank aren't insured by the FDIC. And you don't always do favors just to earn payback. Sometimes you do the right thing just to do the right thing, which might be called the good-karma network, or the "pay it forward" principle.

But whatever your motive, you always want to maintain a positive balance in your favor bank account. You want liquidity, in case you ever need to make an emergency withdrawal. The longer I work in this murky underworld, the more it resembles Tony Soprano's office in the back room of the Bada Bing strip club. Not just Washington, but the business world, too: They're like the Mafia, but without the horse head in the bed. Usually.

Anyway, I knew a guy who worked in a fairly senior capacity at the Transportation Security Administration, the TSA. These are the folks who frisk and wand you and grope you, make you take off your shoes and arbitrarily decide to search through your underwear at airport security gates. Who once seized a toddler's sippy cup at Reagan National Airport a few years back and detained the kid's mother for trying to smuggle potentially lethal infant formula on board. And who not long ago made a lady in Texas remove her nipple rings with a rusty pair of pliers (though the less said about nipple rings the better).

About a year ago, Stoddard Associates was brought in by the TSA to conduct an outside investigation into alleged corruption in the agency—a smuggling ring led by someone inside TSA. For some reason the TSA people didn't want to use the FBI. Something to do with politics and turf, and Jay Stoddard didn't care why.

They'd fingered an operations security administrator named Bill Puccino. I met him and knew right away he hadn't done it. We bonded. His Boston accent was as familiar to me, as comforting, as a pair of old sneakers, after the years I spent in Malden at Grandma's house.

Turned out that his boss had set him up as the fall guy. I cleared Puccino. He was promoted to his boss's job. His boss was punished by being transferred to a more exalted position in Homeland Security, which gave him a medal for his "integrity" and sent him to Paris as their "attaché." Cruel and unusual. The ignoble fate of the political appointee.

TSA was part of the Department of Homeland Security, which itself was part of the vast new bureaucracy created after the attacks of September 11, 2001. Washington responded to 9/11 just like a corporation responds to a bad quarter—by doing a reorg. Shuffle around the boxes on the org chart. In short order, the TSA created the No Fly List, a secret list of people who aren't allowed to board a commercial plane to travel within the U.S. The number of people on that list is also a secret, but it's around fifty thousand.

As I headed up Constitution Avenue toward K Street, I called Bill Puccino's work number. He answered with a bark: "Puccino."

"Pooch," I said. "Nick Heller."

"Nico!" he said. "There you are!"

"How goes it?"

"Doin' good, doin' good."

"Still keeping the world safe from nipple rings, I hope."

He paused, got it, then laughed.

"I need a quick favor," I said.

"For you, big guy, anything."

"I need you to dip into a database."

"Which one?"

"TSDB."

He was silent for a good five or six seconds. "Sorry, Nico. No can do."

And he hung up.

I didn't realize at first that he'd hung up. I thought maybe the call had been dropped—a dead spot, maybe. They're all over the District.

But about two minutes later my cell phone rang. It was Puccino.

"Sorry about that," he said. The sound quality was different; it sounded like he was calling from a mobile phone, too. "I can't talk about that stuff on my work line."

"They monitor your calls?"

"Come on, man, what do you think? I work for Big Brother. So tell me what you want."

"How does someone get put on the No Fly List?"

"Threaten to blow up the White House? Take flying lessons but tell them you don't need to learn how to land the plane?"

Then it was my turn to laugh politely at a lame joke.

"There's a name on your No Fly List," I said. "I want to know how it got there."

He exhaled noisily into his cell phone. "Nick, how important is this to you?"

"Very."

He exhaled into the phone again. It wasn't a sigh of exasperation, though. It was tension, indecision. He was wrestling with it.

"I can check to see if someone's on the No Fly List," Puccino said. "That's easy. Lots of people in law enforcement have access to the Secure Flight program. But when you ask how it got there and what the reason is—well, that's a whole different deal. That means accessing this superduper-double-secret database called TIDE—the Terrorist Identities Data-something or other. That's the one that contains the derogatories."

"Derogatories?"

"The bad stuff they did. The reason someone's a threat. And which agency put 'em there. The originating agency."

"Can you get into that?"

"Sure. But every time you sign in to TIDE, you leave tracks. There's all these information security safeguards now. A whole audit trail. So I gotta be careful."

"Understood. I appreciate your sticking your neck out for me."

"You have a date of birth or a social security number? You wouldn't believe the number of Gary Smiths we have. Or John Williamses."

I told him the name.

He said, "Heller, as in Nick Heller?"

"My brother."

"You gotta be kidding."

"I wish."

"What'd he do?"

"Pissed off the wrong people."

"*I'll* say." He hung up again and called me back just as I was about to pull into the parking garage underneath 1900 K Street. I swung into a space on the street next to a fire hydrant, since the cell reception in the garage was funky.

"Nico, you thinking maybe someone stole your brother's identity or something? That happens sometimes."

"What do you have?"

"The nominating agency is DoD. Means that Roger Heller was put on the list by the Defense Department."

"Does it say why?"

"See, that's the problem. The field in the database where you normally see the reason—you know, 'Mustafa says he wants to blow up the White House'—just has a code. Meaning it's classified beyond my level."

"Okay," I said. "This is a big help. Thanks a lot."

I was about to disconnect the call, when he said, "Nick, listen. I know I'm just a pencil-neck bureaucrat. But I need to protect my pencil neck. You understand?"

"Yeah," I said. "Don't worry about it. You won't hear from me again."

30

Putting my brother on a terrorist watch list was preposterous. He was an asshole, yes. But a terrorist? All it told me was that he had some very powerful enemies who had the power to abuse the No Fly List. Enemies, I assumed, somewhere within my old haunt, the Pentagon.

But how could Roger have made enemies in the Defense Department? And why?

The more I dug into it, the more I came to believe that something strange and disturbing was going on: something corrupt at a very high level, and my brother was just a casualty. And maybe that was an even more important motivation: my obsessive need to turn over the rock, as Jay Stoddard liked to say. To root out the truth. A shrink would probably tell me that it was a logical, if neurotic, legacy of my peculiar upbringing, of being lied to repeatedly by Victor Heller.

But since I'd never seen a shrink, and I wasn't particularly self-reflective, I didn't particularly care where it came from. I didn't need to understand.

All I knew was that I wasn't going to stop until I'd unearthed the truth about what had happened to my brother.

* * *

Dorothy Duval had a plaque on her desk that said JESUS
IS COMING—LOOK BUSY.

I always liked that. That about summed her up. She
was actually a fairly devout churchgoer, but she had a
bawdy sense of humor about it. She also enjoyed pissing people off. She wasn't quiet and demure. She was
in your face—"all up in your grill," as she'd put it. It
was a trait that was inseparable from her stubbornness.
She was brilliant and tireless and methodical, and she
never gave up.

I'd seen her in T-shirts that said things like JESUS IS
MY HOMEBOY and SATAN SUCKS and MY GOD CAN KICK
YOUR GOD'S BUTT. Though not in the office. She always
dressed far nicer than a forensic data tech needed to.
That day she was wearing a black skirt and a peach
blouse and enormous silver hoop earrings.

As a tech, not an investigator, Dorothy didn't get an
office. She got a cubicle in the open area of Stoddard
Associates known as the bullpen, along with the other
support staff. Her desk was always impeccable. Tacked
to the walls of her cubicle were pictures of her parents,
her brother, and a gaggle of nieces and nephews. She
had no kids of her own, and no significant other—male
or female—and I never asked her about her personal
life. As blunt-spoken as she was, she kept her private
life private, and I always respected that.

She noticed me standing there and cast a wary eye at
the laptop under my arm. "That for me?"

I nodded. She took it. "Case number? I don't see a
label on there."

She was referring to the barcode sticker with a case
ID that we put on all pieces of evidence so everything
can be tracked easily.

"It's not a Stoddard case," I said, and I explained.

It took me a few minutes.

She turned the computer over, popped it open. "This is your brother's?"

I nodded.

"You tell me what you want, boyfriend." She looked around. Marty Masur, fellow investigator and petty martinet, strutted by, nodded at us. "Let's talk in your office," she said. "Need a little privacy."

"Yeah, it's hosed, all right," Dorothy said a few minutes later, staring at the screen. "Someone tried to scrub it but screwed it up. Got the operating system, too. What do you want off it?"

"Anything and everything you can get."

"What's on here that's so important?"

"I have no idea," I said. "But I'm guessing there was something there important enough for my brother to try to get rid of it."

"Why?"

"I just told you."

"Uh-uh. You told me what you're looking for. You didn't tell me *why* you want it."

"How about you just do it?" I said, sort of testily.

"Honey, it don't work like that," she said. I'd noticed that her speech turned "street" when she got annoyed, as if for dramatic effect. She extended a forefinger and tapped the long peach fingernail against the palm of her other hand. "There ain't some magic unerasing trick or something that's going to recover permanently deleted data, okay? That's just science fiction. You watch too many movies."

"I don't watch enough, actually. No time."

"Yeah, well, if someone's real serious about scrubbing their computer, there's some hard-core wiping programs out there. That physically overwrite every sector, from zero right to the end of the disc. No way we're going to find any traces, if they knew what they were doing. I can try some data-carving utilities on this baby, and I might get lucky, but that's a crapshoot."

"Well, see what you can do," I said. "I don't understand half of what you said, but I don't need to."

"Man, I think you're actually *proud* of being a Luddite."

"I'm not proud. I just know there are some things I'm good at and some things I'm not."

"Well, maybe you ought to learn this stuff."

"I wouldn't want to put you out of a job."

"I wouldn't worry about that."

"Exactly. Here's how I look at it. Economists call this the law of comparative advantage. I forget where I read this. Michael Jordan can probably mow his lawn faster than anyone else, but does that mean he should mow it himself?"

"Michael Jordan don't even play basketball anymore."

"Tiger Woods, then. Or David Beckham."

"Are you saying you could be the Tiger Woods or the David Beckham of data recovery if you put your mind to it?"

"I think I better just shut my mouth."

"I think that's the first smart thing you said today."

"Fair enough."

"Look, Nick, if you're serious about trying to figure out what your brother was up to, I'm guessing you want a whole deep-dish data-mining job on him. Am I right?"

I smiled, shrugged. "You got me."

"I know you."

"Anything you can do," I said.

"Do I get paid for this?"

"Whatever you want."

"Let's just call it a six-figure deposit into my favor bank. To put it in Nick Heller terms."

I smiled again. "You got it."

She stood up, folded her arms. "Nick, sweetie, can I say something?"

"Can I ever stop you from saying anything?"

"Not hardly. Nick, don't do this."

"Don't do what?"

"Don't get involved in this. This whole thing with your brother—it's too personal. You get too invested, and it just messes you up. You start doing things you shouldn't do. You lose your professional distance."

"You ever see me act less than professional?"

She thought for a second. "Plenty of times."

"But not on the job."

She shrugged. "I guess."

"I can handle this."

"See, I'm not so sure about that. Leave it to the cops. That's their job. You want to help them, feed them stuff, go ahead. But if you take this on yourself, you're going to go too far. I tell you this because I love you."

"And I appreciate it," I said.

"I'm serious, Nick."

"Don't worry about me," I said.

31

Everything's under control," Noreen said. "His regular suite at Hotel Le Royal in Luxembourg, a private room reserved at Mosconi for the Benelux senior managers—"

"The Princière."

"What?"

"When he stays in Luxembourg, he likes the Princière Suite at the Le Royal."

"I know," Noreen said, peeved.

"Did you ask the hotel to stock the kitchenette with bottles of San Pellegrino? Or Perrier? Their usual mineral water is too salty."

"He didn't say anything about that."

"He always forgets until he gets there, then he raises holy hell." Lauren realized what she must have sounded like—the master control freak—and she was embarrassed. Her tone softened. "I'll call the concierge."

"Oh, and Leland's in a meeting with a new financial adviser. For his personal portfolio, not the company's. Nice guy. But ugly? Hoo boy. Must have fallen out of the ugly tree and hit every branch."

"Okay, I've been warned," she said.

"Buffalo Face, I call him. He walks by the bathroom, and all the toilets flush."

"I need to get back to work," Lauren said.

Noreen finally went back to her own desk, and Lauren checked her e-mail.

Nothing from Roger.

But why would there be anything? There had been just that one, heartbreaking e-mail, and now that was gone.

Nick wanted her to dig into what Roger had been doing at Gifford, but truthfully, she was afraid to. How could she investigate without setting off all kinds of alarm bells?

She had to be so careful.

The door to Leland's office came open, and a man in a shapeless gray suit strode rapidly out. She caught only a fleeting glimpse—homely face, horn-rimmed glasses—before he disappeared.

Then Leland came out of his office, and his face lit up.

"I didn't think you'd really be back so soon!" he boomed in his Texas accent. Gifford's father had been a railroad worker in west Texas before starting the family business. Now it had revenues of ten billion dollars a year, managed construction projects in forty-seven countries, and was still in the hands of the Gifford family. Gifford Industries had been headquartered in Austin until Leland had made the wrenching decision to relocate to Washington, D.C., because that was where most of the business had gone. Government, not oil fields anymore.

She rose as Leland came over to her desk and hugged her. He was tall and rotund, with arched bushy eyebrows and sagging jowls, a large head and rosy cheeks and a white crew cut. Those who met him for the first time found him physically intimidating, and indeed, in repose, he often wore an imperious expression, made even more threatening by his arched brows.

Then he stopped abruptly. "Boy hidy, I forgot you're hurt, and here I am crushing the life out of you."

"Come on, Leland, I'm not made of glass."

He put both hands on her shoulders and fixed her with a stern expression. "Nothin' new about Roger?"

She shook her head.

"They don't even know if he's alive?"

"Right."

He closed his eyes. "Why're you even here?" he said softly.

"Because I need to be here," she said.

"You understand you can take all the time you need, doncha? Weeks, months—whatever it takes."

"I need to be here."

"You know, I don't understand half the stuff Roger does, but he's a valued employee. More important, he's your husband. If you ever need anything from me, you just say so, you hear?"

She nodded. "You have to leave in half an hour," she said. "Twenty-five minutes, actually."

She pulled a few magazines from the stack on her desk, handed him a fresh *Business Week* and a *Forbes*. Then she turned back around, opened a drawer, and took out a handful of Metamucil packets and handed them to him, too.

"You think of everything," he said. "You sweetie."

32

Loud laughter rang out from Jay Stoddard's office as I approached. I expected to see Jay in animated conversation with one of his old buddies from the Agency. But he was alone, sitting at his desk, leaning back in his chair, watching his computer screen.

He glanced at me, then turned back to the computer. He extended his left arm and beckoned me in with a flip of his hand. "Nicky," he said. "Just the man I wanted to talk to."

"Okay."

Stoddard was wearing one of his more extreme bespoke suits: double-breasted, double-vented, cut from a hairy tweed fabric. On each cuff four buttons that really buttoned, the last one undone. He looked like he'd just come back from a weekend at Balmoral Castle. My father used to wear suits like that. Before he started wearing orange jumpsuits every day.

"Oh, dear me," he gasped, laughing helplessly. "Oh, sweet Jesus. Have you seen this?"

I entered, leaned across his desk, craned my neck. He was watching a video on the Internet. At first glance it appeared to be porn. Well, it sort of was. An assortment of busty young women in dominatrix costumes were whipping the naked buttocks of a middle-aged man with leather riding crops. One of them was checking his hair for lice. They were shouting at him in bad German. Clearly this was supposed to be a Nazi-themed orgy, though it didn't look like much fun if you were the guy being whipped.

"Their German accents aren't very good, are they?" I said.

"Do you know who that guy is?"

"His butt doesn't look all that familiar, no."

Stoddard told me the name of a prominent British political figure. "He wants to know how this video got out. He's trying to get an injunction to take it down from the Internet. Says his privacy rights have been violated."

I looked closer. "Says there it's been viewed one million, four hundred thousand—"

"I know, I know. He's an Oxford man, you know that?"

"I didn't. Hal—"

"Brophy can wrap this one up in his sleep," he said. Brophy was one of our more senior investigators. "Waste of time, you ask me, but I won't turn it down."

"Maybe Brophy can take on that CEO backgrounder, too."

He brought his chair upright. "No, Nicky, you're our big swinging dick. Don't tell me you have ethical qualms about this one, too?" He raked his fingers through his silver mane.

"No. Not if it can wait. I'm taking a couple of personal days."

"Oh?"

"Family business."

He looked at me expectantly.

I just looked back.

He wanted to know, of course, and I wasn't going to tell him anything I didn't have to.

He looked down pensively at the immaculate surface of his desk, gave a slight shake of his head. "Your family," he said. "Your father, then your brother . . . You sure you're not descended from the House of Atreus?"

"Excuse me?"

"You gotta wonder if it's some kind of blood curse."

"What do you know about my brother?" I said.

His phone buzzed, and the voice of Elizabeth, the receptionist, crisply announced a caller who insisted on speaking with him right away.

I got up as he picked up the phone. His long, tapered index finger hovered over the extension button. "It doesn't look good, does it?" he said, then he punched the button and took the call.

33

Stoddard's parting remark felt like a kick to the solar plexus.

"It doesn't look good"? Meaning what?

That the chances of finding Roger weren't good, I assumed he meant. But how would he know that? And more to the point, who'd told him about Roger's disappearance?

Jay Stoddard seemed to know something I didn't. Sure, he was more plugged in than anybody, knew people and things and all the scuttlebutt before anyone else.

But for some reason he wanted me to know that he knew.

I hesitated in the corridor outside his office for a moment, considered storming back in there and grabbing the phone out of his hand and slamming him against the wall and asking him what the hell he knew. But I came to my senses pretty quickly. There were other, better ways to find out.

One of them was a guy in suburban Maryland who'd been in the FBI a long time ago. Frank Montello was sort of a sketchy character, but a useful one to know. He called himself an information broker. Frank used to be the one you'd call when you wanted to get an unlisted phone number and didn't have the time, or the right, to get a court order. That was back in the day when there was only one phone company. Since then he'd amassed contacts deep inside all the major wireless carriers, too, including T-Mobile, AT&T, and Verizon. I never asked how he got his information; I didn't want to know.

I'd called Frank as soon as I got back from L.A. and asked him to find out who owned the cell-phone number Woody had given me at the airport. He quoted me an outrageous price and told me it might take a day or two.

So I called Frank again.

"Patience, my friend," he said in his deep, gravelly voice. "My girl was out of the office yesterday."

"I'm not calling about that," I said. "I've got another job."

"Let's hear it."

I gave him Roger's cell-phone number, the one whose billing records I couldn't find in his study, and asked him to e-mail me the phone bills as soon as he could. I figured that if my brother went to the trouble of hiding his cell-phone bills, there must be something useful in them. Or at least something he wanted to hide.

The price Frank quoted was even higher.

"Don't I get a volume discount?" I asked, and Frank laughed heartily, meaning no.

I went out to get a cup of coffee, and when I returned, Dorothy Duval was sitting at my desk, leaning back in the chair, her feet up. Peach stiletto pumps with high heels and a cutout at the toe.

"How do I get an office like this?" she said.

"Kiss a lot of ass."

"Then I guess I'm lucky I got a cubicle," she muttered. "You know, it's amazing what you can find out about people these days. I can't decide if it's cool or ter-rifying. Maybe it's both."

"You unerased the laptop?"

"Babe, that'll take hours. A lot of hours. Meanwhile, I did some basic data-mining."

"Tell me."

"How about your brother's medical prescriptions?"

"You serious?"

"As a heart attack."

"How'd you get those?" I said, impressed.

She laughed. "Oh, it's evil. All the big pharmacy chains sell their prescription records to a couple of companies—electronic prescribing networks, they're called. Supposed to be for patient safety, but you know what it's really about." She rubbed her fingers together in the universal sign of moolah. "Man, everything's online now."

"Real protected, huh?"

"Oh, yeah. So, how much you wanna know about your brother?"

"What are we talking about?"

"Well, Viagra, for one."

"He took Viagra, huh?"

She crossed her ankles. Her toenails were painted with peach polish.

"That may be more than I want to know about Roger and Lauren's sex life."

"Might not involve Lauren," she said.

I folded my arms. "How do you figure that?"

She lowered her feet to the floor, then leaned for-ward.

"Because seven months ago your brother paid for an abortion."

I stared at her for a few seconds. "I assume it wasn't Lauren."

She shook her head.

"How do you . . . ?" The words died in my mouth. I was in shock.

I didn't think anything about my brother could surprise me. But that knocked the wind right out of me. More than anything, it made me sad. I thought of Lauren and her admiration for him—her love of him, which I'd never understood. And I thought of Gabe and his suspicions that his father was being unfaithful, and I wondered whether kids just saw things more clearly. As an only child, Gabe probably observed his parents with X-ray vision.

She gave a pensive sigh and spoke quietly. "You know medical records aren't really private."

"But abortions . . . Don't people sometimes use cash to keep it private?"

"Apparently there were complications. That's how I found the records—the woman was admitted from a family planning center in Brookline, Mass., to Mass General Hospital in Boston, and your brother's name was recorded as the accompanying adult."

"Who's the woman?"

"It's a funny name. Candi something?" She looked at her notes. "Candi Dupont. That's Candy with an 'i' at the end."

"Did you find out anything about her?"

"Not yet."

"You think that's a real name?"

"Sounds like a stripper name to me."

"Can you keep digging on it, see what turns up? The usual databases—Accurint, AutoTrack, LexisNexis—see what you turn up on her whereabouts and her employment background and all that."

"Come on, Nick, what do you think?"

"I appreciate it."

"Do you think his wife knows?"

"I doubt it."

"They're always the last to know, aren't they? You going to tell her?"

I hesitated, then shook my head. "I don't see the point. It doesn't have anything to do with whatever happened to him."

"You sure?"

"Her life has already been turned upside down. She might have lost her husband. No need to make things even more painful for her."

"So should I not have told you about this?"

"Of course you should have," I said, surprised she'd even suggest it. "I need to know everything about my brother. Even the things I'd rather not know."

"Nick," she said, "you can't know everything about anyone. No matter how good an investigator you are, no matter how many databases you have access to, no matter how deep you dig. You just can never know another person completely."

"You're too smart to be working in a place like this," I said.

34

For a couple of years during college I was a summer associate at McKinsey, the big management-consulting firm. I shouldn't have even gotten the job. Those were normally reserved for MBA and JD candidates, not for undergrads. But the partner who hired me probably figured that Victor Heller, the fugitive financier, the storied Dark Prince of Wall Street, might throw some big business her way. Which never happened, of course.

I was put on a team assigned to a troubled athletic-shoe manufacturer, which meant I had to interview everyone I could possibly interview, then, at the end of the summer, do a presentation for senior management. My boss seemed to be a lot more interested in what she called the "gatekeepers" and the "decision makers" at the company than in how lousy their sneakers were. I even had to do a Decision Matrix with all the key players' names color-coded—green meant they wanted to buy more of our consulting services. Red meant they were violently opposed. When I went over my presentation with my boss, she kept leaning on me to trash this one division chief, highlight all the problems in his division.

I tried to argue with my boss about this. After all, the division chief was perfectly fine. Finally, one of my fellow associates, a lovely dark-haired woman who was studying at the Tuck School of Business at Dartmouth—and who I was going out with that summer—explained to me what was going on.

Turned out this particular manager was a "red name." He was an obstructionist. He thought consultants like us were a monumental waste of time. My boss wanted him defanged.

So I did what I was told. I did my PowerPoint, dredging up every mistake he'd ever made, every wrong decision.

Shortly afterward, the guy got fired.

Problem solved.

That was when I decided that consulting wasn't for me. But acting and talking like a consultant—well, that turned out to be a skill set that had come in handy on more than one occasion.

I called Lauren and arranged for a visitor's pass to be left for me at the concierge desk in the lobby of Gifford Industries. I was a management consultant with Bain & Company, or so the paperwork said.

That was enough to get me upstairs and wandering around unsupervised.

I didn't arrive at the swanky Gifford Industries headquarters building until the early afternoon. I'd hoped to get out of the office much earlier, but work kept intruding. I couldn't just drop the cases I'd been working; I had to pass along the files to others at Stoddard, brief them on my progress and the outstanding issues. I had to make phone calls to clients I'd been working with to let them know that I'd be taking a few days off for family reasons, which I didn't explain, and assure them they'd be in good hands; and I had to write and reply to a bunch of e-mails. E-mail: the curse of modern office life. I don't remember what we did before it.

I was still reeling from what Dorothy had learned about Roger. The fact that he'd been having an affair and had taken his lover to an abortion clinic. The fact that my brother had been unfaithful to his wife, a woman he was beyond lucky to have found. He wasn't exactly Brad Pitt or George Clooney. I felt the way I often did when I read some Hollywood gossip item about how some supermodel's husband was caught cheating on her: *What do you want, guy? You're married to one of the most desirable women in the world. What else can you possibly want?*

As a single male, I admit I understood the impulse. My brother and I used to tell a joke when we were kids that went something like this: *Hey, did you hear* Playboy *just came out with a magazine just for married men? Yep. Every month the centerfold's the exact same woman.* But being attracted and acting on it were two very different things.

I think that on some deeply buried, subconscious level I was hoping that by investigating my brother's disappearance I'd discover a side of him that I'd never seen, which would make me finally appreciate him.

I didn't expect to find out things that would make me dislike him even more.

Roger worked in the special-projects group of the corporate development division of Gifford Industries. There were three attorneys and just one administrative assistant for all of them. You could tell just by looking at their offices that the special-projects group was sort of a ghetto in the company. It didn't seem to be very special at all. It was hidden in a distant corner of the Legal Department, on the fourth floor, in a warren of identical offices with nothing on the walls except the sort of mind-numbing signs you see in every corporate office in the world—stern notices about floating holidays and how if you don't give sufficient notice you lose them, something about the blood drive, about keeping the kitchenette clean ("We are not your mothers!" it said). My tie suddenly felt too tight around my neck.

The admin for the special-projects group was named Kim Harding. She was shy and bookish, in her early fifties, with hyperthyroidic eyes behind oversized tinted glasses. She had short curly brown hair and small prim lips painted with dark red lipstick. She looked like a scared rabbit.

"Hello, Kim," I said. "I'm John Murray, from Security Compliance." I handed her a business card. That was one of the covers that Stoddard provided its investigators, and it always worked. It identified Security Compliance Partners as a management-consulting firm specializing in security audits of Fortune 500 corporations. It gave the Stoddard Associates address and a phone number there that Elizabeth, the receptionist, would answer the right way.

Every corporation that did business with the Pentagon, as Gifford Industries did, had to suffer regular visits from outside security auditors, who prowled the halls of the company, meeting with people and checking the facilities and the networks, making sure they were in compliance with all the ridiculous, paranoid security measures the government required of any contractor who did classified work. So Kim Harding was conditioned to be cooperative.

She glanced at it and said, "Yes, John, how can I help you?"

"Well, you know, Mr. Gifford has retained our firm to look into certain anomalies concerning someone you work with, a Mr. Roger Heller?"

She looked stricken, compressed her lips, and looked up at me. For a moment I thought she might ask if we were related. Roger and I didn't resemble each other much anymore, but women tend to be far more observant than men, and someone like Kim, who'd worked for him every day, might be particularly keen.

Instead, she said, "I'm so worried about Roger. Do we know anything more—?"

"I'm not really allowed to go into any of that, Kim, but I'd very much appreciate your help."

She blinked a few times. "Yes?"

"Well, let's start with something easy. Do you keep records of telephone calls Roger made or received?"

Kim drew herself up. Her nostrils flared as she inhaled. "The answer's not going to change no matter how many times you people ask me."

"Someone's asked you about this already?"

"Just this morning. Mr. Gifford's office. Why do I get the feeling the left hand doesn't know what the right hand's doing?"

"Who in Mr. Gifford's office?"

She gave me a piercing look. There was a smudge of lipstick on her teeth.

"Noreen Purvis. The woman who's been filling in for Lauren Heller."

"I see."

"I'll tell you what I told her." She held up a pad of pink "While You Were Out" message slips. The kind I knew well. "I write messages on these things and I hand them to the attorneys or put them on their desks, and no, I never keep carbon copies either. You want phone records, talk to the girls in Accounting."

"Well, that's a start," I said. "And I'm sorry for the duplication of effort. Can you show me to Roger's office, please? I'm going to need to take a look at his computer."

"You people really don't talk to each other, do you?"

"Noreen did that, too?"

"No. She asked about it, and I told her that his computer's gone. It was removed by Corporate Security, on direct orders from Mr. Gifford."

A plain woman with thick wire-frame glasses, wearing a gray business suit, passed by, and Kim held up a pink message slip. The woman took it and said, "Thanks, Kim." She glanced at the slip, wadded it up, and dropped it in a metal trash basket next to Kim Harding's desk.

Then she peered at me. "You're asking about Roger?"

"That's right," I said.

"What's this about?"

I handed her my business card and told her about Security Compliance. She shook my hand, firm, like a man.

"You look familiar," she said.

"I hear that a lot," I said.

"You want to know something about Roger, you talk to Marjorie," said Kim Harding, turning back to her keyboard. "Marjorie knows everything about Roger."

The woman named Marjorie smiled and blushed. "I do not," she said. "You make it sound like we were having an affair."

"Did I say that?" Kim said to me. "Did I say that?"

"No, you didn't," I said.

"No, I did not," Kim said with a slow shake of her head. "But Roger always tells me, if he's not here, and I need to know anything about a deal he's working on, go right to Marjorie."

Marjorie shrugged and said, "Oh, that's an exaggeration," but she was still blushing and smiling with unmistakable pleasure.

"Come on, sweetie," Kim said to her. "Roger always says, if Marjorie doesn't know it, she can always find it out. Why do you think he calls you the librarian?"

35

"Why are you so interested in what Roger was working on?"

"Just doing my job," I said. Marjorie Ogonowski worked at a cubicle, so we sat in Roger's office.

It wasn't what I expected at all. I'd figured his office at Gifford Industries would have at least some of the pompous décor of his home library. A decent copy of a George Stubbs painting of horses. Maybe even an antique John J. Audubon print of the Brown-headed Nuthatch. But it was a tiny and dismal cubbyhole with no distinguishing features. His desk chair wasn't an Aeron or anything stylish and emblematic; it looked like overstock from some low-end office-furniture supply house.

There was no computer on his desk.

"But why?" she said. "Does this have anything to do with his disappearance?"

"Do you know anything about it?"

"I asked you."

I didn't feel like getting into that kind of standoff, so I said, "That's the operating theory. What can you tell us, Marge?"

"Marjorie. If you're working for Leland Gifford, you know exactly what he was working on."

I paused for a moment. She had a point. "Mr. Heller indicated in an e-mail to his wife that if anything happened to him, you'd know why."

"He did?"

I nodded.

"Can I see that e-mail?"

"I'm afraid not."

"What did he say about—about something happening to him?"

"He must have said something to you along the same lines."

"You're not going to tell me what he said?"

"That's the problem. He didn't say. Nothing beyond that. What do you think he was referring to?"

She was a plain, mannish woman, with short light-brown hair, straight bangs high on her forehead. No lipstick or makeup of any kind. Even her gray suit was man-tailored. She was immensely smart, no-nonsense, precise in her language and mannerisms.

She blinked owlishly. "He didn't tell me everything. Despite what Kim said."

"He must have told you enough to make you worried about his well-being." That was sheer speculation on my part, of course. She obviously took pride in her special relationship to Roger, which I doubted was sexual—she was defiantly asexual. He might have confided in her, because she was so ferociously competent.

"He told me very little about it."

"About what?"

"About what he'd found."

I waited, and when she didn't go on, I said, "What did he find?"

"Mr. Murray, do you have any idea what Roger did here?"

"John," I said. "No, not really."

"We mostly worked on M&A stuff with biz-dev deal

teams, checking the books, going over the P&L on current and expected, working on rev-rec issues."

It had been a while since I'd heard that kind of biz-buzz English-as-a-foreign-language. Not since my McKinsey days, in fact. It took me a few seconds to do a mental translation, and I said, "You guys buy companies."

"In simple terms, yes. I'm just an associate counsel, so I assist Roger. And I have to say, Roger Heller was the smartest person I've ever met. He was a pure structured-finance genius. And he's never gotten the credit he deserves around here. People far less qualified are always getting promoted over his head. He should be general counsel or CFO. At least he should have become managing director of the global M&A practice. But it was like he was frozen in amber."

"Why do you think that is?"

"Maybe because he's too smart. He intimidates people."

"Is that so?"

She nodded, then pushed at the nosepiece of her glasses. "He always says what he thinks. It's like there's no filter. I guess I'd say that most people don't get along with him. They see him as sort of humorless. But Roger and I—we get along great. He expects the best out of everyone he works with, and I give him my best. He expects nothing less than perfection, and I—"

"You gave it to him."

"I usually don't make mistakes. He knows he can always turn to me." She smiled. "I document everything. He used to call me 'the reference librarian,' and then just 'the librarian,' for short. We always got along great."

"He trusted you."

"I think he did."

"So what did he tell you?"

She'd begun to feel more comfortable with me, I

could tell. "He said he'd found something in the books of one of the companies. During the due diligence. Something he said was 'troubling.'"

"What was that?"

"He didn't say, really. But he said he wished he hadn't. He said he was afraid for his life. He was terrified."

"I don't quite follow. Why would discovering something 'troubling' make him afraid for his life?"

"Well, he—he left out a step, obviously. As I said, he didn't tell me everything. But he sort of indicated that he'd called them on it. He'd let them know what he'd found."

"Called who on it?"

"The company. The one that was doing—whatever."

"Doing what?"

"Corruption of some sort, I guess."

"But why'd he contact them?"

She shook her head. "Obviously, he was upset. But that's just the way he is, you know? He always has to cross every t and dot every i. I think that's why we get along so well."

I was sorely tempted to say something, but I all but bit my tongue restraining myself.

She went on, "You know, his father is this famous— you know who the fugitive financier is, Victor Heller? Is, was—I'm not sure. He's either in prison or he died in prison. But I got a really strong sense that Roger was reacting to his father's criminality. I mean, that's just my take on it—he never liked to talk about his father. Once we were in a car on the way to Dulles, and I kind of summoned the courage to ask him about Victor Heller. I guess I thought we'd worked together long enough that we could talk about that kind of thing? And he said his father was a brilliant and misunderstood man, and he should never have gone to jail. Something in his tone told me not to pursue it, so I just changed the subject. And later I realized that I wasn't really sure what he meant, you know? What did that mean, his father should never have gone to jail? Did that mean that his father shouldn't have broken the law? Or that his father shouldn't have gone to jail for whatever he did? I never got that, really. But I couldn't ask."

"Hmph," I said, not knowing what else to say.

"And another time he said to me—well, it was sort of an aside, sort of a joke—he was talking about some kind of tricky variable-interest entities he noticed on a company's balance sheet, and he said, 'You know, in a good market, this is called financial engineering. In a bad market, it's called fraud.' I never knew what to make of that. What he meant, exactly."

I was sort of lost myself. I said, "Meaning, you couldn't tell if he approved or disapproved?"

She was quiet for a long time. "I'm not even sure what I mean myself."

"But he reacted in a very moral way to what he found in that company's books—what company did you say that was?"

"I didn't say."

"What company was it?"

Now she was quiet for even longer. "That I can't say."

"It's extremely important," I said.

"I understand. But some of the acquisitions we make I'm just not allowed to talk about."

"So it was a company that Gifford Industries acquired recently."

"I can't say."

"That doesn't really help us."

"I know. I'm sorry. But I have to follow rules around here."

Sometimes silence is the most powerful weapon in

an investigator's arsenal, so I looked at her for a long time without saying anything.

But the weapon doesn't always hit its target. She looked back, then looked down, then back up. Then she said softly, "All I can tell you is, Roger was terrified."

"I see."

"You know," she said, "you really do look familiar."

36

By the time I reached Georgetown, it was already mid-afternoon. I backed into a space on Water Street, along a chain-link fence. A few blocks farther down, Water Street turned into K Street. The banks of the Potomac at that point were not exactly the stuff of postcards. No cherry blossoms here; no gleaming Jefferson Memorial. Instead, there were great mounds of dirt and construction trailers and Porta Potties. The city had been working for years to build a waterfront park in place of the industrial blight, the abandoned factories and the rail yards. They'd turned the old incinerator into a Ritz-Carlton. Maybe someday there'd be a park here. But it was a scraggly, weed-choked, trash-littered mess, in the shadows of the Whitehurst Freeway. Truly an urban failure story.

My cell phone emitted four high beeps, alerting me to a text message.

It was a location report from the GPS tracker that Merlin had sent via FedEx to EasyOffice, Traverse Development's mail drop in Arlington, Virginia. The GPS device had just been delivered to the mail drop. The text message linked me to a Google Earth map, where I could see a flashing red dot indicating where the tracker was.

That told me nothing. I already had that address.

I walked up the footbridge to Cady's Alley, crossed over to the restaurant where Lauren and Roger had had their last dinner. A Japanese restaurant on Thirty-third Street called Oji-San.

Then I retraced their route from the restaurant, down Cady's Alley. Back down the footbridge. Across Water Street to their car.

There I stood for a few minutes, thinking. A black Humvee drove by. We'd used up-armored M1114 Humvees in Iraq as our tactical vehicles, equipped with fire-suppression systems and frag protection and mounts on the roof hatch for machine guns and grenade launchers. The air-conditioning wasn't bad either. But I never understood the point of driving one of them around the city, even a civilian model. What did they expect, rocket-propelled grenades in Georgetown?

Lauren had said it was raining the night of the attack. Parking was probably in short supply. The restaurant didn't offer valet parking, but there was a garage nearby. So why did Roger park all the way down the hill on Water Street?

He wasn't a tightwad. You couldn't grow up in our house in Bedford and learn to be a coupon-clipper. At the most, you could grow up to be someone who doesn't much care about money—having seen what it can and can't do. But my brother, unlike me, shared Victor Heller's unhealthy fixation on wealth. He liked to show off. He had to have the fanciest car, the most opulent kitchen. This was not a guy who'd happily park his S-Class Mercedes in the squalor of Water Street, in the underbelly of the freeway, amid the vagrants and broken bottles, a long walk away on a rainy night.

I didn't get it.

And I thought about what Lauren remembered Roger saying the night of the attack: "Why her?"

Not, *Why?* Not, *Leave her alone.*

But, *Why her?*

As in, "Why are you coming after her, when it's me you want."

Or something like that.

I checked my watch, and while I continued to puzzle over my brother's last remarks, I walked along Water Street in the direction of the Key Bridge. I liked that bridge. I liked the rhythm of its five high concrete arches, the open spandrel design. I even liked the irony that, in order to build the bridge named after Francis Scott Key, the guy who wrote the "Star Spangled Banner," they had to tear down Francis Scott Key's house. Or maybe it was to build that eyesore, the Whitehurst Freeway.

It took me six minutes to walk to the ATM where Roger had made his withdrawal. It was one of those twenty-four-hour walk-up cash machines, built into a brick wall next to a gas station. Outdoors and exposed. A young woman was using it, a large woman dressed entirely in black with platinum hair sticking up in the front like a rooster's comb. Tufts of her hair were dyed orange and blue. Either she was doing that whole punk thing, or she was on her way to a costume party. She turned around and glared at me. I was too close. I was making her nervous.

So I backed off a few feet and surveyed the area while I waited. This was a no-name gas station that was open twenty-four hours and advertised fresh pastries and the coldest drinks in town. It sold cigarettes and rolling papers and lottery tickets. The pumps were self-serve.

A black Humvee passed by. The same one that had

driven by on Water Street? I wondered whether I was being watched. I noted the license plate.

I assumed that Roger had been trundled into a vehicle at the scene of the attack, then driven over to the ATM. Why, I had no idea. But from here I could see the entrance to the Key Bridge, which took you across the Potomac to Virginia and the Parkway, the Beltway, any number of highways. Not a bad place to stop on your way out of town.

The large woman was taking her damned time at the cash machine. I approached, my shoes scraping against a scree pile of that white granular stuff used to absorb gasoline spills. She turned, glared at me, extracted her card and her cash, and hurried away.

The brick wall was covered in graffiti. I was pretty sure this was one side of the old Georgetown Car Barn, a nineteenth-century building where they used to store the trolley cars. Probably it was now offices or condos.

At the top of the ATM console was the lens of a CCTV camera—the one that had recorded Roger approaching, some guy with a gun at his side. Moving right up to the ATM, I turned around and watched an old Honda drive into the lot and pull up next to a pump. Assuming that Roger and his captor or captors had driven here from Water Street, I figured they must have come up M Street. Water Street was a dead end.

From here, they could have driven right onto the Key Bridge. But they could have also taken the Whitehurst Freeway. As I turned my head, I noticed something on top of the convenience store: another security camera.

A weatherproof bullet camera, as it's called, attached to the steel arm of a mounting bracket. It was aimed at the cash machine.

37

The gas-station attendant stood at a cash register in a booth behind thick bulletproof Plexiglas. He was changing the paper tape in the cash register. He was a small, squat, dark-skinned man in his fifties. Indian or Pakistani, maybe, with jet-black hair and steel-framed aviator glasses and a serious scowl. He wore a tie. I concluded he wasn't merely the attendant but probably the owner. A black name badge pinned to his white shirt said MR. YOUNIS.

Mr. Younis. This was a man who demanded respect.

"Excuse me, Mr. Younis," I said.

He glared at me, suspicious. "Yes?"

"I wonder if you could help me." I kept my tone matter-of-fact. "A couple of days ago I was mugged over there by the ATM. Couple of thugs took my cash, my wallet, everything."

He shook his head, turned away, went back to changing the register tape. "I know nothing about this."

Right, I thought. He's afraid he'll somehow get ensnared in a crime that had nothing to do with him, just because it took place on his property. Was the ATM in fact on his property? The ATM belonged to Wachovia

Bank. The brick wall was the side of the old car-barn building and probably belonged to Georgetown University, which was the big landlord around here. So why did he have his own surveillance camera pointed in that direction?

The graffiti, I guessed. Kids with cans of spray paint, defacing the wall he looked at every day. Probably made his already high blood pressure shoot up to dangerous levels.

"The cops won't do a damned thing," I said. "They can't be bothered."

He grunted, fiddled with the register-tape roll, pushed it into its slot.

"Know what they said?" I went on. "They said forget it. They couldn't care less. There's a damned crime wave in this city, and the police just sit there on their fat asses."

He shook his head, and his scowl deepened. He closed the cash-register-tape compartment and looked up. "It's a disgrace," he agreed.

A man who installed such an elaborate security system was not someone who had a great deal of faith in law enforcement. He was also a guy with a lot of pent-up resentment.

He was putty in my hands.

"These thugs just run wild around here," I said. "Do whatever the hell they want. They know they'll get away with it. Like all that graffiti on the wall over there."

Some little sprocket of anger clicked into place in the guy's head. He looked up at me. "These vandals—they call themselves 'taggers,' and they call this vandalism 'art.' And the police, they tell me if they have no documentation, they can do nothing. So I put in cameras."

"It didn't stop them, huh?"

"No! Nothing! One of the police even told me this is

freedom of expression, this 'tagging'!" He folded his arms.

"Easy for them to say. They don't have to live with it."

"It is an outrage!"

"But it looks like a terrific surveillance system you've put in. High-res, infrared—"

"—Yet it does me no good! None! Thousands of dollars, and these taggers are still doing their 'art'!"

"Gosh, wouldn't it be great if your system got some video of my mugging, couple of days ago? Hell, might even be the same guys who keep writing on your wall. Let's see the cops try to wriggle out of *that,* huh?"

He looked at me, his eyes narrowing.

"Do you know how to operate a digital recorder?" he asked. "I have to stay behind the counter."

Mr. Younis kept his security equipment in a locked supply closet next to a shelf of beer. On a wire shelf was a low-end digital recorder, eight-channel, a black oblong box. The video images were stored on a computer hard drive. On top of the DVR was a cheap fourteen-inch color monitor. He showed me how to search by date and time, and he returned to his Plexiglas booth to wait on a couple of college kids who wanted to buy a pack of Marlboros and a case of Budweiser.

The supply closet was shallow, so I stood half-in, half-out. It took me five minutes to locate the night I wanted. I pushed PLAY. The recorder was set to take one picture every two seconds until it detected motion, at which point it kicked the recording speed up to a full thirty frames per second. Cars entered the frame and turned and backed up. People walked up to the ATM, alone or in couples, a few groups of three, their movements jerky, then suddenly smooth. I fast-scanned until I reached 11:00 P.M.

At 11:06, a white panel van entered the frame, nosed

in against the brick wall a few yards to the left of the cash machine. A bulky guy in a hooded gray sweatshirt got out of the driver's side, slammed the door, then walked around the back of the van to the passenger's side. It was hard to tell for sure, but it looked like he had a gun in his left hand. When the guy turned slightly, I was able to catch a glimpse of his profile: beefy face, mustache. Late thirties or early forties. With his right hand, he unlocked the front passenger door. He pocketed the keys, switched the gun to his right hand, then pulled the door open.

And Roger stepped out.

The hooded guy raised his gun a little, waved it back and forth. Roger nodded. He looked panicked. His tie was out of place, his suit rumpled.

The guy in the hooded sweatshirt grabbed Roger with his left hand, and the two of them looped around the back of the van. They stood there for a few seconds.

"Dude."

I looked up. A kid with tattoos and a silver barbell through his nasal septum was standing there.

"Zig-Zags," he said.

"What about it?" He also had huge silver plugs, easily half an inch in diameter, through his earlobes. I wondered what this kid would look like at age seventy with big droopy holes in his ears and nose.

"Like, where the hell are the rolling papers?"

"Yeah," I said with a glare, "like I know."

He hurried away.

I turned back to the monitor. The beefy guy in the hooded sweatshirt said something to Roger, then turned around, and I got a full-on look at his face.

No one I recognized, but he was a type—Neanderthal forehead, deep eye sockets, simian features. He could have been any one of a dozen guys I trained with in Special Forces and who washed out before the end. One of those blank-faced muscle-bound cretins who think they're tougher and smarter than they really are and usually end up working as mall cops.

I paused the video and zoomed in until I had a good screen capture of his face, then I cut and pasted the image. Not bad for a computer illiterate. When I returned to the normal view, I moved the cursor over until the rear of the van was in the center of the screen. A Ford Econoline E-350 Super Duty van, fairly new. The kind you see everywhere.

I zoomed in closer and got another screen capture.

The abductor had been careful to hide his face from the ATM camera. But not being all that bright, he hadn't counted on another surveillance camera grabbing a very clear picture of his face.

Or the license plate of the van he was driving.

38

I suppose I could have asked someone at Stoddard Associates to run the plates for me, but I knew that Virginia's motor-vehicle records weren't online—some ridiculous state law—and I didn't want to call in any favors at work that I didn't have to. Not with Stoddard keeping an eye on what I was doing.

But Arthur Garvin was only too happy to run a trace: This was a serious break on a case that had been confounding him. As I walked back to my car, I read off the number and told him that as soon as I got back to the office, I'd e-mail him some of the video-frame captures of the thug who'd grabbed Roger. He warned me it might take him a day or two, but he promised he'd get the information for me.

My cell phone gave off four beeps, and, as I stood next to the Defender, I checked the text message. Another location report from the GPS tracker in the FedEx envelope.

By then it was in Falls Church, Virginia. About six or seven miles from the drop site in Arlington. An address on Leesburg Pike.

That meant that the package had been moved.

Someone had picked it up and was delivering it somewhere else.

I found myself juggling the cell phone and the BlackBerry, which I never liked using as a cell phone, and the DVD copy of Mr. Younis's surveillance tape, in an old cracked CD jewel case he had lying around. I arrayed them before me on the hood of the Defender, my mobile office.

When I clicked on Google Earth and zoomed in on the flashing red dot on my BlackBerry screen, I could see it was some big V-shaped office building.

Success. Maybe. But at least I knew that someone had picked up the FedEx package and moved it from the mail drop to an office building in Falls Church, and that was something. Or it might turn out to be nothing. I wouldn't know until I drove out there and took a look. I pocketed the BlackBerry and cell phone and fished out my car key, the DVD in my left hand.

The Defender is as nonautomatic a vehicle as you can get: even the windows crank by hand. No remote starter; no keyless entry. You open it with a good old-fashioned key just like they did a century ago. I inserted the key in the lock and turned it—

And heard the scrape against the pavement an instant too late.

I turned slowly, but suddenly the car window came at me, smashing into my nose and mouth.

While, at the same time, the DVD was wrenched out of my left hand.

Reeling in pain, I spun, hands out, unsteady on my feet. Miraculously, the window glass hadn't broken, but it felt like maybe my nose had.

Enraged, I took off after my assailant, who was already quite a distance away. A black Humvee came hurtling down the street and slowed for a second. Its passenger-side door came open, and the guy took a running leap into the vehicle.

Once I caught a glimpse of its license plate, I knew it was the same Humvee that had passed me twice before. I'm not the fastest runner, but fueled by adrenaline and considerable anger, I was able to get close enough to the Humvee to thump an angry fist against its left rear quarter panel before it disappeared down the street.

My attacker had been unusually tall, with a steroid-poisoned wrestler's build and what looked at a distance to be a high-and-tight jarhead recon haircut—shaven everywhere except the crown of his head, like a short Mohawk. He looked like an overweight Travis Bickle.

I felt along the bridge of my nose. It wasn't broken. No broken teeth either, though my upper lip was bleeding. I felt and tasted the blood.

I took out my cell phone and hit redial, and when Garvin answered I said, "I have one more license plate for you."

39

The Dean & Deluca's on M Street in Georgetown sold excellent fresh-baked chocolate-chip cookies. I bought a dozen and asked the bakery clerk to pack them for me in a plain white deli box. I placed the box of cookies on the car seat next to me and got onto the George Washington Memorial Parkway. The entire interior of the car at once filled with the sweet buttery smell of freshly baked cookies.

About half an hour later I turned off Leesburg Pike into a semicircular drive in front of a modern ten-story office building built in the shape of a broad V, with a blue glass skin that mirrored the sky so perfectly it seemed at times to disappear.

The name on the front of the building was Skyview Executive Center. It appeared to be a multitenant office building. Like a lot of commercial buildings in Tysons Corner and Falls Church, there was an underground parking garage. Instead, I parked in the Doubletree Hotel down the block and walked over with my box of cookies.

I hadn't gotten any text messages from the GPS tracker in a while, so as I walked I took out my phone and opened the last message I'd received, then clicked on the map. The red dot was gone. That told me that the device had stopped transmitting. Which presumably meant that it had been discovered, then disabled.

I entered the lobby and spent a few minutes inspecting the building directory, one of those big black wall signs with white letters, rear-illuminated. A long list of tenants. Mostly small to midsize firms: health-care consultants, investment managers, accountants, a lot of lawyers. A couple of government-agency satellite offices. A number of companies with cryptic-sounding names like Aegis Partners and Orion Strategy, which were either lobbyists or defense contractors.

But no Traverse Development. Nothing that sounded even remotely familiar. It didn't surprise me that this mysterious company wasn't listed on the building's directory. But one of the companies in the building had to be connected to them, in some way.

The security guard, seated behind a curved granite counter in the middle of the lobby, saw me staring at the directory board and called out, "Can I help you, sir?" He was in his late fifties, with deep-set eyes and a prominent forehead, a shiny bald head and protruding ears.

"You have a list of the tenants in this building you might be able to give me?"

"No, sir, I'm afraid I can't. Management company won't let me hand that out."

"Rules is rules, huh? Thing is, the wife's trying to start a chocolate-chip cookie business?" I held up the white bakery box. "I'm helping her with the marketing. Because she won't let me near the kitchen."

I smiled, and he smiled back, and I went on, "We want to give out free boxes of cookies to all the companies here, sort of a promotional thing?" I came closer and handed him the box. "Here, these are for you. Try a couple and tell me if you don't think my wife's got it nailed."

He hesitated.

"Go on, try one. If you can stop at one."

He opened the flaps on the box and pulled out a cookie and took a large bite. "Mmm," he said. "Soft and chewy and crispy all at the same time. She use dark chocolate chips?"

"Only the best quality chocolate."

He took another bite. "Man, these are *good*."

"Thank you."

He opened a desk drawer and pulled out a stapled set of papers and gave it to me. "Just don't tell anyone where you got this, okay?" He winked.

I winked back. "Not a word."

He peered at me, touched his nose and lip and said, "You get into a fight with the wife?"

For a moment I didn't know what he was talking about, then I remembered that my bruised nose and split lip probably looked pretty bad by then. "Yeah," I said. "I told her I thought she should use shortening instead of butter. Learned my lesson. I'm sticking to the marketing."

Instead of driving back to the office, I stopped at a FedEx/ Kinko's copy shop and faxed Dorothy the tenant list. Not to some fax machine in the halls of Stoddard Associates, where anyone could see it; instead, I faxed it to her E-Fax account, so she'd get it online. While I was there, I rented time on a computer, checked my e-mail, and found an e-mail from Frank Montello, my information broker.

Whenever he wrote e-mails, he used all capital letters as if he were sending a telegram by Western Union.

ATTACHED YOUR BRO'S PHONE BILLS. BIG FILE. STILL WORKING ON THAT OTHER CELL # BUT SHOULD

HAVE SOMETHING BY TOMORROW. INVOICE AT-
TACHED, TOO, PAYABLE WITHIN 10 DAYS AS PER
USUAL.

So he still hadn't located the owner of the emergency
contact number that Woody Sawyer had been given,
back at the airport outside of L.A. But he had been able
to unearth the billing statements for one of Roger's cell
phones, the one whose bills I couldn't find in his study.
The detailed phone records ran for dozens of pages. It
wouldn't have been much fun to read them on my
BlackBerry. I printed them all out and skimmed the list
while sitting in my car.

Mostly meaningless columns of phone numbers. But
then something leaped out at me.

Five calls, all collect, all from a number in Altamont, New York.

"Billed on behalf of Global TelLink," it said, and
gave a phone number with a 518 area code.

The Altamont Correctional Facility, it said.

From Victor Heller, of course.

I hadn't talked to my father in several years. Whereas
Roger had spoken to him five times in the last month.

My brother always got along with our father well—
far better than I did. I'd always thought that was because the two of them were so much alike.

But five phone calls in the last month?

More carefully, I went through the previous year's
phone bills and found just one other collect call from my
father—eleven months ago. Six collect calls in a year
from Dad, five of them in the last four weeks. Just before
Roger's disappearance.

No coincidence.

40

When I returned to Lauren's house—after a quick stop at Mr. Younis's gas station in Georgetown to make another DVD copy of the surveillance video that had been snatched from me—both Lauren and Gabe were home. Her Lexus was in the driveway, and the light in Gabe's room was on. I unlocked the front door. The security system's warning tone didn't sound. They'd disarmed it.

That was not what I wanted. I'd made it clear to Lauren that whenever they were home, they should use the night setting, which would give off a tone whenever someone entered. So I went to find her and explain to her how to use the system.

She wasn't in the kitchen. Nor was she in the TV room or at the computer in the hutch that served as her home office. I became aware of raised voices coming from upstairs, and I walked toward the staircase, climbed the steps.

Mother and son were arguing. I stopped halfway up the landing, heard Gabe shout, his voice cracking: "—But you don't *know* that. You don't *know* that!"

Lauren shouted back, "You listen to me! He'll turn up. They'll find him. I promise you!"

"After all this time? He's dead, don't you get it? Why do you keep pretending?"

"He's not dead, Gabriel! You have to think positive. You have to believe. Your father is *not dead*!"

It was too painful to listen to, and anyway, I was eavesdropping on a private moment. I headed back down the stairs.

I watched TV listlessly for a few minutes, changing the channels, not finding anything I wanted to stay on. I heard a door slam, followed by heavy footsteps, then Lauren entered the room.

"That kid, I swear—"

She stopped short when she saw my face. "Jesus, Nick, what happened?"

I shrugged.

"Who did that to you?"

"It's not as bad as it looks," I said, and smiled.

"Yeah, I get the reference. How'd that happen?"

"Lauren, I overheard you talking to Gabe."

She sat at the end of the same couch I was sitting on. "You call that 'talking'? More like screaming. He just knows how to push every single one of my buttons."

"Why are you telling him to keep the faith? What's the point of assuring him that Roger's alive?"

"*Why?*" Her eyes flashed. "Can you imagine what it's like to have your father disappear suddenly, not knowing whether he's . . ." She faltered, seeing my expression, realizing.

I nodded. "Yeah, I can imagine."

"Why did I never see the parallel?"

"What makes you think there's a parallel? My father took off in the middle of the night. My mother told us he was on the run. We knew that he was out there somewhere, hiding from the authorities."

She said softly, "Maybe Roger is, too. Something like that—I *want* to believe that's what happened."

"I don't think so," I said, and I described the surveillance video I'd just seen: the apparent abduction, the Econoline van, the gun.

She looked stricken, then closed her eyes for five or ten seconds. "Can I see it? Do you have a copy?"

"Yeah," I said. "Someone grabbed it from me. That's how I got this." I pointed to my bruised nose and split lip. "So I just went back and made another one."

I played the DVD for her on her computer, and she responded the way I expected she would: shock, disbelief, then immense relief. And then puzzlement: What did it mean? Roger hadn't been killed in the attack, but he had been abducted. But by whom, and why?

"This means he's alive," she said.

"Maybe," I said carefully. "It certainly means he survived the attack. That much we know for sure. As for whether . . ."

"He's alive," she said. "These people have him."

"Could be."

She pointed to my face. "Who did that to you?"

"Probably the same people who abducted him."

"Who?"

"You'll be the first to know when I find out," I said.

She nodded, compressed her lips. "Nick, you were able to get into Gifford Industries today, right?"

"I was, yes. And I met with the librarian."

"The librarian—?"

"Roger's e-mail, remember—he said something about saying good-bye to a librarian. 'The librarian' turns out to be Roger's nickname for a lawyer colleague of his named—"

"—Marjorie something. Right! I'd totally forgotten. So what did she say?"

I told her about how protective of Roger she'd been, her unwillingness to provide details beyond the fact that Roger had discovered something "troubling" in the books of a company they were acquiring.

"Well, it shouldn't be so hard to figure out which company she's talking about. We've only acquired one in the last three or four months, a power company in Brazil."

"She wouldn't say whether it was a company Gifford acquired or was *considering* acquiring."

"Is she covering something up?"

"That wasn't my sense." I paused. Thought for a second. "I walked around Georgetown a bit. Retraced the route you and Roger took the night you were attacked. So let me ask you something."

"Sure."

"Roger parked his car on Water Street. Quite a ways down the hill from the restaurant. I don't get that."

"What don't you get? Oji-San doesn't have valet parking."

"But there are parking garages a lot closer than where he parked. And it was a rainy night—not the kind of night you'd want to stroll around Georgetown."

"I . . . I suppose I never thought about it."

"It didn't strike you as somehow strange?"

"No, not really. What are you getting at?"

"I don't have a theory. It's just that it doesn't make sense."

"Sense? I mean, Roger's parked there before. It's free, it's easy to get in and out of. I don't see what the big deal is."

"Okay."

"What, you think he deliberately parked there for some sinister reason?"

"Not necessarily."

"Then what are you saying?"

I spoke carefully. "I just wonder how well you know him. How much you know about him."

"How well I know *Roger*? What are you talking about? If you're hinting at something, why don't you just come out and say it?"

I hesitated, blew out a lungful of air. "Did you know Roger was having an affair?" I asked gingerly.

"Stop it."

"Did you know?"

"Just cut it out."

"You had no idea?"

"That's just not true. Now you're listening to Gabe's crazy ideas?"

"I'm not asking if it's true. I'm asking if you knew about it."

She shook her head. "Stop it."

I got up, closed both living-room doors. "What do you know about Candi Dupont?" I asked.

Lauren blinked a few times. "Candy . . . ?"

"Candi Dupont is a woman. Candi with an i. A woman that Roger was having an affair with."

She flushed, looked as if she'd just been slapped. Closed her eyes again.

"Seven months ago—" I began.

"I don't want to hear it," she interrupted. "If he started seeing her again, I don't want to know about it."

"So you did know."

"What does this have to do with what happened to him?"

"It's an important lead. She might know where he is."

"Or not."

"Or not," I agreed.

"Nick, we went through a—a difficult time in our marriage a few years ago."

She looked at me, but I just nodded silently.

"Sort of a crisis, I guess you'd call it. He'd met some woman on a business trip to Boston. We'd had some big fight before he left, and I guess he was angry at me, and he said he was in the bar at the Four Seasons, and in a moment of weakness . . ."

"Candi Dupont."

"I never knew her name. He wouldn't tell me. But this was three or four years ago, Nick. He begged me to forgive him, and he promised it was over. He swore."

"Obviously it wasn't. Seven months ago Roger paid for a woman named Candi Dupont to have an abortion at a clinic in Boston."

"Oh, God."

"We haven't turned up anything on any 'Candi Dupont' in the standard databases, which tells me that 'Candi Dupont' might be some sort of alias. But whatever her name is, maybe it's the same woman Roger told you about. Which would mean the affair didn't end three or four years ago."

She grabbed a hardcover book from the coffee table and hurled it across the room. It hit the wall, rattled a picture frame, and fell to the floor. I couldn't help noticing that the book was called *Anger: Wisdom for Cooling the Flames* by Thich Nhat Hanh. "Enough!" she cried. "I don't want to hear about it! If he didn't stop seeing that . . . slut . . . I don't want to know about it! Don't you get that?"

"I do," I said quietly. "I'm sorry. Forgive me."

She got up and retrieved the book, put it back on the coffee table, and sat back down on the couch, but much closer to me. For a minute or so she was silent, and I didn't say anything either, then she said, "Nick."

"Yeah?"

"I've been lying to you."

41

"Okay," I said gently. I kept my tone light, casual, non-confrontational. I wanted her to feel safe about finally opening up to me. "Tell me."

"Roger did mention something."

"About what?"

"Just that he'd found something he wasn't supposed to know about. Some kind of corruption, it sounded like."

"Which is precisely what Marjorie Ogonowski told me. Did he say whether it involved Gifford Industries?"

"I don't know. He said it involved a lot of money, but other than that, he was completely vague about it. The more I pressed him on it, the more he withdrew. He could get that way. He'd retreat into himself."

"He didn't give you any specifics? Nothing at all?"

"Nothing. But—well, he was afraid that something might happen to him. That he'd gotten threats."

"That's pretty vague, too."

"He admitted it sounded paranoid. Like he was some conspiracy theorist. I asked him if he wanted me to talk to Leland—to see if Leland could do something, help in some way. But he told me never to say anything to Leland about it. He made me promise."

"And did you keep that promise?"

"Of course."

"And he never said who was threatening him?"

She shook her head again. "He never said, and I gave up asking. He said he wanted to protect Gabe and me, and the less I knew, the better."

"So that e-mail he sent—that InCaseOfDeath thing—that didn't really shock you, did it, what he was telling you?"

A beat. Then, ruefully: "No."

"So why did you keep this from me?"

"Ohh, Nick." She sighed, then hugged herself, shivering as if she were cold. "Because what if he—I don't know, surrendered."

"Surrendered? To whom?"

"I mean, what if he gave himself up? I mean, they'd threatened him, threatened his family, and he knew he couldn't unring the bell, you know? He couldn't pretend *not* to know whatever it was he found out. So maybe he made a deal with them. These guys, whoever they are, they attacked me and he saw that and he said, in effect, 'Hey, why her? I'm the one you want. Take me.' To spare me and Gabe. Do you follow? Am I making any sense?"

"I think so," I said. "But what do you think happened to him?"

Very quietly, she said, "He might have sacrificed himself."

She lowered her head almost to her chest, then put her hands on each temple. From the way her head was moving, I knew she was crying. After a moment, she looked up, tears streaming down her face. "You see? Do you understand why I'm so scared?"

"Yes. I do." I reached over and held her in a tight embrace, felt her damp heat. "But I'm not going to let anything happen to you or Gabe."

"What if that's beyond your control, Nick?"

"It's not," I said, and I was instantly ashamed because that was a transparent lie. Plenty of things were beyond my control.

"And you know, just listening to you talk about what happened that night, the night I was attacked—well, maybe you're right. Maybe there *was* something strange about it. And then there was that e-mail from him, and now there's this video, and it all seems to add up to something very different from what I thought it was."

I held her for a long while.

"Lauren," I said, "did he ever tell you why he talked to Victor so often?"

"He called your dad? When?"

"Victor called him, to be precise. Collect calls. Five times in the last month."

"He never said anything about that to me. Are you sure about this? I thought he hadn't talked to Victor in almost a year."

I sat there for a few minutes in front of the TV set after Lauren went to bed—Kyra Sedgwick in a rerun of *The Closer,* saying to a bunch of sullen male cops, in a treacly Southern accent, "Why thank you *very* much, gentlemen"—and then I thought of something.

I went to the entry hall by the front door. The spare key to Roger's car—really, a keyless entry fob—was in a green ceramic Japanese bowl on the hall table. His S-Class AMG Mercedes was parked in the garage, black and gleaming. Inside, it smelled like new leather. I started it up, pressed the navigation system button on the LCD touch screen, hit DESTINATION MEMORY, then LAST DESTINATIONS.

A beautiful car, that Mercedes. A six-liter V-12 engine with 604 horsepower and incredible torque. Invoice price probably around a hundred eighty thousand dollars. And the crappiest navigation system in the world.

But it told me what I needed to know.

Roger had not just talked to Dad on the phone a bunch of times in the last month. He'd also visited him in prison. He'd driven to upstate New York, and at least once he'd used the Mercedes's navigation system to get him there.

The question was why.

The one person who might know what had happened to Roger was the last person I wanted to see.

PART TWO

A man's most open actions have a secret side to them.
—Joseph Conrad

42

The Altamont Correctional Facility had originally been built as a hospital for the criminally insane, a hundred and fifty years ago. The Altamont Lunatic Asylum, as it was then called, was a grand Victorian Gothic complex of spires and crenellated towers. Its forbidding red-brick walls were stained dark with soot from a century of internal-combustion engines. Some forty years ago the mental hospital was shut down and converted into a medium-security prison, but it still looked like the sort of place a homicidal maniac escapes from, then terrorizes the nearby summer camp. It also reminded me a little of the high school I'd gone to in Malden.

They'd done some renovation since the days of straitjackets and lobotomies. There was a concrete perimeter wall thirty feet high, topped with coils of razor wire, watchtowers, and banks of high-mast lights. Inside the walls, the old Gothic prison complex was surrounded by a luxuriant green lawn that wouldn't have been out of place at Pebble Beach.

I'd flown from Washington to Albany, rented a car, and driven a few miles to the outskirts of the town of Guilderland. The nav system was one of those separate portable things that sticks to the dashboard by means of a suction cup. It spoke in an officious, nasal female voice, which might have been tolerable if she hadn't got me lost for twenty minutes. So I bore her some resentment for making me a little late. Though it wasn't as if my father was going anywhere.

I filled out a form, showed a driver's license, went through a metal detector, then an ion scan, for drugs. I had to empty my pockets, leave cell phone and keys in a paper bag with my name on it. The visitor-control system was fairly automated—they took my picture and printed out an adhesive pass with my photo on it and a bar code.

After I passed through a second metal cage, I turned to the guard who was scanning my pass with a barcode reader and said, "Pretty high-tech."

The guard, a bored-looking, obese black guy with sad eyes and a wide mouth, nodded.

"Big old scary building like this, I was expecting, you know, one of those huge ledgers and a quill, right?"

He broke out laughing. It obviously took very little to amuse him.

"Hey, so I guess that means you keep track of every visitor in your computer."

"Oh yeah."

"Anyone can see I visited?"

"Not unless they have access to the computer," he said.

I nodded. "Okay."

"You visiting Victor Heller?"

"Right."

"Who's that, your brother?"

"Father."

"Father, huh? Been inside a long time?"

"A while."

"Guess you got scared straight, right?"

"You could say that."

* * *

The visitors' room looked like the cafeteria in my high school—the same molded-plastic chairs, the same greenish linoleum floor, the same high ceiling with stained white drop-in panels. The same smell of ammonia mixed with human sweat and desperation. A long, undulating counter snaked through the room, bisecting it: prisoners on one side, visitors on the other. On the visitors' side, a cheery mural was painted on the wall, primitive art depicting the countryside, probably done by inmates. There were maybe half a dozen visitors. A couple of little kids were running around, oblivious to the setting. Only three prisoners.

Sitting at the far end of the counter was my father.

In the twelve years since I'd last seen him, I'd aged, of course. But he seemed to have aged at the speed of light. Victor Heller, the Dark Prince of Wall Street, was an old man. His shoulders were stooped. He had a big white beard and looked like an Old Testament prophet. His eyebrows were heavy and unruly, like steel-wool pads that had seen too much use. He was wearing a dark green shirt and matching pants, his prison outfit, which looked like a janitor's uniform.

He looked up as I approached. His eyes were rheumy, and he looked lost. His chronic psoriasis had gotten much worse since I'd last seen him: large flakes of skin were coming off his cheeks and forehead. He reminded me of a molting reptile, a snake shedding its skin, as if the scales were falling away to reveal his corrupt inner core.

But then he smiled when he saw me, and the old familiar glint was in his eyes.

He waited for me to sit down, adjust my chair, the legs scraping against the linoleum. Then he said, "They must have told you."

"Told me what?" I said.

"About the cancer."

"The cancer," I repeated, then I understood. The reason he and Roger had spoken five times. But why hadn't Roger said anything to me, or at least to Lauren? Why hadn't my mother called to tell me the news? The old man was dying. Suddenly, I felt hollow.

I looked down. "Dad, I—my God, I had—"

He was laughing raucously, his head thrown back. His beard extended down his neck. That hollow place inside me filled slowly with something ice-cold.

"Why else would you lay down your arms and come visit your poor old Dad?" he said, his words half-choked by laughter. "No, I'm not dying. But there's gotta be one hell of a reason why you're here. I figured you must know something they're not telling me."

"No, Dad, I don't."

"You've never been here before, have you?"

I shook my head.

"Of course you haven't. The day I reported, Roger drove me. Your mother was quite ill."

"She was too depressed to get out of bed."

"Yes, that's right. And you—you had a *study* to finish at McKinsey, was that it?"

"I'd enlisted by then."

"Ah, yes. The few. The proud. Nick Heller."

"It was the army, not the marines. Special Forces."

"Special," he said. He rolled the word around in his mouth like the first sip of a Château Lafite. His lips curled at the edges. "Hooah."

The day he entered prison, Dad gave Roger his most prized possession, a gold Patek Philippe watch that Mom had given him when he made his first hundred million. Inscribed on the back was a line from Virgil in Latin: *Audentes fortuna juvat.* Fortune favors the bold. He'd been bold all right, but Fortune hadn't gotten the memo.

"So to what do I owe the honor of your presence?"

"I want to know what Roger's been talking to you about."

His eyes went blank. "What's he been *talking* to me about? What do sons talk about with their fathers?" A slow, mirthless smile. "Been so long, you've probably forgotten."

One of the inmates down the row was arguing with his visitor, a young black woman who appeared to be the mother of the two little kids running around. Maybe he was the father. I wondered whether the prisoners were allowed conjugal visits.

"He's been in touch with you a lot recently."

"He calls his dad. He worries about me. He sends me packages. Your mother sends me packages. Everyone else does." He cocked his head, raised his heavy brows, looked at me through drooping lids. "Maybe it's a financial hardship?"

Of course, I knew that Roger hadn't actually called Dad. Incoming calls weren't allowed. Dad had to place collect calls to Roger.

"Roger's come to visit you, too." The nav system in his Mercedes confirmed it.

"They allow visitors between seven thirty and three. They encourage visits, in fact. They say visits can be a positive influence, you know that? They say inmates who receive regular visits adjust much better once they're released from prison. Which, in my case, is a mere eighteen years from now. When I'll be, assuming I'm still alive—"

"Why?"

"Why does he visit me? Maybe because he's concerned. Silly, I know. An old man like me locked up with rapists and child molesters and perverts—what's to worry about?"

"I mean, why so often?"

"Often? That's a relative concept when you're in here." He licked his lips. They were chapped, startlingly red against the snow white of his Methuselah beard.

I tried again, came at it head-on. "When did you last see him?"

He frowned, folded his arms, leaned back. "I haven't seen your brother in, well, easily a year." He looked up and to his right. One of the telltale indicators that he was lying. Another one, some might say, was when he moved his lips. "Roger's got a family and a serious career. It's not so convenient—"

"He was here last week," I said.

He slowly shook his head. "I think I'd remember that, Nicholas. There's not much to do here if you don't lift weights, and you've seen all the *Law and Order* reruns."

"Roger's name is in the prison visitor-control system three times in the last ten weeks."

He hesitated only a split second while he decided whether to brazen it out. His smile spread slowly, eyes gleaming.

"You know me too well," he said with a laugh.

43

The summer before Roger went off to Harvard, we were hanging out in the body shop of Norman Lang Motors, the used-car dealership owned by a buddy of mine.

Timmy Lang was watching a guy spray-paint an orange-and-yellow flaming pony on the side of a red Mustang. The paint fumes smelled bad, and we'd always thought that Timmy, not the brightest bulb, had probably breathed too much of them over the years, so Roger and I were standing as far away as we could get. I was going on about how unfair it was, what they'd done to Dad. The way he'd had to go on the lam, become a fugitive somewhere in Switzerland, and all because he'd made some powerful enemies. He was innocent: He'd told us so himself.

Roger cut me off. "Look, Red Man," he said, "you really shouldn't talk about things you don't understand."

"What's that supposed to mean?"

"All I'm saying, Nick, is that sometimes things are . . . complicated, that's all."

"What are you saying?"

"Figure it out," he said.

Then I did something I'd never done before: I slugged Roger in the stomach. He doubled over, came back up a minute later, red-faced. But he wasn't angry. He smiled. "You're the last true believer, aren't you, Nick?" he said. "You'll learn."

If a cynic is just a bruised idealist, then Roger wasn't really a cynic. He was no idealist. He was just more clear-eyed than me.

See, I'd taken Dad at his word.

"All phone calls here are monitored and recorded," I said to my father. "So if you want to talk about something sensitive, it's got to be in person. What did Roger want to talk about?"

He raised his chin slowly, pursed his lips a few times. "Yes, why in the world would he waste his time coming all the way out here to talk to an old fart like me?"

"Dad," I said, refusing to give in to his rancor, "this is important. It's for Roger's sake."

But he didn't want to be deterred from his tirade. His voice rose steadily. I could smell the goatish fug of his body odor.

"There was a time when you worshipped your brother. You thought he peed Perrier. You thought he hung the moon. But I understand why you despise him now. You can't stand the fact that he stood by me all these years while you did the easy thing and succumbed to all the peer pressure and turned against me."

"Are you finished?" I said patiently. The mother with two little kids had stopped arguing with her boyfriend or husband. Her kids had gotten tired of exploring the featureless room and were sitting on the floor with markers and coloring books.

"Do you know that I still get producers from Fox News and CNN and even *60 Minutes* calling the prison and writing me, wanting to interview me? MSNBC wants to feature me on some show called *Lock-up*. And do you know why I refuse? Because of you. And your mother. And Roger. And my grandson. Because I don't want to stir things up. I don't want to embarrass you. I want people to forget. I know what they want. They want a nice juicy video segment, a tight close-up of the billionaire in his prison uniform, brought low, humiliated and *filled* with regret and expressing remorse for his terrible crimes. They want a morality play. So their viewers can feel a little better about their lives of quiet desperation."

"Dad—"

"Do you know—do you *know*—that I'm locked up in the same cellblock as murderers and rapists? I'm in here for *thirty years*, Nicholas. There are *child molesters* who will be out long before me."

"You can be released early for good behavior," I said.

He smiled bitterly. "If I'm very *very* good, they'll put me on a prison bus and let me pick up garbage on the side of the road. Are you aware that there's a man in here who murdered his own father? Beat him with a baseball bat, then gutted him with a fish knife and put the body in the woods, and this lovely fellow was convicted of manslaughter in the first degree, and he's serving five years. *Five years.* While I'm in here for three decades. And do you know why?" A gob of spittle had formed at the corner of his mouth.

I nodded. "Securities fraud and grand larceny."

He waggled a finger. "Wrong. I'm here because of ambition."

"I suppose that's one way of putting it."

"Oh, not my own ambition. Believe me. I'm here because some very greedy and grasping young turks in the U.S. Attorney's Office in Manhattan wanted a scalp. They wanted to advance their grubby little careers. They wanted to land a plum job at some white-shoe law firm.

Or run for mayor. Or governor. It's all about ambition, Nicholas. Theirs versus mine. I was merely a stepping-stone on their path to greater glory. There's no more Mafia, so now they go after the rich guys. 'White-collar crime,' they call it. Isn't that what you do for a living now? Some sort of gumshoe? A private dick? You don't think that's beneath you, Nicholas? A little déclassé?"

I let my eyes roam the visiting room slowly, pointedly. "It's hard to measure up to your accomplishments," I said. "You set the bar awfully high." I smiled. "Also, Stoddard Associates wasn't too déclassé when you wanted them to save your ass."

"When you need a plumber, you call a plumber. Doesn't mean you become one."

I shrugged.

"And yet you dare to pass judgment on me," he said.

"Not at all. I don't need to pass judgment on you. I already know what I think of you."

He gave me his raptor's smile.

"Anyway, I wasn't asking about you," I said. "Fascinating as you are. I need to know what Roger came here to talk about."

He licked his lips very precisely, with just the tip of his tongue. "Your brother and I spoke in confidence. I won't betray that confidence. You can ask him yourself."

"I wish I could. But he's gone. And I'm thinking it had something to do with whatever you two talked about."

"That's between father and son." He said it with a cruel twist, as if he and I had a different, less privileged relationship.

"Okay," I said. I pushed back the chair and got up. The guard looked up from his small wooden table at the door. "Nice to see you, Dad. A pleasure as always."

"Sit down," he said. "Don't be silly. Your brother can tell you whatever he chooses to tell you."

"Not likely. He and Lauren were attacked in George-town a couple of days ago, and when she woke up in the hospital—"

"Hospital? Is Lauren all right?"

I nodded, backed away from the counter a few steps.

My father stared at me levelly. Blinked a few times. "And Roger?"

"No one's been able to find him since then. No one's heard anything from him."

A look of panic darted across his eyes, and he suddenly gave a loud, guttural cry. "No! Dear God, *no*! God damn it, I told him not to do it."

44

My father ran a hand over his forehead, his eyes, flecking off some snowflakes of dead skin. "What does this mean, no one's been able to find him? They haven't found a—?"

"No body, Dad. Maybe he's alive. Maybe he's just fine. Then again . . ." I returned to the plastic chair and sat down. "So tell me what you and Roger talked about."

He cradled his scaly forehead in his hands. His large blunt fingers massaged the skin deeply, and I had to look away. Psoriasis often flares up at times of severe emotional stress. I imagined that being in prison might be stressful. Funny how the condition made him more repellent, more reptilian, rather than more sympathetic or vulnerable.

"He said he'd found something he wanted my input on," Victor said, his words muffled.

"Your input."

He looked up, sighed. He folded his hands on the counter in front of him. "Yes, Nicholas, it turns out I know a thing or two. Even though you never wanted to learn anything from me."

"What do you mean? I learned plenty."

"Your sarcasm doesn't escape me. Roger told me

he'd come across a phony expense from one of his subcontractors—a security firm."

"A subcontractor?"

"They'd been providing installation security for Gifford Industries—armed guards for their power plants and construction projects and such."

"What do you mean, a 'phony expense'?"

"He was convinced this was a bribe, a kickback, to some Pentagon big shot, and he wanted proof. But that was a tall order, even to someone as brilliant as your brother. It's a little like understanding algebraic combinatorics if you still don't get long division."

Ah, the old Victor Heller arrogance. Even talking about his revered and adored son, he had to establish his superiority. "Like a toddler trying to run the Boston Marathon, is that it?"

"Give it a rest, Nicholas. Roger knows this stuff on a fairly deep level. But not like me. I've done it."

I assumed he meant that he'd set up all kinds of shell companies in offshore tax havens. I'd often wondered whether he'd squirreled money away, money the government hadn't been able to locate and seize. How else could he have lived as a fugitive for all those years?

"So Roger wanted to prove that this security firm was making kickbacks to the Pentagon," I said skeptically. That fit with what he'd told Lauren and what Marjorie Ogonowski had told me. "Why? So he could report it to the government? Earn a merit badge, maybe? Why does this not sound like Roger?"

My father sighed impatiently, waved a hand around as if trying to swat away a cloud of mosquitoes. "Oh, please," he said. "Spare me. Roger was tired of being poor."

"Poor?" I said. "Good God. He was making a six-figure salary."

He snorted. "A six-figure salary. These days, that's poverty."

"What do you earn, working in the prison laundry?" I said. "Ten cents a day?"

He didn't even bother granting me one of his famous withering glares. "He'd had it with being sidelined. He was fed up with seeing mediocrities being promoted above him while he remained stuck. One of a hundred vice presidents. He could have run Gifford Industries, and he knew it."

"So what was he trying to do?"

"Quite simply, he wanted to make it clear what he had on them. What he knew. And how much he wanted."

"Hush money," I said.

He nodded.

"Extortion."

"You always did have a way with words."

Yes. Now that sounded like the Roger I knew. "How much did he want?"

"Ten million dollars."

"That all?" I said as dryly as I could.

"Actually, that was quite reasonable. Quite the bargain. If you consider the public furor that would have erupted if the kickbacks became public. They'd have lost many times that in government contracts."

"Government contracts, huh? What's the company?"

"You might have heard of Paladin Worldwide."

"Ah," I said.

Paladin Worldwide was the world's largest private military contractor. It began as a supplier of armed guards for businesses like Gifford Enterprises and eventually morphed into a full-fledged army for hire. Paladin was infamous, controversial, and generally despised. Paladin soldiers—"contractors," they were called—were widely regarded as trigger-happy cowboys. But what really ticked off U.S. soldiers was that, while a typical sergeant might make a hundred bucks a day, the Paladin guys were making a thousand.

When I was in the service, in Afghanistan and Bosnia, Paladin mercs fought alongside the U.S. troops. They were all recent vets, and in truth they were as well trained as anyone, but since they were legally classified as "consultants," they weren't subject to the laws of the country in which they were fighting—or even U.S. military law. That meant that they could fire at civilians with impunity, and some of them did. They couldn't be prosecuted. Not one was ever charged with a crime. It was like the Wild West. In Iraq, in fact, there were more private contractors than U.S. Army troops. And Paladin Worldwide was the biggest contractor there.

"He was trying to extort ten million dollars from Paladin? Not the smartest idea. Those guys are armed and dangerous."

"I warned him that the whole idea was reckless."

"Did you, Dad? Or did you give him tips on how to do it?"

Another sigh, this one more peeved than impatient. "I told him he was playing a very dangerous game."

I was silent for a long while, then I said, "Did he ever get the ten million?"

"I don't know. I assume not."

I recalled Roger's e-mail, sent through that InCaseOfDeath website. "This has to be the strangest letter I've ever written," he'd said. "Because if you get it, that means I'm dead."

And: "Who knows what they'll do? Will they try to make it look like I committed suicide?"

He talked about "the people who are trying to stop me."

The people who were trying to stop him—from

blackmailing them, from extorting them—were Paladin Worldwide, it was clear. Somehow Roger had learned about a phony expense they'd submitted to Gifford Industries, a kickback they'd tried to bill Gifford for. And Roger being Roger, he moved in for the kill. Demanded ten million dollars in hush money.

From Paladin Worldwide. The world's largest private army.

There could scarcely be a more lethal adversary.

"So what do you think happened?" I said. "You think Paladin grabbed Roger? Or maybe Roger disappeared in order to escape them?"

He put his hands over his eyes, and a large silver flake sloughed off. "Disappeared? No, Nicholas. It's far more likely that they . . . did away with him. That's how they work."

"I wonder." I didn't bother to explain my reasoning—the fact that Lauren had been knocked unconscious rather than being killed. "I don't believe in corporate hit squads."

"Then you're either naïve or you're not paying attention. You don't remember that vice chairman of Enron who was just about to testify before Congress, about to name names in the biggest corporate scandal ever, but before he could get on a plane to Washington, he was found shot to death in his car? 'Suicide,' they called it, of course. Then a couple of months later, a consultant for Arthur Andersen whose big client was—you guessed it, Enron—was found shot in the head in a forest in Colorado? And then a banker with the Royal Bank of Scotland who was about to testify against his colleagues in guess what case—that's right, Enron—was found dead in the woods outside London. Another apparent suicide."

"This is grassy-knoll, tinfoil-hat stuff, Dad. Black helicopters."

"A woman named Karen Silkwood works in a nuclear plant in Oklahoma and gets plutonium poisoning and gets in her car to meet a *New York Times* reporter to spill the beans about unsafe working conditions in the nuclear industry, only her car runs off the road. Suicide?"

"I saw the Meryl Streep movie. Good flick. What's your point?"

His tone had become fierce. "I have no doubt they killed Roger. Probably meant to kill Lauren, too, not just give her a concussion."

I decided to let the argument drop. It wasn't getting me anywhere.

"I need names," I said. "Who at Paladin he talked to. Who might have threatened him."

Dad looked at me for a long while as if deciding how much to say. Then: "He tried to contact their founder and CEO, Allen Granger, but Granger refused to talk with him."

I knew a bit about Allen Granger, the billionaire founder of Paladin Worldwide, but it was limited to what I'd read and heard. A former Navy SEAL from northern Michigan. Rich guy, sort of a recluse. A born-again Christian evangelist, far-right-wing conservative.

"Did he talk to anyone else at Paladin, then?"

Victor nodded. "The head of the Washington office, a man named Carl Koblenz. I think he may be the president of the company—the number two, just under Granger."

"Carl Koblenz," I repeated to myself. "Was Koblenz the one who directly threatened Roger?"

"Did I say anything about any direct threats?"

"No, you did not," I replied.

"You're planning something," he said. "I can tell."

"Maybe."

"Don't. At least learn from your brother's mistakes. I don't want to lose my only remaining son."

"I'm touched. But that won't happen."

"Surely you know the *Thirty-Six Stratagems*."

I shook my head.

"The ancient Chinese art of deception."

"Oh, right. Sun Tzu. Jay Stoddard's favorite."

"Forget Sun Tzu's *Art of War*. That's so common-place." He held up a gnarled, age-spotted finger. "Far more interesting than Sun Tzu is Chu-ko Liang. Perhaps the most brilliant military strategist ever. One of his stratagems was to defeat your enemy from within. Infiltrate the enemy's camp in the guise of cooperation or surrender. Then, once you've discovered the source of his weakness, you strike."

Somehow the setting—the visitors' room of the Altamont Correctional Facility—made my father's advice a little less authoritative.

As I walked out of the visitors' room, I savored a feeling of relief.

Because at that moment I knew that my brother was alive.

45

Probably meant to kill Lauren, too, not just give her a concussion, Victor had said.

But I hadn't said anything about a concussion.

All I'd told him was that Lauren had been attacked and had woken up in the hospital. He had another source of information, I was sure. Even though he'd pretended that this was the first he was hearing about it. And given how many times the two of them had spoken in the last month, it was likely that his source was Roger.

If so, that meant that Roger had talked to him after his disappearance.

And thus that Roger was not only still alive but able to receive phone calls. Which meant that he was not a hostage, not a kidnapping victim, not imprisoned somewhere. He was in hiding.

But he was reachable. Since Victor couldn't receive incoming calls, that meant that he had called Roger.

And that phone number had to be on a list here at the prison. Inmates were allowed to make outgoing collect calls only, to an approved list of up to fifteen telephone numbers.

After I spent a few minutes schmoozing with my new friend, the guard who sat outside the visitors' room, I confessed to him my concern that my father might be trying to reconnect with some of his old business colleagues. Wasn't that against prison rules?

He was only too happy to go on the computer and pull up Victor's approved telephone list. I gave him fifty dollars for his research assistance and thanked him for helping keep my father on the straight and narrow.

As I drove into the Albany International Airport, I called Frank the information broker.

"Didn't I tell you to be patient?" he said before I could even give him the one number from Victor's phone list that I didn't recognize.

"This is about something else, Frank."

"Yeah, well, I got the information you wanted on that cell number you gave me."

It took me a second to remember which number he was talking about: the one that Woody, from the cargo company, had given me in Los Angeles. "Great," I said. "What have you got?"

"It's a corporate account. Registered to a Carl Koblenz."

"Paladin Worldwide," I said.

"You already knew this?"

"I know the name."

So the president of Paladin Worldwide had hired Woody to steal almost a billion dollars from Traverse Development. That was corporate theft on a truly grand scale.

And then the pieces began to click into place. If my father was telling me the truth—which, of course, wasn't a given—then Roger had discovered evidence that Paladin Worldwide had been paying kickbacks to the Pentagon. Once they found out what he had, they began to threaten him. He knew they planned to kidnap him, maybe even kill him.

And so he vanished before they had the chance.

But what about that billion dollars? Maybe Paladin, which did a lot of work in Iraq, had learned that Traverse Development—whoever they were—was shipping all this cash back to the U.S., and Paladin had decided to help themselves. A billion dollars was a lot of bribes.

"I sent you your brother's phone bills," Frank said, interrupting my reverie. "You ever get them?"

"I did, thanks," I said. "And I have one more for you."

46

Throughout the morning, Lauren found herself checking her e-mail far too often.

She was checking for e-mails from Roger. As foolish as that was.

Give it up, she told herself. *There won't be any more from him.*

Stop torturing yourself.

She'd gotten to work late, because she'd had to let in Nick's friend to overhaul the home-security system. That was okay: Leland was out of the country, so things were slower than usual. Just before lunch, she looked up from her e-mail and saw a man sitting in one of the visitor chairs. She did a double take.

She remembered seeing him come out of Leland's office. The man was remarkably . . . well, homely. Ugly, not to put too fine a point on it. His face was deeply pitted with scars, obviously the victim of a terrible case of adolescent acne. He wore horn-rimmed glasses and had thinning brown hair, round shoulders, a pigeon chest.

"Hi?" she said.

"I didn't want to disturb you," the man said. He stood up awkwardly, and a leather portfolio slipped out of his hand and hit the floor. He leaned over to retrieve it, and when he came back up his scarred face was flushed. Looking embarrassed, he approached her desk, extended his hand to shake. "Um, I'm Lloyd Kozak. I don't know if Leland mentioned me—I'm his new financial adviser?"

Lauren looked over at Noreen, who said, "Hello there, Lloyd."

"Oh, yes—Noreen, right?" He went over to Noreen's desk and shook her hand, too. "I'm sorry, I didn't see you." He looked over at Lauren, back at Noreen, seeming trapped between the two women. "I just—did Leland leave any computer disks for me?"

Lauren shook her head. "He didn't say anything—"

"Oh, sure, right here," Noreen said, and she produced a manila envelope and handed it to the man.

"Thank you," he said to her, then he went over to Lauren's desk and said, "I'm sorry to disturb you."

"No worries," Lauren said.

The man hurried away.

Lauren waited until he was gone then said to Noreen, "Leland didn't say anything to me about a financial adviser."

"I thought I told you about him."

"Well, yes, you did. But Leland didn't mention it."

"Cool your jets," Noreen said. "Leland told me the guy was going to stop by today and asked me to give him some stuff. It's no big deal."

"Well, he didn't say anything, that's all."

"You don't expect him to explain everything twice, do you?"

"Of course not."

"Well, all right, then."

Lauren made a mental note to ask about this financial adviser when Leland got back. She couldn't help feeling a little hurt, though. Normally, she handled everything for him. He kept no secrets from her. It was silly, she realized, but she felt a little left out. And no doubt Noreen loved it. She was preening over a tiny piece of Leland's personal life that she, and only she, knew something about.

Lauren really disliked the woman.

In the early afternoon, right after lunch, she checked her e-mail again and found a message from an address she didn't recognize. Its subject line read: "For Lauren—Personal."

She clicked on it.

Inside the message box there was no text. Just a dark gray rectangle that she could tell right away was a video player, the sort you see all over the Internet: a frame with video toolbar buttons at its bottom edge. A big pale gray circle right in the middle containing a white triangular play button. It virtually shouted to her, *Click me! Click me!*

She thought for a moment. The thing looked suspicious. Possibly dangerous.

She checked the sender line and saw that it was blank. Which was strange—she was certain there'd been something there a few seconds ago.

But the sender's name was gone.

There was only the video-player window. The big white triangular play button taunting her.

After a few seconds, she couldn't resist any longer. She clicked on the triangle. The gray rectangle came to life: a streaming video image began to move. Black-and-white. Fuzzy and indistinct at first. Shadowy shapes. She couldn't make anything out.

But then the video became sharper, as if the fog had cleared, and there was something eerily familiar about the scene she was watching. Something she couldn't put her finger on, but familiar all the same. A white-shrouded figure, shifting slowly, which became a lump beneath rumpled bed sheets. Someone asleep in bed. There was a voyeuristic, quasi-porno quality to the movie she was watching. But what was it? Why was it so familiar? She clicked the full-screen button, and the video took over her entire monitor. The resolution wasn't great; the contrast was harsh, as if it had been shot at night, using infrared light or something.

The restlessly sleeping figure turned over, and she recognized the long eyelashes, the curly hair. Her head swam, and her heart skittered as the camera zoomed in and held tight on Gabe's face.

Her son, asleep in bed.

She gasped aloud.

Suddenly the video stopped playing, and the dark gray window shrank back to the size it had been at first, the white triangle at its center. With unsteady fingers, she fumbled for the computer mouse and tried to click the play button again, but the dark gray square was gone. It had vanished, like the Cheshire cat in *Alice in Wonderland*.

Leaving not a trace.

As if it had never been there.

47

I had plenty of time before my flight left the airport, so I held on to the rental car awhile longer, left the parking lot, and drove around, just thinking. The roads here were broad and newly paved, with far less congestion than Washington, and in a few miles I passed the Colonie Public Library. On an impulse, I turned in.

In the Internet age, public libraries are immensely undervalued as resources. Sometimes there's just no substitute for books on shelves and old newspapers, even microfilm copies. Far too many local newspapers just aren't searchable through Google. Even those that have search engines accessible on the Internet are often poorly indexed. Most of the good stuff you have to find the old-fashioned way.

I found a set of indexes for a Michigan newspaper, the *Grand Rapids Press,* and began searching year by year for articles on the reclusive founder of Paladin, Allen Granger. Since his family was from northern Michigan, I figured there was a chance I'd find some interesting local coverage, something that might tell me something that I hadn't read in *Time* or *Newsweek.*

While I leafed through volume after volume, my cell

phone rang. The periodicals librarian gave me a look, and I shut it off without glancing at the caller ID. I found quite a few articles on Granger, but almost all of them were wire-service dispatches, and none of them was news to me. Lots of pieces on Paladin and various controversies their employees had run into in Iraq. Articles about Allen Granger testifying before Congress. He hadn't testified before Congress in a year, though. Neither had he done any in-person interviews, as far as I could tell. An interview in which "Mr. Granger spoke to the Associated Press by telephone from Paladin headquarters in southern Georgia." In the last year, Carl Koblenz, identified as chief executive officer of Paladin Worldwide, based in Falls Church, Virginia, seemed to have taken over the public-spokesman role. Granger hadn't been seen in public in over a year.

I had to go back quite a few years before I was able to find any local interviews with Allen Granger. Fifteen years, in fact.

I went to the periodicals desk and requested the roll of microfilm from the *Grand Rapids Press*. Ten minutes later, I was scrolling through the scratchy old microfilm, trying to suppress a wave of motion sickness, and finally located the interview, done by a Grand Rapids reporter, who described Allen Granger as the "handsome scion" of a "waste-management empire" and "former Navy SEAL." The photo they ran confirmed the handsome part, anyway: He had a clean-cut, blue-eyed, wholesome Midwestern look. Granger told the reporter about how he'd just recently purchased ten thousand acres of pine forest in southern Georgia as a training facility for what he envisioned as "the FedEx of national security," whatever that meant.

The last line of the interview said, "For Allen Granger, it's a long way from Traverse City."

Traverse City, Michigan, was Granger's hometown.

And Traverse Development? Could that be another one of his firms?

I was thoroughly confused. Why would the president of Paladin Worldwide have hired some guy in a shipping company to steal a billion dollars' worth of cash from *another* one of Allen Granger's companies?

Unless Granger didn't know what Koblenz was doing.

I couldn't begin to make sense of this.

Stepping outside into the blindingly bright sunshine, I checked my voice mail.

"Heller," Dorothy Duval said in a quiet voice. "Call me. We got trouble."

48

"What's wrong?" I said.

"I didn't think Stoddard even knew where my cubicle was. He just walked up to my desk and told me that I've been abusing office resources."

"You getting all your work in on time?"

"You know it doesn't work like that around here. I'm not on the clock."

"Exactly. You tell him what you do on your own time is your business."

"First of all, Nick, I've never talked to Stoddard that way, and I'm not going to start now. I'm not like you. I'm disposable."

"You're the best, Dorothy, and you know it. None of the other forensic techs get invited to the Monday morning meetings."

"Yeah, well, as far as Jay Stoddard is concerned, I'm one of about a thousand data-recovery specialists out there, most of whom would jump at the chance to work here." She lowered her voice. "And he's probably right."

"He's not going to fire you for helping me locate my brother."

"Oh no? He as much as said so. He said if I do any more database searches on Traverse Development or

Roger Heller or anything that's not a Stoddard project, I better update my résumé."

"Dorothy," I said. "You know I've got your back."

"Must be why they always get me from the front," she said acidly. "You don't have the power to keep him from firing me, Nick."

"Don't be so sure of that."

"Uh-huh," she said. "Right. I'll believe it when I see it."

"Let's hope it doesn't come to that. Any luck on that list of office-building tenants I faxed you?"

"Nothing. I'm sorry."

"What are you doing, running every company name to see if they're subsidiaries of other companies?"

"That would take forever. No, I'm running them against this Traverse Development. But no luck yet."

"And Roger's laptop?"

"Looks like it's mostly personal stuff. E-mails and all that."

"Can you send it to me?"

"No. But I'll give you what I got when I see you."

Call waiting came on, and I saw that it was Garvin. "Dorothy," I said, "would you mind—?"

"Take the call, Nick."

"Thanks. You're the best."

"I'm glad you appreciate it," she said. "Because this is the last job I can do for you. See, Nick, I need a paycheck."

When I clicked over to Garvin's call, he began abruptly, without even identifying himself: "This is interesting."

"Let's hear it."

"I got back a trace on both of those tags—the Econoline van and that black Humvee?" Like most cops, Garvin called license plates "tags."

"And?"

"And they both trace back to the same owner."

"Makes sense," I said. "Who is it?"

"The registration on file in both cases seems to be a holding company."

I waited.

"Something called A.G. Holdings."

"Is there an address?"

"Just a P.O. box."

"Okay," I said. "That helps. That helps a lot."

I hung up, and a minute later I was talking to Dorothy again.

She cut me off: "I told you, Nick, I can't do any more work for you."

"I just need you to look at that tenant list I faxed you."

"Just look at it?"

"Right."

"I got it right here."

"Is there a tenant in that building called A.G. Holdings?"

There was a long pause, a rustling of paper. Finally: "Seventh floor," she said.

"Nice," I said.

"What?"

"A.G. Holdings is Allen Granger."

"I don't understand."

"I'm not sure I do either," I said. "But I intend to find out."

49

It seemed like the more I knew, the less I understood.

Paladin Worldwide and Traverse Development and A.G. Holdings—they were all the same company. Or to put it more accurately, they all shared ownership, which wasn't quite the same thing. One of them owned the other. Maybe it didn't make any difference which company owned the other. They were all Allen Granger.

Okay, fine. So one of Paladin's subsidiaries, Traverse Development, secretly shipped a billion dollars' worth of cash into the United States, only the cash went missing. Why? Because it was stolen by the security director of the shipping company.

Who'd been hired by the same company that shipped it over in the first place.

So in essence, Paladin Worldwide was stealing from itself.

Or, maybe more to the point, Carl Koblenz was stealing from his own company. Maybe that was it. Maybe he was embezzling money on a grand scale.

Maybe Carl Koblenz had tried to steal a billion dollars, and Roger had found out and tried to extort hush money from him to keep it quiet. And Koblenz had decided it would be easier just to abduct, perhaps kill, Roger.

And Roger had somehow managed to escape their clutches.

Okay. But then why would Paladin—under the name of one of its subsidiaries, or holding companies, Traverse Development—hire my firm to track down the missing cash?

The only explanation that made any sense to me was that Stoddard Associates had been hired not by Carl Koblenz but by Allen Granger. In other words, Paladin's CEO had no idea that his own president had stolen a billion dollars from the company.

And Roger had stepped into the middle of that mess.

And so had I.

As I returned to the airport parking lot, I called a guy I didn't know, a friend of a friend who worked for Paladin Worldwide. His name was Neil Burris, an ex–Navy SEAL, and he worked out of Paladin's Falls Church office in their private-security division.

He didn't sound very friendly on the phone. But after I identified myself as Marty Masur of Stoddard Associates and told him that Stoddard was interested in possibly hiring him, at a salary at least twice what he was making at Paladin, he warmed up.

We arranged to meet for drinks.

50

With a trembling hand, Lauren picked up the phone to call Nick.

Her heart was racing. Her mouth was dry. She was nauseated, light-headed. The room seemed to be spinning slowly, and she had the physical sensation of falling through space.

How could someone have taken video of Gabe sleeping? Had someone sneaked in during the night? Was there some sort of hidden camera in his room? Could it possibly be?

And who could have done such a thing?

Feeling as if she were about to vomit, she put the phone down. No. It would be a mistake to call Nick. He'd already unearthed things about Roger and about their family life that she wished he hadn't. How in the world had he discovered Roger's affair, that terrible, gut-wrenching thing that had so blighted their marriage? She wished Gabe had never asked Nick to help.

Then she opened the St. Gregory's website—Harvard crimson, elegant font, the school's coat of arms—and found the main switchboard number on the bottom of the page. She picked up the phone again and called the school.

She recognized the voice of the woman who answered—the receptionist, Mrs. Jordan—and began speaking all in a rush. "Ruth, this is Gabe Heller's mom, Lauren Heller? I wonder, do you think you could check to see if Gabe's in school today?"

"Oh, hello, Mrs. Heller. Is there a problem?"

"No, not at all, I left the house early, and you know how late these boys sleep, and . . ."

Mrs. Jordan chuckled softly. Lauren could hear her typing. She stared at the school's seal. The Latin motto: *Mens Sana in Corpore Sano.* What did that mean, "A Healthy Mind in a Healthy Body"? She wondered what the Latin was for "More Rich Assholes Than You Can Shake a Stick At."

She couldn't breathe.

"He's in today," she said. "I think he's in science right now. Did you want to get a message to him?"

Lauren let her breath out slowly. "No, I—" She hesitated. "Actually, yes, Ruth. Can you tell him that I'll pick him up from school today?"

She looked up the cell-phone number of Kate Vaughan, the mom who was scheduled to drive the car pool in the afternoons this week. She called Kate and told her not to drive Gabe home.

She could leave work early today. Leland wasn't here, and Noreen would be more than happy to hold down the fort.

She needed to see her son and make sure he was all right.

51

That headache was back.

The same throbbing in her temples and her forehead, the feeling that her head was a lightbulb that could explode at any moment. That sensation of needles jabbing into the back of her eyeballs.

She could barely concentrate on the road. Since she never left work so early, she had no idea how bad the traffic on the George Washington Parkway was in the midafternoon. It was only two thirty, not even rush hour, and it was already bumper-to-bumper.

And her head was about to explode.

In her mind she kept replaying that video of Gabe asleep in bed, over and over until she wanted to scream.

St. Gregory's School was located on a verdant campus off Wisconsin Avenue, near the National Cathedral. It looked like an Ivy League school. It sure cost like an Ivy League school. She drove in past the tennis courts, past the huge new athletic facility, and pulled into a long line of very expensive SUVs. In front of her was a Range Rover. Behind her was a Porsche Cayenne Turbo.

The whole scene felt unfamiliar to her. Yet at the same time sort of nice. Picking your kid up from school—that was something she really missed. Not since Gabe was in first grade had she picked him up from school and taken him home. That was in the early years of working for Leland, and it had been hard to arrange time off, but she'd done it. Seven years ago. Apart from a few days when he was sick, anyway.

There was a time when Lauren knew she could keep Gabe safe. Once she'd been able to pick him up in the palm of one hand. She could still his cries by offering him a bottle or her breast, by patting his back until he gave a tiny burp, by wrapping him up in his blankets as snugly as an egg roll.

But then you send your kid out into the world and anything can happen.

The pickup area was jammed with SUVs pulling in and out, jousting with one another like some high-end monster-truck rally.

The tap of a car horn. A blue Toyota Land Cruiser had pulled up alongside her. The window glided down.

"Lauren?"

Kate Vaughan. A pretty blond woman, very jocky, who wore her hair in a ponytail. A major squash player. Lauren had heard that the Vaughans had had a squash court built in their home. She had three sons, two of them at St. Gregory's, all three serious squash players, the eldest one nationally ranked. Four boys were in the back two rows, tussling and arguing.

Lauren looked up, waved.

"I got your message about Gabe. You guys going somewhere?"

"No, just—boss is out of town. Did you see Gabe up there?"

"Haven't seen him, sorry. Are you okay? I heard you were in an accident."

"Oh, I'm fine, thanks."

"And, um . . . Roger? Do they know anything more?"

Lauren shook her head.

"God, Lauren, you must be so *worried*." A huge black Cadillac Escalade behind Kate's Toyota was trying to lumber by and honked loudly.

"I am."

Kate's son, Kip, in the front seat, said something to her, and she swatted him away. "Will you chill, kids, okay? God, Lauren. You know, I once heard about something called wandering amnesia? It's like a . . . fugue state? It's triggered by stress—you just all of a sudden forget who you are, and you could be wandering around, and—"

The Escalade blasted its horn.

Kate flipped the bird out the window at the Escalade's driver. "Sheesh, can you believe this guy? All right, I better move it. Keep me posted, okay? I'm sure it's totally nothing. But God, it's so scary, huh?"

"I will. Thanks."

Hers was one of the last cars to reach the pickup spot. The crowd of boys waiting there, laughing and shoving and shouting to one another, was thinning, and she didn't see Gabe.

Her forehead was throbbing, and she felt a tightness in her chest.

Maybe he hadn't gotten the message that she'd be picking him up.

Unlikely. Mrs. Jordan, the school secretary, was a hundred percent reliable. St. Gregory's was scrupulous about keeping track of its students' whereabouts at all times. The sons of some very rich and important people—senators and Supreme Court justices and presidents of foreign countries—went here. The parents had to be assured that their kids were safe.

Gabe tended to be pretty spacey, though. He could easily have forgotten she was coming. But then he would have gotten into Kate Vaughan's car, and she'd have told him to wait for his mom.

The car in front of her pulled away, and she drove up to the curb, and there was no one there.

No Gabe.

She called his cell phone.

It rang four, five, six times, then went to voice mail. Or whatever you called that blast of hideous music that she didn't have the patience to get through before his recorded voice came on.

Maybe he'd forgotten to carry his cell phone. That was very Gabe. He didn't use it much, often left it at home or in his locker at school.

She switched off the engine and got out. You weren't supposed to park here, but she didn't care. She ran up the concrete path to the Middle School building, heart thudding.

A small pile of backpacks in the foyer, and three boys were sitting on the floor, one of them showing the others something on his iPod.

"Any of you kids seen Gabe Heller?" she asked.

They shrugged. They weren't in his grade, didn't know who he was. She kept going, up the big stone staircase to the school secretary's office.

Mrs. Jordan, a handsome middle-aged black woman, was on the phone, smiled at her, nodded, put the phone on hold.

"Mrs. Heller, why are you—?"

Lauren, trying to sound casual, trying not to sound like the crazed neurotic mom, said, "Have you seen Gabe?"

Mrs. Jordan, who monitored all the students' absences and late arrivals and early departures from her command post, looked perplexed. "He got picked up half an hour early, like you told me."

Lauren shook her head. "No, I said to tell him that *I* was going to pick him up today. I didn't say anything about coming early."

"Right, but then you called back to say the police needed to talk to him."

"The *police*—?"

"A couple of policemen stopped by just like you said, and I sent them over to his English class to get him and—"

The room seemed to revolve.

"I never called—"

Lauren turned around, her legs feeling wobbly, lurching out of the office.

"I'm sorry, Mrs. Heller? What you said was—"

But Lauren, running toward her car, heard no more.

52

When my Delta flight landed at Reagan National, I switched my phone and my BlackBerry back on. I had five voice messages on my cell. Three from Lauren.

Gabe had gone missing.

My first thought, before I returned her call, was that Gabe was probably just acting out. After all, he was upset, under pressure, worried sick about his dad. On top of his problems at school. And . . . well, just being Gabe.

But when I finally reached her, she told me he'd been picked up by a couple of uniformed D.C. cops, and she'd been unable to reach him on his cell phone. She was terrified. I tried to calm her down, assured her it was very likely Lieutenant Garvin or his guys, and that I'd give him a call.

But then she told me about an anonymous e-mail she'd gotten at the office—a video clip of Gabe asleep in his bed, clearly a surveillance video taken by a concealed camera in his bedroom.

At that point I knew something was very wrong. I reached Garvin on his cell phone and asked him whether he'd sent uniformed officers over to St. Gregory's School to talk to Gabe for some reason.

He hadn't. They weren't from Violent Crimes, or he'd know about it.

I asked him to check the radio runs to see if any police officers had been dispatched to Gabe's school for some other reason. None had.

I drove to Chevy Chase at top speed.

Lauren let me in. Her face was flushed and her makeup was smeared and she'd obviously been crying.

"We'll find him," I said.

She shook her head, sniffled, rubbed her nose with the back of her hand. She was still dressed in work clothes, still as gorgeous as ever, but she looked gutted.

"He's here," she said.

"He's been here the whole time?"

She shook her head again. "They brought him home. They picked him up at school and brought him home."

"Who did?"

"I don't know. It just sounds totally bizarre. It doesn't make sense to me. . . . Just, can you talk to him, Nick?"

"What happened?"

"Maybe he'll talk to you. He won't talk to me."

"Is he okay?"

"*He's* fine. But we can't stay here anymore. It's just not safe."

"Lauren."

"I'm taking Gabe, and I'm getting out of here. Go stay with my sister, maybe."

"Lauren," I said. "Let me talk to him."

53

I could hear the tinny rasp coming from Gabe's iPod earbuds even before I opened the door. He was lying on his bed, wearing a black *Nightmare Before Christmas* T-shirt, reading a paperback. On the cover was some guy in a Roman-gladiator outfit holding a gleaming sword and flying through the air. No doubt one of the sci-fi/fantasy series he devoured along with every comic book ever published.

He didn't look up.

I sat down on the side of the bed. "Hey," I said.

He kept reading. Maybe it was a generational thing, but I didn't understand how he could read at the same time he was listening to music like that. I couldn't.

Actually, I couldn't floss my teeth while listening to music like that, but whatever.

"I want to hear what happened," I said.

He kept looking at the book, but his eyes weren't scanning the page.

"What happened, Gabe?" I said.

No response.

I reached over and yanked the earbuds out of his ears with one hard tug.

"Hey!" he squawked.

"What'd they do to you?" I said.

He glared at me. "Why? So you can tell Mom? She's all whacked out over it."

"She was scared. Can't blame her. What'd they do?"

"Like, did they arrest me or something?" He gave me that prototypical teenage glower and put his book facedown on the bed. "They wanted to ask me stuff."

"Like what?"

"I don't know, all kinds of stuff."

"Did they take you somewhere?"

"No. They just talked on the way."

"On the way?"

"They picked me up at school and brought me home. They knew where I lived and everything. I didn't even have to give them directions."

"And what did they ask you?"

"Lots of questions."

"Like?"

"Like, does Dad have any safe-deposit boxes, and where he keeps the keys, and like that. Does he stash stuff anywhere in the house? Is there like a panic room or some kind of hidden room in the house where he might have kept stuff? Where do we go on vacation, and do Dad and Mom have any places they like to travel to? They wanted names of Dad's friends and relatives and like that. Anything I could think of."

"Did they tell you why they wanted to know all this?"

"Of course. They said they're trying to find him. They said maybe he left files or notes or something. Stuff that might tell them where he went. People who might know where he'd gone."

"And . . . you answered all their questions, right?"

"I sure did."

My stomach sank.

"I told them Dad has a safe-deposit box at Chevy

Chase Bank, only I forgot which branch. I told them I was pretty sure Dad was hiding out at our house on Cape Cod."

"House on Cape Cod," I repeated.

"Wellfleet."

"No one told me about this house in Wellfleet," I said.

"That's because we don't have one. He also doesn't have a safe-deposit box at the Chevy Chase Bank. As far as I know. Come on, dude, what kind of detective are you, anyway?"

54

Momentarily stunned, I noticed the little smile pulling at the edges of Gabe's mouth, and I couldn't help smiling myself. "You lied to them," I said.

"Misled them," Gabe said. "Okay, I lied to them."

"You figured out they weren't real cops."

"Thing is, Uncle Nick, they were driving a Crown Vic like all plainclothes cops drive, and they were wearing blue uniforms with shoulder patches that said MET-ROPOLITAN POLICE, so at first they looked totally for real. They even showed me their badges. But you can buy badges and police uniforms and all that stuff on the Internet."

"So what made you realize they were fake?"

"They didn't have a police radio installed."

"Excellent."

"And they didn't have those strobe light thingies, the kind the cops take out and put on the roof of their car when they're chasing speeders."

"Very nice."

"And I didn't smell doughnuts." He grinned, and I grinned back.

"You did good," I said.

"Tell that to Mom."

"I will." I leaned over to pat him on the shoulder, and I noticed his face had gotten strangely contorted, and there were tears in his eyes. He made a hiccuping sound. He was trying not to cry.

"I was scared out of my mind, Uncle Nick," he said.

"I know," I said. I tried to hug him, but it was awkward, the way he was lying back on the bed. Then he leaned forward and gave me a hug.

"Who are they?" he said.

"I don't know."

"You don't know, or you won't tell me?"

"At this point, I can only guess, and I don't want to do that."

He let go, turned around, sat on the edge of the bed, looked back at me. "So what was the point of all that? Were they just trying to scare Mom and me?"

"Maybe."

"For what?"

"I don't know."

"Are . . . are we safe?"

I hesitated far too long. "I don't know."

"Are you going to stay in the house, or are you going back to the fortress of solitude?"

"I told you, Gabe. You can't get rid of me that easy."

"Are you going to teach me how to use a gun?"

"No."

"Why not?"

"Have a little faith in me," I said.

He made a derisory snort.

"What's the matter?" I said. "You don't trust me?"

He rolled his eyes.

"Listen," I said. "There was once this legendary French acrobat named Charles Blondin, okay? He was famous in the nineteenth century for doing these impossible daredevil tightrope-walking stunts. He strung a rope across Niagara Falls, a thousand feet long. And this crowd gathered and he walked on the tightrope over the falls, hundreds of feet above the gorge, and the crowd went crazy when he got to the other side, clapping and cheering."

Gabe gave me a skeptical glance. "Yeah?"

"And then he said to the crowd, 'Do you believe I can do it again?' and the crowd cheered, 'Yes!' And he did it. And the crowd cheered even louder, and he said, 'Do you believe I can do it wearing a blindfold?' And some people in the crowd got scared and shouted, 'No, don't do it,' and others said, 'Yes! You can do it!'"

"And he fell," Gabe said.

I shook my head. "He did it, and the crowd cheered even louder, and he said, 'Do you believe I can do it on stilts this time?' And the crowd shouted out, "Yes! You can do it!' And he did it, and the crowd roared and got even wilder. So then he said, 'Do you believe I can do it pushing a wheelbarrow along the rope?' And the crowd roared and cheered and said, 'Yes!' And Blondin said, 'You really think I can? You believe it?' And they shouted, 'Yes! Yes, you can!'"

Despite himself, despite his teenage cynicism, he was actually listening. For a moment he almost seemed to be a child again, listening to a bedtime story. "Is this true?"

"Yes."

"He actually did it?"

"Yep. He did it. He walked across the tightrope hundreds of feet above the gorge pushing a wheelbarrow, and when he made it to the other side the audience had grown huge and frenzied and totally worked up and they cheered. Really went crazy. So Blondin said, 'Do you believe I can do it again but this time pushing a man in this wheelbarrow?' And the crowd roared and said, 'Yes!' He said, 'You really believe I can do it?' And they all went, 'Yes, definitely! You can do it! We believe in you! Yes! Absolutely!' By that time the crowd was completely behind him. They thought he could do anything. So Blondin said, 'Then who will volunteer to sit in the wheelbarrow?' And the crowd suddenly went quiet. Totally silent. And he said, 'What's the matter? You don't believe in me anymore?' And they were silent for a long time before someone from the crowd finally said, 'Yes, we believe in you. But not *that* much.'"

"Huh. Did anyone ever volunteer to get in the wheelbarrow?"

I shrugged.

"How'd the guy die?"

"In bed. Forty years later. From diabetes."

"Bummer."

"Better than falling to his death, don't you think?"

"Can I use that in my novel?"

"All yours."

"So what's your point, Nick? We all die someday, is that it?"

"No. I'm just telling you, sometimes you just gotta have a little faith." I stood up. "Good night, Gabe." As I walked out of his bedroom, he said, "Hey, Uncle Nick?"

"Yeah?"

He hurled something at me, and I caught it in mid-air.

His notebook. His graphic novel.

"Let me know what you think," he said.

Then it was my turn to tear up.

55

Lauren was racing wildly around her bedroom, tossing clothes into a couple of suitcases on the bed. Her face was flushed, glistening with perspiration.

"Chill," I said. "Take a nice, deep breath."

"No, Nick. I can't. We can't stay here."

"Lauren, sit down, please."

"Will you at least tell me what happened to him this afternoon?"

"I will if you sit down."

Slowly, grudgingly, she lowered herself onto the ottoman of the big overstuffed reading chair in the corner. I gave her a quick summary of what had happened to Gabe and how deftly he'd handled it.

"So they were fake cops," she said. "Impostors."

I nodded.

"They're trying to find Roger, aren't they?"

"Maybe," I said. "But I don't think getting information was the point of that exercise. That was a threat. Just like that video clip you got today. We're watching you. You and your son, you're vulnerable. You're not safe anywhere."

The blood seemed to drain from her face. "And this is supposed to calm me *down*?" she said, her voice rising.

"I'm not here to calm you down."

She began speaking quickly, almost muttering to herself. "My sister doesn't have room for us. But we can stay with Mom for a few days while I look for something."

"What makes you think you'll be any safer in your mother's apartment? Or in some Comfort Inn somewhere? You think they can't track you down? I don't think there's any hiding from them."

"Jesus, Nick!" She got to her feet.

"Did my guy Merlin come by today to put in the new security system?"

"Yeah?"

"I want you to start using it."

"For what?" she said sharply. "So we can stay locked up inside the house all day with the alarm on like, like, it's a fortress? You think we're really safe here? And what happens when Gabe goes to school? You think they're not going to grab him again? And this time—"

"If anyone wanted to hurt you or Gabe, they'd have done it already. I don't think that's what they want."

"Then what do they want?"

"My guess? Cooperation."

"Cooperation? On *what*?"

I answered her question with one of my own: "What are you keeping from me?"

"I'm not keeping anything from you."

"Lauren. You have something they want."

"I have no idea what anyone could possibly want from me."

"Look," I said. "I saw my father this morning."

"Victor? In prison?"

"Where else? And he told me that Roger tried to extort a lot of money from a private military company called Paladin Worldwide."

Eyes wide, she shook her head. "I don't believe that. Roger? No way."

"Well, whatever Roger did or didn't do, I'm sure that's who these people are. Paladin. And they're not messing around. You have something they want. Maybe something Roger left for you, whether you're aware of it or not. And if you don't give it to them, they'll take something from you. Something very important to you."

"Don't say that. God, Nick, don't say that."

"The meaning of the threat was obvious. But it didn't contain a single explicit demand. So what do you have that they want?"

"I don't have the slightest idea!"

"Roger said in that e-mail that he'd taken precautions to protect you. That he'd given you the means to hold them off. What else aren't you telling me?"

She shook her head again, this time more violently. "I don't know what he meant by that. He never told me anything about any extortion. He never mentioned this . . . Paladin. You have to believe me. I'm telling you everything I know."

"You told me everything was fine between you two," I said.

She paused, frowned, and said, "That was different. That was . . . personal. I didn't think it was right to talk about that with you. I'm not withholding anything."

I was tempted to press her on that point. But instead I said, "Look, I want to do everything I can to protect you guys. So I need you to think really hard about anything Roger might have said to you, maybe something that didn't mean anything at the time. Or something he gave you."

"I'm telling you, Nick, I can't think of anything. You think I'd ever hold out on you, with Gabe's life at stake?"

"Of course not. Not knowingly. Not consciously. But I need you to think really hard."

"I will."

"And give me the chance to find these guys. The only solution is to flush them out and neutralize them."

" 'Neutralize'? Meaning what, exactly?"

"I'll know when I get there. Have a little confidence in me, please."

She paused, swallowed hard. "All right," she said. "But one more threat—one more phone call or e-mail or anything like what happened today, and I'm taking Gabe and driving as far away from here as I can."

"Deal."

She reached out her hand, and we shook. Once, up and down, firmly. Then for the first time she noticed Gabe's notebook in my other hand. "He gave that to you?"

"He just wants my expert opinion."

"Why you?"

"No idea," I said.

"I'm his *mom,* for God's sake."

"Maybe that's why he didn't want you to see it."

The doorbell rang, and she looked at me, her eyes wary. "Who could that be?"

"Merlin again. And Dorothy, a colleague of mine at work. They're here to sweep the house."

"Sweep it . . . ?"

"For electronic devices. Hidden cameras and microphones, all that sort of thing. And I'm going to have them start in Gabe's room."

"Gabe's room? I don't want him to know about that video thing, Nick. He'll freak out."

"Yeah, maybe," I said. "At first. But give him a little credit. He can handle it."

"You have no idea what it's like to have a kid," she said.

"Can't argue with that."

"It's like you go from all-powerful to powerless. You—you produce this *being* that you want to protect with all of your heart and all of your strength, but then you discover that you can't. You realize that at some point you just can't protect them anymore."

"You know what you can do?" I said softly. "If you really want to protect Gabe and yourself?"

"What?"

"Open up. Level with me. Whatever you're hiding, you need to let me know what it is."

56

Walter McGeorge, aka Merlin, was small and compact, like a lot of Special Forces guys. He had a black buzz cut, a porcine nose, and a pencil-thin mustache. He had deep vertical furrows carved into his forehead, which made him look permanently angry.

I helped him carry his equipment upstairs to Gabe's room: a couple of ridged aluminum cases lined with black polyurethane egg-crate foam and something that looked like a big old video camera out of the early eighties on a tripod.

Gabe gaped as we entered.

"I'm sorry," I said, "but we need to borrow your room for a while."

"For what?"

"Your mom will explain everything," I said.

For a few moments I watched Merlin moving something that looked like a metal detector or a small mine-sweeper along the wall. It was wired to a pair of black headphones he was wearing.

"You haven't found anything yet?"

"Nothing. You sure there's something here?"

"Positive."

"This here's our top-of-the-line spectrum analyzer. Costs a fortune. Sees RF signals in real time. Stuff you normally can't detect."

"And it's not finding anything."

"Right."

"Meaning there aren't any wireless bugs, right?"

"Apparently not. Nothing transmitting right now, anyway. But that thermal-imaging camera over there?"—he pointed at the thing on the tripod—"that's laboratory-grade instrumentation. I mean, that baby can pick up hot spots in the walls to, like, one-eighteen-thousandth of a degree."

"And nothing?"

"Nothing."

"If you do find anything, don't you expect it's going to be a GSM bug?"

He nodded. "If it's really Paladin, yeah. They use government stuff."

The old days, when the guys monitoring an eavesdropping device had to sit in the back of a van on the street close enough to pick up the transmission, were over. Instead the state-of-the-art bugs used the same technology you find in cell phones. They *were* the guts of cell phones, in fact, minus the keypad and the fancy trappings. You could call in to them from anywhere in the world, and they'd answer silently and switch on their microphones, and you could listen in. From anywhere. They were smaller than a pack of cigarettes, sometimes as small as two inches long, and if you wired them to an existing power line, they'd work forever.

They broadcast using cell-phone signals, but only when they were on. So he used the thermal camera to look for any electronic circuitry. Something about the tiny amounts of heat generated by electricity moving through the diodes.

"No luck with that thing either?"

"Nonlinear junction detector," he said. "Sends out a high-frequency pulse, then analyzes the harmonics that bounce back. Should find any electronic devices even if they're off."

"And?"

"I found plenty."

"Oh?"

"Yeah. Clocks, telephones, DVD player—a bunch. Just no bugs. Am I allowed to smoke in here?"

"No."

"Prisons use these bad boys to find contraband cell phones hidden in the walls or floors."

"Really?"

"Yeah. But I'm telling you, Heller, there's nothing."

I tried to help by searching the old-fashioned way—a visual inspection, looking for minute traces in the walls and ceiling. I unscrewed light-switch plates and power-outlet covers and the ceiling light fixture. There were all sorts of ways to conceal cameras these days in things like air purifiers and wall clocks and lamps. There was no end to the possible hiding places.

Merlin and I both worked fast, but half an hour later, he sounded discouraged. "Nothing," he said.

"Some Merlin you are," I said.

"Are we done here?"

"Not yet," I said. "Not until you find it."

57

I could hear Dorothy Duval's raucous laugh as I entered the kitchen. Lauren was making coffee, and Dorothy was helping, or maybe just female bonding. But I knew that Dorothy had a hidden agenda: She was putting Lauren at ease, cajoling her out of her state of anxiety.

"You've been hiding this girl from me," Dorothy said, sipping from a mug.

"I never mix business and pleasure," I said.

A throaty, knowing laugh. "Right. Tell me about it. You didn't tell me she's from C-Ville. I used to spend every summer there, at my grandma's house."

Lauren poured a mug of coffee from a glass carafe, the kind from one of those simple automatic drip coffeemakers, and she handed it to me. I took a sip. "Delicious," I said. "How come I can't make coffee this good?"

"Because you're not using the right machine," Lauren said.

I noticed the beat-up old Hamilton Beach coffee machine on the counter. "You've been hiding that from me. That one I know how to use."

"Roger never liked having it out on the counter. He didn't like the way it looked."

She poured coffee into another stoneware mug. "How does your friend upstairs take his coffee?"

"I have no idea," I said. "We used to boil the freeze-dried instant crap on a folding Esbit stove. Sometimes we'd just chew the coffee granules right out of the MRE bag. If we were in a hurry. But his tastes might have gotten more refined since Afghanistan. Where's Gabe?"

"In the living room, reading."

"You told him?"

She nodded.

"How'd he take it?"

"He said he wasn't surprised."

"Nick," Dorothy said, "can I talk to you for a second?"

"You found something?"

"Right."

"That's all right," I said. "I want Lauren to hear this."

Dorothy looked from me to Lauren, then back at me. "None of my malware-detection kits picked up anything," she said. "So I ended up having to put a box on the line—a network forensics appliance. I finally captured some encrypted traffic going out."

"Encrypted?" I said.

"Bunch of hash marks. Nothing I can read."

"We're talking spyware?" Lauren said.

"That's right," Dorothy said. "Some pretty sophisticated code. Not a commercial, off-the-shelf product like eBlaster. Government-grade, looks like."

"Government-grade?" Lauren said. "Meaning, it's the government that's doing this?"

"Or a government contractor with access to government code."

"So every e-mail we get or send out, every website we visit—"

"Every single keystroke," Dorothy said.

"All my user names and passwords on all my e-mail accounts?"

"Right."

"Paladin's a government contractor, right?" Lauren asked me.

"The U.S. government's their main customer."

"But how could they have installed it? Does that mean they were inside the house?"

"Not necessarily," Dorothy said. "They could have installed this program remotely. But honey, that video they sent you confirms they've been in your house. To plant the camera."

Lauren nodded, bit her lip. "Did that other guy find the camera?" She pointed toward the ceiling.

"Not yet," I said. "But he will."

"I don't understand how that video clip of Gabe could have disappeared," Lauren said. "How could they make it just disappear that way?"

Dorothy nodded. "I know what that is. That's something called VaporLock. It's a kind of private web-based mail system. For recordless electronic communication. Once you open it, the sender's name disappears, then the message disappears."

"Okay," Lauren said. "What's the point of this spyware? They think Roger might contact me, so they want to read any e-mail I might get from him? That it?"

"Maybe."

"So doesn't that tell you they think he's alive?"

I was silent for ten seconds or so. "Possibly," I said.

"And maybe that they really *don't* have him? They don't know where he is?"

"I suppose," I conceded. "But there's a more likely explanation."

"Which is?"

"That they think you have something. And they want it."

"And I keep telling you I have no idea what that could possibly be."

"Maybe it's money," I suggested. "A lot of it."

"That's crazy."

"Or information. Files."

"Well, I don't have anything. Believe me, I don't. They may think I do, but I don't."

"Okay," I said, though I didn't know what to believe.

"Another question," Lauren said. "When parents put spyware on their kids' computers, they sometimes get reports on their e-mail at work or whatever, right? So can't you tell where this program is sending the reports? By looking at the IP address? Won't that tell you who's doing this?"

Dorothy grinned slowly, looked at me. She had a slight gap between her front teeth that I always found cute.

"This girlfriend is extremely clever," she said. "I see computer ignorance doesn't run in the family."

"We're only related by marriage, not blood," I pointed out.

"Clearly," Dorothy said. "The packets are all going out to a botnet in Ukraine—probably one of those Eastern European guys who's put together this illegal network of thousands of infected Windows XP computers all over the world into a Tier 2 Network."

"I think I get some of what you're saying," I said. "I assume the data going out of the DSL line here isn't actually ending up on some illegal network in Ukraine, right?"

"Right. It's just a way to hide where it's really going. So I suggest we keep all the spyware and the bugs in place, and I keep monitoring the traffic until I figure out its final destination. If I can."

"Sounds like a plan," I said. "Do whatever it takes. I'm going upstairs." I took the mug of coffee from the counter. "Merlin's gonna drink it black whether he likes it that way or not."

Merlin still hadn't found anything.

"If there was something here," he said, "it's gone now. How do you know that video wasn't taken a week ago? A month ago, even?"

"I don't," I admitted.

While he searched, I sat at Gabe's desk chair and read his graphic novel. I was astonished at the quality of the drawings. I had never been a big comic-book reader, but for a couple of years, as boys, Roger and I used to exchange old Batman and Superman comics, the occasional *Green Lantern* and *Captain America*. And Gabe's drawings were at least as accomplished as those. He'd done them with an ultrafine-tip black pen, done shadows with cross-hatching. The lettering looked almost professional, too.

But it was the story that blew me away.

He'd titled it *The Escape Artist*. It was the story of a strong-jawed superhero called The Cowl, who fought evildoers in the nation's capital, which was a decaying version of Washington, D.C. The Cowl—so named because he wore a black cowl like Batman—was a dead ringer for me. He even had my black hair, although Gabe had given me a Supermanesque whorl on my forehead, a gleaming forelock, which I don't have. The Cowl had a Dark Past, which seemed to involve a dead wife, and had a dark, brooding temperament. He had a fortress of solitude, which bore more than a passing resemblance to my real-life loft in Adams Morgan. He was able to break out of any prison, escape confinement like Houdini, and he basically beat the crap out of bad guys, most of whom were evil, oversized adolescent boys who dressed like the boys at St. Gregory's, with blazers and slacks, but also seemed to have come out of the pages of *The Lord of the Flies*.

His mother didn't make a single appearance. The archvillain was named Dr. Cash, who looked an awful lot like Roger except that he was hideously deformed, had blue skin, the result of taking colloidal silver. He was the CEO of an evil corporation who had somehow taken over the government in a postapocalyptic coup d'etat and now tyrannized the land from his underground bunker beneath the crumbling ruins of the White House. He was often seen with a busty blonde on his arm, a villainess named Candi Dupont.

Candi Dupont.

Not a name you could easily forget.

Candi Dupont was the woman Roger had been having an affair with, whose abortion he had paid for. An alias, surely: Dorothy had turned up nothing on her in any database. But whatever her real name, obviously Gabe knew about her as well.

Dorothy entered the room, interrupting my reading. "You didn't turn the kid's computer back on, did you?"

I closed the notebook.

"No," Merlin said.

"Because I thought I turned off both computers, and I'm definitely detecting outgoing network traffic. Something's still transmitting a signal over the Internet."

"Thanks," Merlin said mordantly. "That helps a whole lot."

"That tells us there's something in the house," I said. "Something that's broadcasting, right?"

Merlin shrugged. "So we keep looking."

"Man, this kid's Richie Rich," Dorothy said, ogling all Gabe's stuff. "Look at all this junk. He's got video games and iPods and boom boxes and a Game Boy and a Nintendo Wii and a PlayStation 3 and an Xbox 360.

And I thought *my* nephew was spoiled. Did you check all the electronics?"

"Yeah," Merlin said. "I found a number of semiconductors."

"Yeah, thanks," she replied. "All electronic devices have semiconductors. I get your sarcasm. But isn't that where you actually *want* to look? In with a lot of other electronic circuits?"

"Yeah," Merlin said, unwilling to let go of the sarcasm. "That's just where I'd hide a camera. In a Game Boy that gets moved around everywhere."

"I don't know why you're even bothering to look over there," Dorothy told him. "The camera angle's all wrong. Lauren described the shot to me, and that camera's gonna be just above eye level." She sliced the air with her hand flat, moving back and forth along a precise horizontal.

I nodded, approached Gabe's desk, looked at the giant iPod/CD player with the built-in speakers. The one he put his iPod in to use as an alarm every morning. It was covered with a fine film of dust.

A small area on the front console, though, was dust-free.

Right around an LED light that didn't seem to belong. I grasped the tiny bulb and pulled and out came the long black snake cable that was attached to it.

"Holy crap," Merlin said.

"Mm-hm," Dorothy said.

In a few minutes Merlin had carefully disassembled the CD player and placed the components on top of a pile of Gabe's books. "Hoo boy," he said excitedly. "This is really cool. I've never seen one of these ultraminis before. It's a Misumi—a Taiwanese company. Hooked up to a wireless video IP encoder that takes the analog signal and transmits it over the Internet."

"So how come *you* didn't find it?" Dorothy said.

"Because they wrapped it in neoprene to hide the heat signature. Very clever. But how'd they know where to put it? They must have checked out the house in advance."

I thought of the disabled sensors in Roger's study and said, "For sure." Then I looked at my watch. "Thank you, guys. I owe you big-time."

"Just add it to my favor bank account," Dorothy said.

"You got it."

"Man, I'm looking forward to cashing in," she said.

"Substantial penalty for early withdrawal," I warned her as I walked toward the door. "I'll catch up with you guys soon."

"You have a date or something?"

"Nah," I said. "I'm meeting an old buddy for a drink."

58

The Anchor Tavern was a dive bar's dive bar a few blocks from Capitol Hill. There were dead animals on the wall. Wednesday was dollar-beer night, they had the best burgers in town, and they didn't serve appletinis.

I sat for ten minutes in a red Naugahyde booth that was sticky and smelled sourly of spilled beer, waiting for a man named Neil Burris, a security officer with Paladin Worldwide.

I expected that in the time since I'd called him from the Albany airport, pretending to be Marty Masur, he'd done his due diligence. Which in his case probably meant not much more than asking around to find out what kind of money Stoddard Associates paid, then drooling when he found out.

Just when I was about to leave the bar, a compact, muscle-bound guy with ridiculously broad shoulders and a scruffy goatee approached my booth. He had the look of a tough guy gone soft. He wore a black nylon body-hugging muscle shirt that zipped up at the top. The point was probably to show off his shredded biceps and pecs, but it had the unfortunate side effect of displaying his muffin top.

"*Hola,*" he said. He didn't even try to make it sound like Spanish. He reached his hand across the table and gave me a bone-crushing shake. "Neil Burris."

"Marty Masur," I said. "Nice to meet you."

"Real sorry I'm late. Couldn't find parking."

"It's bad around here," I said.

He slid into the booth across from me. Looked at me for a long moment. "Funny," he said. "You don't look like your picture."

"I've been working out."

He stared a little longer, then smiled slowly. His teeth were small and pointed and discolored. The brown was probably from chewing tobacco. "Listen, man," he said. "This is, like, between us, right? I don't want—"

"You don't want anyone at Paladin to know we're talking. Gotcha. We don't either."

"Good."

I signaled for the waitress. "Koblenz won't let you go without a fight, what I hear."

"Well . . ." Neil said with a shrug and a slow, embarrassed smile.

"I mean, it *is* Koblenz who's the real power there, right? Not Allen Granger?"

"Never met Granger, you wanna know the truth. He kinda keeps to himself down there in Georgia. Like a hermit or something. No one ever sees him."

"Why, do you figure?"

His eyes slid from side to side, and he leaned closer. "What I hear, there's guys who want to kill him."

"I don't get it. He runs the world's largest private army. He's got all the guards he needs, right?"

"Doesn't help if the guys who wanna wax you work for you."

"What do you mean?"

He nodded. "Oh yeah. For real. Remember a couple

years back when there was that big mess over in Baghdad, eight or ten towel heads got shot, right? Civilians? Coupla Paladin guys got some serious heat for that."

I vaguely remembered. Some Paladin security guards had fired at Iraqi civilians and killed them. "The victims' families filed a lawsuit in U.S. courts, wasn't that it?"

"Yeah. Screwed up big-time, man. Pentagon was threatening not to renew our contract, so Granger handed over the guys."

"Handed over?"

"He coulda fought it if he wanted. But he made some deal with the government. Like, he said these guys are just bad apples, you know? Take 'em and do whatever, and that kinda crap won't happen again. Well, a lotta Paladin guys just went whacko. We figured they'd always protect us, something bad happens. Like always." He shook his head. "Way I heard it, some buddies of those guys, working Paladin security down in Georgia, tried to off Granger."

"Off him? Like, kill him?"

"I don't know, man. Just what I hear. Screwed up, huh?"

The waitress, a pretty young girl with spiky blond hair and multiple piercings in her earlobes, took our order. Burris introduced himself and attempted to flirt with her, but without success. Maybe it was the name. "Neil" is a perfectly good name, but not for a tough guy. He probably wished his name were Bruno or Butch or at least Jack.

"So here's the deal, Neil," I said. "Old Man Stoddard wants to expand. Build the brand. He wants to get into the Paladin business, and he's looking for someone to spearhead that effort."

"Spearhead it," Burris said.

"Set it up for us. Means we need someone who knows the lay of the land."

"The lay of the land," Burris repeated. He was looking nervous. I could almost see the thought balloon floating above his head, as if he were a cartoon character: *You got the wrong guy. I'm just muscle. I don't know that stuff.*

But he didn't want to miss out on a chance like this. So maybe he wasn't qualified. Let the buyer beware.

I went on, "Business like this, you got one main customer, right? The U.S. government."

"Right."

"You gotta know who the players are. How to approach them. Know what I'm saying?"

He nodded. "Absolutely."

"Gotta know the right palms to grease, you know? The old baksheesh." I rubbed my fingers together to underscore the point.

"Speaking of which, you know, Paladin pays me in cash."

"Cash? You serious? All you guys?"

"My guess, they don't want records all over the place. Cash doesn't leave a trail."

"Cash? For real?"

"Not all of us. I don't know, I think it has to do with, like, the fact that we're independent contractors, not employees. I always figured it was some kinda scam, some way for them to avoid paying taxes, but I don't ask too many questions. I like cash."

"Can't blame you."

"That a problem for you?"

"I'm sure anything can be arranged," I said.

A couple of minutes later, the spiky-haired waitress set two draft beers on the table in front of us. Budweisers. Thin and watery and almost flavorless, just the way I liked them.

We toasted each other, and I said, in a confiding tone, "I probably shouldn't tell you this, but Jay Stoddard's real desperate to get into this business, and soon.

That means, if you can show me a sample of the wares, I can probably hold him up for a lot more than I told you on the phone. I mean, we might not be able to pay you in cash. Maybe, maybe not. But we're talking three-quarters of a mil to start. Plus stock options."

He was in midswallow, and some of the beer must have gone down the wrong way, because he started coughing, and his face turned red. He held up his palm to let me know he was okay, or maybe to tell me to hold on a minute. When he finally stopped coughing, he said, "I'm at your service, uh, Marty."

59

"So what kind of sample you guys looking for?" Burris said.

"Names, mostly. Something I can take back to Stoddard so he can feel confident you know who the real players are." I smiled. "See, you don't need to do a résumé. All you need is a name or two."

"I could probably find out," he said.

"You don't know?"

Hastily, he said, "I'm kinda like—I like to leave that kinda stuff to others, you know? But I can ask around."

"Sounds like you're out of the loop."

"Nah, nah, it's not like that. I just focus on other stuff, mostly." He was making it up and not doing a particularly convincing job of it. He didn't know.

I sidled out of the booth and made to stand up. I threw down a twenty. "Beer's on me, Neil. Sorry I wasted your time."

He reached out, grabbed me by the elbow. "Slow down, there. I can find out anything for you." He waved me close. "Like, there's all kinds of dirt."

"Uh-huh."

"Seriously. I can ask around," he said.

"Ask around?" I said. "Come on, man. Anyone can ask around."

Burris shook his head emphatically. "Not if you want the good stuff. The serious, secret stuff—that's real protected, like."

"Protected," I scoffed.

"For real." He lowered his voice still more. "Koblenz keeps this, like, smart card in his office safe. He uses it to get onto the secure part of the network, so he can make payments and transfers and so on."

I was intrigued, but I looked both bored and skeptical. "Yeah, every major corporation gives those out. It's a key fob—a secure hardware card that generates random one-time passwords you type in. Big deal."

"No. No. I'm not talking about those. This is a smart card with a cryptochip-thingy embedded in it. It's like a whole new generation. Like superduper high-tech. I heard about it. Developed by the NSA. No one else in the private sector has it yet."

"So, Neil," I said, "can you get this for me? As a sample?"

"I think so. I might be able to. His secretary has the combination to his safe—I think I know where she keeps it."

I looked away. I couldn't have looked less interested. "Uh-huh."

"I'm pretty sure I can," Burris said, handing me back my twenty. "Oh, and hey—beer's on me. Really."

He slapped down a crisp new one-hundred-dollar bill.

I looked at it, couldn't help glancing at the serial number on the front. It began with DB. Just like the ones in the shipment I'd recovered outside Los Angeles.

Burris probably figured I'd be impressed he had hundred-dollar bills to throw around. "Like I told you," he said. "I get paid in cash."

His cell phone rang, and he glanced down at it. "Gotta get it," he told me. "The boss." He picked it up, and said, "Yes, Carl."

I stood up, gave him an abrupt wave. Pantomimed *we'll talk* by making a little phone symbol out of my left hand and holding it to my cheek.

He gave me a thumbs-up.

I fought my way through the bar, twisting and turning and squeezing between pods of very different types of patrons: neighborhood customers in HVAC uniforms with name patches sewn on, and Hill rats in charcoal suits from the Men's Wearhouse, letting off steam after a long day of making photocopies and kissing butt in some minor congressman's office.

As I stepped out of the bar and into the refreshing cool air, I noticed a commotion behind me. Neil Burris was bulldozing a path through the crowd, elbowing people aside.

"Hey," he said, following me out onto the street. "You're not Marty Masur."

"No?" A couple of motorcycles roared by.

Burris drew so close to me I could smell his foul breath. "You're that guy's brother," he said. "You're Nick Heller."

60

Cars whooshed by. Somewhere nearby a dog was barking. A couple of girls in halter tops were smoking, which they couldn't do inside the Anchor. A gang of overgrown frat boys were jeering, and one of them was pissing in the alley next to the bar. The restrooms there were so malodorous that no one ever used them more than once.

Somehow Carl Koblenz had learned that I was meeting with Burris. I had no idea how, but I suppose I shouldn't have been surprised.

"And I thought we looked nothing alike," I said.

"You son of a bitch."

"Where is he, Neil?" A shot in the dark. Maybe he knew; maybe he didn't.

Burris answered with an obscenity, and suddenly he lunged at me. I saw him move a split second too late. He slammed me against the side of a building, cracking my head hard against the brick. With his right hand, he clamped my throat just below the Adam's apple and pincered hard. He was strong, even stronger than I expected, and he put his whole overdeveloped body into it. At the same time, he pinioned my left arm with his right shoulder and grabbed my right hand, just above the wrist, and jammed his right knee into the inside of my leg.

Now I knew for sure he'd really been a Navy SEAL. He was doing everything by the book.

Which was good, actually.

His face was so close to mine that I could feel the bristles of his goatee. "Your brother . . ." he said, breathing hard, "wasn't as smart as he thought." His face was red with exertion, and he sounded short of breath. "He thought he could rip us off and get away with it. Not gonna happen." Flecks of saliva sprayed my eyes.

Then I relaxed my shoulders and contracted my neck to make it hard for him. I stared back into his adrenaline-crazed eyes. Blinked slowly. Said nothing.

He expected me to fight back. He didn't expect me to do nothing, so that's what I did. Nothing.

For a few seconds, anyway.

"Your brother ticked off some very powerful people. He got too greedy. Went too far. So get this straight, Heller. Anything your brother left behind—like files or documents or *anything*—you're gonna want to share it with us. You hold back, and there's going to be collateral damage. I'm talking family members. You decide if it's worth it. Believe me, you don't want to make an enemy out of us."

He had that triumphant look of someone who knew he'd overpowered his opponent. He was intoxicated with confidence.

I shot my left hand out and jammed it against his right shoulder, which momentarily eased his hold on my throat, while I grabbed his right hand with my left and twisted his wrist clockwise. He let out a roar, scrambled his feet around to try to gain some purchase, but I levered his arm down and around, sending him sprawling to the gravel-strewn pavement.

I had his right hand in both of mine, the fingers pulled back so far that he only had to move too suddenly and his wrist would snap. He was helpless, and he knew it. But he was too stupid, and too truculent. He tried to swing his legs around, so I kneed him in the face—harder than I intended to, actually. He roared, and I heard something snap, and I knew that I'd broken his nose, perhaps even a cheekbone as well. Blood gushed down the lower part of his face.

"Was that a threat?" I said. "Because I really hate threats."

He bellowed, and I torqued his wrist around some more just to remind him of the price of any further struggle. He let loose with a string of obscenities, but his heart wasn't in it, I didn't think. He didn't seem to have much energy anymore.

Breathing thickly through the blood in his mouth, he said something about what he planned to do to Lauren.

"I don't think so," I replied. "Not with only one hand."

I grasped his right hand by the fingers and pulled them all the way back. His wrist made a muted *snick* noise when it broke, not the loud snap I expected. He let out a loud, agonized scream. His right hand—his gun hand, I assumed—dangled uselessly, like a marionette off its strings.

Burris summoned a final burst of strength, tried to rear up, but I kneed him in the chest, heard a few ribs crack. His head snapped backwards, reflexively, slamming into the pavement.

He went *uhhh,* looked dazed. All the wind went out of him.

I stood up, brushed the dirt and debris from my pants, surveyed the damage.

His eyes were going in and out of focus. He was hovering somewhere between consciousness and unconsciousness. His head had collided with the asphalt pretty hard.

"Hey, Neil," I said.

His eyes shifted slightly in my direction. I doubted he could see me very clearly, but I was sure he could hear me.

He said nothing.

I leaned over him, jamming my knee into his solar plexus, and said softly, "What do you know about my brother?"

He blinked, once. He grunted, barely audibly, the faintest indication that he was listening to me, though he couldn't form words. A small bubble of blood formed at the corner of his lips.

I knew I wasn't going to get an answer out of him even if he knew anything.

I'm not one of those guys who get a perverse pleasure from beating people up. Often it makes me feel guilty. But inflicting pain on Neil Burris, I have to admit, was not entirely unpleasurable.

My satisfaction faded somewhat a few minutes later, when I crossed the street and found the Defender with a deep white gouge running across the driver's side door all the way to the rear quarter panel. It looked like someone had keyed it, but with a screwdriver. Maybe some drunken frat kid.

It was annoying, but I had larger concerns. I took out my phone and dialed the number that Woody the cargo guy had given me in L.A. The number that belonged to Carl Koblenz.

I got a generic phone-company female voice telling me the number I'd just called, and after the tone I left a message for Carl Koblenz.

As I was finishing my message, another call was coming in. The caller ID showed "private," but I picked it up anyway.

It was Frank Montello. My information broker. "That phone number your father called from prison?" he said.

"Yeah?"

"It's a prepaid disposable cell phone. Bought with cash, I bet."

Very good, Roger, I thought. I'd expect nothing less. "Does the cell provider have billing records?"

"What do they need billing records for? It's prepaid, right? Ten bucks, twenty, fifty—whatever. They don't need to keep track of the calls."

"They do sometimes. All I want to know is where Roger was when he received a collect call from my father."

"No go. These cheapo phones don't have GPS locator chips in them. Most don't. Anyway, this one didn't."

"What about the location of the cell tower where the phone was when the call came in."

"They don't record that data, not on these disposable phones. I get a feeling your brother's going to a lot of trouble to conceal his location."

"Tell me about it," I said. "So how about one more job?"

61

By the time I got back to Roger's house, Lauren and Gabe were asleep. I cleaned up the nasty cuts and scrapes on my face and neck with some peroxide, checked to make sure that the alarm was set properly and the house secure. Then I crashed for a few hours. I had an important meeting to prepare for.

The headquarters of Paladin Worldwide was in southern Georgia, on ten thousand acres of swampland that also served as a training facility. This was where Allen Granger, Paladin's chairman, apparently spent most of his time.

But you couldn't do business with the U.S. government and not keep a base in or near Washington, D.C. So Paladin had a small office in Falls Church, Virginia, on the seventh floor of the Skyview Executive Center on Leesburg Pike, out of which they ran most of their government operations, their lobbying efforts, and so on.

This time I parked on the third level of the underground garage. But instead of taking the elevator right up to the seventh floor, I walked up to the street level and took a leisurely stroll around the outside of the building. Checked out the corporate landscaping, the artificial copses of trees out back, the contours of the shallow plot of land on which the building had been sited. Standing on the highest promontory I could find, I took out a pocket monocular spotting scope, located the bank of windows belonging to the offices of A.G. Holdings, which was either Paladin or Paladin's holding company—but for all intents and purposes, the same thing. After all, it was where Carl Koblenz worked, where he'd told me to come. For about twenty minutes I watched as much of the comings and goings as I could see from that angle.

It wasn't like in the movies. I didn't see much. I was pretty sure I saw Koblenz—I'd seen his picture on Paladin's website—sitting at his desk, conferring with his assistant and a couple of large men. In any case, I saw enough to get a sense of the flow of office traffic.

Then I entered the lobby and headed over to the directory sign. Nowhere did the name "Paladin" appear. On the seventh floor was a Japanese intellectual property firm and A.G. Holdings. Paladin's holding company. Or maybe just another name for Paladin. It made sense. Maybe they didn't want it publicly known that Paladin's offices were here. They probably didn't want protesters or crazed intruders trying to storm the gates.

"Hey, cookie man!"

I turned, saw my old friend the security guard, gave him a smile and a wave.

"Got any more free samples for me?" he said.

"Next time, I promise. I have an appointment with Paladin. Carl Koblenz."

"Oh, yeah? Excellent. Bunch of real big guys work there. Betcha they'll go crazy for your wife's cookies." So: as I thought. A.G. Holdings *was* Paladin.

I gave him my name, and he printed out a security pass for me to stick on the front of my shirt.

* * *

I was wearing jeans and a slightly grubby polo shirt, partly to remind Koblenz that I wasn't on official Stoddard Associates business. And to let him know I wasn't playing by the rules of the suit-and-tie world. Also because it was more comfortable than a suit.

The elevator rose smoothly and swiftly to the seventh floor. I got out into a small lobby with dark wooden doors at either end. Each door had a brass plaque. One said NAKAMURA & PARTNERS. A law firm, according to the lobby directory sign. The other said A.G. HOLDINGS.

A small black dome camera, almost undetectable, was mounted high on the wall on Paladin's side, but not on Nakamura & Partners' side. That told me Paladin had their own private security system, in addition to whatever the building provided its tenants. I'd have expected nothing less. Mounted to the doorframe was a proximity-key reader, where Paladin's employees would swipe to enter.

I pushed the lever handle down and entered a reception area with a long black granite desk.

The receptionist was a cute young blonde with carefully applied makeup and an expensive haircut.

"Mr. Heller?" she said.

"Right."

"Please have a seat, and Mr. Koblenz will be right with you."

Mounted to the front of the receptionist's desk was the Paladin logo, a navy blue globe with white continents and white crosshairs superimposed over it. As if to say: *We're taking aim at the world.*

Or maybe: *Overcharging governments around the world and killing innocent civilians since 1994.*

The globe reminded me of the one in the Gifford Industries lobby. Maybe all rapacious international firms were required to have a globe in their logo. The coffee table was black and marble and coffin-shaped. There wasn't much to browse: the *Post*, the *Wall Street Journal*, a couple of security magazines. I glanced over the front page of the *Journal*, but I didn't have time to read it before the inner door opened and three large guys entered.

One of them had his right hand in a splint.

62

"Hey there, Neil," I said. "Gosh, what happened to your hand?"

Neil Burris just glared at me. He was wearing a shopping-mall suit, not that there was anything wrong with that except that the tailoring obviously wasn't included. It was too tight across the shoulders and too short in the arms and made him look like a circus gorilla.

The two other guys also wore cheap suits, which seemed to be the uniform of the Paladin security staff. One of them had longish hair, flecked with gray, and a droopy mustache. He had the lean muscular build of a Navy SEAL. The other looked like something out of WrestleMania—one of those mean-looking three-hundred-pound Ukrainians. He had a jarhead haircut. I recognized him, too.

He was the one who'd grabbed the surveillance-video DVD from me in Georgetown and in the process smashed my face against the window of my Defender.

The long-haired guy, who was older and seemed to be in charge, said, "You're going to have to surrender your cell phone and BlackBerry."

" 'Surrender' them?" I said. That was smart of Koblenz, actually. Both cell phones and BlackBerrys could be used as eavesdropping devices. That told me that he wanted to speak freely, which was a good thing. He didn't want whatever he said to be recorded or transmitted to anyone else.

The other two tried to stare me down. The pretty receptionist was examining a copy of *People* the way a rabbi might study the Talmud.

"Mr. Koblenz won't meet with you if you have any RF equipment on your person."

I shrugged. "I never surrender," I said.

He handed me a gray RF-isolation pouch. I'd used pouches like this in secure facilities, but never outside of the military or intelligence community. I slid the Black-Berry and cell phone inside, closed the Velcro flap, and put the pouch into my leather portfolio.

"Thank you, sir," said the long-haired one. He also seemed to be the only one allowed to speak. "This way, please."

"This is great," I said. "I even get my own entourage."

The long-haired guy waved his proximity badge at the reader mounted next to the inside door. The door buzzed, and he pushed it open, and the two other guys fell in, Burris beside me and Andre the Giant behind. Either they were trying to intimidate me or they were concerned I might shoplift.

We walked down a hall that had the generic look of a midrange hotel.

"Hey, Neil," I muttered to Burris. "I'm still waiting for your references."

He stared straight ahead. His hand and arm were encased in a hard brace made out of some kind of light-weight resin over foam, with Velcro straps around the whole thing.

"Hello, Mr. Heller."

Carl Koblenz was in his late forties but had a youthful appearance, despite the bags under his eyes. He had a pink-scrubbed face and clear green eyes and sandy brown hair clipped short. He wore a natty blue blazer over a striped dress shirt and a regimental tie. Maybe the tie was from Eton, where Koblenz went to school, or maybe it was from Sandhurst, where he did his officer training. I'm not very good on British regimental ties.

"Carl," I said. We grasped hands firmly. He grasped my hand at the knuckles, so I couldn't shake back. A power move. He was probably full of them.

"Thank you for coming out to Falls Church." He spoke so quietly I could barely hear him.

"Thank you for taking time to see me."

When he'd returned my phone message, I insisted we meet in Washington, and naturally he refused. He was too important a man to leave his office, his power place. He said, in what I surmised was an Eton drawl, "I'm afraid I've got a full calendar of appointments, Mr. Heller. I wish I could get out of the office, but I can't possibly."

Just as I'd expected, and hoped, the same reverse psychology that works so well on a three-year-old worked on him, too. I reluctantly agreed to go to the Paladin office in Falls Church.

"I think you've met Neil, haven't you?"

"Old friends," I said. I reached out to shake Burris's wounded hand, but he didn't offer it.

"Don Taylor and Anatoly Bondarchuk," he said, indicating the others. "I hope you don't mind if they join us." Bondarchuk, I assumed, was Andre the Giant.

Sitting at the desk right outside Koblenz's office was a small, plain woman with short, mousy brown hair. The fake wood plaque on her desk said ELEANOR APPLEBY.

"You know, I do mind," I said apologetically. "I was hoping we could have a candid talk."

"I'd prefer to loop them in."

"I'm not going to hurt you, Carl," I said. "I promise."

"Hurt me?" A twinkle of amusement came into his eyes. "You don't know much about me, do you?"

I knew more about him by now than he probably wanted. I knew that after Eton and Sandhurst, he joined the Scots Guards, and was then selected to the SAS, the British equivalent of the Special Forces that was widely believed to be even tougher than our own, though of course I doubted that. He was sort of a legend during Desert Storm. He was part of the assault team that tried to sneak into an Iraqi communications facility, found themselves facing three hundred Iraqi soldiers, but planted the explosives anyway and pulled out of there under fire. Not a single SAS man was injured. A lot of rich Arabs in Kensington wanted to hire him to do their security after that, but instead he cashed in, joined an international mercenary firm. He ran guns for the government of Sierra Leone, in violation of the U.N. embargo. Then he got involved in a coup attempt against the president of Equatorial Guinea and was arrested and locked up for six months in Black Beach Prison in Malabo, which made the Altamont Correctional Facility look like Canyon Ranch.

"Enough not to mess with you," I said with a generous smile, and he smiled back. With his hand on my shoulder, he guided me into his office, which was as generic as the rest of the place. It smelled like old cigar smoke.

The three security guards filed in behind me. I stopped short, then turned around. "Thanks, guys," I said. "You got me here safely. Well done. Now, your boss and I have some personal business to discuss."

Koblenz shook his head, sighed, and said, "All right, mates, wait outside, please."

He sat behind his desk, I sat in the chair in front of his desk, and he said, "Well, you've certainly got quite the track record."

"Lies, all lies," I said modestly.

I noticed his office safe, where—according to Neil Burris—he stored the smart card with the embedded cryptochip that enabled access to the most secure layer of the Paladin computer network. The safe was black, about as tall as his desk, and looked like a three- or four-drawer model. An electronic keypad. Formidable-looking.

Despite the great safecracking scenes we've all seen in movies, in reality it's become extremely difficult to crack a high-security safe. The technology has evolved far too much in the last dozen or so years. But with the right plan, nothing was truly impossible.

"Hunting war criminals in Bosnia, huh? With some triple–top secret army unit—what was it, the ISA, right?"

"Couldn't be all that secret if you know about it."

He'd done his homework. The Intelligence Support Activity was a classified military intelligence unit that roamed Bosnia looking for Serbian war criminals. Snatch-and-grab strikes on "high-value targets," as we called them. I never talked about what I'd done in Bosnia or Iraq during the first Gulf War, not to anyone. So Paladin obviously had some excellent sources deep inside the Pentagon.

"What you did to that Serb guy . . . Drašković?" His pronunciation was excellent. He shook his head, smiled. "Well done." An admiring, conspiratorial chuckle.

I said nothing. Just pulled out a folder of photographs and handed it to him.

One was a close-up of the license plate on the Econoline van in which one of his guys had abducted Roger. The other was a close-up of the same guy's face. The third was a medium view showing Roger and his abductor next to the van.

"Your employee was careful not to let his license plate be seen by the bank's surveillance camera," I said, "but he didn't think about the gas station having its own security cameras."

"Yes," he said. "I've seen the tape."

Well, that's a start, I thought.

"Am I supposed to know what this is about?" he asked.

"It's about fifteen years in prison for abduction," I said. "For you and for your boss. And millions of dollars in lost government business. If you had him killed, well, I think we're looking at forty years to life."

"You might want to be a bit more careful about tossing around legal threats."

"I have no interest in the legal process." I folded my arms and gave him a lethal smile. "See, I just want my brother back."

63

Koblenz went quiet for a few seconds, seemed to be thinking. He blew out air through pursed lips. "Where do I begin, Heller?"

"Maybe with the container of cash in Los Angeles. You could start there. I'm sure Allen Granger would love to hear about that."

"So much ground to cover."

"I'll bet. Or else we could talk about my brother's attempts to extort money from you. I'm sure it seemed a lot easier just to get rid of the guy than risk exposure of all the kickbacks you give the Pentagon."

He shook his head, looked mildly amused. "Ah, well, let's see." He held up the picture, then let go. It fluttered and slid across his desktop, finally landing on the floor. "First of all, I have no idea who this fellow is. The other one is obviously your brother."

"We're running a search right now," I bluffed. "The PATRIOT Act makes it much easier these days. That and facial-recognition software."

"Well, let me know what you find. And if you find the guy, maybe you could ask him why he stole a license plate off of one of our vehicles."

"You can do better than that, Carl."

"We don't own a single Econoline van, Heller."

"Who doesn't? Paladin? Or one of your twelve subsidiaries?"

"More than twelve. But no. No Econoline vans. I assure you, Heller, we didn't abduct your brother. Although I do wish we'd thought of it."

"I hope you're not denying that's your license plate," I said.

"I can neither confirm nor deny," Koblenz said with a wry smile. "I can barely remember the license-plate numbers of my own cars. But the prefix on the plate suggests it's one of ours, so I'm not going to argue. You'll find it's registered to either a Hummer or an Escalade, though. As for who switched the plates, well, I have no idea."

"The D.C. police aren't going to care what kind of vehicle it belongs on."

"I doubt that seriously," Koblenz said. "And as for the cash—well, all I can say is, you have my deepest thanks. You're every bit as good as Jay Stoddard said you are."

"A billion dollars in cash," I said. "That should about cover your off-the-books payroll for a month or two."

"Guilty as charged. But surely you don't think we're the only security firm in Baghdad who had to pay cash bribes to Iraqi officials to get things done. It was like Nigeria over there." He slid a cigar box across the expanse of desk. "Have you forgotten how it worked, Heller? It was a cash economy. The biggest dispenser of cash bribes was the U.S. government. I'd love to see them try to prosecute. Have a Cuban?"

I shook my head. "No, thanks."

"Are you sure? Hoyo de Monterrey Double Coronas. Handmade in Cuba by only the most skilled *torcedoras. Totalmente a mano.*"

"No, thanks."

"Your father's favorites. Though I don't imagine he gets much of a chance to smoke them these days." He selected one, took a guillotine clipper from his desk, held the cigar at eye level, then decisively circumcised it.

I paused, smiled, thought of at least three possible rejoinders. Then I took one of his cigars and studied it for a few seconds before handing it back to him. "My father, whatever his flaws, would never smoke counterfeit cigars."

"Counterfeit? I don't think so, Heller." He flicked a silver butane lighter and held the end of the cigar near the flame, rotating it slowly before putting it in his mouth and drawing on it slowly like a baby enjoying his first reassuring suck on a pacifier.

I pointed to the green-and-white tax stamp on the left front side of the box. "Put it under a blacklight and you'll see. You won't see the microprinting above REPÚBLICA DE CUBA. That's not a Cuban Government Warranty Seal."

Wreathed in smoke, he examined the box suspiciously. "You can't be serious." He sounded uncertain.

"Sorry. Shouldn't have said anything. Didn't mean to spoil it for you. You'd never have known the difference."

He stared at me through narrowed, glittering eyes.

I continued, "It took me a while to figure out why you'd hire the security director of Argon Express Cargo to steal your own shipment of cash. Until I realized that you didn't want U.S. Customs discovering the cash, maybe on a random inspection. So you arranged a bogus theft. To make sure Paladin wasn't charged with bulk-cash smuggling by some government bureaucrat."

"I like your theory."

"Thank you."

"The only hole in it, of course, is that the U.S. government hired us to round up the cash in Baghdad and ship it back. Everything was aboveboard, or at least as much as it can be with the government." He smiled.

"Sorry. Your mistake was giving Elwood Sawyer your cell-phone number as an emergency contact."

"And on that slender reed you're building a case against me? That someone gave him my cell-phone number? Now I'm wondering whether Jay Stoddard gives you too much credit."

"No doubt," I said.

"And as for your brother, well, he simply took on the wrong people."

"Yeah," I said. "He probably meant to go after Mother Teresa instead."

"The hellbat of Calcutta is dead, alas," Koblenz said with a lopsided grin. "Though I always wanted to have a tablecloth made out of her sari. Do we pay kickbacks to certain influential individuals in the Pentagon? Sure."

"You admit it."

"Well, not on the record, no, of course not. I'm not *that* stupid."

"How much money did he demand from you for silence?"

"Not a cent, as far as I know."

"Then why was my brother such a threat to you?"

"Who says he was a threat?"

" 'I got a stone in my shoe, Mr. Corleone,' " I said, quoting from the third *Godfather* movie. Another Stoddard favorite, but I liked it, too.

He got the reference. "As I said, we had nothing to do with your brother's disappearance. Whoever's on that surveillance tape, it wasn't us. Do a little legwork, and you'll see." He smiled. "And no, we didn't give your brother a poisoned cannoli either. Why would we?"

"Maybe for the same reason your goons are threatening to kidnap Roger's son. Or e-mailing videos to his wife. And the spyware and the video cameras you planted in his house? The data went out to some Eastern European botnet and eventually right back to Paladin. Which I'll admit took us a lot of digging. But every step was documented." Only half of that was true. Dorothy still hadn't been able to figure out where the network traffic ended up after it went to that Ukrainian network. But let him think we were more on top of things than we actually were.

He shook his head. "I don't know anything about any surveillance device or any Eastern European . . . whatever. But *arguendo,* as the lawyers say—just for the sake of argument—let's say my employees have been applying pressure on your brother's wife. Why would they do that if we'd taken Roger prisoner? Where's the sense in that?"

"Because he left something behind, and you want it."

"Now you're starting to make sense. You're half-right."

"Am I?"

"Absolutely. He does have something we want. That's absolutely true. But I doubt he left it behind. That doesn't fit with my understanding of your brother's character. Though maybe that's presumptuous. You know him far better than we do. Am I wrong to assume that he takes after your father?"

"What's your point?"

He spun around in his chair and took a brown file folder from a wire rack on the credenza behind him next to a couple of generic office plants. He opened it, took out a sheet of paper, and looked at it for a moment. Then he handed it to me.

It was a fax from a bank in the Caymans called Transatlantic Bank & Trust (Cayman) Limited, located on Mary Street in George Town, Grand Cayman. A copy of a copy of a copy, festooned with smudges and photocopier artifacts. It was a letter from Roger, on Gifford

Industries letterhead, to the bank's manager. A letter of instruction.

Roger was instructing the bank manager to move two hundred and fifty million dollars from one account—a subsidiary of Paladin whose name I recognized—to an account in his own name.

"What does that look like to you?" he said.

"A forgery."

He shrugged, snorted quietly. "That's right, Heller. We have teams of forgers at work creating phony documents just for you." His sarcasm was subtle. "Now do you see? Starting to recognize your brother's modus operandi? Steal a bunch of money, then, when you realize that you've messed with the wrong guys, do the cowardly thing and run? Wonder where he got that from."

"Screw you." I no longer felt bad about making up that story about his cigars.

"Oh, believe me, it's the truth. Maybe to Victor Heller's sons that's nothing more than loose change you find under your sofa cushions. But not to me. And certainly not to Allen Granger."

"Roger worked for Gifford Industries. Not for Paladin. He wouldn't even have had the legal authority to make a transfer."

"Sure he did."

"It doesn't work that way," I said.

"Your brother had Leland Gifford's proxy."

"What does Gifford have to do with Paladin?"

Koblenz tipped his head to one side. "I'm disappointed you don't know."

"Know what?"

"Gifford Industries is our parent company. Gifford owns Paladin. Has done for five months."

At that point I didn't know what to say. I just looked at him.

"This is not public information, obviously," he said.

"As a privately held corporation, Gifford isn't required to tell anyone about the acquisition. But Allen was looking to sell for years. So it's not just me or Allen Granger who wants this money back. It's Leland Gifford, too. And the gentlemen out there. They each have a significant cash incentive to find your brother, and more important, to find the money he's stolen. Call them bounty hunters. The profit motive always works."

"Screw you," I said. My vocabulary had become very limited all of a sudden.

"Roger's wife may require a different type of incentive to cooperate."

"That's not going to work anymore."

"Heller, there are so many ways to induce her to cooperate."

"I don't recommend you try any of them."

"And I'd rather not. But I'll do whatever it takes."

I rattled the sheet of paper he'd just handed me. "If this is the only proof you have—"

"I don't need proof," Koblenz said calmly. "I'm like you—I have no interest in the legal process. We just want our money back. Whatever it takes. If there's collateral damage, so be it."

"That kind of sounds like another threat," I said.

He shrugged. "It is what it is."

I stood up, put the piece of paper down on the desk, tapped it with my forefinger. "It's actually a good forgery. Though it would have been more persuasive if you got the bank's SWIFT code right."

The SWIFT code is a series of numbers or letters that banks use to identify themselves for the purpose of transferring funds.

"I see," Koblenz said. "Since of course you have every SWIFT code memorized."

"No, not at all," I said. "I just know that the SWIFT code for Cayman Islands banks always includes the letters KY. Like K-Y Jelly. I'm sure you know what that is. And this one doesn't have those letters. Close, but no cigar, as they say."

Koblenz, who didn't seem to be a guy who was ever at a loss for words, was momentarily silenced. He blinked a few times, and his mouth made fishlike motions.

Then I said, "You've been a big help, Carl. You've told me exactly what I wanted to know."

He recovered, gave a tart, skeptical smile, and I went on, "See, I know where my brother is. I just wanted to find out whether you do. And now I've learned you don't. So, thanks for the help."

And I walked calmly out of his office.

64

It was, of course, an outrageous bluff, pure and simple, though I soon wished I hadn't done it.

And not until I'd left Paladin's office and was riding the elevator down to the parking garage did what Koblenz had told me finally sink in.

I had to assume, of course, that every word Koblenz had told me, including "and" and "the," was a lie. That was a given. But I operated on that assumption most of the time anyway: Washington, D.C., is to lying what Hershey, Pennsylvania, is to chocolate.

Was Paladin Worldwide really owned by Gifford Industries?

Why not? That wasn't inconceivable at all. This was the age of corporate consolidation. Big companies buy smaller companies all the time. It's part of nature, the corporate food chain. The same way microscopic phytoplankton are eaten by zooplankton, which are in turn eaten by little fish, which get eaten by bigger fish and so on up to the orca killer whale.

I'd heard rumors that Allen Granger had been looking to sell Paladin. Maybe he realized that things had changed in Washington, that the new administration didn't want to do so much business with him.

For instance, one of Paladin's subsidiaries was an aviation company that did secret "extraordinary rendition" flights for the CIA. Which basically meant that when suspected terrorists were seized by masked men on the street somewhere in Europe and blindfolded and tranquilized and spirited away, it was a Paladin-owned Gulfstream or Boeing 737 that flew the guy off to be tortured in a secret CIA prison in Egypt or Macedonia or Morocco or Libya or another such country that took a more broad-minded view of human rights than the U.S.

With a new president in office and the secret rendition program cancelled, maybe that wasn't such a great business to be in anymore.

Allen Granger was known to be a shrewd businessman. Why wouldn't he want to cash out at or near the top of the market? Made sense.

And if Gifford Industries owned Paladin Worldwide, that would explain why Roger had had access to Paladin's offshore financial records.

That made sense, too.

It would certainly explain his meetings with and phone calls to our father, the master thief. Victor had been giving Roger tutorials.

I told him he was playing a very dangerous game, Victor had said.

I warned him that the whole idea was reckless.

So Roger had finally figured out a way to get the money he'd always felt entitled to. Even if it meant leaving behind his wife and son. A wife he was unfaithful to, and her son. Not his.

He hadn't stolen money from Paladin, though. He'd tried to blackmail them, which was a very different thing. He'd found out about bribes, kickbacks, whatever, that Paladin made to the Pentagon in order to make sure they got their no-bid contracts—that was my theory, anyway—and had threatened them with exposure. Threatened to report them to some law-enforcement authority, maybe. Unless they paid up.

Roger was tired of being poor.

He wasn't a thief. He was a blackmailer. An extortionist.

Not that extortion was any better than stealing. I didn't care one way or the other. But I was certain that Carl Koblenz had handed me a forgery, because he didn't want me—or anyone—to know that Roger had tried to blackmail them.

Because to admit that Roger had tried to blackmail them would mean admitting to the sleaze, the illegality, that Roger had threatened to expose. And that Koblenz didn't want to do.

I found the Defender where I'd parked it, in a row that branched off the third underground level. As I inserted my key in the lock, I hesitated.

Call it paranoia. Call it instinct.

Call it the realization that someone had unwittingly disturbed the pattern of gravel I'd placed on three sides of the car—tiny pyramids of gravel fragments. I wasn't a fool. I was parking my car in the garage underneath the building where Paladin had an office. Not to assume they'd do something would be naïve.

Kneeling down, I ran my hand across the undercarriage, feeling for anything that might have been added while I was upstairs meeting with Koblenz. A bomb, say. I peered underneath the car, scanned carefully, and saw nothing.

Paranoia, I thought.

Just because you're paranoid doesn't mean they're not really out to get you.

I opened the car door; then, just to be thorough, I got out and knelt in front of the bumper.

And found it, magnetically affixed to the back of the license plate. I pulled it off: a miniature GPS tracking

device. A box about three inches by one containing a
GPS receiver and a cellular modem. That little toy could
transmit a vehicle's location over a cell-phone network.

That meant that my friends at Paladin could track
my car's every move on their computers at the office or
even on their PDAs or iPhones. The technology in those
things was light-years beyond the days of "bumper beep-
ers," when you slapped a radio transmitter on a straying
wife's car so you could follow her to her rendezvous with
the UPS guy at Motel 6.

I heard a scraping sound, and I looked up.

Three Day-Glo traffic cones had been placed across
the mouth of the lane.

And coming at me slowly, steadily, were my three
friends from upstairs.

65

Three against one, I thought: *Not exactly a fair fight.*

Though they weren't expecting much of a fight. I could see that.

"What's up, guys?" I said.

The guy with the long grayish hair and the droopy mustache—Taylor, I think—rasped, "Got a quick sec to talk?"

He was the only one of the three still wearing a suit, though he'd taken off his tie. The others had changed into jeans. Taylor looked like a washed-up country-and-western music star doing a late-night TV talk show.

Except for the weapon he was holding. An aluminum-frame Ruger .45 with a black polycarbonate grip, I guessed. Probably a P90. After a couple of years in the field, I'd gotten good at identifying weapons, a skill that could save your life.

But these guys weren't here to kill me. I took Taylor at his word: They wanted to talk to me. Ask me questions.

The steroid-poisoned WrestleMania reject with the jarhead haircut—Bondarchuk, I remembered—was dangling a handful of yellow nylon flex cuffs. I wasn't sure

why Burris was here, though, unless it was for the personal satisfaction of seeing me restrained and maybe
bruised a bit in the process. Otherwise, with his broken
wrist, he was mostly a liability.

They advanced toward me slowly, moving into position. Burris swaggered, torquing his yard-wide shoulders back and forth, though I noticed that he kept back
a good safe distance. Placing the traffic cones was a
thoughtful touch. They wanted to make sure no car came
by and got in the way.

"This doesn't look like a bible-study group," I said.
I stood next to my Land Rover, at the back end, not
moving.

"Let's just do this quick and easy," Taylor said.

"Always happy to talk," I said, hands outspread.
"Though I thought Carl and I said all there was to say."

Taylor stopped about ten feet away and raised his
weapon slowly, adjusting his grip, and thumbed up the
safety to the fire position. Bondarchuk came around to
my other side, flex cuffs at the ready. In his giant hand,
the yellow nylon straps looked like loose threads.

A couple walked past the traffic cones, did a double
take, then rushed to their car.

Neil Burris had a little smirk on his moon face,
wreathed by his scrubby goatee—a chin mullet. Now
I could see a weapon in his left hand, his only good
hand. A black pistol-like object with yellow markings
and a muzzle that was too broad to be a gun. A Taser,
law-enforcement model. He stood about twenty feet
away.

The operating manual that came with the
professional-grade Taser told you that twenty-one feet
was the maximum effective distance. Theoretically, the
compressed nitrogen cartridge in the Taser would fire
its two barbed aluminum probes, which were connected

by wire filaments to the handheld unit, up to twenty-one feet. The miniature electric harpoons would penetrate clothing then let loose with a paralyzing fifty thousand volts and eighteen watts. Theoretically.

But Burris should have spent more time reading the manual.

Fire the thing at a distance of twenty-one feet, and the probes spread too far apart. If both probes don't hit your subject, you won't get an electrical circuit. It won't work. Seven or eight feet is probably the farthest you want to be.

But Burris was afraid to stand that close to me.

"Hands up and turn around," Taylor said.

It didn't take me long to decide that I had no choice. A Ruger and a Taser. Three men on one.

They only wanted to talk.

Then again, some of the most ruthless interrogators at Abu Ghraib and Guantánamo had been supplied by Paladin. So maybe it was all in how you defined "talk."

I shrugged, put my hands up, and turned around, my back to Taylor. Bondarchuk scuffed into an orthogonal position to my left, just far enough away that I couldn't jump him.

"Hands behind your back, please," Taylor said.

Burris had shifted position so that he was directly in front of me, and still a good twenty feet away. He raised the Taser in his left hand and pointed it at me and squinted one eye as if he were aiming. That was pure theater. You didn't need to aim a stun gun that precisely, and if he did fire it, it wouldn't work, and I was fairly certain he wasn't planning on using it anyway.

I brought my hands down to my side. Bondarchuk stepped close to loop the flex cuffs around my wrists.

These were pros, and I couldn't let them establish a tactical advantage, or it was all over.

I felt Taylor clap a hand on my left shoulder. "Hands behind your back," he shouted, jamming his Ruger against my spine. "Do it *now*!"

At that instant, I stumbled, but not forward.

I fell backwards, right into him, catching him off guard. The momentum sent his gun hand sliding forward, through the gap between my torso and my right arm.

I didn't have time to think. Lightning-fast, I slipped my hands over his wrist while twisting to my right, his elbow vised tight against my side, and pulled down on his straight arm with a sudden sharp force, hyperextending it.

The elbow is a complicated joint. It's a hinge made out of three bones that come together with a lot of ligaments and tendons. Most people can flex their elbows nearly one hundred and eight degrees. Force it beyond that, and you'll wedge the bony tip of the ulna under the end of the humerus, and bad things can happen. The bones can separate, or fracture, or simply snap.

I heard a snap.

Taylor's scream was almost inhuman. It echoed off the concrete walls as he doubled over in pain and sank to the floor.

His Ruger clattered to the ground.

I couldn't risk leaning over to retrieve it. Instead, I gave the gun a sideways kick, sending it skittering across the floor and underneath my car.

And then two things happened almost simultaneously.

Bondarchuk lunged at me and threw a straight punch at my head, his enormous fist coming at me with all of his vast body weight behind it. I raised my left arm to deflect the blow, which threw him off-balance. He leaned forward just as I smashed my elbow into his chin. He grunted, wobbled, righted himself, somehow managed to land a punch on my shoulder.

Immensely painful, but nothing compared to what Taylor was experiencing. He lay writhing and bellowing like a dying beast, clutching his grotesquely distended joint.

Then Neil Burris, who'd been striding toward me, raised his Taser and fired.

66

Here's the thing about close combat in real life: It's almost always over in a matter of seconds. Not like in the movies, where your hero has the luxury to strategize and maneuver and grapple for minutes on end.

Fortunately, when your life is in danger, your brain kicks in. Deep inside your brain this little almond-shaped gland called the amygdala sends out the signal to make your body start pumping out dopamine and adrenaline and cortisol. Time seems to slow, your focus sharpens, you suddenly start perceiving way more stimuli than normal. Neurologists call this *tachypsychia*. Everyone else calls it the fight-or-flight response. Cavemen who didn't have it got eaten by saber-toothed tigers.

So I made a quick decision. I could either be incapacitated by a Taser, or I could put myself within the reach of Bondarchuk's fists.

No choice.

I dove at the giant, kneeing him in the stomach as I did so. He toppled to the ground, and I landed on top of him.

There was a loud pop and then a metallic *chink-chink* as Burris's Taser fired its two fishhook probes into the

Defender's steel rear door. He'd missed me by about one second. Then came the rattling, frying-bug-zapper sound of the Taser sending out its electrical current.

Burris cursed. He couldn't use the Taser again until he'd replaced the spent cartridge, which wouldn't be easy with only one working hand.

Meanwhile, Bondarchuk reared up, taking me up with him like a forklift. But I really didn't want to give him the chance to swing at me again. I kneed him in the chin, snapping his head upward. He sagged to the floor, finally knocked out.

"Tase him!" I heard. "Tase him, *now*!"

Taylor was on his knees, trying to get up. Behind him, Burris was fumbling with the holster clipped to his belt using the fingers of his wounded hand. Not a handgun. A replacement cartridge for the Taser. Both men were badly hurt, and neither was giving up.

The profit motive always works.

I guess I was motivated, at that precise moment, by pure raw anger. Winded and aching, I struggled to my feet, grabbing on to the side-view mirror of the Toyota Camry parked next to my car to hoist myself up.

But with a metallic groan the damned thing wrenched loose and I almost fell backwards. I got back up, kicked Taylor at the back of his head, and he, too, went down.

Burris managed to seat the new cartridge into the Taser.

I grabbed the Camry's dangling side-view-mirror assembly, twisted it free, then hurled the heavy chrome mirror object at Burris. It clipped him on the forehead with a loud *thud*. He wobbled, the Taser slipped from his hand, and he toppled slowly, like a felled tree.

Leaning back against the Camry's passenger-side door, I took a few deep breaths. The flex cuffs lay scattered on the floor near Bondarchuk's feet. I snatched them up. Four nylon temporary restraints: He'd brought enough to bind my hands and my feet, with a few left over for good luck.

In a little over a minute I had all three of them cuffed. I figured they might regain consciousness in a few minutes. Even if they were out longer, why not slow them down as much as possible?

But just as I was pulling the cuffs tight on Burris's wrists, he came to. He moved his head, groaned, opened his eyes. They were glassy and bloodshot.

"Big mistake," he said.

"Hey there, Neil. We meet again."

"Think this is over?" His speech was slurred.

"Yeah," I said. "I think so."

He didn't reply.

The Taser was on the floor between his feet, calling out to me. It was already powered on.

He saw where I was looking, and he said, "Don't even f—"

"Tell Koblenz that if he wants to ask me anything, he can make an appointment with my secretary."

"You have any idea what Granger's going to do to you? You'll beg for death."

"I haven't used one of these in years," I said.

Burris snorted. "Go ahead. Did the kid tell you he pissed his pants when my buddies gave him a ride home from school? Yep, that's what I heard. He was probably too embarrassed to tell you that, huh?"

All of a sudden the Taser seemed too impersonal. I aimed my fist carefully at a small area behind his ear, at the base of his skull, a bony outgrowth called the mastoid process. I knew that if I wasn't careful, I could break my hand.

So I was careful. I hit him hard and fast, and I didn't break my hand.

Burris went right out.

Clipped to his belt was his keycard. It had his photo

printed on the front, along with his name and employee number and the Paladin seal.

The others, I knew, would have their cards with them as well. They might be mercenaries and ex–Navy SEALS but they were also corporate employees, and like cube dwellers everywhere, they never went anywhere without their keycards.

I jotted down their full names and dates of birth and employee numbers. I checked their wallets and noted the information on their driver's licenses and wrote that down, too. Each had a rugged little push-to-talk Nextel cell phone. No car keys. Nothing else of interest.

I took Taylor's phone, on the theory that the most senior guy would probably have the most access to higher-ups, meaning that he'd have the most useful phone numbers programmed into his phone.

I retrieved the gun from under the Defender. Always useful.

But it was the keycards that most interested me. They would get me into the building. Maybe into Paladin's office suite as well.

Taking a keycard, however, was out of the question. Once Koblenz realized I'd taken it, that card would be deactivated, frozen. And I wasn't yet ready to use it. Not quite yet. I needed time to prepare.

I examined Taylor's card, and confirmed that it was the same exact type that Stoddard used, a PVC proximity card. Convenient, but not a huge surprise. The vast majority of corporations around the world issued keycards just like the ones Paladin used.

It was the size of a credit card, with printing on one side. Actually, it was a sandwich: a layer of PVC, then a layer containing an antenna coil and an integrated electronic chip, then another layer of PVC, with an adhesive backing designed to go through the company's on-site printer.

Most companies recycle keycards—they just reprogram them and peel off the label and stick on a new one. It wasn't hard to peel the top layer off Taylor's keycard, once I wedged a fingernail in there. I was able to swap his picture for mine in a matter of minutes. That way, they wouldn't realize I'd taken one of their proximity cards. Taylor's wouldn't work, but that wouldn't worry them too much. Maybe it had gotten damaged in the struggle.

Anyway, Taylor and his colleagues had bigger concerns than a nonfunctioning keycard.

I got in my car and headed out of the garage, and as I drove, I made a phone call.

67

Leland Gifford, who could barely use a computer, had become a BlackBerry addict. He no longer went anywhere without it.

That was not quite true. He never left the building without it. When he was in the building, he usually left it in his office.

At the moment he was in a budget meeting with the CFO and the EVPs, down the hall in the Executive Conference Room. His BlackBerry was in its usual place in his office.

Normally, Lauren went into Leland's office only to put notes and files on his desk. He didn't like her in his office too much, which was understandable. He wanted some zone of privacy.

Noreen was typing something at her desk. Lauren glanced at her quickly, then stood and walked quickly to Leland's office.

Her heart was pounding.

She knew that she was about to betray a man she loved deeply. But she also knew she had no choice. If she wanted to save her family—to save Roger's life, to protect Gabe—she had to do this.

In life you sometimes have to make terrible choices, and she'd finally made hers. Her true family over her work family.

To anyone watching, she wasn't doing anything furtive. She was going into her boss's office. But she couldn't help being nervous.

His BlackBerry wasn't where he normally left it, on the left side of his desk.

"Can I get you a sandwich?"

Noreen was standing in the doorway, hands folded across her ample bosom.

"That would be great."

Go, she thought. *Just leave me alone.*

"The usual? Cracked pepper turkey on wheat, mustard and lettuce, no cheese or mayo?"

"Perfect. Thanks." She smiled, examined Leland's desk, intent and focused and very, very busy. She straightened a pile of folders. Looked up, saw Noreen still standing there.

Noreen smiled back, seemingly about to say something, then turned and left.

She waited until she heard the glass doors of the executive suite close.

On the floor next to the desk, on the far side, Leland had left his briefcase. A battered old cordovan leather case handed down from his father.

She lifted the flap, found his BlackBerry in one of the front pockets.

Slipped it out.

Told herself that she was *checking on something.*

Her mouth was dry.

By then, Noreen would have been in the dining room downstairs, waiting in line for sandwiches. Leland was in his budget meeting. She looked at her watch. The meeting would go on for another twenty minutes at least.

She powered his BlackBerry on. The T-Mobile screen came up, then a message: HANDHELD IS LOCKED.

Since when did Leland use the password protection on his BlackBerry?

She clicked UNLOCK.

ENTER PASSWORD:

She hesitated. Entered the password he used for his regular office e-mail account. She'd helped him come up with something he'd remember: Don17. For his favorite Dallas Cowboys player, Don Meredith, the famous quarterback from the 1960s, plus his jersey number.

INCORRECT PASSWORD!

She clicked OK, and a message came up: ENTER PASSWORD (2/10):

Meaning the second try of ten. What would happen when she hit ten?

She tried again, entered "DandyDon17."

INCORRECT PASSWORD!

What was it? She tried several more variations on Don Meredith, kept getting INCORRECT PASSWORD!

On the fifth try, it told her to enter the word "black-berry" to keep going. She did, then tried other passwords. His daughter's name. His wife's name. His birthday. The year of his birth.

Before her tenth try, a warning came up. One more incorrect entry and the handheld would be wiped.

"No line today."

Noreen was standing before her. She handed Lauren a sandwich wrapped in brown recycled chlorine-free deli wrap. "That's Leland's BlackBerry, isn't it?"

Lauren felt a jolt in her stomach. Looked up, a bored expression on her face. "Oh, yeah," she said with an exasperated sigh. "If he's going to ask me to install a firmware update one more time . . ." She let her voice trail off. "Anyway, thanks."

"Sure," Noreen said, a suspicious look in her eyes. "Anytime."

68

My apartment was dusty and had that closed-up smell, since—between travel and staying at Lauren's house—I had barely been there in weeks. But it made for a convenient command center. Merlin took the afternoon off—his boss didn't mind, since the work had been slow—and this time I'd insisted he accept payment. We devised a plan, came up with a shopping list, then split up. It was a little like a scavenger hunt. A handful of disposable cell phones. A laser pointer from an office-supply store. From a hardware store, a couple of chandelier bulbs, a few bags of plaster of paris, some bell wire. From an auto-parts store, aluminum powder, which is used to stop leaks in radiators. From a supermarket, a couple of five-pound bags of granulated sugar and some vegetable oil. Three ski masks from a sporting-goods store. A Super Soaker pressurized water gun from a toy store.

The rest of the equipment was stuff Merlin had in his garage at home.

He was easily able to find white smoke grenades at a gun shop. By far the hardest item to find was potassium chlorate. It's one of those chemicals that the U.S. government tries to control, particularly since 9/11, but

Merlin was able to turn up a couple of dusty bags at a garden center, where it was sold as weed killer.

At fifteen minutes after midnight I was back at the office building on Leesburg Pike in Falls Church.

The ten-story building was mostly dark, but not completely. Lights were on in a few windows here and there, though none on the seventh floor. Paladin Worldwide's Virginia office was a nine-to-five business.

I positioned myself at the back of the west wing of the building—the western leg of the inverted V—in the location I'd picked out earlier in the day. From there, behind a row of perfectly spaced trees that had been planted to provide an illusion of woods for the building's tenants, I knew I wouldn't be spotted if anyone happened to be looking out the window. Though at that time of night, there wasn't likely to be anyone.

The mirrored blue glass skin of the building looked black and opaque in the moonlight. There was a little ambient light from the distant streetlights. The wind howled, gusting a few drops of rain. I looked up. The sky was black and murky and threatening. It appeared that it might really start coming down at any moment.

Much quieter here at midnight than it had been during the day, when the traffic on the Leesburg Pike was a constant high roar. Instead there was only the occasional *blat* of a motorcycle, the full-throated growl of a truck.

I looked at my watch, unzipped the nylon Under Armour duffel, and pulled out a small black sphere, soft and squishy.

A stress ball, roughly the size of a baseball. Lycra over a semisolid gel. Apparently squeezing this little ball helped office workers relieve the tensions of their workday.

I lobbed it at a second-floor window. It was dense

enough to make a *thud* as it struck the glass, but not hard enough to break it.

Then I hurled a second one, and a third, and a fourth. All at the same window.

A few seconds later, I heard the rapid whooping klaxon, an alarm that was broadcast over a couple of sirens inside and out. The exterior windows were wired to glass-break detectors. That meant they'd detect the specific shock frequencies generated by breaking glass—or simply by the vibration caused by a good hard impact that didn't actually break the glass.

I checked my watch again, then strolled over to the Defender, parked on a side street in direct view of the building's main entrance. I got in and waited.

The security guard showed up nine minutes later.

He got out of his company vehicle, a Hyundai Sonata, the logo painted on the side. Middle-aged, a comb-over, gin-blossom face. A blue uniform. Armed only with a walkie-talkie. A retired cop, by the look of him, which meant that he'd do everything by the book.

He did.

He switched on a flashlight and walked around the perimeter of the building, shining his light up and down the glass exterior, looking for a broken window, for evidence of any intruders. Most office buildings don't have glass-break sensors above the third floor, on the theory that no one's going to break a window and try to enter that high up.

So he only had to check out the windows on the first two stories, which wouldn't take long. Once he realized there weren't any broken windows, he'd relax. He'd know he wasn't dealing with a burglary or even an accident but a technical glitch of some sort. Something had set off the glass-break sensor, he'd figure. A stray gust of wind. Or a defective window frame. Maybe he'd investigate further inside, but his heart wouldn't be in it.

He finished his survey of the building's exterior in six minutes, which was longer than I expected. He was more thorough than he had to be. Definitely a retired cop. A lot of rent-a-cops who haven't been in law enforcement will do the bare minimum. This guy was going beyond that. He was doing his job. I liked that.

Plus, it helped me out considerably. If he limited his inspection to a cursory walk around the building, I'd be screwed.

But he didn't. He came around to the front of the building again, casting a cone of light in front of him. He took a key from a large ring on his belt and unlocked a door to the left of the revolving doors.

I watched him disappear into the lobby. He was probably going up to the second floor to investigate further, whether by the stairs or the elevator. But I could tell from his body language that he'd already decided there was no crime in progress.

He didn't lock the door behind him.

I didn't think he would—it's the sort of detail most people, even security guards, don't think about—but if he had locked the door, then I would have gone to Plan B. Which was to wait until he'd left, gone back to the monitoring station, and then lob some more stress balls at the window.

And he'd come back again, annoyed at being pulled away from his book or his newspaper or his TV show, and he'd investigate again, but this time it would be more perfunctory. He'd be convinced that there was some mechanical glitch in the system. Eventually, after two or three callbacks, he'd leave the door open behind him. They always did.

But he'd just saved me a half hour or more.

I moved the Defender to the back of the building, then got out and crossed the narrow strip of lawn that I figured wasn't covered by the CCTV cameras mounted on this side of the building. There are always blind spots.

I reached the southwest corner of the building, then risked a quick appearance on a security monitor—I had no choice—by sidling close to the building and slipping in through the unlocked door.

Of course, if it had been daytime, the Paladin key-card I'd filched from Don Taylor—swapped, really—would have gotten me in to both the building and the Paladin office suite on the seventh floor. But then the Paladin office suite wouldn't have been unoccupied. And that wouldn't have worked at all.

So I had another plan, one that required the help of my friends and a shopping list of supplies and some carefully coordinated execution.

And the one thing that you can't buy or plan on or wheedle. The one thing you can never count on.

Luck.

69

Fortunately, I only had to hide in the utility closet off the lobby for fourteen minutes. The space was small and close, the smell of rancid wet mops and strong cleaning fluids overpowering. I heard the elevator doors *ping,* then open. The squawk of the guard's walkie-talkie. The *click* of his heels against the marble tile as he walked to the exit.

I waited another ten minutes. I wasn't able to hear his car start up, not at this distance. But by the time I emerged, his car was gone.

He'd found nothing. He would blame it on errant technology, the bane of our existence. He'd done his job, and he'd served my purpose, and he wouldn't be back.

Then I hit a preprogrammed number on my cell.

Three minutes later I unlocked the side door for Dorothy and Merlin.

"It's the A-Team," I said.

"I guess that makes me Mr. T," Dorothy said.

"Wasn't that show a little before your time, Dorothy?" I said.

"Honey, I watched it in reruns, come on."

"Never seen it," Merlin said, sounding cranky. He was carrying a couple of green clothlike recyclable shopping bags from Whole Foods, which held the improvised devices we'd assembled.

I placed one of them outside the lobby men's room, where it couldn't be seen through the glass doors at the front of the building. Then I led them through the lobby to the fire stairs at the back. The door was unlocked.

Each floor was accessible from inside the stairwells, of course—it's a fire-safety law—so I was able to make a quick stop on the second floor to drop off the second device. When I returned to the stairwell, I noticed that Merlin was looking even more sullen, and I decided to say something.

"You're having second thoughts."

He nodded.

"It's too late." I gave him a steely stare, and he returned it.

Then I half smiled, and said, "Look, Merlin. There are no guarantees. We have a solid plan of action and a fallback, and at a certain point we just have to rely on luck."

"Never believed in luck," he said. The stairwell was dark and empty, and his words echoed hollowly.

"I think luck is essential. You can never count on it, I agree. But we don't have much choice. Bail if you want to. I'll understand."

We stood there in silence for almost a minute. Dorothy looked from Merlin to me and waited.

Finally, he said, "I just want to be clear about something. This isn't for you, or your brother, or whatever kind of revenge thing you've got going on. This is because I hate everything that Paladin stands for."

"Okay," I said.

"Just to be clear," he said. He turned and started climbing the stairs, and Dorothy and I followed.

She flashed me a furtive smile. "How many floors?"

"We're going to seven," I said.

"Why the hell couldn't we take the elevator?"

She was just complaining for the sake of complaining. She knew that the stairs were at the end of the lobby farthest from the Paladin surveillance camera, which was trained on the elevators.

Neither Merlin nor I said anything as we climbed.

"I'm not doing the elliptical trainer for a week," she muttered, breathing hard.

Then Merlin said, "The problem is, we're all relying on your observations from one quick walk-through. You didn't have a chance to get in there and really look around. We really don't know what their full security setup is like."

He was right: All we knew was what I'd seen. No keypad access at the door to Paladin's offices. That was so the cleaning people could get in at night. Don Taylor's keycard would get us right in, I expected.

That was assuming, naturally, that Carl Koblenz hadn't gone into some state of DEFCON 1 alert after discovering that three of his professionals had been dispatched by a guy whose field skills he'd probably expected were pretty damned rusty. I hoped, and assumed, that he'd thought it through and decided that my response had been mere, understandable, self-preservation: I didn't want to be taken in and questioned by three bad guys. Who could blame me?

He wouldn't think to check his guys' keycards to see whether they'd been tampered with. He wasn't going to deactivate any of them. That I was sure of. He'd never expect me to come back in the middle of the night.

At least, I didn't think so, and one way or the other, we were about to find out soon.

In terms of surveillance, there appeared to be a single CCTV camera in the lobby outside their main office door, fixed and not pan-tilt-zoom. Another camera inside, in the receptionist's area. No other visible surveillance cameras. It was possible that they were monitored live somewhere, but that wasn't likely. That would be overkill for an office that mostly handled administrative stuff. I've done jobs at corporation headquarters that had more than two hundred security cameras and maybe three monitors. Live monitoring at night, for a small office like this, was almost unheard of.

We stood at the door to the seventh floor. I pushed the crash bar, opening the door an inch or so. Enough to confirm that it wasn't locked from inside.

"I'm not going to argue with you," I said. "It's a crapshoot. You're just going to have to rely on me."

Merlin sighed, long and loud.

Dorothy made a sarcastic *mmm-hmmm* sound. "Then we're all screwed," she said.

70

Merlin was the first through the door. He wore a black ski mask, which made him look like a small-town bank robber. He quickly found the surveillance camera, mounted on the wall outside the Paladin office, then carefully aimed a laser pointer at its lens. The tiny laser beam would dazzle the camera's sensor, temporarily blinding it so that it would see only a white blur.

He held it steady, aimed at the lens, while walking slowly toward Paladin's mahogany front doors. Dorothy and I followed. I pulled out the Super Soaker water gun from my duffel bag, pumped it twenty times or so to build up pressure, then pointed it at the camera lens. A thin stream of fluid jetted out: a mix of vegetable oil and water. This coated the lens with a cloudy film of grease, which would fuzz out the image for as long as the grease film remained. Even if someone were monitoring the feed live, unlikely though that was, they'd blame the camera. Merlin lowered the laser pointer and kept on going.

I passed the Paladin keycard over the reader and heard a click. The door was unlocked. Merlin readied the laser pointer in his right hand and switched on his

LED flashlight in the other. Then I pulled the door open a few inches.

"Where the hell—?" he said.

"Ten o'clock," I said.

"How high?"

I closed my eyes, called the memory of Paladin's lobby to mind. "Roughly eight feet."

" 'Roughly' doesn't help."

"You're wearing a mask."

He shrugged, stepped into the dark office. He planted his feet and directed a beam of light into the reception area. Then he raised the laser pointer and waited a few seconds. "Okay."

We entered behind him, and I squirted that camera with the Super Soaker as well.

Merlin washed the walls with the LED beam, his eyes scanning the room quickly. "Motion detectors?"

"No," I said.

"You're sure."

"No."

"Great," Dorothy said.

"Not likely," I said. "Building cleaners probably come in here at night."

"Not likely," Merlin echoed. *"Probably."* He lowered the flashlight beam to the floor.

"Life's a risk," I said.

"Especially around you," Dorothy said. "Are we cool here? I'm going to get to work."

I nodded, handed her an LED flashlight, and shined mine along the floor to the next room, illuminating a path to the windows. The Paladin offices seemed a lot smaller in the dark. Starting at the leftmost window, I tugged the venetian blinds closed. Then I directed Dorothy to the desk where Koblenz's admin, Eleanor Appleby, normally sat.

Meanwhile, Merlin busied himself with his equipment, looking for stray microwaves that might indicate a microwave-based motion detector, and an RF detector to search for hidden cameras.

"Clear?" I said.

"So far."

Dorothy made a *pssst* sound, and I came over, shining my flashlight. She was sitting at Eleanor Appleby's computer, looking frustrated. "They do take precautions here," she said. "It's logged out."

"Did you check the usual place?" Merlin asked.

"You mean, the Post-it pad in the middle drawer? Yeah, I checked it, but there's nothing there. What's *wrong* with these people?"

"Can you crack the password?" I asked her.

"If you don't mind me sitting here until morning, I might be able to. I'll need a pot of coffee, though."

"Maybe not such a good idea," I said.

"That means I can't install any spyware. But maybe that's just as well. Place like this, they probably have antivirus software that'd pick it up."

"Now what?"

"I'm stumped."

This was a disappointment. If we wanted to capture any of Eleanor Appleby's passwords, we needed to put some kind of eavesdropping device on her computer.

"How about a piece of hardware?" Merlin said. He'd brought a couple of different keyloggers—plastic devices that looked like one of those barrel connectors you might—or might not—notice in the rat's nest of cables behind your computer.

"Uh-uh," Dorothy said. She pointed at the back of the admin's computer. "They're making life hard for us. Check it out."

I trained my flashlight at the back of the computer, saw only smooth wood. "What am I looking at?"

"All the computer cables are routed through the desk so no one can tamper with them."

"That rules out the hardware keylogger, too," I said.

"No," said Merlin. "It just means Plan C. The keyboard module."

That was another little electronic component he'd brought along, which you installed inside the keyboard. Even harder to detect than the barrel connector, but time-consuming to put in. He put his messenger bag on Eleanor Appleby's desk.

"Dorothy, can you put it in?" I asked.

"I can figure it out, yeah," she said. "Though Walter might be faster at it."

"Faster and better," Merlin said, "but I've got another job to do."

"Then you'll just have to settle," Dorothy snapped. She reached into his messenger bag and took out a crimping tool, a screwdriver, and a tube of Superglue. She flipped the keyboard over, began loosening the miniature screws.

"You realize," Merlin said, "that this means you're going to have to get back in here and retrieve this thing in a day or two, right?"

"*We* are," I said.

He grunted. "Then you really better hope nothing goes south tonight."

I nodded. "Let's get lucky."

I approached Koblenz's office door, turned the knob slowly, pushed it open. Merlin followed right behind, carrying a second messenger bag full of equipment.

I looked back at Merlin. "You didn't detect any motion detectors in here, right?"

"Not microwave-based," he said. "Passive infrared I'm not going to pick up."

"You think he might have passive infrared?"

Merlin shined the light quickly around the office,

saw the immaculate desk, the perfectly squared piles on the credenza behind it. "Nah. He's too orderly."

Unless the cleaning people had been given instructions not to clean his office, Koblenz wouldn't have a motion detector of any kind inside his office. I agreed with Merlin: Koblenz seemed the fastidious type, the sort of guy who'd want his office carpet vacuumed every night, the wastebaskets emptied. And, although it was possible, I doubted his admin cleaned his office for him.

Merlin sighed. "That's a TL-30X6."

"I thought it was a Diebold."

"That's the rating. The most secure safe they make. And an electronic lock. Oh, man."

"Like I told you."

"Yeah," he said.

"Right?"

"You said electronic lock. I didn't know it was a TL-30X6."

"I don't like your tone, Merlin. You sound very pessimistic. Maybe even defeatist."

"Heller, listen to me. I brought my StrongArm safe cracker diamond-core drill bits, okay? But drilling through one of these, that's a five-hour job at least. That mother's made from inch-and-a-half-thick steel and cobalt-carbide matrix hardplate, okay?"

"If you say so."

"Then they've got sheets of tempered glass mounted inside, rigged to break when a drill hits it. Triggers a relocking mechanism that even the right combination won't open."

"Merlin," I said. "I get you. I think we're going to have to change your name to Eeyore. Now, why don't we try the keypad? I'd prefer nondestructive means."

He gave me a look, telling me that was his plan anyway.

The safe had an electronic keypad on the front: nine numbers, on black keys, inset in a round black dial with a red LED light at the top. Instead of turning a dial, you punched in the combination.

He knelt before the safe, took out a small jar and brush, and began dusting the keypad with white fingerprint powder. When he shined the flashlight beam at it, I could see distinct fingerprints on only four of the keys: 3, 5, 9, and ENTER.

"That's a start," I said. "That limits us to three numbers."

"It's a six-digit combination of 3, 5, and 9," Merlin said. "How many possible permutations does that make? Like a million?"

"Less than that, Eeyore."

"Not a lot less. Anyway, we get four tries before we go into penalty mode."

"And then?"

"Then a five-minute lockout before we can try again."

"So let's hope we guess right. What about the manufacturer's tryout combo?"

"It's 1-2-3-4-5-6."

"That's not it, then. You're just going to have to try randomly."

As far as I knew, there were no six-digit numbers that Koblenz had any obvious connection to—his house number had four digits, the number of the office building had five, the suite number had three.

"Right. Great." He hissed in a breath. "All right, here goes." He punched in one sequence.

And nothing happened.

"Try again," I said.

He punched in another sequence.

Nothing.

And a third time. Nothing.

Merlin gritted his teeth and entered another sequence.

Then something happened. But not what we wanted. The red LED light flashed. On, then off, with a ten-second delay between flashes.

"Crap," he said. "Now we have to wait five minutes."

"No. Try spiking the solenoid."

He shrugged, gave me a dyspeptic scowl, and twisted the keypad off the safe door. It's meant to be easily removed, so you can change the battery. He pushed on a couple of clips, releasing a plastic cover, then pulled out the black rubber membrane. This exposed a circuit board and a row of eight tiny metal posts.

Then he took a nine-volt battery from his bag and clipped on a pair of leads. One end he held against the leftmost post. When he touched the other lead to the top right post, there was a crackling sound and the smell of electronic components burning.

And nothing else. It didn't unlock.

"That's it," he said. "We're screwed now."

"Try the drill."

"I thought you wanted nondestructive."

"I want the card," I said. "At this point I want it any way we can get it."

"If you told me in the first place, I could have brought in a thermic lance."

"What, from the *Ocean's Eleven* prop room?"

"No, man, it's for real. Cuts through concrete and rebar steel and everything. But it's huge, and you need an oxygen tank."

I was about to tell him to try the drill anyway, despite the long odds, when, out of the murky darkness of Koblenz's inner sanctum, a tiny red light winked at me from high on the wall near the ceiling.

"You see that flashing light?" I said.

"Yeah," Merlin said impatiently. "Told you, that's the penalty mode light. Means we gotta wait five minutes."

"No. Up there." I pointed.

He looked up.

Saw the blinking red light.

"*Damn* it, Heller."

"What?"

"PIR. Passive infrared."

A motion detector.

"We gotta get out of here," he said, his voice rising.

"What's going on?" Dorothy called from the desk right outside.

"We just set off an alarm," I said.

71

"His guys are probably already on their way," Merlin said.

"Oh, good Lord," Dorothy said.

"*Move* it," Merlin said. "Let's go. Won't take them more than ten minutes to show up, I bet. Damn it to hell!"

"No," I said. "We're not leaving here with nothing. Dorothy, how much more time do you need?"

"I don't know—three, four minutes. But I can't rush it."

"Don't rush," I said. "Get that thing in there and clean things up so they can't tell we've been here."

I swung the flashlight beam around Koblenz's office, saw the built-in ventilation system beneath his windows. Raced over to it and flipped open the control panel.

"What the hell are you doing?" Merlin said. Perspiration had broken out on his forehead. "Let's get the hell out of here."

"Calm down," I said. "This is why we have the backup procedure." The air-conditioning had gone off for the evening, as an energy-saving measure, but I switched it back on and turned the fan on full blast. Then I adjusted the louvers on the front of the unit so that air was blowing up at an angle, rattling the papers on top of the file cabinets and the credenza. On top of the credenza were a large rubber plant and a smaller jade plant. I tipped over the jade plant. The plastic pot went in one direction, the plant and its clump of earth went another. Then I took a pile of papers from the credenza and scattered some of them to the floor.

"What the hell?" Merlin said.

"Establishing a plausible explanation," I said. In reality, the gust of air probably wouldn't be strong enough to tip over the jade plant, but Koblenz would probably accept it. Especially since nothing would appear to have been stolen. He'd focus on the real anomaly, which was why his AC had gone on in the middle of the night. But he'd dismiss that as a malfunction in the building's ventilation system. People always blame technology.

I pulled out the four disposable cell phones, found the one that I'd labeled in Sharpie marker with a big number "1."

"All right," I said. "Here goes." I hit the preset number on the first cell phone.

I couldn't see the result right away. I didn't need to. The incendiary devices we'd jury-rigged were rudimentary, but the effect would be dramatic. Not that we wanted to burn the building down; not at all. We just wanted to make it look that way.

Inside each Whole Foods bag was a simple contraption: a cell phone wired to a relay, a nine-volt battery, the filament from a chandelier bulb. Phone rings, bulb filament gets hot, sets off a mixture of sugar and potassium chlorate inside a smoke grenade. That in turn sets off the plaster-of-paris and aluminum-powder mix, which we'd poured into a flowerpot and let harden. That mixture would get incredibly hot. It would actually burn underwater.

Basic explosives training; nothing fancy. But within thirty seconds, the entire lobby would be filled with smoke, billowing from a blazing hot fire. Hot but contained. And extremely dramatic. The smoke would pour out of the building.

Even before I made it to the window and saw the clouds of grayish white smoke in the moonlight, the building's smoke alarm started clanging.

Dorothy announced, "All set." She adjusted the keyboard on Eleanor Appleby's desk, restoring it to where it had been before she tinkered with it, then she stood up.

"The fire trucks should be here in five minutes," I said. "We'd just better hope none of our Paladin friends is closer than that."

"I thought you said it would take the Paladin guys ten minutes," Dorothy said.

"That was an estimate."

"You didn't know? You were *guessing*?"

"An educated guess."

"Heller, why didn't you tell me that?"

I didn't reply. The answer was simple: It was a gap in the plan I was hoping to just finesse. I was hoping for good luck. But if I'd told them that, I'd have been doing this alone.

For the first time, I was nervous.

Our escape plan rested entirely on the likelihood that the firefighters would get here before the Paladin guys. Once the fire department arrived, they'd secure the scene and allow no one to enter. But if Paladin got here first, they might well decide to race upstairs, smoke or no smoke. It was entirely possible that they'd connect the two things—the motion sensor in Koblenz's office going off and an apparent fire raging in the lobby—and conclude that their office had been the target of vandals. Then they'd be all the more motivated to rush up here.

I could hear the sirens, louder and closer, heard the shouts and the braking of the trucks and the clatter of the equipment as the firemen jumped out, and I heaved a sigh of relief.

"They're here," she said.

I pressed the second preprogrammed number, detonating the second incendiary device, which I'd placed in the lobby of the second floor.

"I'm not deaf," I said.

The loud squealing of tires.

"No, Heller, I mean Paladin. Two black Humvees. That's Paladin."

"I'm *out* of here!" Merlin shouted.

"Walter," Dorothy said. "Man up."

The last thing I saw before we raced out of the Paladin office and down the stairs was a shouting match between some intimidating-looking Paladin employees, a couple of Falls Church policemen, and a few firemen.

Not a contest the Paladin security people were going to win. The police and the fire department would never let them enter what appeared to be a burning building.

We raced out through the loading-dock entrance at the ground level. No one was waiting for us there. Both smoke devices were at the front of the building, so that was where the firefighters were gathered.

"Merlin," I said as we parted, Dorothy running ahead toward the Defender. "Thank you."

He turned toward me, gave me a dark look, and didn't say a word.

72

Dorothy and I didn't talk for a long while. Maybe it was the adrenaline crash, that low-level anxiety and mild depression that often sets in after a time of great stress. You see that a lot after a battle.

Finally, she said, "Now what?"

"There's always another way."

"Well, I sure can't think of one."

"I can," I said, and I explained.

"Oh man," she said. "That's either incredibly bold or incredibly stupid."

"I like to think positive."

"You know, if Koblenz really has one of those Raptor-Cards, that's just incredible."

"Is that what it's called?"

"I've only heard rumors about this. Remember a couple years back how it came out about the U.S. government tapping into the whole SWIFT banking consortium? So they could monitor suspicious movements of money?"

"For terrorist surveillance, sure."

"Right. But then it turned out the government could spy on every single funds transfer, every single financial transaction—everything. No more bank secrecy. Big Brother was watching, right?"

I didn't want to argue with her, but I'd always believed that there was a whole lot less secrecy in banking than most people thought. Rich folks assume that when they stash money offshore, it's going to remain a deep, dark secret. But bankers are human beings. Even offshore bankers. All you have to do is pay off the right one, or make the right friend, and you can find out all sorts of things.

Which wasn't necessarily a bad thing for people in my line of work, of course.

And then there was a report that was leaked on the Internet not so long ago about how Cisco Systems was secretly building a backdoor into all its routers to enable the government to eavesdrop on all network traffic, including e-mails and phone calls.

"So a RaptorCard allows you to move money around without the government watching."

"Right. By embedding private-key cryptography in an appliance that looks like a credit card. The strongest encryption ever devised. The closest thing to a true random number generator. Authentication's built right in. You can use it anywhere."

"Numbered accounts are just so twentieth-century, huh?"

"Right. So my question for you, Nick, is what do you plan to do with it?"

I thought for a long moment. The answer was complicated, and in truth, I hadn't yet figured it out. Not entirely, anyway.

But I didn't get a chance to answer before my cell phone rang.

"Got something for you," Frank Montello said. "Something really interesting. That cell phone you asked me to track?"

I hesitated, then remembered. "Yeah?"

"She just called the same throwaway cell phone number your father called."

"Roger's cell phone," I said, and I began to feel queasy. "You're not serious."

"Yeah," Frank said. "Just about an hour ago, Lauren Heller called her husband."

73

Marjorie Ogonowski parted the curtains and looked out her living-room window.

A dark blue Buick Century sedan pulled up to the curb. She took note of the white license plate with the dark blue lettering that said U.S. GOVERNMENT. The license-plate number started with a J, denoting the Justice Department. Marjorie, whose cousin was married to an FBI employee, knew a fair amount about the FBI.

After the FBI man had called her to arrange an interview concerning a matter at work, she'd been sorely tempted to call her cousin and see what she could find out. But he had instructed her not to speak to anyone. She hadn't stopped worrying since the man called. She wondered if it had anything to do with her boss, Roger Heller. She was pretty sure it did. Especially after that man John Murray from Security Compliance had come to talk to her at the office about Roger and why he'd gone missing.

Well, at least the FBI man was right on time. Seven o'clock P.M., just as he promised. She liked that. Marjorie was always on time, always precise. She was orderly in all things. She was nothing if not detail-oriented. This was one of the qualities that made her such a good lawyer, she was convinced. That, and her brains, and her willingness to work long hours without complaining. Right out of Georgetown Law she'd landed a job as an associate counsel in the corporate development division at Gifford Industries, working on mergers and acquisitions, and she was convinced that she was on the fast track to general counsel.

Her salary wasn't great, but that would change in short order. In the meantime, it had allowed her to buy this tiny ranch house in Linthicum, Maryland. The real-estate salesman had called it "an investor's dream," which meant that it needed a lot of work. She had done most of it herself, stripping the yellowed wallpaper, painting, even installing a new laminate hardwood floor in her kitchen by herself over a long weekend.

This was the advantage of not having a social life. You got a lot of work done around the house.

The FBI agent rang the doorbell, and she tried not to answer it too quickly. She didn't want him to know how nervous she was. Nor that this was the high point of her week, although it was.

In the other room her cockatiel, Caesar, whistled loudly.

She opened the aluminum screen door and shook his hand. Something about his unhandsome face made him seem trustworthy.

"Were my directions okay?" she said.

"Perfect," he said. "The Parkway wasn't bad at all. Took me exactly thirty-seven minutes."

She liked his precision.

She let him in and offered him tea or a soft drink, but he declined. He showed her his FBI badge and credentials, which she inspected carefully, though she'd only seen things like that on TV. The gold badge with the eagle and the embossed letters, in a black leather wallet. The laminated credentials with his photo and signature were clipped to the breast pocket of his cheap suit. He handed her a business card.

They sat facing each other at an angle in the two easy chairs, which she had slipcovered herself with remnant fabric from a shop in Laurel. Her Apple MacBook laptop was open on the narrow desk. She glanced at it. She could see the screen from where she sat and wondered whether he could, too.

His name was Special Agent Corelli, and he had a slight stammer that sounded like a residue from childhood. He was not slick or arrogant, as she was afraid an FBI agent might be, and she liked that, too.

From his black nylon briefcase he took out a notepad.

"Ms. Ogonowski, how well do you know Roger Heller?" he said.

So it was about Roger after all. "Marjorie, please."

"Marjorie," he said with an abashed smile.

"Did something happen to him?"

"I'm afraid I can't talk about an active investigation. I'm sorry."

An active investigation! "Well, Mr. Heller is my boss—I mean, I just know him that way, of course." She found herself looking at the business card, turning it over, evading his eyes.

"Of course."

"He's my direct supervisor, and it's been superbusy lately—"

"He's been out of town a lot, hasn't he? Out of the office?"

"He travels a lot for business, yes."

"And for other reasons."

She hesitated. She drummed her fingers on the end table next to her chair, then reflexively, compulsively, began realigning the objects on the table, lining up the tiny Apple remote alongside the TV and cable and DVD remotes, making them all nice and parallel and evenly spaced. "I'm sorry, what's the question?"

"You recently tried to reach him when he was out of town. Not on company business."

How could the FBI possibly know about this? She'd promised never to tell anyone. Could that Security Compliance consultant, John Murray, have found out and told him? "I don't remember."

"I think you do," the FBI man said quietly.

Something in him had suddenly switched off. No longer was he the trustworthy and sincere-seeming federal agent. Now there was a coldness in the man that frightened her even more than the question.

Caesar started whistling again.

"I'm sorry about the bird," she said. "I need to change the cage liner, so he's getting a little cranky."

"Not a problem," the FBI man said.

She slid her hand across the end table again, shifting, then straightening the remotes back into parallel lines.

"Would you mind if I called the Bureau," she said abruptly. "Is that all right? Just to—I don't know . . ."

He lifted his chin, turned up his hands, smiled. "Go right ahead. We always encourage that. The number's right there on the card."

She stood up, went over to the wall phone in the hall outside the kitchen, within view of the FBI man. "My cousin's husband works there," she said. "I'm going to call him, if you don't mind."

"Of course," he said. "I don't mind at all. Whatever puts your mind at ease."

Taped to the wall was a long list of phone numbers that included her cousin Beverly and Beverly's husband, Stuart. She found Stuart's office number and dialed it.

The number on Agent Corelli's card had a different exchange, she noticed, though she wasn't sure that meant anything. Maybe main FBI had a different area code from the Washington Field Office. Then something else about the card attracted her notice, too.

"Did they redo the business cards recently?" she asked, looking at Corelli's card closely. "The seal on my cousin Stuart's business card—"

A hand shot out and depressed the plunger on the wall phone, breaking the connection. She hadn't even heard him approach.

She tried to scream, but a hand was clapped over her mouth. "I need you to tell me everything," the man said softly, so quietly that she could barely hear his words over Caesar's shrill whistle.

74

I was waiting for Lauren to emerge from her bathroom.

In the meantime, Gabe and I talked a bit in his room. I handed his graphic novel back, and he wanted to know what I thought. I told him I thought it was incredible. That I was honored and humbled to be The Cowl.

"What are you talking about?" he said.

"The hero. The Cowl. With the fortress of solitude in Adams Morgan."

"That's not you," he said.

"I thought he looked a little like me. No?"

"Huh? No way."

I sneaked a glance at his face. He looked awkward and extremely defensive. Deeply embarrassed. I had brought out in the open something he didn't want to admit to out loud. "No," I said. "Of course not. I mean, I *wish,* right?"

"Don't flatter yourself, dude."

"Gabe, who's Candi Dupont?"

He was too young, or maybe too honest, to have learned how to cover. His eyes flashed with fear. "Just a name," he said.

"Candi Dupont is Dr. Cash's girlfriend. Dr. Cash is your dad, Gabe."

"Oh, man. This is *fiction*. Don't you understand how fiction works, dude? You take little bits and pieces from your real life, and you weave it into this—"

"Gabe. You read your dad's e-mails, didn't you?"

"Screw you!" he shouted hoarsely. He shoved me away with one hand and turned away.

"Gabe." I put both of my hands on his shoulders and rotated him to face me. "Your dad used the same password on all of his accounts, didn't he? His Gmail and his iTunes and whatever. And you accessed his e-mail."

He was crying by then. His face had gone scarlet, his acne like droplets of blood sprinkled over his nose and cheeks.

"That's how you found out about Candi Dupont, isn't that right? That's how you knew your dad had a . . . a relationship."

"He was cheating on Mom!" he gasped.

"Gabe, it's okay. I'm not going to yell at you. I really don't care about that. I just need that password. If there's any chance of saving your father."

He looked at me. "Why?"

"Because you're right: Candi Dupont is just a name. It's the name that your father called his girlfriend, I'm guessing. A name she used. An alias of some sort. But it's not her real name. Which is why we haven't been able to locate her. But if we can find out what her real name is, we might be able to find your dad. Because maybe she knows. Gabe, I know how horrible this is for you—"

"I don't *know* her real name! How would I know that? All I know is that he was sending all these gross, like totally explicit, *sexual* e-mails to this woman named Candi Dupont, and she was writing back, and she was even more explicit, and he was lying to Mom the whole time, and it just made me want to puke."

"Of course it did," I said gently. "Of course. But if

you give me his password, we can find out her e-mail address. And that might be enough to find her."

His head was on his chest, his right elbow shielding his eyes from my gaze, and tears were spilling onto his T-shirt.

"Gabe," I said. "Come on."

When Lauren came downstairs, I asked her to go with me to Roger's library so we could talk privately. We sat in the antique French club chairs, which were positioned so that each of us had to shift uncomfortably in order to look at each other.

"How's Roger?" I said.

Her immediate reaction—a microexpression, I think they're called—was shock. A split second later she had regained her poise. "You're asking *me*? How could I possibly know—?"

"Lauren," I said. "You called him. A few hours ago. On the same disposable cell phone number that my father called him on."

She blinked quickly. "Nick . . ."

"You've been lying to me since the beginning of this whole mess. You've known all along where he was."

"No," she whispered. "I don't."

"Well," I said, and I cleared my throat, "I wish I could believe that. But you've lost all credibility. If you ever had any to begin with. Is this some kind of a scam that you're helping him pull off?"

"Nick, will you *listen* to me?"

"Yeah," I said. "I'd love to hear your explanation. And while you're at it, maybe you can tell me how you justify putting Gabe through the hell you've put him through."

"Nick," she said. "I didn't know what happened to Roger until last night. I didn't know anything more than you did. Yes, I admit it—I've been concealing a few things from you—but if you'd just hear me out—"

"Last night," I interrupted. "That was the first time you heard from him?"

"Check my phone records."

"He called you? E-mailed you?"

"He sent me a text message. With a number to call." She lifted her purse from the floor, began rummaging through it. "Here, you can check my phone's text-message in-box if you don't believe me."

"So where is he?"

"He said he's being held somewhere in Georgia."

Paladin's training facility and headquarters were in Georgia, I realized. "Yet he was able to call you?"

"Yes."

"And he was able to receive a call from my father. What kind of imprisonment is that?"

"He didn't say he was in any kind of prison. Or even that he was a hostage."

"He said he was 'being held,' isn't that right?"

"Yes, that's what he said. He kept saying he had to make it fast, that he only had a minute to talk—I had the feeling that wherever he was they didn't know he had a phone. But listen—the main thing is, he said they were going to release him."

"'Release' him."

"That they were going to let him go free, finally. They were going to make a deal."

"Who's 'they'?"

She shook her head. "He didn't say. I didn't ask—there wasn't time, and I didn't know how freely he could talk."

"What kind of a deal?"

"I don't *know*, Nick. He just said that I should be careful, I shouldn't do anything or make any phone calls or screw things up in any way, and they were going to let him go free. I mean, we talked for maybe a minute before he hung up."

"You must be relieved to hear from him."

"Of course I'm relieved. This has been a nightmare."

"You're getting your husband back," I said.

For a long time she was quiet. "The truth is that our marriage has been over for a while now."

I felt something cold begin to coil in the pit of my stomach. "I see." That didn't surprise me. But it did surprise me to hear her say it.

"I mean, ever since I found out about that affair he had—I haven't been able to forgive him. We haven't had a romantic life. He's still a great dad to Gabe, though, and—"

I stood up. "You know what, Lauren? I don't really care anymore."

75

The Surgeon unfolded his black canvas surgical instrument kit and removed his favorite scalpel, a Miltex MeisterHand #3. He carefully inserted a blade made of the finest carbon steel.

Marjorie Ogonowski was crying, the sound muffled by the duct tape over her mouth. Her hands and feet were bound to the bedposts by means of duct tape, too.

He'd left her glasses on so that she could see him clearly.

She'd stopped struggling a few minutes ago, but when she saw him put on the latex gloves, her writhing grew frenzied, her screams agonized. Seeing the scalpel escalated her terror considerably. But that was to be expected. One of the maxims of what was often euphemistically called "enhanced interrogation techniques" was that the fear of pain was always far more effective than the pain itself.

Of course, he wasn't actually a surgeon—he'd been expelled from medical school after an unpleasantness he didn't like to think about—but he'd gotten the nickname at Bagram, in Afghanistan. The CIA had needed to hire outside contractors to conduct interrogations in their secret prisons, in order to insulate the Agency politically. He'd so impressed his employers that they later sent him to Abu Ghraib. But when that whole mess became public, he'd been hung out to dry. There wasn't much call for his talents in the private sector. He was fortunate to have been hired by one of the few buyers out there, Paladin Worldwide.

Torture—to call it by its true name—was a greatly misunderstood art. It had become politically correct in recent years, during the backlash to the war in Iraq, to claim that torture didn't work. But if torture didn't work, why had mankind been using it for thousands of years? Why had all those members of the French Resistance given up the names of their comrades, even their own family members, under Nazi torture? Torture was only ineffective if it wasn't done right. This wasn't just a matter of creative techniques. You needed people skills. You had to know how to read people and how to establish your authority.

He spoke softly, calmly, as he always did. To raise your voice was to lose control. "Let's try this again. Mr. Heller was out of town, and you needed to reach him urgently, isn't that right? I believe you were working on a big acquisition. A power plant in São Paolo. Yes? Nod if I'm correct."

Her eyes were wide, and tears spilled down her face. She gave an exaggerated nod, up down, up down.

"Something had come up suddenly. You needed to reach him right away. But he was out of the office on a personal day. Correct?"

She nodded.

"There was a big mergers-and-acquisitions committee meeting first thing the next morning, and the slide deck had already been prepared, but you found something in the due-diligence process that you were afraid might derail the acquisition. A showstopper, you thought. Am I right?"

She nodded slowly. He could tell that she was puzzled as to how he knew this. Let alone who he was.

There is nothing we fear so much as the unknown, and the Surgeon was not going to enlighten her.

"But you had no way to reach him. You needed to reach him immediately, but he didn't have his cell phone with him. You couldn't e-mail him on his BlackBerry, because he didn't have that with him either. Am I right?"

She hesitated a few seconds before nodding.

"Strange, isn't it? A hardworking man like Mr. Heller didn't have his cell phone or his BlackBerry with him while he was traveling at such a very busy time, when he needed to be reachable at all times?"

Her eyes slid to one side. Her deception flashed like a neon sign.

"Yet somehow you reached him. You talked to him. How so?"

She looked away.

"I'm going to remove the tape from your mouth," he said. "But first I want you to see this scalpel up close. I want you to feel how sharp it is."

Her eyes widened, filled with tears. She began to shake her head—as if to say, No, please don't—but then she stopped. She didn't want him to misinterpret the gesture as an unwillingness to cooperate.

He came in close, the scalpel in his right hand, and he moved it very close to her right eyeball.

She closed her eyes, shook her head violently.

"No sudden moves, please," he said. "You'll hurt yourself badly."

Her eyes remained scrunched closed.

"Open your eyes, please, or you'll be hurt much worse."

He waited a few seconds until her eyes came open. She squinted, blinked.

"The skin of the eyelid is less than one millimeter

thick. This scalpel will slice through it quite easily. And then the sclera, beneath. The aqueous fluid will leak right out. The damage to your eye will not be reparable."

Her blinking became rapid. She moaned.

"Do you know the term 'enucleation'?"

She closed her eyes again, her moaning louder.

"Enucleation is the surgical removal of the eyeball. Usually it's done only in drastic circumstances like traumatic injury or a malignant tumor."

He could see her jaw working up and down, could hear her trying to shout the word "please" over and over.

"You'll still be able to work as an attorney without your eyes, of course," he explained. "They have screen-reading software now and scanners. You'll be able to use Westlaw that way, I believe. But you can forget about handwritten notes, and very few websites are accessible to the visually impaired, unfortunately. The adjustment will be onerous."

He laid his left hand on her forehead, right above her glasses: an intimate gesture, almost a caress.

"Now, I'm going to remove the tape from your mouth, and if you make any noise—if you shout or scream or call for help—I'm going to perform some very quick surgery. Are we clear?"

She nodded, her eyes closed.

"As soon as the tape comes off, I want you to tell me how you reached Mr. Heller. Clear?"

She nodded.

He held the scalpel about a half inch from her eye. With his left hand, he ripped off the duct tape.

She gasped loudly, gulped air.

Her words came all in a rush, high-pitched and mewling. "He left me a message on my voice mail. He told me to go to his desk, he had a cell phone in one of the drawers, one of those prepaid phones, and he said it was already activated, and he wanted me to take it and go down to the street and call him."

"Call him where?"

"He gave me a phone number."

"What was the number he gave you?"

"I don't know, I don't know, how can I possibly remember? I didn't memorize the number, how could I know what the number is? I called from work. I didn't keep a record. He told me not to!"

"Of course you don't have the phone number memorized. But the number you called will be listed on the phone you used."

She hesitated, just for a second, but long enough for him to realize that she was inventing a reply. "I put the phone back in Roger's desk."

"No, I don't think you did. I think you brought it home because he told you to do so."

She shook her head. She was trembling.

"You're a very loyal colleague," he said. He'd stopped using her name. He never used their names. "You're protecting Mr. Heller. That's commendable. But he's gone now, and you no longer need to protect him. Right now you face a choice. You will give me that phone, or you'll undergo some very painful surgery without the benefit of anesthesia."

"Please, *no.*"

"Where is the phone?"

After she told him, he went to the dresser. The throwaway cell phone was in the top drawer, just as she said. He nodded, turned back to her.

Just to be sure, he powered it on, then checked the list of outgoing calls.

It had been used only once.

"Very good," he said.

"Please," she said in a whisper, "please, can you

leave now? You have what you want, don't you? I don't know why you want it or who you are, and I don't *care*, but I just want you to leave now, please. I promise you—I give you my *word*—I won't talk to the police. I won't talk to *anyone*."

"I know you won't," the Surgeon said, ripping off a fresh length of duct tape from the silvery roll and swiftly placing it over her mouth. "I know you won't."

76

Even after all that time, I still knew very little for certain about what had happened to Roger.

The most I could do was to mull over several different hypotheses. Think them through, turn them over and over and try to calculate which one was the most likely. What I eventually settled on was something like this: my ever-scheming, ever-dissatisfied, megalomaniacal brother had finally discovered a way out of his middle-class purgatory. After his company, Gifford Industries, had secretly acquired Paladin Worldwide, he'd combed through Paladin's financial records, come across evidence of some mammoth kickback scheme, and made the brazen error of trying to extort millions of dollars from Carl Koblenz, Paladin's president. But instead of simply buying Roger's silence, Paladin had come right back at him. Threatened him. Targeted him. Then, one night in Georgetown, grabbed him.

After that, well, my hypothesis got even shakier. Had he managed to escape his abductors? That seemed awfully unlikely. Roger was no superhero. Was he being held prisoner at the Paladin training facility in Georgia in such a lax, loose way that he was actually able to use a cell phone? That was only marginally more likely.

So maybe he was being used by his captors instead. Maybe they were forcing him to make the calls, to Dad and to Lauren, urging them to cooperate with Paladin, give them what they wanted, so he could win his release.

Maybe.

But what my father had to do with it—what my father could have that Paladin might want—I couldn't imagine.

So maybe there was yet another explanation entirely, something I hadn't even begun to fathom.

Nothing would surprise me anymore.

I called Dorothy Duval a little later. I tried her work number first, but was put into her voice mail. Then I tried her cell, and she picked right up. A television was playing in the background, loud, wherever she was.

"Hope I'm not disturbing you," I said.

"Oh, no. I've got nothing going on." She sounded down.

"You okay?"

"I'll get by. You wanted to go over today?"

"The thing is, we have to do this in the middle of the workday, which I realize is a problem for you."

"No," she said. "No problem at all." There was a grim, yet singsong, quality to her voice.

"Are you going to tell me what's wrong?"

"Heller, I have all the time in the world. Jay Stoddard just fired me."

"You? For what?"

"He said I was misusing company resources."

"Meaning that you've been helping me out," I said.

"He didn't feel I deserved an explanation. The bad thing is, I'm not going to be able to help you anymore. Because I won't have any more access to any of Stoddard's databases."

"No," I said. "That's not right."

"Maybe not. But it's what happened."

"No," I said again. "This is just not acceptable."

"Tell me about it. Plus he says he's gonna blackball me. Make sure I never get a job in this town again."

"I'll talk to him."

"No," she said. "Don't bother. I can't go back there. Not after he fired me. Uh-uh."

"I'll talk to him," I said. "In the meantime, do me a favor. I need you to go into my brother's laptop and look for something."

"There's not much there."

"He has a Hotmail account. You can find out the account's user ID, right?"

"If it's there, sure. But the password—"

"That's the easy part. Victor10506."

"How do you know that?"

"Long story," I said. "But 10506 is the zip code for Bedford, New York. Where we used to live when we were kids."

"You want me to go into your brother's e-mail. No problem. But what am I looking for?"

"I want you to do a search for all e-mails to and from CatLvr74@yahoo.com," I said. "There's going to be a cell-phone number in one of them."

"And what am I supposed to do if I find one?"

"Well," I said, "I've got an interesting idea."

77

I found Jay Stoddard at breakfast in the Senate Dining Room with a senator from Virginia who was the chairman of the Armed Services Committee and was facing a nasty reelection battle.

I stormed into the elegant room—yellow walls, patterned red carpet, white tablecloths, the hush of power— wearing jeans and a T-shirt and hiking boots. Stoddard was in one of his finest handmade suits: dove gray, double-breasted, with a crisp pale blue shirt and red tie. Before him were a cup of coffee and a bowl of cornflakes. His second breakfast, I guessed. He'd always told me never to go to a business breakfast without eating first.

The maître d' had followed me in, protesting, "Sir! I'm sorry, but jeans aren't permitted. Sir, I'm afraid you're going to have to put on a tie."

The commotion attracted a lot of attention. A lot of stares. Stoddard glanced around curiously, then did a double take.

"*Heller?* What the hell are you—?"

"We have a little unfinished business," I said.

He exchanged a look with the senator—*indulge me*

for a second—and said, "I think this can wait till I'm back in the office."

"You didn't seriously believe you could get rid of Dorothy Duval so easily, did you?" I stood before his table, arms folded.

Stoddard rose. "Excuse me, John," he said to the senator. "Personnel matter." He came around the table, very close to me, and said through gritted teeth, "Heller, get the hell out of here. You're making a scene. If you want to talk about this, make a goddamned appointment."

"Right now works for me," I said.

"Damn you, Heller," he said, and crossed the dining room. I followed him out to the corridor. He stood a few feet away and poked my chest with his index finger. "Don't you *ever* do that again," he said, his voice a low, ominous rumble.

"You want to explain to me why you assigned me to that stolen-cargo case in Los Angeles?"

"I assigned you because I thought you'd do the job."

"Yeah," I said. "No one else in the firm was qualified, huh? So is that the reason you didn't want me looking too hard at who Traverse Development really is? So I wouldn't put it together that Traverse is just a Paladin holding company? Meaning that the real client was Leland Gifford?"

"I don't know what you're talking about, Heller."

"And maybe Leland Gifford figured that I'd have some inside knowledge because of my brother?"

"Why would your brother know anything about this? You're not exactly making sense."

"Or did you think you'd be able to control me if I found out what was in that container?" I was, I admit, speculating wildly. I just knew it was no accident that I was put on the job.

"*Control* you? When have I ever been able to control

you? I've seen the surveillance video of you and Dorothy and some other guy breaking into the Paladin offices."

"So you're singling Dorothy out?"

"I haven't had a chance to talk to you."

"So you were planning to fire me, too, that it?"

"I can*not* have you doing that sort of thing."

I took a small metal object from my back pocket and showed it to him. A USB flash drive that held three gigabytes of files and e-mails. "Yeah," I said. "It would be wrong. Like the illegal wiretap you had us do on the Ogilvie case."

"Oh, please," he said. "Don't tell me you're growing a conscience all of a sudden."

"Your breakfast companion might be interested in hearing about the work you did for his colleague, Senator McBride."

He knew just what I was talking about: a senator who'd hired Stoddard to expunge a domestic-abuse charge before it became public. And then a couple of years later, the senator's opponent hired Stoddard to do a little background research on Senator McBride, and what do you think Stoddard turned up? Lucky for Stoddard that Senator McBride didn't demand his money back.

"So what's this supposed to be, your job insurance?"

I shook my head slowly. "You don't have to worry about me."

"You're quitting, huh?"

"Before you fire me."

"You think anyone's ever going to hire you in this town?"

"Nope."

"You got money in a piggy bank somewhere, Heller? Money your dad buried under a rock for you in the Alps?"

I just looked at him. Let him think it. "Know what this really is, Jay?" I wiggled the flash drive in my fingers. "It's your retirement package. This effectively puts you out of business."

"What do you want?"

"Dorothy doesn't want to work for you. But you're going to do everything in your power to get her an even better job, somewhere else. You're going to give her a sterling recommendation, and you're going to get on the phone and use that famous Stoddard charm and pull every string you have. I'm talking a really *great* job. And if you don't . . ."

I wiggled the flash drive again. Its brushed-metal case glinted in the light from the chandelier overhead.

He stared at me, mouth jutting open. Dumbfounded.

"Don't disappoint me, Jay," I said.

Then I turned to leave.

"Heller," he called after me. "I don't know what you have up your sleeve, but I suggest you not bother. Like Sun Tzu said: 'All battles are won or lost before they're fought.'"

"He never said it," I pointed out. "That's from the movie *Wall Street*."

"Doesn't make it wrong."

"Well," I said. "I guess we'll see."

78

My cell phone kept ringing while I was accosting Jay Stoddard in the Senate Dining Room and outside of it. When I was finally able to check my voice mails, I found six. Two from Dorothy, confirming that she'd been able to rent all the equipment and uniforms I'd asked for. One was from Lauren. One was from an old friend named Pat Keegan, who now taught explosives at the Aberdeen Proving Ground in Maryland and sounded very happy to hear from me. One was from an irate client who hadn't been told that I was on leave from Stoddard Associates. He would not be happy to hear that I most assuredly was not coming back.

And one was from Lieutenant Arthur Garvin. He'd just gotten a heads-up from Anne Arundel County police about an apparent homicide that might have been connected to one of the cases Garvin was working. He wanted me to meet him at the crime scene in Linthicum, Maryland. At that time of the morning, it was more than an hour's drive. There was no way I could do it. I had far too much going on that day.

I called Garvin to extend my apologies.

But when he told me that the victim had worked at Gifford Industries, I raced to my car.

* * *

The neighborhood was cordoned off. A uniformed patrol officer from the Anne Arundel County Police Department was stopping all traffic. His cruiser was parked perpendicular to the street, its light bar flashing red and blue, the strobes pulsing a glaring white.

Garvin met me at the barricade and escorted me through, and together we walked the hundred feet. The neighborhood reminded me of my grandmother's: modest houses set close together, big cars, manicured lawns. The victim's house was tiny, the smallest on the block. The street on either side was choked with police vehicles; the driveway was crawling with uniformed officers and crime-scene techs. A patrolman was standing at the door to the bungalow, taking the crime-scene log. Radios were crackling. Neighbors were huddled together at a safe distance, talking. Probably neighbors who'd never spoken before.

"Here's the deal," Garvin said. "I don't know the lead on this case, but he's an old-timer like me, and he was willing to admit you to the scene on the condition that you don't move or touch anything. Unfortunately, it's daytime, so we've got everyone and their brother showing up here—all twelve guys from the Homicide unit, the unit commander, the duty official, the ME's Office, you name it. I told the detective that you're a buddy of mine, and I trust you."

"I appreciate it," I said.

"And I told him that you knew the victim."

"Barely," I said.

"I told him you could be a time-line witness. Guy's not stupid, he wants any help he can get. So just don't stir up trouble, and we'll be fine."

I was issued Tyvek coveralls and shoe covers and a polypropylene hairnet. I had to put on a double set of latex gloves before entering the house.

In the small front room were a couple of easy chairs and a desk with an open MacBook on it: a small white laptop computer. Someone was dusting the window for prints, someone was taking pictures, and someone else was doing a diagram.

The lead detective on the case was a big bluff man nearing retirement named Lenehan. Without even introducing himself, he gave me a litany of orders, everything I couldn't touch or move or look at, and as he ushered Garvin and me through the crowd in the front room, he said, "So you met with the victim just a couple of days before her death."

"Three days ago," I said.

"Did she indicate any concerns, like anyone stalking her, any enemies, anything like that?"

"No," I said.

"One of her neighbors says he saw a government vehicle parked in the street in front of her house last night. Did she say anything about talking to the FBI, maybe related to her work?"

"Not at all."

"I want to warn you, this might be upsetting."

"I've been to crime scenes," I said.

"Yeah, well," the cop said, and his voice trailed off.

"Defensive wounds on the palms," Garvin said.

Marjorie Ogonowski had clearly died struggling. Both of her hands were rigid claws. Duct tape over her mouth. Her glasses broken on the floor, a number marker next to them.

When I saw what had been done to the woman's eyes, after the first wave of nausea had crested and subsided, I felt a surge of fury.

"The tape on her mouth," I said. "You can see where it was taken off, then put back on."

Garvin leaned close, lifted his glasses to his forehead, nodded.

"Whoever did it had to remove the tape so she could talk," I said. "But put it back on when he got what he wanted."

"Or didn't," Garvin pointed out.

"Who found the body?" I asked.

"She didn't show up for work, and apparently she never missed a day without calling. When her secretary couldn't reach her on the phone, she called a neighbor and asked them to check in on her, see if everything was okay."

"The secretary knew who the neighbors were?"

"Nah. She said she searched for phone numbers by address online."

"The neighbor had a key?"

"Not the one who the secretary called. That was the guy who lives across the street—the one who noticed the car. He called the neighbor who lives next door, and that woman had a key. Unlocked the front door and walked in and found her here. Didn't take long. It's not a big house."

"Mind if I take another look at the front room?" I said.

79

I stood amid the bustle, looking from the open front door to the little desk with the laptop on it to the two easy chairs. "Was there a desk chair?" I asked.

"Nothing's been moved," Lenehan said.

"She didn't work at that desk," I said. "There's no chair. She used the laptop at the desk in her bedroom."

"Your point?" Lenehan said.

I approached the two chairs, saw the end table next to one of them, several remote controls neatly lined up. "No sign of forced entry, right?"

"She opened the door for him," Lenehan said.

"She was expecting him," I said. I pointed at a small white remote control, much smaller than the ones for the cable box and the TV. "That's for her MacBook."

"Maybe she watched movies or TV shows on it," Garvin suggested.

"No," I said. "Too far away. Twelve-inch screen. Plus, I don't think she was the type to watch TV or movies. She worked all the time. The computer's on, isn't it?"

"Looks like it's off," Lenehan said.

"No, it's just gone to sleep," I said. "Okay with you if I touch the touchpad."

"For what?"

"Take the computer out of sleep mode. See what's on it."

"I don't think Crime Scene's going to want you to do that," Lenehan said. "Prints, DNA, all that. But hold on a second." He grabbed someone, had a quick conversation. He turned back to me after half a minute. "Okay, go ahead. They've got to fume it for prints under the hood anyway."

I ran a gloved finger across the MacBook's touchpad, and a screensaver appeared—an image of a planet, which looked like Mars. I clicked the touchpad's button, and the screensaver went away. A large box appeared on the screen: a photograph of me.

It was moving as I moved, as my face moved in closer to the camera lens on the lid of the laptop. Recording my image in real time. You clicked a button, and it froze the picture.

Beneath the big box was a row of smaller snapshots. They were all pictures of the room we were in. All showed a man and a woman sitting in the chairs.

Marjorie Ogonowski and a man in a suit and tie with hunched shoulders and a fleshy, pockmarked face.

Lenehan and Garvin approached. "What's that?" Lenehan said.

"Photo Booth," I said. "It's a Macintosh photo application." I clicked on the touchpad button to enlarge the large photo still more, zoom in on the figures in the chairs.

"She took the pictures while they were sitting there talking," I said.

I document everything, she'd said.

"How?" said Garvin.

"Using the computer's remote control." I pointed. "On the table next to where she was sitting."

"That's our guy," Lenehan said, but it sounded more like a question than a statement.

"That's our guy," I said.

"He let her take his picture?"

"He didn't notice. The computer's sound was turned off, so he didn't hear that simulated camera-shutter noise it usually makes."

"She took his picture without him knowing?" said Lenehan.

"Right," I said. "Which indicates she didn't trust him. She wasn't sure he was who he said he was."

"He didn't leave prints anywhere," Lenehan said. "He was probably wearing gloves. No wonder she was suspicious."

"I'm sure he didn't arrive at her door wearing gloves," I said. "He was just careful about what he touched, and he made sure to wipe down afterward. He's a pro. Now, if you don't mind, I'm going to e-mail myself his picture."

"What for?" Lenehan said.

"We've got a workstation at my office with Face-Examiner on it."

The Maryland homicide cop didn't know what I was talking about, but that wasn't surprising; they weren't likely to have access to technology like that. "It does face recognition by running a mug shot against a database of known images. Same technology the Las Vegas casinos use to catch card counters."

"What does that mean, 'known images'? Where's this database from?"

"We'll have to get cooperation from the government," I said. "So we can tap into their facial databases of all security ID photos. State, Defense, Homeland Security, the intelligence community." I turned to Garvin. "It'll go a lot quicker if you make the call."

"To who?"

"I have a theory," I said. "I think our guy used to be a government employee."

80

Dorothy answered her cell phone abruptly: "Heller, if you keep calling me, I'm not going to be ready in time."

"I need you to go back in to the office and do something," I said.

"I don't think you heard me when I told you I got fired."

"You've got to go back in there and pack up your stuff, right?"

"You don't get it, do you? Stoddard had me escorted out. I had to pack up my cubicle right then and there. I'm out of there for good."

"Actually, I just had a talk with Stoddard."

"He fire you, too?"

"I quit before he could. But our talk was about you."

"What'd he want to know?"

"Nothing. The talk was my idea. I told him to get you another job."

"And he laughed in your face."

"He tried, sure. But he'll do it."

"Yeah, right. A job hanging off the back of a garbage truck, maybe."

"I think he's going to fall all over himself to help you."

The silence on the line was so long that I thought the call had been dropped. Then Dorothy said, "What the *hell* did you do, Nick?"

"You don't want to know."

Another long silence. Then, very softly, something I hardly ever heard her say: "Thanks."

"No problem. So what about it? But would you be willing to go back to the office? To run a photo through FaceExaminer?" I explained quickly about the photo of Marjorie Ogonowski's murderer, which she'd captured on her laptop computer.

"No," she said. "But who says I have to?"

"Care to explain?"

"I've got a backdoor into all the Stoddard databases. Hardly ever use them. Didn't want to. But I sure will, if you want."

"Can you do it now?"

"Not this morning. I've got to head over to Ryder right now and get the truck."

"Change of plans," I said. "I'll send you a picture on your cell phone, and you run it through, and *I'll* get the truck. Then I'll pick you up, and we'll head over to Paladin together."

"You think we have time?"

"We have to," I said.

A little over two hours later, I pulled the rented Ryder truck up to the curb on K Street, where Dorothy was waiting for me.

"You were right," she said as she got in. "I got a match on the photo. The guy works for Paladin Worldwide."

"As I suspected."

"And get this. You know he was one of the interrogators at Guantánamo *and* Abu Ghraib?"

"Sounds like a one-man party," I said, and I handed

her my cell phone. "Do me a favor and hit the speed-dial entry for Arthur Garvin."

"That's the detective in the Washington police?"

"Right. He's going to want to interview Carl Koblenz. So Garvin can help his buddies in Anne Arundel County Homicide clear a case. But tell him to wait until we're finished."

81

Leland was in a finance committee meeting on the sixth floor, where he'd be for at least another hour, maybe even two. Noreen was taking a long lunch: a doctor's appointment.

Lauren entered Leland's office and closed the door behind her.

Took a deep breath.

She found his battered old briefcase and located his BlackBerry in one of the front pockets. Slipped it out of its leather case, which she'd ordered for him, and pressed the power button. Why was the ON button red, she'd always wondered, and not green? Red was supposed to mean off, not on. When the screen lit up, she moved the track wheel until it highlighted his personal e-mail account, then she pressed down on the button.

Scrolled down until she found the e-mail from the Cayman Islands. Its subject line read, "Private."

She clicked on the track wheel to open the message, then clicked again to reply.

And then she composed a message.

When she was finished, she hit SEND, then she stood still for a moment, breathing in and out, trying to remember whether Leland had left the thing on or off. If she left it on when he'd had it turned off, he'd know.

She heard a throat being cleared, and she looked up.

Noreen's arms were folded on her bosom. "What are you doing?"

Lauren's heart began jackhammering. "I'm doing my job," she said. "What business is it of yours?"

Noreen took a few steps into the office. "You're using his BlackBerry," she said quietly. "Does he know what you're doing?"

Lauren realized she was holding Leland's Black-Berry up in the air as if it were an exhibit in a court-room, and she was the prosecutor. She set it down on the desk. "I'm his administrative assistant," she said. "I know you wish it was you, but it's not. Now, don't you have anything better to do?"

But Noreen wasn't budging. "I think you're reading his e-mails," she said.

Lauren widened her eyes dramatically. "You caught me," she said. "I confess. I've been reading his e-mails." Then her voice became harsh and louder. "I read all his e-mail, Noreen. I also answer all of it. That's my job. How about you—don't you have a job to do?"

Noreen shook her head, a smug look on her face. "I mean his private e-mail. You don't have access to his private e-mail accounts except when you use his Black-Berry."

"Are you done?"

"No," Noreen said. "A couple of days ago Leland asked me if I'd moved his BlackBerry. He said he re-membered putting it in the left-hand front pocket of his briefcase, but it was in the right-hand pocket, and he was sure someone had moved it. So I said maybe you did. And you know what he said?"

Noreen paused, and Lauren said nothing. Her heart

was thudding so loudly she wondered whether Noreen could hear it.

"He said, 'Lauren doesn't use my BlackBerry.' He said, 'I keep it password-protected.' He said, 'No one uses it but me.'"

"Why don't you just turn around and get back to your desk?" Lauren said. Her mouth had gone dry.

"You see, he doesn't know what you're doing. And I wonder what he's going to say when I tell him."

Lauren came around from behind Leland's desk and walked up to Noreen until she was right in her face. She could see the lines on her upper lip, the cracks in her lipstick. "Would you say the Katharine Gibbs School trained you well, Noreen?"

Noreen backed up a step. Her mouth came open just a fraction of an inch, then closed again. "What the hell are you talking about?"

"When you first got hired here, umpteen years ago, you lied on your application, and you lied in your interview. You told them you'd graduated from Katharine Gibbs. But you never went there, did you? You didn't even graduate from high school."

"Where are you getting this?" Her perfume, Lauren noticed, smelled a lot like Deep Woods Off bug spray.

"And when your boss found out the truth and asked HR about it, you begged and pleaded with him not to fire you, and he felt bad for you, and he decided he was willing to overlook your lie because you'd been so loyal to him, am I right? And he agreed to keep it quiet. Just a note in your personnel file confirming that the matter had been resolved. No one would ever know about it."

"How—where are you—?"

Lauren had never seen Noreen at a loss like this, and she had to say she was enjoying it. "I see everything,

Noreen," she said. "I see all kinds of files. So let's be clear, you and me. Next time you feel like threatening me, ask yourself whether it's worth your job."

Noreen turned and hurried out of Leland's office.

82

The burnished-mahogany door to the Paladin office suite opened, and the receptionist stood there, looking at us with a puzzled expression.

For an instant I thought she might have remembered me from the day before. But I was barely visible, standing behind the hydraulic pallet truck on which a huge cardboard box rested.

Dorothy took the lead. She stepped up to the receptionist, holding her metal clipboard. She was wearing gray twill pants and a light blue shirt with a patch above her left breast pocket that said HVAC OF RESTON. My uniform was identical, except that I was wearing a dark blue trucker cap that also said HVAC OF RESTON on the front. The uniforms, the pallet truck, and the huge empty Trane carton had all been borrowed from the heating, ventilation, and air-conditioning company owned by Dorothy's second cousin.

"Can I help you?" the pretty blond receptionist said.

"You've got a defective fan-coil unit in one of your offices," Dorothy said. "Building management wants it replaced pronto."

"Fan-coil . . . ?"

"Mind if we move this unit in and get to work? I'm

going to need an authorized signature." She held out
the clipboard and pointed to a blank signature box.

I began pushing the dolly through the double doors.

"But where is this supposed to go?"

"Your boss's office? What's his name, Koblenz or
something? Anyway, management wants this done now,
while Mr. Koblenz is out of the office, so we don't dis-
rupt him any more than we have to."

"I don't understand," the receptionist said. "Who did
you say authorized this?"

"Lady, we don't got time for this," Dorothy said.
"The blower on the fan-coil unit is bad, and it has to be
replaced immediately or it's a fire hazard, are you understanding me? And from what I hear, this building
already had some kinda problem with fire last night, so
if you want to be the one who refuses to let us fix this
unit . . ."

"No, no," the receptionist said. "Come on in."

I kept my head down behind the Trane carton and
hoped no one recognized me. Koblenz wasn't there, I
knew. He was, at that moment, on his way over to an
emergency meeting with Leland Gifford, at Gifford's
home in Great Falls, Virginia.

Though Leland Gifford's wife would no doubt be
surprised when Carl Koblenz rang their doorbell. Leland was at his company's headquarters, at an afternoon meeting of his executive team.

Dorothy—using the name Noreen Purvis—had
scheduled the urgent meeting with Koblenz's admin,
Eleanor Appleby, who was accompanying her boss, as
usual.

Dorothy guided me through the corridor to Koblenz's office.

When we got inside, I began pounding on the cooling unit with a hammer, making a great racket, and
Dorothy considerately shut the office door. I'm sure the

others in the Paladin office appreciated it. They'd gladly stay out of our way.

Then I immediately set to work, taking the empty carton off the hand truck, lowering the hydraulic bed, and sliding its steel lift plate underneath the front of the safe. While I pumped the hydraulic handle, raising the bed, and the safe, a few feet, Dorothy neatly broke down the empty Trane carton and slipped it over the safe. It was quite a bit larger than the safe, but no one would notice.

Then we moved the hand truck out of the Paladin office suite and onto the freight elevator to the basement before anyone happened to notice what was missing from Carl Koblenz's office.

A little less than two hours later, the rented Ryder truck pulled in to the Ordnance Center at Aberdeen Proving Ground in Aberdeen, Maryland, the U.S. Army's oldest testing and evaluation facility for weapons and explosives. A couple of eager soldiers, students at the Ordnance Center & Schools, hopped onto the back of the truck and helped unload the safe.

They were all very much looking forward to learning how to use controlled explosives to open a high-security safe without damaging its contents. It was a rare educational opportunity.

A professional "safe engineer," as they're called, would surely have refused to do the job. He'd have made me fill out all sorts of forms and maybe even asked the local police to witness the opening of the safe. The situation—a large high-security safe brought to him on the back of a rented truck—would have rung every warning bell. But my old friend, Staff Sergeant Patrick Keegan, one of the instructors, was grateful to me for offering up my old safe so they could practice on it.

We all stood back a few hundred feet while Keegan finished wiring the blasting cap to the small morsel of

C-4 explosive that he'd molded to a corner of the safe's rear panel.

He joined the rest of us and pressed the detonator, setting off a loud explosion with the sharp concussive sound of a rifle shot. The back of the safe flew into the air and landed maybe twenty feet away from us.

But the RaptorCard inside was unharmed.

"I wanted to grab that keyboard," Dorothy said as we drove the truck away about an hour and a half later.

"Off Eleanor Appleby's desk? The one with the key-logger in it?"

"Yeah. So we still have to get back in there."

"That probably wouldn't have been a good idea. They might have wondered why a couple of HVAC repair people stole a keyboard."

"Yeah. So let me ask you something."

"Yeah?"

"How the hell did you come up with the idea of stealing the whole damned safe?"

"Not sure," I said. "Maybe it was that cargo job I did in L.A."

My cell phone suddenly emitted four beeps, alerting me to a text message.

I pulled over to the side of the road and flipped the phone open.

NEW TXT MESSAGE
From: Anon@AnonTxt.com
You have something of ours We have something of yours Let's trade

83

My heart began to pound.

Paladin, of course.

From a blocked e-mail address. I hit REPLY. I struggled with the keypad, with how to enter letters. Teenage girls text on their pink Razrs like court reporters on speed—OMG! BRB! LOL! ROTFLOL!

It took me a while. Finally, I was able to enter: "What do you have?"

"What's going on, Heller?" said Dorothy.

I held the phone, waited.

Then, a minute later, four beeps. A photo appeared on the phone's display.

My brother.

Taken at an odd angle, in low light. He looked haggard, seemed to have aged five years. But it was definitely Roger.

A picture that could have been taken at any time. Hardly proof of life.

Dorothy said, "My God."

I entered: "Proof?"

The answer came back a minute later:

No time

Not good enough, I thought. This smelled like a setup. I thought for a few moments, then entered: "What R's nickname for me?"

If, as I suspected, this was Koblenz's trap, that would trip him up. He—or whoever was holding my brother hostage—would have to ask Roger. And if Roger wasn't cooperating, he would either refuse to reply or give a wrong answer.

The four beeps came less than a minute later, and then the words:

RED MAN

"Jesus," I said aloud. "It's him."

"How do you know, Heller? Talk to me."

"Do me a favor," I said. "Drive the truck."

Dorothy took over behind the wheel, and I thought, staring at the phone. What if Roger had used the phrase in some e-mail to me years ago? Had he? I certainly didn't remember, and it wasn't as if he'd e-mailed me much at all in the last few years. A couple of times, maybe. But if he had, and they'd captured his e-mails to me and analyzed them . . .

It wasn't impossible that they'd discovered Roger's nickname for me that way. So this wasn't really proof. Though maybe there was no definitive proof.

I tapped out: "What on back of Dad's gift to R?"

That they couldn't know without asking him. No way. He never put anything like that in an e-mail to me. We never talked about the Patek Philippe watch, Mom's gift to Dad, which he'd handed over to Roger when he entered prison.

The text-message alert took much longer this time. I imagined Roger telling his captors, spelling out the Latin words repeatedly. His frustration at the ignorance of the men who'd taken him prisoner. Men who didn't know Latin the way Roger did.

If, of course, they truly had Roger.

But then came the four beeps.

AUDNTES FORTUNA JUVT

A couple of typos. Missing a few letters, like the Latin inscription on the pediment of an old building. Typed out rapidly. But close enough. *Fortune favors the bold.*

I entered: "Where?"

The answer came back quickly:

Union Station Center Cafe 6:00 pm Alone

I looked at my watch. It was 4:30. That left me barely enough time to return to Washington and make the arrangements I needed to make.

I texted back: "OK"

84

In normal circumstances, I'd always found Union Station to be one of the most beautiful places in Washington, and one of the most impressive train stations in the world. It was meant to evoke the Arch of Constantine in Rome. The barrel-vaulted ceiling in the main waiting room was almost a hundred feet high, with gold leaf all over the place. Not that long ago—twenty, twenty-five years ago—the station had been boarded up. Mold grew on the ceiling, toadstools in the bathrooms. Now it gleamed, freshly painted and re-gold-leafed.

Just then, though, it seemed a teeming, chaotic place. Dangerous. The Paladin people had deliberately set our rendezvous for rush hour, when hordes of commuters flowed through the main hall, in and out of shops, up and down the escalators, to and from the train platforms and the metro station.

They wanted to watch me without being seen themselves. Though I wasn't likely to recognize any of them anyway. The ones who'd already gone after me were probably collecting disability and spending a lot of time in chiropractors' offices.

I'd found a space on the second level of the parking structure adjacent to the terminal. As had become my habit recently, I'd done a quick check for any concealed GPS tracking devices on the undercarriage of my car. There were none.

I took the escalators down, then went through the sliding glass doors to the mezzanine level. There I stood at the balcony and looked down over the main hall. It was impossible to identify anyone who might be watching me. There were far too many people here, moving in irregular patterns or just standing around and browsing. I descended the winding staircase to the main level and crossed the west hall, past a sports-memorabilia shop.

In my peripheral vision I noticed a man in his sixties wearing an old Baltimore Orioles baseball cap pulled down low over his head and a pair of black-framed glasses. Lt. Arthur Garvin of the Washington Metropolitan Police Violent Crime Branch was inspecting a Washington Redskins coffee mug.

He glanced vaguely in my direction, didn't acknowledge me, and I kept going.

By the time I returned to the main pavilion and was circling the Center Cafe, my phone vibrated. I glanced at the number, answered it.

"Yeah?"

"Nothing?" Garvin said.

"Okay," I said. "Twenty-two minutes. There's a couple of stores within direct sight line of the Center Cafe."

Koblenz, I assumed, was counting on my eagerness to see my brother making me sloppy. I hated to disappoint him. But this whole thing felt more and more like a setup.

I was now convinced that they really did have Roger. Between the photo they'd sent to my cell phone and the two pieces of information, one of which no one but Roger could possibly have known, there was little doubt.

But that didn't mean that they actually planned to turn him over. As much as Koblenz wanted his RaptorCard back, he wasn't going to give up leverage like that. At least not so easily.

Instead, they were probably planning on grabbing me, too. He'd use men I didn't recognize. They'd get me somewhere and stick a needle in me and, finally, they'd be rid of the last threat of exposure.

That was, I assumed, their plan, anyway.

But plans are made to go wrong.

Garvin had his department-issue Glock. I had the Ruger .45 I'd liberated from Taylor, the Paladin guy. It was perfectly good, and if there were any legal complications later, I preferred to have the firearms trace lead back to Paladin rather than to me. The Ruger was tucked into an ankle holster, under a loose-fitting pair of jeans.

Still, it was just the two of us, and Garvin was not exactly in shape. He was a desk jockey. Nor could he call in any of his friends on the force, assuming he still had any. On the off chance that Koblenz's swap was actually on the level, we didn't want an unusual police presence in Union Station scaring his men off.

At five minutes before six, I stood in front of the information booth next to the Center Cafe, pretending to study the arrivals-and-departures board. The crowd surged, making it difficult to identify any obvious Paladin types nearby—ex-SEALS or ex–Special Forces guys wearing surveillance earpieces with the distinctive coiled audio tube running down the backs of their necks. Or holding mobile phones to their ears. Or wearing Bluetooth headsets.

There were a number of beefy guys talking into cell phones. Any of them could be Paladin. Or stockbrokers, for that matter.

But none of them seemed to be looking in my direction. Or if they were, they were being subtle.

Garvin was standing at the end of a bar. He looked

like he was caught up in an argument with another
patron.

At exactly six o'clock, my phone beeped four times,
and I checked the text message.

Alone?

I texted back: "Yes."

I waited. A row of gray statues high above gazed
down, solemn Roman legionnaires.

Then another message:

Enter code on reverse of card

I understood at once. They wanted to confirm that I
really had the RaptorCard with me, that I wasn't trying to
pull off a swindle. I took out the card and noted the eight-
digit serial number on the back, which I assumed was a
unique code. Then I entered it on the phone keypad.

And waited.

Then came the four beeps, and a message:

OK Buy ticket Camden Line to Laurel

Tickets to the commuter trains were sold just outside
the doors at the back of the main hall. I walked through
a set of glass doors and got in the long line that wound
around stanchions to a ticket counter. No marble gran-
deur here; it could have been a Trailways bus station in
Poughkeepsie.

About a minute later my phone beeped again.

No time Use machine

They were watching.
But where were they?

I looked around, saw dozens of people milling around, waiting for trains, standing in line. None of them familiar, none of them obviously a Paladin type. Garvin was in range, talking to a shoeshine guy, laughing. As if he had all the time in the world. But he was watching.

Maybe I'd underestimated him.

On either side of the counter was a bank of electronic ticketing machines. The lines there were much shorter. I chose a machine to the right of the counter. Only one person ahead of me; I had to wait just a few seconds. I inserted my credit card and selected the Laurel, Maryland, stop on the northbound MARC train.

I looked around again, trying to catch someone suddenly looking away, averting his eyes. Someone with a cell phone, punching away at the keys—texting, not talking on it.

But saw no one.

I considered calling Garvin's cell to let him know where I was going but decided that was too risky. They were watching. Maybe they'd hear his phone ring, see him answer it at the same time that I was placing a call. I didn't want to endanger him that way. Let him figure out what I was doing.

I'd offered Garvin the use of a tiny Bluetooth microearbud from Merlin's stash. It was government-grade, used by the Secret Service, not available commercially. You slip it into your ear canal, and it's just about invisible. But Garvin was old-school, and he wasn't comfortable sticking something that tiny into his ear. He was afraid it would get stuck.

I wished at that point that Garvin had taken me up on the offer.

The ticket popped out. I grabbed it, found the track number on the departures board. Through the automatic doors at Gate A and outside to the platform. The air was cool and crisp and acrid from uncombusted diesel fuel and smoke. The Camden train was idling, its doors open. Already crowded with passengers. Some of them had put briefcases on the vacant seats next to them. I found a seat in a row of two on the right side, next to an elderly lady. The compartment was just about full to capacity. Passengers started having to take their bags off the empty seats, letting people sit next to them.

Garvin, who'd been following me at a discreet distance, walked past my compartment, decided to board the next car down. A smart move: He didn't want to be recognized.

An announcement came over the train's P.A. system warning that the doors were about to close. The train was about to depart.

My phone beeped, and I flipped it open.

Get off train now Do not take this train

I sighed in annoyance: I didn't like being toyed with. But I jumped out of the train just as the doors began to close with a pneumatic hiss. Garvin, in the next compartment, saw what I was doing a few seconds later and pushed at the doors, tried to force them open. The train picked up speed and several seconds later was gone. Along with Garvin.

My phone was beeping again. The message said:

Penn Line train

Across the platform.
I entered: "To where?"
I was getting good at texting. By then I could have given a teenage girl a run for her money.
The answer came at once:

Just get on

85

The Penn Line train was about to depart, a minute or so after the Camden Line. I raced across the platform and found a seat, and my phone vibrated. A call, not a text message.

"Dammit," Garvin said, "what was that all about?"

"I think that was their way to make sure I'm alone," I said as quietly as I could.

"Where are they sending you now?"

"I don't know. This train heads into Baltimore. Terminates in Perryville."

"Call me back when they tell you which station you're getting off at," he said. "I'll grab a cab or something."

"I'll call you when I get off," I said. "I have a feeling the games aren't over yet."

The conductor came by with a handheld punch and asked for my ticket. I didn't know how far I was going, so I bought a ticket for the end of the line, Perryville.

And for a long while the phone stayed quiet. No text messages; no calls from Garvin.

The train was old and decrepit, the seats worn and permanently soiled. The man next to me kept ripping out articles from the *Washington Post*. I wondered whether he was senile. Very few passengers were talking on cell phones. It was quiet, the silence of people who were depleted after a long day. A few snoozed.

We passed the used-car dealerships in Seabrook, then the landscape became rural. Twenty-two minutes out, we reached Bowie State. Five minutes later, Odenton.

And still no text message with instructions. I'd begun to wonder whether I was being led on a pointless errand, a mind game. The next stop was BWI Marshall Airport. Most of the other passengers got out there, probably to board buses to the airport.

Five minutes later the train stopped at Halethorpe. The suburban outskirts of Baltimore. Tract housing. Residential. A cemetery on the west side.

So maybe they wanted to meet in Baltimore. In seventeen minutes the train would arrive at Baltimore's Penn Station. But still no text message. I wasn't going to call Garvin; not yet. Not until I was certain of the destination.

Just three passengers remained in my car. The old man next to me, obsessively ripping out swaths of newsprint. He looked like the kind of guy who lives in a studio apartment surrounded by towering stacks of dusty yellowed newspapers until one of them topples and he's crushed to death. A young guy, too small and nerdy and fragile-looking to be Paladin. A middle-aged black woman, likely a government worker.

Five minutes later my phone came to life, signaling a text message.

Exit here W Baltimore

An announcement came over the loudspeaker: "Next stop, West Baltimore. Doors open on the last car only. Passengers wishing to depart here should move to the last car."

I got up, walked into the next car and the one after that, and as I did, I hit redial to call Garvin.

"West Baltimore station," I said.

"Jesus Christ. I'm at Annapolis Junction. I'll grab a cab if I can find one."

The train came to a stop, the doors opened, and I got out along with the middle-aged black woman from my car and a young, black-haired guy in a hooded sweatshirt wearing a backpack.

It was a grim-looking area. Down below, to the left, was an old, abandoned red-brick factory, soot-stained, all of its windows broken. Narrow row houses along a steep hillside, many of them boarded up. The train platform was elevated, traffic running underneath. The black-haired guy clomped down the stairs ahead of me.

A text message popped up:

W Mulberry St to Wheeler Ave

So they were going to lead me block by block.

Twilight had begun to settle. Not many people on the streets. I paid close attention to everyone passing by, vigilant to the possibility of an ambush.

Fifteen or twenty minutes later, my phone beeped again.

R on Winchester St North on N Bentalou St

By then I'd walked about a mile. The streets got more desolate, more deserted. More abandoned buildings. It had that sort of bombed-out, urban-wasteland-of-the-future look you see in some of the old sci-fi movies like *Blade Runner* and *Escape from New York*.

Four more beeps:

Cross st

On the other side of the street was an old brick building as long as a city block. One of the many crumbling remains of Charm City's long-vanished industrial era. Faint remnants of painted letters on the brick indicated it had once been a meat-processing plant. It was surrounded by a rusted chain-link fence, bent and ruined and caved in here and there.

Another text-message alert:

Go to E side of easternmost bldg and wait by old loading dock

I could see that it wasn't just one building but an entire factory complex. Three identical block-long buildings parallel to one another, maybe a hundred feet apart, along the west side of the railroad tracks. Each building was four stories high. Broken windows boarded up. Occasional grimy smokestacks. The sort of place that, in a nicer part of a city, would have been converted into condos for yuppies five or ten years ago and named The Meat Factory or something.

I easily stepped over a caved-in section of the chain-link fence.

The no-man's-land inside was littered with old tires and trash and broken bottles. The wind swirled plastic-bag tumbleweed. The buildings were covered with graffiti and plastered with DO NOT ENTER and CONDEMNED notices. It took me a good five minutes just to reach the end of the first building. Then over to the third building, where I found an old loading dock, boarded up like all the windows. Each building was at least a thousand feet long. Far longer than an average city block. More like the length of an east–west block in New York City.

And there I waited.

Looked around at the now-dark, desolate landscape, the wind whistling, the distant sound of car horns.

I understood why they'd chosen the location, or at least I had a pretty good idea. From a distance, anyone watching through binoculars could see I'd come alone. I was on foot and had no backup—they'd made sure of that—and the site was so deserted that they could enter and exit and know they weren't being followed.

I also realized how vulnerable I was, standing here. One man alone, a pistol holstered to my ankle. No one covering me. The Paladin guys could be waiting inside the abandoned building, aiming sniper rifles through the gaps in the boards.

They could take me out in seconds.

But the truth was, they could have taken me out at any number of points if they'd wanted to. Killing me wasn't going to solve their problems. They could have done that easily, long ago. Instead, they probably wanted to force information out of me, which would require taking me alive, as a hostage.

The way they must have taken Roger. Or maybe they planned something like what had been done to Marjorie Ogonowski.

But what could they want from me if they had Roger already?

Or else they really meant what they said, and they simply wanted the RaptorCard back. It was, in my hands, truly a threat. It would enable me to access their computer files.

So maybe they actually did want to trade Roger for that little piece of hardware. Maybe this truly was a swap. The way East and West used to exchange imprisoned spies on the Glienicke Bridge in Berlin.

Maybe. Or maybe not.

At that point, though, I had no more leverage. Not if I wanted to see my brother again.

I waited a little longer. Reached down and pulled the

Ruger from its holster. Thumbed the safety up to the ready position.

My phone rang: a call, not a text message. Garvin.

"Where are you?" I said.

"No goddamned cabs around here. I had to call for one. I'm waiting. Where are you?"

I told him.

"Get out of there," he said. "Don't do anything until I get there."

"No," I said. "I don't control the timing here."

"You can if you want to. Just leave."

"No. Get over here as soon as you can."

"Heller, you idiot."

"Just get here when you can," I said, and I ended the call.

Then I heard the squeal of tires, and two vehicles careened around each end of the building, the timing synchronized. Two black Humvees barreling toward me.

I stood still.

Looked to either side.

The two Humvees pulled up about thirty to forty feet in front of me, nose-to-nose, two feet apart, their brakes screeching. Dark-tinted windows: I couldn't see inside. Mud on the license plates.

I waited. The Ruger in my right hand, at my side. The driver's side door of the Hummer on my right opened, and a guy got out. Tall, bullet-headed, his head shaven down to the skin. Odd-shaped head, too. He looked like a human-sized penis.

In his hand was not a gun but something small and oblong that looked vaguely familiar but I couldn't immediately identify.

"Don't move," the guy said.

"I'm not," I said.

He held up the device. A garage-door opener, I realized, but I knew what it was for.

"Drop the weapon."

"Convince me."

"This is a detonator," the penis-shaped man said. "Do anything sudden, and your brother dies."

"Just like that, huh?"

"Drop the gun."

"Drop it? Rather not scratch the finish."

"Drop it now."

"Why?"

"You want to find out?"

I didn't. I lowered the Ruger, safety still off, still fire-ready, and set it gingerly on the hard-packed earth.

He signaled with his free hand, and the back door on the other vehicle opened. I heard it open, didn't see it. Heard voices. Commands uttered in a low voice. A figure came around the far side of the car, walked between the two vehicles, stopped to the right of the bullet-headed guy.

A figure in baggy, shapeless clothes. Dun-colored overalls that were too big for him, under an old trench coat.

Roger.

PART THREE

We are never deceived; we deceive ourselves.
—Goethe

86

He looked as if he'd been drugged. He appeared even older and more haggard than in the picture they'd sent me. He was sweating profusely.

"Nick," he said, his voice cracking.

"Stop right there," the bullet-headed guy barked to Roger.

"Hey, Red Man," I said softly.

"Hold up the card," the guy said. "Take it out slowly."

I pulled it from my pocket, held it up.

"You understand the deal," he said.

I nodded. Roger was wearing some kind of vest, maybe a fly-fishing vest, that had been rigged up with blocks of M112 demolition charges wrapped in olive drab Mylar film. C4 explosive, army-manufacture. I could have recognized them a mile away. Wires came out of each block. The whole thing duct-taped to him. Sloppy, but professional.

He was a walking bomb.

A second guy got out of the Humvee on the left, the same one Roger had emerged from. He, too, was holding a garage-door opener in one hand and a pistol in the other. That guy was beefy, had a goatee. A real type.

Like Neil Burris, like a hundred other guys I'd served with.

Both Humvees had been left idling. This was going to happen quickly. They wanted to make a speedy getaway.

"Here's how it's going to go down," the first guy said. "Your brother's going to get the card from you and hand it to me. I check it out. If it's good, I take off his vest."

"Sounds like you don't want to get too close to me," I said.

"Try anything stupid, one of us hits the detonator. Got it?"

"Got it."

"In case you're thinking maybe you grab your gun and try to take us both out, lemme tell you, you don't want to do that. The detonators are on a dead man's switch. So either of us lets go, the bomb goes off. Then there's a pressure switch on the vest, and you don't know where it is. You try to take off the vest, it's gonna blow, and both of you get vaporized. You getting all this?"

"Seems sort of complicated."

"It's not. It's real simple. Don't play games, and you and your brother go home. All there is to it."

I glanced at Roger. His eyes were closed, and he appeared to be trembling.

"No," I said.

"Excuse me?" the first guy said.

"No," I repeated. "I hand you the RaptorCard, what's going to stop you from setting off the vest and killing us both anyway? Your sense of honor?"

The second guy said, "We don't need this. Let's get out of here."

"*Here's* how it's going to go down," I said. "I'll hand my brother the card. Only you're going to stand right next to him. Then you take off the vest, and he gives it to you. And we all go home."

There was a beat of silence. The goateed guy looked at the bald guy.

They really wanted to keep their distance from me. I suppose I should have been flattered.

The bald guy nodded. "Go," he said to Roger.

Roger walked toward me slowly, unsteady on his feet. By then, his eyes were open, and staring, and frightened. His face was ashen. As he approached, the two Paladin guys watched, gripping their detonators, thumbs at the ready.

Roger seemed to be trying to tell me something with his eyes. I looked at him as he came closer, step by step.

He was shaking his head ever so subtly.

Telling me *No*.

I gave him a puzzled look in return: *What do you mean?*

He mouthed the word *No*.

He was just a few feet away. Slowly he reached out his left hand. Dad's Patek Philippe was on his wrist.

I handed him the RaptorCard.

He whispered, "They're going to kill us both."

I shook my head.

He spoke a little louder: "I won't let them kill you, Nick."

His eyes were wide. "Run," he said.

I whispered back: *"No."*

The bald guy shouted, "Hey, let's *move* it!"

"Run," he whispered again.

"No," I told him.

Suddenly he lurched to his right. He spun, raced toward the Hummer on the left. Collided with the goateed guy. Knocked him to the ground.

The detonator dropped to the ground.

But nothing happened. There was no dead man's

switch on the detonator. That had been a lie. What else were they lying about?

Then I saw Roger fling the car door wide open, ramming it into the goateed guy just as he was getting back to his feet, knocking him over again.

"*No!*" I shouted. "*Roger, don't!*"

"Hey!" the bald guy shouted.

Roger leaped into the Hummer, and I propelled myself toward the bald man, slamming his body to the ground. His detonator went flying, and even as I had him down on the ground, I braced myself for a terrible explosion.

But nothing happened that time either.

The Hummer roared to life, speeded forward, raced to the end of the building. The bald guy wrenched himself free of me and jumped into the other vehicle. The goateed guy vaulted into the car as well, and it took off in pursuit of Roger.

One of the garage-door openers still lay on the ground, abandoned by the bald guy.

I picked up the Ruger and took off on foot, but both Hummers were gone. I could hear them squealing around a corner, then I heard the screech of brakes.

Shouted voices.

I kept running. They must have headed him off. Trapped him.

I ran.

About five seconds later the explosion came, deafeningly loud, a blast as loud as anything I'd ever heard in wartime, echoing off the buildings. And I knew what had happened. They'd set off the C-4.

But I kept running.

I reached the end of the building, looped around, saw nothing.

I ran until there was a stitch in my side so painful it almost brought me to a halt, but I ran through it.

A yellow-orange blaze illuminated the sky on the far side of the next building over.

As I raced, I did something I'd never done before: I prayed.

Then I reached the second building and saw the conflagration. A bonfire twenty feet high. The wreck of a Hummer, its carcass barely visible behind the veil of flame.

"No!" I shouted.

Only one car. The other was gone.

I got to within twenty feet of the fiery wreck before the wall of heat hit me. I stopped, tried to get closer. The Hummer's windows had blown out. Shattered glass was strewn for dozens of feet.

I shouted, moved in closer, saw the shape inside.

A hand clutching the pillar between where the driver's window had been and the window behind it. A human hand, yes, but blackened. Burned almost to a husk.

Roger's wedding ring on one of its fingers.

On its charred wrist was my father's Patek Philippe.

87

Afterward, I wandered the streets of West Baltimore for a long while. I don't know how long. I lost track of time. I felt my cell phone vibrate several times but ignored it.

Eventually I answered the phone and heard Garvin's voice.

He came by in a Maryland cab and took me to the Union Station parking garage. A long, silent ride. Expensive, too. My jeans and sweatshirt were ripped and soiled and reeked of smoke, and pretty soon the entire cab smelled of it, too.

I retrieved the Defender, drove over to Lauren's house, and let myself in.

I'd faced all sorts of danger back in the day, in Bosnia and Iraq. But I couldn't bring myself to tell Lauren what had just happened. I couldn't bear to tell her— and Gabe—that I'd failed them after all.

I'd made a promise to Gabe, and I'd broken it.

As devastating as my brother's death had been, the thought of telling Lauren and Gabe about it was worse.

I needed to make things right before I could face

them. So I quickly and quietly gathered up some of my things from the guest room, intending to slip out of the house while they both slept and head over to my apartment.

Gabe was in the hallway when I emerged.

"What are you doing awake?" I whispered.

"You smell like smoke."

"Yeah," I said, my hand on the doorknob. "It's late. You should be asleep."

I had to get away from him because I was afraid I couldn't hold things in anymore. I didn't want to be the one to tell him about his father. That was his mother's responsibility.

"Something wrong?" he said.

I pulled him into me and gave him a hug, long and hard.

When he let go, he said, "What was that for?"

"I need to leave," I said. "I just wanted to say goodbye, and I wanted you to know I love you. And that I'll always be there for you. No matter what happens. Okay? You can't get rid of me so easy."

Gabe looked even more confused at my words. "Did something happen?"

I ignored the question. "Oh, and you know how you're always asking me to teach you how to use a gun?"

"You serious?" he said, excited.

"No, nothing like that. Next best thing. I left you a Taser. It's in the TV room."

"Awesome," he said.

"It's not a toy."

"Dude, I know that."

"It's only for emergencies."

"Sure. Of course. Cool!"

"You'll figure it out. You don't need me for that."

"Okay, Uncle Nick."

"But Gabe? Read the manual, okay?"

"Okay." He paused. "Uncle Nick, where are you going?"

"I just have another job to do," I said.

88

When I got back to my loft, I fell fast asleep on the couch, still wearing my ripped and filthy jeans and sweatshirt and boots. At around eight in the morning my cell phone woke me up. My head was pounding, and my clothes gave off the stench of an ashtray, and for a moment I forgot where I was and what had happened.

And then I remembered.

"Nick." It was Dorothy Duval. "Did I wake you?"

"It's all right," I said. "I had to get up to answer the phone anyway."

"Sorry about that. But you left me a voice mail last night?"

"Oh, yeah. Right."

"You okay? You sound lousy."

I told her about how the swap had gone bad, and we talked for a while. I'd never heard her sound so gentle. "You know, I did get into your brother's e-mail after all. And I found that woman's cell phone number."

"Woman?" I had no idea what she was talking about.

"She called herself Candi Dupont, but her real name is Margaret Desmond. But I guess this is a little late, huh? I'm sorry, Nick."

* * *

I spent a fair amount of time examining the Defender for any tracking devices until I was satisfied there weren't any. Then I left my cell phone and BlackBerry in my loft, just to make sure the GPS locator chips inside them couldn't be used against me, and I gave Garvin and Dorothy the number of one of the disposable cell phones I'd bought.

I was about to make a long drive, and I didn't want Paladin knowing where I was or where I was heading.

At least, not until I got there.

The drive took me twelve hours, but I didn't mind it. I finally got to spend some quality time in the Defender. Alone behind the wheel, in my own head. Listening to music. Burning tank after tank of petroleum. Thinking about my brother, mostly. I still didn't know what to believe about him, what had happened to him. Whether he'd been taken hostage or had arranged an intricate disappearance, abandoning his wife and son. Why Lauren had been attacked. How much of her husband's plan she'd known about—or had even been involved in planning.

There were so many questions, and there was one person, I was convinced, who'd have the answers. At least, if my analysis of the network traffic was correct.

Though I knew he wouldn't exactly volunteer them.

Most of the drive was straight down 95, through Virginia and North Carolina, through South Carolina and finally into Georgia. The Defender is a great vehicle, but it's really meant for desert maneuvers, not the interstate. It doesn't like to go much faster than seventy miles an hour.

While I drove, I played a lot of Johnny Cash CDs—I was down South, after all. I listened to "All I Do Is Drive" a bunch of times, and when my mood turned darker, I put on his cover of a Nine Inch Nails song,

"Hurt." That one could always wrench the heart out of me. Johnny—or is it Trent Reznor?—sings about how everyone he knows goes away in the end. How "I will let you down" and "I will make you hurt."

Outside of Savannah, I stopped at a hunting outfitter and a hardware store. When I got back on 95, I took the exit for Waycross. Route 187 meandered south and then west for a while until it hit 129, at which point I drove south, on a road so straight it must have been drawn with a ruler.

I was in Echols County, in southernmost Georgia, on the Florida border. It's the least populous county in the state: just over four thousand people. Almost all of it is privately owned. A few unincorporated towns and a lot of pine forest. The county seat, Statenville, used to be called Troublesome. No joke.

Twelve years ago the family that owned most of the county sold ten thousand acres to Allen Granger. It had been advertised as "perfect for a hunt club," but it became the training facility and headquarters of Paladin Worldwide.

An unmarked road came off of Route 129, cut through the dense pine forest: newly built, freshly paved. According to the handheld GPS receiver I'd picked up in Savannah, it led directly to the Paladin facility. Half a mile down the road, the forest ended abruptly, and a clearing began, as far as the eye could see. The road ended in a large asphalt-paved circular drive.

There were a gatehouse and a barrier arm and a road-spike barrier and a large sign that said PALADIN WORLDWIDE TRAINING CENTER with the Paladin logo, that stylized blue globe.

On either side of the gate was a high chain-link fence, topped with coils of razor wire, cutting through the woods. How far into the woods, I had no idea. Various articles and Internet reports about Paladin had mentioned the chain-link fence and the razor wire, but I had no idea how far the fence extended. A chain-link fence enclosing ten thousand acres? That seemed excessive. Hugely expensive.

It was amazing, actually, how much I did know about the Paladin training center, all of it from the public record, mostly the Internet. The most useful information came from Google Earth, which had overhead satellite reconnaissance photos of the place, even precise geographical coordinates.

But nothing can take the place of what you can see in person. "Route reconnaissance," as they called it in the Special Forces.

So I turned around and headed back down the freshly paved road until I found a gap in the trees, a natural path, and drove into the woods as far as I could. Finally, some true off-road driving, and here the Defender performed like a champ. I stowed the car in a thicket that was far enough from the road that it wouldn't be spotted by anyone driving past, but just to be safe, I hauled some downed limbs and branches and managed to camouflage it reasonably well.

Before I set off, I switched my cell phone on and found four voice mails, all from Arthur Garvin.

He picked up right away.

"Nick," he said. "I reached out to the Baltimore Homicide guys. To get your brother's remains."

"You know what?" I said softly. "I don't really care about that. No offense—"

"Listen to me. Did your brother have a hip replacement?"

"A *what*?"

"The Maryland ME's Office found something interesting in the wreckage. A piece of a high-grade stainless-steel alloy called Orthinox. It's a stem used in a total hip replacement."

"No," I said. "He never had a hip replacement."

"I didn't think so. Also, Washington Hospital Center reported a body missing from their morgue. A sixty-nine-year-old white male."

I said nothing for a long time.

"Nick?" he said. "You there?"

"Yeah," I finally said. "I'm here."

"Oh, and listen. We got a warrant for the guy in the Marjorie Ogonowski murder," he said. "Nice work on that. The photo match thing."

"Not me," I said. "Friend of mine. Like I said, we have some fancy databases at my high-priced firm."

"Still," he said. "Good going, there."

"Do me a favor," I said. "Keep an eye on Lauren Heller and her son, please?"

I disconnected the call and set off through the woods to do my reconnaissance.

89

Lauren picked up the phone in the kitchen.

"Is this Ms. Heller?" A pleasant baritone, halting in its delivery. "You don't know me, but my name is Lloyd Kozak, and I'm Leland's financial adviser?"

She remembered suddenly: that homely man who'd come by one day to get some disks from Noreen. "Yes? What can I do for you?"

"It's just that—well, I know you're Leland's personal assistant, and you probably know him better than anyone, but I really hope I'm not sticking my head someplace where it doesn't belong."

"I'm not sure what I can do for you," she said.

"Something's not right with Leland," he said. "I need to talk with you if you have a couple of minutes."

"What's this about?"

"I'm in Chevy Chase. I could come by soon, if you're not busy. I think we need to talk."

"About what?"

"About Leland," he said. "I think—I just think something's wrong with him."

The doorbell rang around half an hour later.

Lauren went to the front door and looked out the

fish-eye and saw a pockmarked face, oversized horn-rimmed glasses. She opened the door.

Lloyd Kozak stood on the other side of the screen door in a sad-looking suit and tie. Parked in the driveway was a Buick that had to be at least ten years old.

"Thank you so much for seeing me," he said, and she opened the screen door and let him in.

The foyer was dark and chilly. The central air-conditioning was set too high. She led him down the hall toward the kitchen, her default meeting place.

"Leland's told me so much about you," he said. "He admires you so much. *Trusts* you so much. I figured you were the one person I could talk to about him."

"You've got me worried sick," she said. "What's the problem?"

"You," he said, and suddenly he was next to her, and he placed a hand over her mouth.

90

My first response was anger, of course—great, towering fury toward this most contemptible of men. But as I walked through the woods, my anger subsided enough for me to realize that my brother had learned from a master, after all. Nothing he did should have surprised me.

Like a great illusionist, he was always one step ahead of his spectators. He understood that magic is all about misdirection: that sudden burst from a flash pot that gives us retinal burn so we don't notice him palming the queen of hearts.

A professional magician once told me that the greatest magic tricks are never, in fact, a single trick at all. They're always a sequence of tricks, and the true magic lies in how they're presented. The audience watches a magic act in a state of high suspicion. They're fully expecting to be fooled, and they watch, gimlet-eyed, convinced they *know* how the magician's going to pull it off. But what they never know is that it's this very suspicion that enables them to be mystified in the end. The magician directs their scrutiny away from what he's really up to and toward a phony explanation of how it's being done. They think it's going to be one sort of trick, but then it becomes something else. And just when they're sure they've got it figured out, it's over, and they've been totally fooled.

I thought about Victor and the way he had misled me so cleverly. Maybe that was the real reason why Roger and he had talked so many times. Roger wanted to make sure Dad knew what to say. How to point me toward Paladin in such a way that I would believe I'd figured it out on my own. Roger *wanted* me to investigate Paladin. He wanted them to feel the hot breath on their necks.

The question was why.

In the end, I drew strength from my anger.

Still, you never want to let your emotion, your impatience, get in the way of an operation. It's always the times when you most want to rush to the finish line that you need to slow down, take stock, do it right.

That was why I spent the night in the woods.

I did a loop around the Paladin compound—ten thousand acres, which meant a perimeter of close to sixteen miles. Too long to circumnavigate on foot. I took the Defender out of concealment and managed to zigzag through the woods, stopping periodically to approach the fence.

Remarkably, the entire property really was fenced in. The apparent excess confirmed what Neil Burris had told me, that Allen Granger was a man with something to worry about. Why else would he spend so much money to put up a fence sixteen miles long? I'd been to top secret government areas before, located in places that weren't nearly so remote, and none of them was so well protected.

Allen Granger, who hadn't been seen in public in over a year, was known to be a recluse and intensely private. I realized he was also probably paranoid.

As far as I could see, there weren't any fiber-optic sensors buried in the ground next to the perimeter fence.

That would have been outrageously costly. Unnecessary, too. Instead, the facility was protected by a twelve-foot chain-link fence, six-gauge galvanized steel—extremely difficult to cut through—and topped by coils of razor wire.

But that wasn't all. There were guards, too. One guard was stationed at the gatehouse at the main entry and was relieved every six hours. Two others made a circuit just inside the fence. Their shift changed every six hours as well, and every half hour they radioed in to a command post.

I knew that because I listened in on their traffic using my handheld Bearcat scanner. That, and a pair of good German binoculars, were all the instruments I needed to learn what I had to about the place. There were an airstrip and several helicopter landing pads, a high-speed driving track and a running track. Rock-climbing walls and drop zones. There was a pound for bomb-sniffing dogs: I could hear the baying of the hounds late into the night. There were barracks for the trainees, a mess hall, administrative offices, and a club where the trainees could go for drinks. It closed down at two in the morning. The lawns were luxuriant and regularly irrigated and mown short like a golf course. There were a few man-made ponds. In fact, the place could have been a country club—if not for the shooting ranges and the ammo-storage bunkers. And the mock village, used for assault exercises, and a fake town with a plaque that said LITTLE BAGHDAD, even though it looked nothing like the real Baghdad and we weren't fighting there any longer. So far as I knew, anyway. And the black Hummers that came and went at regular intervals.

Fairly close to the entrance was an impressive two-story lodge, the sort of faux-rustic home you might see in Aspen.

Granger's house.

I paid particular attention to the patterns there. Which lights went on in which rooms and when. What time they were switched off. How many guards—two, one inside and one outside—and when their shifts ended. Allen Granger was guarded twenty-four/seven—within the well-protected confines of the compound. Like paranoid old King Herod, ruling from a fortress within the fortress city of Jerusalem, a moat and drawbridge protecting him from those he feared most of all: his own subjects.

Granger lived here alone, I was fairly certain, though I never once saw him emerge. I knew what he looked like from photographs: a clean-cut, handsome young guy, early forties. Sandy brown hair cut short, but not enlisted-man short.

The radio traffic indicated that the boss was in residence. The cook—a tiny Hispanic woman—arrived a few hours before dinnertime and went in through a separate kitchen entrance. There were meetings throughout the day. Vehicles pulled up to the front of the lodge— black Humvees for Paladin officials, and the occasional black Lincoln Town Car bearing politicians, some of whom I recognized—and were always greeted by the outside guard.

I got several hours' sleep in the woods, in a sleeping bag in a pup tent, with enough food and water to get me through. Once I knew which room Allen Granger slept in and when his bedtime was, I put away my Leitz binoculars and my Bearcat scanner and prepared to make my move.

91

"You need to tell me," Lloyd Kozak said softly, gently, "how to reach your husband."

She couldn't have replied even if she'd wanted to, not with the duct tape over her mouth. All she could do was shake her head and give him her fiercest glare. She couldn't move her arms or legs.

She hadn't expected him to be so strong, to subdue her so easily.

He had taped her into one of the dining-room chairs, her arms bound to her side, and wound silver duct tape around and around her torso. No matter how she twisted her body, she couldn't move, couldn't get the chair to move, and he kept talking to her in that soft, gentle voice as he unfolded a cloth parcel, the jingling of metal inside, instruments of some kind.

She grunted—angry, defiant.

The sound of a key in the lock of the front door, and she thought, *Oh please, not Gabe, not now, not with this madman here.*

Kozak—or whoever he was, whatever his name was—turned. "Maybe Gabriel will know how to reach his father," he said.

She tried to scream, to warn Gabe, but nothing came out.

He had something in his hand, something shiny that glinted, caught the light from overhead. Something that looked like a blade. A razor? No. A . . . scalpel?

Fear wriggled deep inside her, a living organism, cold and scaly and serpentlike.

She felt the cool sharp edge of the scalpel as he placed it against the delicate skin just beneath her left eye. She closed her eyes, tried to scream again.

She couldn't move, couldn't shout, couldn't warn Gabe to stay away.

Where was he?

Maybe he'd gone right up to his room.

But he must have noticed the strange car in the driveway. Or the light on in the kitchen, which would tell him that someone was home. Or the fact that the alarm tone hadn't sounded, which would tell him that it had already been disarmed by someone, and wouldn't he wonder why?

She heard a series of high electronic tones, faint but distinct.

Had to be Gabe, punching in the alarm code. Spacey as he always was. He was disarming the alarm even though it was already off.

Which told her that he hadn't even noticed anything wrong. Hadn't noticed the strange car in the driveway, or if he had, he hadn't wondered about it.

Please don't come in here, she thought. He'd be overpowered in a second by this lunatic.

Unless . . .

Unless he walked into the kitchen and saw his mother bound to a chair with a strange man there, and he turned and ran, out of the house, ran to get help. That he could do. Get help.

She didn't even know what she wanted him to do.

But it made no difference anyway. She didn't control her son's actions. She could no longer keep him safe and wrap him up in his baby blanket like an egg roll. She could no longer pick him up in the palm of her hand.

She heard him go upstairs. Up to his bedroom.

Maybe that was for the best.

"Lauren," the man murmured. She felt the prick of the blade against her eyelid, cold and hot at the same time, then warm and wet and terribly painful. "If I have to remove your eyes, I will."

For a moment she didn't think she could possibly have heard him right.

She squeezed her eyes tight, but it didn't stop the pain because he just pressed the blade in harder and slid it slowly to one side and she screamed but the sound that came out was a keening, small and frightened.

"You'll never look at your son's face again," he said.

"Back off," someone said, and for an instant she didn't recognize Gabe's voice. It sounded deeper, as if his voice had suddenly changed.

The voice of a man.

But Gabe's voice. That she knew for sure.

She opened her eyes and the scalpel was no longer there, and Lloyd Kozak had turned around to see what she now saw, too.

Gabe, standing in the doorway, holding the Taser. Pointed at Kozak.

The weapon was shaking in his hand.

92

At that point it was mostly a matter of timing.

I needed at least a fifteen-minute window to enter the compound. When the radio traffic indicated that the perimeter guards were at the far end of their circuit, and my Leitz binoculars confirmed they weren't in sight, I unfolded the lightweight, portable aluminum ladder next to a section of the fence by the rifle-shooting range. The backstop was easily twenty feet high, which provided good cover. Placing a big square of carpet on top of the razor wire coils, I climbed up, straddled the top of the fence, and hoisted the ladder up after me. Then I set it on the ground on the other side and climbed down.

Easy.

I'd already determined my route, based on which parts of the compound seemed to be deserted at night and which weren't. There was no way to be sure I wouldn't be seen by someone who happened to be wandering the grounds at two thirty in the morning, or maybe just standing around smoking, but it was the best route I could devise, with the lowest probability of being spotted. Nothing was certain, of course. But nothing in life is certain.

Carrying the folding ladder and my duffel bag, I

looped around the driving track, where there was no one. Then past the airstrip. Adjacent to that was a helipad, well marked with a big white *H* painted on the concrete and recessed landing lights, though the lights were off. No helicopter was expected that night.

A landscaped path wandered by the trainees' mess hall, which was dark, then a smaller building that apparently served as the dining hall for VIPs and Paladin executives, which was also dark. If the Paladin compound were a military base, which it resembled, that would have been the officers' club.

Here the path forked, the left fork leading to the barracks where the trainees bunked. A few lights were still on there. Some of the trainees kept late hours, and I couldn't risk being seen. I took the right fork, which meandered past a man-made pond, bordered by ornamental grasses and flowers. Definitely more country club than army base.

Up ahead loomed Granger's lodge. I stopped behind a cluster of trees where the path bent so I could observe unseen. The house was surrounded by thick, waist-high hedges: too low for privacy. Probably to delineate a border, a sort of moat. A line beyond which you dared not cross. In front of the house was a white-gravel parking area. When you walked over it, your footsteps would crunch audibly. The only vehicle parked here was a black Hummer.

I went closer, then crouched down behind the Hummer and watched the house for a few minutes. The only light on was in the front room, probably where the interior guard was stationed during Granger's sleeping hours. I plugged an earphone into the Bearcat scanner and listened for transmissions. There weren't any.

A guard was making a long, slow, counterclockwise circuit around the lodge. He was smoking a cigarette, toting a machine gun, and looking bored.

I didn't envy the guard his job, protecting a paranoid shut-in during the small hours of the night. He couldn't read, couldn't listen to music, and had no one to share the tedium with.

Then again, some of his colleagues were working in various death zones around the world, so maybe he had the better gig. Boredom was generally better than death or mutilation.

But boredom makes you less alert. You're likely to tune out, get distracted, let your mind wander. You expend all your mental energy trying to stay awake and get through your shift.

I hoped that was the case here.

Somehow I had to approach the house undetected. I also needed at least three minutes. Ideally, five. That wasn't likely to happen, not with a guard constantly circling the property.

I removed a cell phone from my pocket, switched it on, and slid it behind the Hummer's rear tire. When the guard had rounded the southeast corner of the lodge, I made my move, taking long quiet strides, from time to time ducking beneath the hedges when I thought I might have moved into the guard's peripheral vision. Then, when he'd circled around the back of the lodge and disappeared around the northwest corner, I stepped over the hedge, hoisted the ladder and duffel bag after me, and ran to the kitchen entrance.

I looked at my watch.

I had around sixty seconds before the guard circled around again and spotted me. Maybe a bit less. I took out a second cell phone and dialed the first one.

A few seconds later, I could hear the phone ringing. Even at this distance, the sharp trill pierced the stillness.

Before setting down the ladder, I hooked up the earpiece of the radio scanner again and heard: "Alpha Three to Alpha Two."

"This is Alpha Two."

"You hear that? Sounds like a . . . *phone,* huh?"

"I don't hear nothin'."

"It's out here somewhere. Out in front. I'm gonna go check it out."

The disturbance was irresistible, of course. Just as I hoped it might be.

After five rings, I disconnected the call.

At both the front and the back of the lodge were entrance porches with wood-shingled shed roofs, lower than the roof of the main building. That made it easy to climb to the second story. I set up the ladder against the peeled-log exterior wall and started to climb, and I heard in my earpiece:

"Alpha Two to Alpha Three."

"Alpha Three here."

"What'd you find?"

"Nothing."

"You think someone dropped a phone, maybe?"

"I don't know. I'm coming back in."

"Back in" probably meant back on his circuit. Which meant he'd be here in forty-five seconds.

As I clambered onto the roof of the porch, I hit redial, and I heard the faint ringing from the other side of the lodge.

"Ahh, dammit, there it is again," I heard in my earpiece.

"I hear it now. You check the porch?"

"Nah, it's farther out there."

I chose a second-floor window that had remained dark at night. It seemed the safest point of entry.

"Alpha Three, I still hear it."

"Yeah, me, too. I'm lookin'."

That bought me another minute at least.

I switched off the cell phone to stop the ringing. I wanted him to look but not find it. From my duffel bag

I pulled out a glass cutter and suction device, set them down on the flat of the roof outside the window.

But I saw no alarm contacts and the window slid right up.

The screen was unlocked, too, and I managed to slide that open.

Then I pulled the ladder up after me, folded it, and set it on the floor of the darkened room.

And then I entered the house in search of Allen Granger.

93

"Gabriel," Kozak said, softly, coaxing, "you don't want to be responsible for mutilating your own mother, do you? Put that toy down."

Gabe snarled, *"You goddamned—"* and there was a loud pop and Kozak, anticipating the shot, sidestepped, and the thing shot out of the Taser, the metal probes striking the granite kitchen island, trailed by a silvery filament, *click-click-clicking*.

And Lloyd Kozak lurched forward, quick as a rattlesnake striking, grabbing her son, while she screamed again, the high, desperate, choked cry, tears blurring her vision, and she knew it was over, the whole terrible nightmare was ending, and this sadist would—

"Police!" barked a voice. Another voice.

A whole bunch of them, blue-clad policemen in her kitchen, weapons drawn. The one who knocked Kozak to the floor, a knee to Kozak's throat, was older than the others, a man with thick glasses she recognized from the hospital room so long ago. Not much more than a week ago, though it seemed much longer.

"Who punched in the duress code?" Arthur Garvin asked.

"Me," Gabe said.

"You did good, kid," Garvin said. "Saved your mom's life."

Gabe nodded.

"We need to get your mom to the emergency room. Get a doc to take a look at that cut on her eye. Probably need stitches."

The emergency medical guys had bandaged the slice under her eye, which stanched the flow of blood. It no longer hurt. Her mouth hurt more, actually, from where they'd ripped off the duct tape.

"Was he in the house when you got home?" Garvin asked, meaning Kozak.

She shook her head. "He called and asked if he could come over. Who is he?"

"He works for Paladin."

Yes, she thought. Paladin. She knew it was only a matter of time.

"You knew he'd come here?"

"No. I have a warrant for his arrest, and we've been looking for him all over, most of the day."

"But what made you come here?"

"Truth?" Garvin said. "Nick asked me to check in on you. Make sure you guys were okay."

94

The room was dark and cool and smelled both recently cleaned and rarely used. The floor had been washed with oil soap and the furniture polished with lemon oil. But at the same time there was that faint musty odor of a room that's normally kept closed up. Enough light from outside filtered in for me to see that it was a guest room. Twin beds, two night tables, a TV set, a bureau. A private bathroom. Not much else.

I placed the folded ladder and the duffel bag on the floor by the window, out of sight and yet easy to get to. Unzipped the bag and removed one last piece of equipment: the Ruger.

The floor creaked as I walked across it.

I slowed my pace, trying to minimize the creaking. Listening for any sounds. I had a rough idea where I was headed. I'd figured that Granger's bedroom, the largest room on the second floor, was at the front of the lodge, on the southwest corner.

I'd also observed that no other lights stayed on up here. No lights in the corridors. That indicated that there were no guards outside his bedroom, unless they sat in the dark, which would be highly unusual.

Though not impossible. Nothing could be ruled out.

The door was heavy and solid, well balanced on its hinges. I turned the knob and pulled the door in slowly a few inches. No squeak. Almost silent. I peered out, saw no one.

Pulled it in a few inches more.

Waited.

There was less ambient light in the hall than there'd been in the bedroom. The window was farther away. But when my eyes adjusted I saw no guard, no one sitting on a chair with a weapon. Just a corridor that was empty except for a narrow table, a vase of flowers at its center.

I emerged slowly, carefully, gripping my weapon, and pulled the door almost shut behind me.

A pair of double doors down the hall to my right.

The doors to Allen Granger's room.

Was he really in there? I hadn't seen him enter or leave the lodge since I'd arrived. But the radio transmissions had made reference to him—to "the boss," to "the Big Guy," and once even to "Mr. Granger." Plus, the security procedures would have been relaxed considerably if he hadn't been in residence.

He had to be here.

Walking slowly, keeping my tread as light as possible, I made my way down the hall until I reached the double doors. Then I stopped. Listened.

Heard the faint buzzing of someone asleep. Gentle snoring.

He was asleep in there.

Ruger in my right hand, I clutched the left knob and turned it slowly. Hoping it wasn't locked.

It wasn't.

Pushed the left door open slowly, slowly. Glimpsed a large bed in the darkness. A sleeping figure beneath the covers. Heard the soft snoring.

Darker in here than it had been in the hall. The

shades were pulled down: room-darkening shades, which made the room almost pitch-black. The only light spilled in from the hall.

I left the door ajar. Entered the room. The floors were covered in deep wall-to-wall carpet, which muffled my footsteps. I crossed the room to the right side of the bed, closest to where Granger lay swaddled in covers.

I'm sure my father had some line from one of his beloved ancient Chinese military tracts about the advantages of a sneak attack. But I didn't need an ancient Chinese strategist to tell me what I already knew.

My heart had begun to thud. Not fear. But anticipation. Anticipation of what I would do to the man. Anger. Adrenaline.

As I reached the side of the bed, a tone sounded.

Loud.

Like a doorbell chime.

Too late I realized that I'd set off a pressure-sensitive switch concealed beneath the carpet.

I froze.

The sleeping figure suddenly lurched, the covers flying off, and a pajama-clad man sat up, grabbing a gun from under a pillow in one smooth movement.

Aimed it about three feet to the left of where I stood.

Nowhere near me.

"Freeze," he said.

My eyes had adjusted to the darkness by now. I recognized Allen Granger: the neatly trimmed hair, the handsome young face I'd seen in photos hundreds of times.

But I didn't expect to see the terrible scarring that marred the top half of his face. The raised welts of flesh where his eyes should have been.

Allen Granger was blind.

95

"Don't move," he said.

He was gripping a Glock, still aimed a few feet to my left.

I didn't move. I didn't breathe, said nothing.

I didn't want Granger to be able to locate me by sound.

He moved the gun slowly to his right, even farther away from me. He was guessing.

From the hallway behind me came footsteps. Someone running.

Quickly I reached out, grabbed the barrel of his Glock, jammed it upward, and wrenched it out of his hands. He struggled, made an angry growl, but he seemed to have no strength.

He had no leverage because he didn't have the full use of his body. Granger was not just blind; he was partly paralyzed as well.

"You're not going to make it out of here alive," Granger said.

"Don't you want to know why I'm here?" I said.

"I know why you're here, and you'll never get away with it."

The door to Granger's bedroom burst open, lights came on, and a guard entered, weapon drawn. A submachine gun. A Heckler & Koch MP5.

"Take him down," Granger said.

I spun around, my Ruger leveled at the guard. He looked vaguely familiar. Tall, fit, around my age.

A pistol versus a submachine gun. Like using a water pistol against a fire hose.

Then again, eight hundred rounds per minute didn't mean much if the guy holding the submachine gun was dead. A bullet was a bullet.

I noticed the tattoo on his right biceps: crossed arrows over a dagger and the words DE OPPRESSO LIBRE. The Special Forces motto. Misspelled, but then, tattoo artists aren't always known for their spelling.

"Drop the gun," he said.

For several long seconds we stared at each other.

I lowered the Ruger.

"I said, drop it."

I let go. The pistol fell noiselessly to the carpet.

Then I lowered my gaze to his submachine gun and smiled. I looked into his eyes again. "I don't know how many rounds you plan on getting off," I said, "with the fire selector on safe."

He couldn't help himself: He glanced quickly down at his weapon.

And I lunged.

Grabbed the barrel and twisted it upward as I kneed him in the stomach, knocked him to the floor. He expelled a great lungful of air, made an *ooof* sound.

I said, "Your tattoo guy spelled it wrong, you know."

The Special Forces motto was "De Oppresso Liber," not "Libre." Which meant "To liberate the oppressed."

"Who the hell are you?" he said.

"Heller," I said. "I'm here for my brother. And I don't plan on leaving without him."

"Did he say Heller?" I heard Allen Granger say from behind me. "That's Roger Heller?"

"No," I said. "Nick Heller. Roger's brother."

"Dear Lord," Granger said. "We need to talk."

96

"Can I offer you a drink?"

"I thought you don't drink."

We'd moved to a spacious room downstairs. A fire roared in the large stone fireplace. Hand-hewn beams crisscrossed the ceiling.

Granger sat in a wheelchair, dressed in a white cardigan sweater, blue button-down shirt, and gray woolen slacks. His hair was neatly combed.

His once-handsome face was ruined.

Press-shy, a recluse: of course. It must have happened within the past year.

"Oh, not alcohol," he said with a quiet chuckle. "Heavens, no." He gave me a conspiratorial look. "I'm talking genuine Dublin Dr Pepper."

"Excuse me?"

"The oldest Dr Pepper bottling plant in the world. Dublin, Texas. They make it with real cane sugar, not that nasty high-fructose corn syrup. In six-and-a-half-ounce glass bottles, too. You can hardly find the stuff anymore. And if you've never had a Dublin Dr Pepper, this is gonna change your life. It's my weakness. Now you know."

"No, thanks."

"Please accept my apologies," Granger said. "I've had difficulties with some of my employees."

"Is that what happened to you? You were attacked by one of your own employees?"

He nodded. "I was fragged, I guess you could say."

"Civilians can't be fragged."

"Technically, I suppose you're right. But civilians usually don't use grenades."

I'd put the Ruger back in my ankle holster. I'd handed him back his Glock. There no longer seemed any point in weapons.

Softly, Granger said, "Have you found him?"

"No," I said. "Until a few hours ago, I thought he was dead."

"I don't mean your brother. I mean *Him*. The Lord. Have you found Him?"

I blinked a few times. "I've been sort of busy."

"Jesus is never too busy for us," he said. "We must never be too busy for Him."

"I'll keep that in mind."

Granger gestured toward his face, then toward his lap. "He's gotten me through."

"Why?" I said.

He paused, then said, "Why was I attacked?"

"Right."

"There was a time, not so long ago, when private military contractors were outside the law, you know."

"Above the law."

"No. Outside the law. We weren't covered by military law, and we weren't covered by civilian law."

"Neat little loophole. So your guys got to be cowboys. Shoot first and ask questions later. Kill whoever they wanted."

"Some did, it's true. Not all. Just a few."

"But you realized that if you wanted to keep doing business with the government, you'd have to hang a few of your guys out to dry."

"That's awfully harsh, Nick."

"The cost of doing business."

"I won't argue. And the men blame me for selling them out."

"Who else should they blame?"

"I'm not in charge anymore. I'm little more than the figurehead. The front man."

"Because you're a division of a larger corporation? You're part of Gifford Industries?"

He didn't reply.

"So who is in charge now? Leland Gifford?"

He turned his unfocused blind eyes toward me. "You really don't know, do you?"

"Don't know what?"

"What your brother did?"

"Yes," I said impatiently. "Roger tried to extort a lot of money from you. He threatened to leak information on the bribes and payoffs you've made to the Pentagon."

"That's just a cover story."

"And what's *your* cover story? That my brother embezzled from the company?"

"No," Granger said. "Your brother didn't steal *from* the company. That's not it at all. He stole the company itself."

97

Allen Granger offered me the use of his Gulfstream 100 and one of his best pilots.

I took the Gulfstream to New York.

I had no idea what to expect as I crossed Lexington Avenue in Manhattan.

The ornate exterior of the Graystone Building hadn't changed at all since I was a kid. It still looked like a Babylonian temple. Inside, though, you could see how the once-magnificent lobby had gotten run-down. The mural of Prometheus stealing fire was chipped and faded, but a couple of painters were perched on ladders, carefully restoring it. Some other guys were retouching the art deco ceiling panels. One of the elevators was being repaired.

But the brass elevator doors gleamed, and the elevator cabin still smelled of warm brass machinery and old leather. It still ascended slowly yet smoothly, the *whir* and *clunk* of gears somehow reassuring.

It seemed impossible, but the penthouse floor still had the aroma of my father's pipe smoke.

There were a lot more workers up here, buffing the granite floor and replacing broken tiles and retouching the paint. I'd once read a piece in *The New York Times* about how the Graystone Building had fallen upon hard times, its occupancy rate had fallen to under forty percent, and its owners had been looking to sell for years.

It looked like the building had a new owner.

A couple of carpenters, who were restoring the mahogany wainscoting in the elevator lobby, glanced at me without interest. I walked slowly down the hall to the big corner office.

A woman was coming out: a tall, buxom blonde. Very attractive. Far more beautiful than the photo Dorothy had sent to my cell phone. I nodded, but she didn't nod back.

Empty of any furniture or carpets, its oak parquet floor covered with white dropcloths, the office seemed even more spacious than I'd remembered it.

The sunlight flooded through the floor-to-ceiling windows, and he stood, his back to me, looking out over Manhattan. His arms were spread, his hands pressed against the glass.

I wondered whether he remembered that Dad sometimes used to stand exactly like that.

He must have heard me enter, because he turned slowly. He flinched, but almost imperceptibly. Only a brother would have sensed it.

"Hey, Red Man," Roger said.

98

I didn't say anything.

I approached, arms outspread, and when he opened his arms for a hug, I punched him in the stomach. Hard.

He doubled over, glasses flying. For almost a minute he dry-heaved, clutching himself, head down, then he managed to stand erect, if unsteadily, crimson-faced.

"That wasn't very brotherly, Nick."

"No?" I said.

He took a few faltering steps and picked up his glasses and put them back on.

"Great view," I said. "I'd forgotten how great."

"Best in the city, I always thought."

"You lease the whole floor? Just like Dad?"

"Actually, Nick, I own the building," he said softly. Proudly. "Good price, too. A very motivated seller."

"Nice."

"Did Lauren tell you where to find me?"

"Don't worry," I said. "Lauren's done a far better job of protecting your role in this than you had any right to expect. No, I got your address from Candi. Or should I say, Margaret."

For a few seconds he looked stymied. He tilted his head to one side: his skeptical expression. I knew it well.

"Oh, not from her personally. From her cell phone. In your booty e-mail."

"Booty e-mail?"

"The secret e-mail addresses you and Candi used to arrange hook-ups."

"I thought I deleted all that stuff."

"It's nice to be underestimated sometimes," I said.

"You're good," he said with a short laugh. "And, what? Once you got her cell number, you used some sort of private-eye hocus-pocus to find out where she'd made calls from? Including right here?"

"Hocus-pocus," I said, nodding. "Yep. Magic." The GPS locator chip in the cell phone used by "Candi Dupont"—Margaret Desmond—had yielded the location of her phone calls to within fifty meters. Which gave me the building address pretty quickly. "Though I couldn't decide where to look first: the old house in Bedford, or here. She called from both places. That surprised me, the Bedford house. I thought some rich hedge-fund manager bought it a couple of years ago. I didn't think he'd want to sell so soon."

"Hedge funds are in trouble these days. Besides, everyone has a price."

I nodded. Smiled. *Tell me about it, bro.* "And sometimes the family has to pay it."

"Believe me, Lauren and Gabe aren't going to suffer. They're not exactly going to be paupers."

"Her payoff, right? Her divorce settlement? For all she did to help you?"

"No, bro. Because I still love her."

"Heartwarming," I said. "No one shows it the way you do. At least Dad didn't arrange a hit on Mom before he disappeared."

"Oh, come on, Nick. You really think I'd hire someone to bash Lauren's head in? What kind of guy do you think I am?"

"I don't think you want me to answer that."

"My guy was just supposed to knock her out. Nothing more than that."

"She almost died, you know. And then, thanks to you, Koblenz sent one of his guys to kill her. Who came very close to succeeding."

Roger looked ashamed suddenly. He hung his head. "She's okay now. Thank God."

"Maybe. But not Gabe. After what you've put him through in the last couple of weeks. That leaves scars. Not that you care."

"Of course I care. I still love the kid. Lauren, too."

"What a guy."

"I did what I had to. To protect them."

"No," I said. "You did what you did to try to pull off the greatest heist in history. Even if it meant a little collateral damage. Like Marjorie Ogonowski, who seemed to be the only friend you had at Gifford. You know about her by now, right?"

I could tell from his expression that he knew about her murder. *And me,* I thought. *I almost became his collateral damage, too.* But I'd never give him the satisfaction of hearing me say it out loud. "Well, I guess you can't make an omelet without breaking a few eggs, huh?"

"I had no choice."

"So you staged the greatest vanishing act of all time," I said. "With the help of a couple of guys you lured away from Paladin. While you were in the process of taking their company over. Well played."

"Actually, Nick, you disappointed me, I have to say. I was convinced you'd identify my 'abductor' "—he made air quotes with two fingers on each hand—"as a Paladin employee."

"With a little more time we would have. The license plate was good enough to finger Paladin. Which was the point, wasn't it?" Obviously, they'd switched plates with a Paladin vehicle. And meant for me, or someone, to locate that gas-station surveillance camera and make the connection. "Though I'm surprised you trusted any of those Paladin guys."

"They're all for sale. Look who they work for. Whoever writes their paychecks buys their loyalty."

"So you had someone steal a body from a hospital morgue to set up your final trick," I said. "No matter how it might traumatize your son."

A pained expression wracked his face. "That was unfortunate, but necessary."

"All to convince Gifford and Paladin that you were dead? Just to buy yourself a little time while you arranged to steal the company?"

"Not just that. Also to protect Lauren and Gabe."

"Whose lives you endangered in the first place," I pointed out.

But he ignored that. "After Paladin started putting pressure on Lauren, I had no choice. She started panicking. I almost lost her. I had to keep her from giving the whole thing up. I mean, look, when it comes right down to it, she's a mother first and foremost."

"Yeah," I said dryly. "What's wrong with her?"

"Nick," he said, "I'm sure you know the story about the family that's hiding from the Nazis, right? They're in the basement, or hiding under the floorboard—I forget, a mother and father and a couple of kids and a tiny infant. And the Nazi soldiers are searching the house—"

"Yep," I said impatiently. "And the baby starts to cry so the mother puts her hand over his mouth to stop his cries. Smothers her own child. Feels it go limp."

He nodded. "She kills her own baby to protect the rest of the family. A hard thing. A haunting thing. But what choice did she have? The life of a tiny child weighed against the life of an entire family?"

"You have a point?"

"Whatever Gabe and Lauren had to endure, it was for their own protection."

"Protection? No. This was about bread crumbs."

"Bread crumbs?"

"Easter eggs, maybe. Laying down a false trail for me."

"Well, not for you. For the cops or the FBI. I certainly never wanted Lauren to call you in. That was Gabe's doing."

"Sorry to screw up your plans."

He shrugged. "But you didn't. Not at all. If it hadn't been you, it would have been someone else. See, diversion is a major part of every magic act. Haven't you learned that yet?"

I thought of the story that Victor and Lauren both told about Roger's attempt to extort money from Paladin—which I doubted was true. He was after far more than ten million dollars. And everything buried just deep enough that I'd have to dig. Which made it all plausible. And then I thought of that "missing" billion dollars in cash, which Stoddard put me onto, which led me to Carl Koblenz, and I knew that Roger had somehow set that up as well. All in the interests of creating a false trail that pointed toward Paladin. But why? To neutralize them? To keep the heat on them? That part I hadn't figured out yet.

"So you hired the cargo guy yourself," I said. "To steal the container. Which you knew Paladin was shipping."

He tipped his head to one side modestly. "And gave him Koblenz's cell phone number to use only in case of an emergency." He chuckled. "I can only imagine what Koblenz would have said if he'd gotten a call from the guy."

"What if Stoddard hadn't put me on the job?" I said.

"Why would he assign anyone else? Leland Gifford

specifically requested you." He gave me a wink, and I immediately understood that it was actually Lauren who'd put in the request, in her boss's name. "I knew I could count on my little brother to protect me like you always did. That's the thing about families. Even when we grow up, we play the same roles."

"And yours was always as Dad's Mini-Me. Has he been pulling the strings the whole time from his prison cell? The greatest swindle of his career? He wanted his empire back, didn't he? Probably his idea, too, this whole scam."

"Give me a little more credit than *that,* Nick."

"I do. You always saw Dad for what he was."

"You can't be disillusioned if you never had any illusions to begin with."

"And you couldn't have done this without him."

"Probably not," Roger admitted. "I know a lot about offshore finance. But he really knows all the ins and outs. His firm was structured just like Gifford Industries, you know. Both family firms, both privately held by offshore entities. For tax reasons. Liability reasons."

"I see," I said. "So you convinced Leland Gifford to restructure his company after he acquired Paladin, right?"

"You been going to night school, Nick? You got it. I told Gifford he had to create another layer of offshore insulation, in order to shield himself from liability. He knew about all the kickbacks Paladin gave the Pentagon. He was smart enough to see that, with a new president in the White House, the worm was turning. He knew he might have to take the fall. He could be facing Congressional hearings, maybe even prison time, if he wasn't protected. So he did what I urged him to do. He temporarily transferred beneficial ownership."

" 'Beneficial ownership,' " I said. "In other words, the title to the company. To all of Gifford Industries, which included its new subsidiary, Paladin. Am I right? Since Gifford's privately held?"

"And I always thought you had no interest in finance."

"Just the bare minimum," I said. "Just enough to catch the assholes."

"Just enough knowledge to be dangerous, huh?"

"Guess that makes me dangerous, Roger. So—what, you had to disappear until the transfer became permanent? Until the mandatory waiting period had expired?"

"And everyone always said *I* was the smart one." He smiled with what could almost pass for admiration.

"But you couldn't have pulled this off without the RaptorCard," I said. "Having your name on the paperwork was only part of it. You also had to transfer the company's assets to your own personal accounts, right? Which is why you needed me to break in there and steal it."

"Not quite," he said. "You almost screwed the whole thing up."

"Sorry to hear it. How so?"

"I gave Koblenz's admin a boatload of money to go into his safe and get me the RaptorCard. Would have gone much more smoothly if you hadn't broken in and stolen the damn thing. So I had to improvise."

"Well done," I said, and I meant it. I continued leading him along: "But I'm still not clear about something. That fake swap—trading you for the RaptorCard—how'd you know for sure I actually had it?"

Roger hesitated, but only for an instant. "Koblenz."

"I see." I saw the lie at once, but I didn't pursue it. I knew the truth. "Well, you finally got your payback, didn't you?"

"Payback?"

"Leland Gifford never really respected you. Never promoted you. I guess you got the job you deserved all along. So what happens to Leland Gifford now? You're going to park him in a nursing home somewhere? Give him a monthly allowance?"

"Don't worry about Leland Gifford. I paid him off handsomely. He'll retire an extremely wealthy man. But I'm keeping him on. I'm not really an operational guy."

"And he's not going to talk anyway, is he? It's not in his interest."

"Very good. You got it. If the details of Paladin's kickback arrangements with the Pentagon ever became public, the spigot would get turned off. The Defense Department would be forced to cancel all of its contracts. Paladin would be worthless. Gifford would lose his multibillion-dollar investment in his own company. So he's better off with some money than nothing. It's win-win."

"You seem relaxed and calm," I said. "Secure, even. You really think you're safe?"

"Who's going to come after me? Gifford? Granger? Koblenz? They all work for me now."

"Tell that to Allen Granger. He lives in fear of his own employees."

"That's why I'm keeping him on. Let them all think he's still their boss. Some of these ex-military guys are crazy."

"I'm an ex-military guy. Don't forget."

"But you're not crazy."

"Not everyone would agree with that. Anyway, bear in mind, people aren't always rational when they get angry. And you've got a lot of enemies."

"Why do I get the feeling you're talking about yourself?"

I shrugged.

"What are you going to do, kill your own brother?"

"No," I said, after waiting just long enough to make him nervous. "I'd never do that. But some courts might consider what you did theft. Criminal, even. Crazy as it might sound."

"Who's going to charge me with theft? Leland Gifford? He doesn't want to go to prison. He'd be liable for all of the kickbacks Paladin made, because he knew about them. From the due diligence I did. I made sure to let him know."

I nodded slowly, felt for the cell phone in my pocket, looked up. "For all the due diligence you did, you're entrusting your entire financial empire to some fleabag offshore bank? Really, Roger. That's where you really blew it. Don't you realize how quickly those offshore havens fold when the U.S. government puts the squeeze on them? Look what happened to Nauru."

Roger always hated it when I knew more than him about anything. "Yeah?" he said. "You consider Barclays, B.V.I., fleabag? Come on, bro. Nothing but the best."

"Barclays in the British Virgin Islands?" I said. "That's in, what, Tortola? All right. I underestimated you."

He smiled. "You know, Nick, there was an ancient Chinese philosopher who once said that battles are always won or lost before they're fought."

"Someone told me that," I said. "You know a lot about war, Roger?"

"Just theoretically. And just enough to be dangerous. So are we done here, bro? Because I have a lot of work to do. I've got a conference call scheduled, and we don't even have phones yet."

"Almost," I said. "Hold on a second."

I pulled out my BlackBerry.

"Can you repeat that again?" I said.

Roger looked at me, bewildered. "Repeat what?"

"Sorry," I said. "I was talking to my phone." The cell phone in my pocket had been on and transmitting our conversation to Dorothy the whole time. It took her just a few seconds to pull up the SWIFT code for Barclays' British Virgin Islands branch. As she read it to me again, slowly, I typed the numbers into a message field on my BlackBerry.

I've always hated Bluetooth headsets—I don't like walking around with a thing clipped to my ear like an extra in a *Star Trek* movie—but the one I was wearing was nonstandard. It was one of Merlin's government-grade miniature earbuds. Roger'd never noticed it.

"There we go," I said, this time to Roger. I smiled, held up the BlackBerry. "The cool thing about the Raptor Card," I said, "is how easy it is to build in a backdoor, if you know what you're doing. Every single transaction you made, it sent me a copy. Right here."

Roger didn't seem to know how to react. I could see the skepticism mixed with anxiety. "Yeah," he said. "Like you know what you're doing."

"Oh, not me," I admitted. "But one of my colleagues. Comes in handy to have friends sometimes. Now, watch closely. Nothing up my sleeve."

"What do you think you're doing?" A tendril of panic had entered his voice. Slowly he came around to my side of his desk. "What's this all about? Because I did what you were too much of a candy ass to do?"

"Shhh," I said. "Never interrupt a magician in midact. And now—"

"You understand that I fully intend to share this with you, right?"

"—Watch as I click this ordinary-looking button on this very ordinary-looking BlackBerry, and your entire digital trail is sent, by the magic of the Internet, to FinCen. The U.S. Treasury's financial-crimes enforcement network—"

Roger leapt at me. "You're a *Heller*!" he thundered. *"This is the life we were meant to have!"*

I sidestepped his lunge.

"And . . . abracadabra!"

With an unnecessarily theatrical flourish, I clicked the SEND button.

Then, without even turning to look at him, I strode across the wide expanse of his office. "If they give you a choice, I hope you request Altamont Correctional Facility," I said. "It would be nice for Dad to have company. Maybe you two can work in the laundry together."

And then I opened the door for the FBI.

99

A few days later I tried to slip into Lauren's house to retrieve the rest of my things, at a time I thought she and Gabe would be gone. I figured it would be easier on everyone if they just came home one day and found my stuff gone. No scene. No muss, no fuss.

I'd forgotten about private-school schedules, though: The more money you pay for school, the shorter the academic year. St. Gregory's was out for the year, and Gabe was upstairs, listening to music. Lauren was doing something on her home computer. Another thing I didn't expect: that Lauren would be at home and not at work.

That was actually okay, though. We had a lot to talk about. She told me that she'd decided to take a leave of absence from her job. A long one. The leave she should have taken in the first place, after the injury.

"For the first time in I don't know how long, I actually need to work for a living," she said pensively.

I suppose I could have let my brother get away with it, which would have meant that Lauren and Gabe might have shared in the spoils, or so Roger had said. But in the end, they'd never have been safe—you never get away with something like that.

And it just didn't sit well with me. Bad karma, maybe. I knew a little about living off tainted money.

And—call me a starry-eyed idealist, but I did sort of like the idea of doing the right thing.

"Have you started looking for a job yet?" I asked.

She looked at me with surprise. "I'm not leaving Leland," she said. "Why would I?"

"He'd take you back?"

"Take me back? What's that supposed to mean?"

I felt a pang of sadness. She hadn't stopped concealing. "Lauren," I said.

"Lee doesn't blame me for what Roger did. That wouldn't be fair."

"So Leland still doesn't know," I said. "Well, I'll say this much for my brother. He may have used you, but he did protect you."

"Protect me? In what way?"

"He could have turned you in when he was arrested, but he didn't. And I doubt he will."

"Turn me in for what?"

"For what you did. For your role in all of this."

"My role?"

"Lauren, come on."

"What?"

I was really disappointed in my people-reading skills. It had taken me far too long to learn to read her. Maybe my usual perceptiveness had been blunted by my love for her and her son. "Well, for one thing, Roger couldn't have stolen all of Gifford Industries' assets without the RaptorCard. And there's only one way he could have known that I had it. From you."

Her eyes were opaque, hard to read. "I told you he contacted me. He left me a voice message. He gave me a—an untraceable cell number to call. Because he wanted to make sure this deal went off without a hitch. So, yes. I told him."

"Right," I said. "But that was only part of it."

She looked wounded. "What are you accusing me of?"

"I'm not going to turn you in," I said. "No point in that. I blame my brother for dragging you into this."

"I wasn't dragged . . ." she began.

"Lauren," I said. "Don't even bother. Leland didn't trust Roger. He didn't like him. He'd never have gone along with the idea of creating a holding company—and designating Roger as the full, temporary, owner—if you hadn't urged him to do it."

She winced as she shook her head.

But I kept going. "Dorothy told me you asked her how to access a password-protected BlackBerry. You told her you wanted to help me out. Get into his e-mails. Of course, you didn't bother to tell *me* about it."

Hollowly, she attempted, "I didn't?"

"Of course not. Because that wasn't true. You weren't trying to help find Roger. You were sending out e-mails under Leland Gifford's name. To a bank in the Caymans. Authorizing the transfer. Replying to the bank's queries. And later, I assume, deleting all evidence of the correspondence so Gifford wouldn't find out."

"Nick," she began.

"Roger needed a confederate in the CEO's office, or none of this would have worked."

She looked away.

"And—oh, yes—you made sure that Stoddard assigned me to locate the missing cargo. That billion dollars in cash. A theft Roger arranged. More bread crumbs, to lead me to Paladin."

Her expression confirmed my theory. She'd e-mailed Jay Stoddard as Leland Gifford to be certain he put me on the case.

"I don't like what you're implying. You don't seriously think I'd risk Gabe's life for money, do you?"

"No, I don't. I'm sure this wasn't your idea in the first place."

"Of course it wasn't! The worst you can say about me is that I was naïve. I *trusted* him. When he told me he had to disappear because that was the only way to keep us safe, I believed him. And then things just started to spin out of control, and Paladin started making all those threats—"

"I know. That's when Roger took the risk of calling you. To make sure you stayed with the program."

A single tear streamed down her left cheek in a perfectly straight line. "He told me if I didn't, they'd kill him. He said it was the only way to save him and protect Gabe. He used me. He manipulated me."

"He's good at that. I understand."

"His relationship with Gabe is over. He's destroyed it."

"He doesn't deserve Gabe."

"No," she said. "He doesn't deserve Gabe."

"I don't think Gabe's going to be visiting him in prison. You see how often I visit my dad."

She nodded sadly. "And . . . what about you?"

"I'll figure something out."

"You think you might move?"

"I might. I'll see. I've never loved Washington, you know that."

"I hope not. That wouldn't be easy for Gabe."

"Or for me."

"So don't move. Stay in town."

"I'll figure something out," I said. "I'm not worried."

"You never worry, do you?"

"Sure I do. All the time," I said. "I just don't like to show it."

Before I left, I took Gabe for a walk around the block. The old oak trees shaded the path, their leaves rippling gently in the wind, the light dappled. He was wearing black shorts and his black Chuck Taylors and a red Full Bleed T-shirt with a big white fingerprint on it.

"Can you freakin' believe it?" he said. "Dad asked Mom if I'd visit him in jail."

"You're not going to?"

"Are you kidding me? I told him I never wanted to see him again."

"He loves you. You should know that. He may be a flawed person, but he does love you."

"So? I don't really care. He cheats on Mom, and he lies to us and almost gets us killed?" He shook his head. "And now I don't think Mom can afford to send me to St. Greg's anymore."

"I thought you hated the place."

"I never said that."

I shrugged. I didn't feel much like arguing.

"And we don't even get any of that money he stole. If you hadn't had him arrested, we could be *rich*."

"Yeah," I said. "Justice sucks sometimes. I get that."

He glared at me.

"It's like Batman," I said.

"Huh?"

"Well, think about it. Batman these days, he's an angst-ridden vigilante, right? Dark and brooding and tortured. He has these inner demons."

He looked at me in surprise. "You've read *The Dark Knight Returns*?"

"Nah. Saw the movies. But when I was a kid, Batman was this really cool superhero. He was the Caped Crusader. He was millionaire Bruce Wayne, and he had the Batmobile and the Bat Cave, and he was always saving Gotham City from the Joker or the Riddler. He always *won*. The bad guys always ended up behind bars."

"You're talking about the TV show."

"Point is, real-life justice is a little more complicated. More like the dark and brooding Batman, you could say."

"Yeah, well, you're totally wrong. Batman was originally this, like, tragic figure. Bruce Wayne's parents are killed in a holdup, and he makes this solemn promise on their grave to rid the city of crime."

"Okay, okay," I said. I should have known better than to talk comic books with Gabe. "What I'm trying to tell you is, the right thing isn't always the easy thing."

"Do I get a cookie with that fortune?"

"You might want to watch the way you talk to your elders," I said sternly.

"Yeah, right," he said, and he smiled, and I smiled, too.

This was getting way too heavy for me, so I changed the subject and asked him about his summer plans, but he didn't really have any, except for finishing his graphic novel. We circled back to their driveway and stood in front of my Defender.

I'd paid one of Granger's guys to recover it from the Georgia woods and drive it back to D.C. The guy had had the car washed and polished, and it gleamed. Of course, that just made the long white scratch on the driver's side stand out more against the glossy Coniston green.

"What happened here?" Gabe said, tracing the mark with his finger.

"Some jerk keyed it."

"That's a bummer."

I shrugged. "Not my biggest concern right now."

He looked uncomfortable for a few seconds, as if he wanted to bring something up.

"What?" I said.

"So how come you're moving out?"

"I have my own apartment."

"I mean, out of Washington. I heard you talking to Mom."

"I haven't decided what I'm doing. I might move back to Boston."

"So, what, that's it? You're just going to move, and I'll, like, never see you again?"

"You'll see me plenty, you poor guy. More than before, probably."

He smiled again. He had a terrific, totally winning smile when he actually used it. His mom's smile. "You can run, but you can't hide, Nick."

"Don't worry about it," I said. "You can't get rid of me that easy."

ACKNOWLEDGMENTS

I'm immensely grateful to a few people who've given generously of their time to make me look so much smarter than I really am. Most of all: Lieutenant Robert "Buzz" Glover of the Washington, D.C., Metropolitan Police Department's Special Operations Division, whose assistance with the specifics of crime and law enforcement in the D.C. area was invaluable; and two extremely savvy international private investigators who helped make Nick Heller real: my old friend Harry "Skip" Brandon, of Smith Brandon, and Terry Lenzner, of the Investigative Group.

Once again, Dick Rogers—the FBI legend who led the Hostage Rescue Team—was terrific in helping choreograph some of the most intricate action scenes and keep them plausible, along with Nick's martial-arts trainer, Jack Hoban.

Kevin Murray, a specialist in eavesdropping-detection, audits, and counterespionage consulting, gave me extensive information about what's actually possible in the realm of surveillance technology, which was even more than I'd imagined. Bill Spellings briefed me about the business of TSCM (technical surveillance countermeasures) and how it works in real life, and

Mark Spencer of First Advantage Litigation Consulting made the complex technology of computer forensics and data recovery not only understandable but very cool, as did Simson Garfinkel (who helped come up with the "RaptorCard").

Thanks to my security experts, including Jeff Dingle and Roland Cloutier, director of Global Security for the EMC Corporation, who devised some creative mobile phone ruses. Dave Wade advised me on the tracing of cell phones, and Jerry Richards helped me understand the intricacies of surveillance cameras and their possible manipulation. My longtime source on explosives technology, the remarkable Jack McGeorge, was there for me again. I was advised as well by Christopher Morgan-Jones, formerly of Kroll; and Gene Smith, of Smith Brandon.

I'm particularly indebted to my friends at ASTAR Air Cargo, who came through for me when I needed access to a cargo flight (and some hard-to-find details) for Nick's opening scene. Thanks to Travis Hall, Martin Godley, Rob Miller, Ron Long, Tom Halpin, Dominick Deleto, Jason Stupp, and CFO Steven Rossum.

Pam Buote—assistant to the CEO of the EMC Corporation, Joe Tucci—told me about the life of an executive admin to a CEO (and understood that I needed to take some liberties for plot reasons). My good friend Bill Teuber, the vice chairman of EMC, helped in all sorts of ways once again. Paul Dacier, EMC's general counsel, guided me through a number of legal complexities, as did Jay Shapiro of Katten Muchin Rosenman and Eric Klein of Sheppard Mullin Richter & Hampton. For safecracking tips, my thanks to Ken Doyle of Advanced Safe and Vault Engineering in Novato, California.

On offshore banking and shell companies, I was advised by Dennis Lormel of Corporate Risk International, Philip R. West of Steptoe & Johnson, Don Meiers of Miles & Stockbridge, and the encyclopedic Jack Blum of Baker Hostetler. Steve Aftergood of the Federation of American Scientists and Steve Kosiak of the Center for Strategic and Budgetary Assessments helped me understand the Pentagon's "black budget." Michael Wilson of Integrity Partners guided me through forensic accounting, and Edward Hasbrouck had some useful suggestions on passports and forgery (all theoretical, of course).

My medical consultants included David Adelson, M.D., and my brother, Dr. Jonathan Finder. On a flight out of L.A. one day I happened to sit next to a private pilot named Ody Pond, who gave me some great plot ideas.

I'm a Boston guy, but this was a Washington, D.C., book, so I spent a lot of time walking the streets, taking notes. When inevitably I needed follow-up details, I was quite fortunate to get some great research assistance from both Amy Petersen and Will Dickinson, who meticulously retraced Nick's steps, took loads of photos, and dug up all sorts of obscure tidbits for me. Tiffany Kim helped with additional research.

My consultants on Gabe, none of whom are in fact "emo" or troubled or alienated, so far as I know, included John Thomsen, Austin Lang, Ben Moss, and Emma Finder.

For advice on comics and graphic novels, thanks to Will Dennis of DC Comics and Brian Azzarello.

As always, Giles McNamee of McNamee Lawrence was my unindicted co-conspirator in devising corporate scams with a mystery writer's sensibility. Even more important, he lent me his Coniston Green Land Rover Defender long enough for me to decide that Nick had to drive one too.

At St. Martin's Press, my U.S. publisher, my deepest thanks to John Sargent, Sally Richardson, Matthew Shear, George Witte, Matthew Baldacci, Lisa Senz, Nancy Trypuc, John Murphy (fellow olive loaf connoisseur), Ann Day, Ami Greko, Jeff Capshew, Brian Heller, Tom Siino, Martin Quinn, Ken Holland, Jerry Todd, and Kathleen Conn. At Audio Renaissance: Mary Beth Roche, Laura Wilson, Jeanne-Marie Hudson, and Kristin Lang.

At Headline, my UK publisher, I thank my wonderful editor (and champion), Vicki Mellor; Alice Shepherd, Siobhan Hooper, and everyone in Sales and Marketing. Thanks as well to my redoubtable UK agent, Clare Alexander of Aitken Alexander, and my foreign rights agent, Danny Baror.

I'm fortunate to have the greatest literary agent in the U.S., Molly Friedrich, who's not only a trusted adviser but also a valued reader. Lucy Carson and Paul Cirone at the Friedrich Agency were important early readers. Clair Lamb was a trusted editor and researcher as well as a valued part of the team that makes my website so good, along with Karen Louie-Joyce. And my assistant, Claire Baldwin, is truly the definition of invaluable. Thanks so much.

I'm indebted to my brother Henry Finder, for all of his brainstorming and editing, and to my amazing editor at St. Martin's, Keith Kahla, who wouldn't let me stop revising until he felt I got it just right.

Finally, my love and gratitude to my wife, Michele Souda, and my daughter, Emma, for their constant love and encouragement—and maybe most of all for their great sense of humor, which keeps me grounded and sane. Most of the time, anyway.

—JOSEPH FINDER
Boston, Massachusetts